Desprite Measures

The Caledonian Sprite Series, Volume 1

by Deborah Jay

Published by Deborah Jay, 2013.

DESPRITE MEASURES

First Edition. 13thDecember, 2013

Copyright © 2013, by Deborah Jay.

Written by Deborah Jay

Cover art by Alexandria N. Thompson

GothicFate.com

This one is for Kimberley - my harshest critic and my greatest supporter. You've always believed in my storytelling. Thank you.

1. MAGICIAN

It's just as well I'm not claustrophobic.

Even so, being held captive in a bottle was *not* how I'd planned to spend my weekend.

It was also one of the most undignified positions I've ever been in; a water sprite can be squished down pretty small, but it doesn't mean we enjoy the process.

Rainbows played across the clear glass walls of my prison, refracting through the swirling liquid of my elemental form. Taking a deep breath, metaphorically speaking, I tried to slow my agitated motion, in danger of over-heating. If someone would uncap my bottle, I'd be able to let off steam.

I prowled the confined space. It stood around ten inches tall, or should that be twenty-five centimetres? I can't keep up with the speed humans alter things. My existence had flowed serenely through the millennia without need for change until the human race invented plumbing.

I'd known there might be drawbacks to living in human form but, after one too many close encounters with the local sewage farm, I'd taken the risk. It had its upsides. Elementals are solitary by nature, but I'd found that I liked having friends—not to mention the thrill of experiencing human emotions.

I don't understand them all yet, but I'm learning.

Perhaps I should also have considered potential pit-falls, but I was still quite new to all this, and when Alison had come to me for support I'd wanted to help. Replaying the fateful conversation in my mind, I realised I should've smelled something fishy from the outset.

"I know it's not your kind of thing, but will you come with me, Cassie? Please say you will," Alison pleaded.

I considered my flame haired friend for a millisecond before committing. "Aye, of course I will, as long as you're certain it's what you want."

She frowned. "What, to become a witch or go to this meeting?"

"The meeting, dear heart. I have no problem with you trying out witchcraft; all that communing with nature is so you. I'm just none too sure about this group."

We both studied the website on Alison's laptop.

"Look at this list of events." I pointed to one corner of the screen. "Like this one: 'Self-development through equine partnership'. What's that all about?"

"But that's only one thing," Alison protested. "Look at the rest. Crystal dowsing, aura reading, herbalism, etcetera, etcetera."

"Okay, okay! Of course I'll come with you. It can't hurt to go to one meeting, can it?"

How wrong could I have been? I know that at the first whiff of strong magic I should have run in the opposite direction. But no, that whiff had been *so* enticing: aromas of strawberries and cream and chocolate all rolled into one. Someone had studied the Facebook group I'd set up for my gym clients, and discovered exactly what would make me hesitate just that fraction of a second too long.

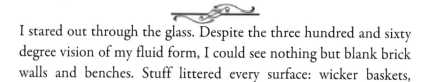

I stared out through the glass. Despite the three hundred and sixty degree vision of my fluid form, I could see nothing but blank brick walls and benches. Stuff littered every surface: wicker baskets, beakers, jars of herbs and cages of fluffy bunnies, guinea pigs, mice, rats, chickens.

Several computers peeked out of the mess, and some weird-shaped metallic objects that looked like they should buzz and whirr, but I couldn't be sure as no sound penetrated my thick glass prison. I didn't know if this meant there *was* no sound—unlikely given the number of animals out there—or that I was under a sound-muffling spell. Perhaps the glass containing me was simply too dense. I *did* know it was too thick for me to bust out of by expanding myself—a trick I've used to shattering effect in the past.

Movement caught my attention. A door, swinging shut behind a stick-thin figure. The magician stalked over to stand in front of my bottle. He lowered his face to stare at me.

I retreated as far as I could. It was like being on the wrong side of the glass with a spotty teenager leering into the magic mirrors on a fairground stall. His elongated face showed scratchy stubble that belonged more to a youth trying to grow a beard than to a man in need of a shave. A bulbous nose ballooned as he pressed it against my bottle, peering short-sightedly through wire-rimmed spectacles. His eyes behind the two layers of distorting glass were like a pair of fried eggs with vivid blue yolks.

I cringed and tried to move further back, but there was nowhere to go.

He straightened up and sauntered over to one of the benches. His retro Led Zeppelin t-shirt and the baggy jeans with waistband sagging below the elastic of his boxers confirmed my initial impression that my captor was a nerd, and a young one at that. However, his youth was no excuse for his atrocious manners, nor would it save him from my wrath when I gained my freedom.

So, back to escape plans.

Pity I had none. I'd already tried everything I could think of.

This left me with nothing to do but watch the nerd tapping on a keyboard. For all I knew he was answering emails, but even through the glass walls of my prison I sensed a certain excitement. I've become pretty good at reading humans over the centuries, and his twitchy movements along with frequent palm wiping on his jeans screamed anxiety.

Without warning, he whipped around and lunged towards me. The feverish glow on his face set my already jittery nerves jangling. Before I knew it I was swinging through the air, my bottle clasped in his hands. His sweaty palms left smears on the outside of my prison after he dumped it on the floor.

Now that I could *see* the floor, I could also see the large circle chalked onto the granite slabs. Typical Highland flooring, and even through the numbness of the spells I could feel the pull of the tides and the rush of a river not too far away. Wherever we were, we hadn't gone far from my native Scottish waterways.

With his back towards me, the magician fumbled amongst the clutter on another bench. He turned with a triumphant grin and strode back into his circle carrying a metal thermos, his hands encased in huge padded gauntlets. He put it down a few feet away from me.

I had a bad feeling about this.

He returned to rummaging through the contents of another bench, and I realised that I'd plastered myself against the rear of my bottle. Silly, I chided myself. As if a few extra inches might make a difference.

I cringed as the magician re-entered the circle, and was a tad miffed to see him treat the thermos with far more caution than my bottle. If he thought he would be safe once I was free, well, he'd learn otherwise. That was assuming we all survived this insane experiment of his, which I seriously doubted.

He pressed a lump of sticky stuff to the neck of my bottle, and then taped on a small black box with a winking red light. He repeated the procedure with the thermos, again handling it with infinitely more respect.

Now I was truly offended.

I had a pretty shrewd idea what the contraption was designed to do, although I'd only seen suchlike in movies.

Satisfied with his preparations, the magician stepped back out of the circle and picked up a bowl. He proceeded to sprinkle a white powder—salt, I guessed—in a continuous overlay of the chalk, his lips moving all the while as he muttered what I had to assume was an incantation. At least he was taking precautions, but I doubted he had any real idea of what he was about to unleash.

Next, he opened one of the wicker baskets and extracted a frantically flapping cockerel. One swift machete chop later, and he was marching around his circle again, this time holding the headless corpse so that its blood drained to mingle with the salt. The poor bird's legs were cycling as if trying to run away, not yet realising it was dead. The exercise kept the blood flowing freely from its severed neck.

Gross.

He completed the circuit and stood back to view his handiwork. He appeared satisfied. Nervous, but satisfied.

After the magical preparations, he took some time laying thick, heavily insulated cables around the exterior of the circle. These black hi-tech snakes were interrupted at intervals with gizmos sprouting coloured wires, which in turn trailed off beneath the various benches around the perimeter of the room.

After a final lengthy survey of the completed layout, Nerd-Features reached up to a large junction box on the wall and pushed up a lever. A double row of green lights lit the board below, and a deep hum penetrated my prison, vibrating the stone floor. Mesmerised by the rows of ready lights, I realised with a start that I'd lost sight of my captor before spotting him near the door, behind a stainless steel unit. Visibly agitated, maybe worried that his nerve might fail, he snatched a wallet-sized black box off the work surface, pulled out a stubby antenna and ducked down behind the metal barrier. A disembodied hand appeared above the work surface and, despite my silent scream of <*NO!*>, his thumb depressed the red button.

My bottle imploded, showering slivers of glass through my vapour as I drew myself together and pulled every molecule up and away, retreating as far as the warded circle would allow. I hung somewhere near the high ceiling, plastered against the dome of magic that flared into the visible spectrum when I brushed against it.

Damn, but that smarted! Like getting zapped by an electric fence.

Just the top of the thermos had blown off, leaving a ragged lip of melted aluminium and an ominous orange glow deep inside. Even as I watched, the golden light rose up, emerging as a tiny flicker of flame which blossomed into a miniature inferno.

Salamander!

A fire elemental.

My opposite.

I caught a glimpse of movement outside the circle. The idiot who'd trapped together two inimical elementals stood there watching. Did he have any idea what might happen if we inadvertently touched? Or was that the experiment? Dear gods, was he that stupid?

At the very least I'd expect a severe earthquake, far higher on the Richter scale than anything Scotland had experienced in thousands of years. It could even sunder the rift that runs through the Highlands—the Great Glen, stretching from Inverness to Fort William—splitting the top section of Scotland away from its adopted home, cracking the south-eastern edge off the Island of Mull and running on to play havoc with Ireland.

At its worst, there might be a large smoking hole where Scotland used to be. I wasn't sure, and I had no wish to find out.

Yet I was clueless about how to prevent it. Salamanders have notoriously short fuses, and for all I knew this one might lash out without thought of consequences. It was already uncomfortably hot in our joint prison, and my extremities were vibrating with increased energy. If I was forced to expand into steam I wasn't sure I'd be able to keep enough distance between myself and my fiery companion to prevent the unthinkable.

There *had* to be a way out of here. Keeping half my attention on the angry swirl of flames prowling the circle at ground level, I quested out with my senses, seeking the water I could feel so tantalizingly close by.

There! A tumbling, quick-running river, not more than a few feet away. I placed the building: an old hydro-electric power station. Whatever the reason it had been moth-balled, the river that once supplied its power still flowed past undisturbed.

I poked at the spells containing us, and a sense of calm spread through me. The magician had made his first mistake. When the bottle shattered, so too had the binding spells that blocked my powers. Oh sure, we were still enclosed in the warded circle, unable to escape. But I was no longer helpless.

Failing to recognise his miscalculation he stood there watching, hoping that my fiery friend and I would do what—touch each other? *Mate* with each other? Did he think he was going to create a new breed of elemental?

Queasiness roiled where my stomach would have been had I been in human form. The possibilities were too horrifying, not to mention bizarre, to contemplate.

Returning to the matter at hand, I reached out and gathered together a few stray water droplets. Stretching further, outside the building and on the banks of the dark river that bounced and bubbled over a small waterfall nearby, I drew moisture to moisture, forming a puddle on one of the flat slabs of black rock. Spray doused my puddle, aiding its growth, peaty dark water on dark stone. The puddle became a pool, and—

<*Ouch! That was too damned close!*>

The lower parts of me smarted where a tongue of flame had licked upward and almost touched me. <*I'm trying to get us out of here, you dimwit. Keep away from me!*> I thought as hard as I could at the salamander.

He seemed to understand and withdrew, smouldering down as far away from me as possible until the heat in our prison dropped a little.

A muffled noise drew my attention back to our jailor, standing with his toes almost touching the outermost of his thick black cables. One look at his face and the muted swearing that made it through the warding told me he was displeased by the status quo I'd achieved. He was waving his arms in what looked alarmingly like incantation-mode and, sure enough, something stung me across the back.

I yelped as the force-bubble zapped me again, and realised with a sickening sinking feeling that the dome was inexorably contracting, forcing me to move downward towards the floor and my dangerous co-captive.

No time for second chances. If he squashed the dome flat enough we would never be able to keep sufficient distance between us, and then, BOOM! Bye-bye Scotland, at least as we know it.

I sent my awareness shooting back outside. Some of my puddle had started to leach away, dragged back into the torrent rushing towards the Moray Firth and thence on out to the North Sea.

Abandoning any finesse, I reached fluid fingers from the puddle into the river flow, joined my water to the wild water and drew it towards me as an adult draws a curious child towards a treat. Clasping the river more firmly in my watery fingers, I drew it over the rocky bank and towards the door of the old power station. It came with surprising ease, almost as if it were keen to try out a new course. A puddle outside the door became a pool, and then a waist-high flood filling the stairwell that led down to the door. For a panicky moment I thought the door might be too well sealed, but it yielded suddenly to the pressure and slammed open.

It was as if a dam had broken and the building stood in its path. The river flowed in through the door, sweeping all manner of flotsam before it; twigs and branches, sweet wrappers and plastic bottles, detritus from the floor of the abandoned power station. I had a glimpse of the magician's face—damn, but he was quick to realise the implications—before he plunged through the raging knee-high torrent and out the door. The black boxes connected to the cables hissed and sparked before being extinguished along with the pervasive hum, and I wished uncharitably that my captor had stayed long enough to be electrocuted by his own contraption.

Unfortunately the spell-driven dome continued to contract, and I spied another problem coming my way. With water swirling around the outside of the magical circle at ever increasing depth, the panicked salamander shot upward. I pulled my moisture in tight, hissing as the ball of fire scorched past me close enough to singe my edges, although not quite close enough to touch. Perhaps he had presence of mind enough to avoid me, perhaps it was sheer blind luck, but whatever, I breathed a sigh of relief and expanded down to cover the ground in as thin a film as I could make of myself.

The river had found some broken bricks in the farther wall, and settled to flow through the room at a stable depth. If only that flow would be *fast* enough.

The blood and salt overlaying the chalk circle had been swept away in the first onslaught, but the chalk itself was more resistant, wearing away little by little as the dome sank lower, forcing my flaming nemesis ever closer to where I lay, helplessly plastered across the floor.

What a way to go; plastered thinly rather than just plain plastered.

As I was about to give myself over to the higher powers, a tiny fraction of the chalk circle washed clean away and the spell bubble collapsed. My fellow prisoner streaked upward towards the ceiling, throwing flickering golden light across the higgledy-piggledy stuff on the benches. A cacophony of animal whines and shrieks battered my senses, so long used to the silence of the bottle followed by the deep hum of the spelled circle.

As the river swept across the stone flags where I lay, I drew myself up and coalesced into human form. A tad premature, I decided, as the water tugged at my knees. I thinned out a bit and drifted upward until my feet rested on the bubbling surface.

Taking a deep breath, I wrinkled my nose at the stench of shorted electrics and soiled straw. A flicker of light caught my attention and I realised that the scorching smell was not all due to the submerged cabling. On his way up, my erstwhile companion had set a dozen tiny sparks amongst the clutter on the work surfaces which were even now expanding into small fires. The shrieks from the cages redoubled.

I couldn't let those poor animals be burnt alive.

With water flowing past my feet in abundance it was an easy task to lift some into the air and split it into smaller droplets, to fall as soft rain onto the workbenches, quenching the flames.

What I failed to take into account was the effect this might have on the salamander, still lurking up there near the high ceiling. The animal noises were drowned out by the sudden eruption of an incandescent firestorm that threatened to engulf the roof.

Damn, but I was going to have to do this the hard way.

2. SALAMANDER

I grabbed the nearest cages, hurried out the door and up the steps to the car park.

The sight that greeted me was so beautiful I wanted to stop and weep with relief that I was still alive to see it. Despite my hijack of one branch of the river, water still thundered over the rocks of the falls above the building. The banks to either side were verdant with ferns and overhung by tall, ancient trees draped with old man's beard. A footpath disappeared beneath the trees, following the course of the river. I could picture it in high summer, with tourists leaning against the newly-installed 'Elf 'n' Safety' post and rail fence that separated the track from the slippery rocks at the water's edge. From there, they would watch salmon struggling to fling themselves upstream against the current and bouncing off the boulders of the waterfall.

I knew this place. In less than an hour's drive I could be back in Inverness and away from the madness.

Of course that required a car.

Indignant squawks recaptured my attention. I dumped my collection of mismatched cages onto the concrete beyond the stairwell and dashed back inside. The salamander still roiled around the roof space, trapped up there by the rain clouds I'd created. I guessed that was pissing him off, and by this time he had the roof well and truly alight.

It took me seven trips to get all the animals out, and then several more to get them transferred to the edge of the forest. Inspecting each cage and basket, I released those that could survive on their own. That left two chickens, two lop-eared bunnies, three guinea pigs and an American mink. I'm sure the mink would have done fine living out here, but I was loath to unleash him on the local wildlife when he didn't belong in this ecosystem.

Turning back to the old building, I was in time to witness the roof cave in with a roar and a whoosh. A gout of flame detached itself from the collapsing rafters and streaked in my direction. Dear gods! Had I upset the salamander so much that he intended to finish what the magician had started?

Surely I could not encounter two such insane entities on the same day?

Lucky for me, the stream I'd diverted into the power station still flowed across the rocks behind me, so the salamander could not get between me and the river. If all else failed I could slip into the water and ride it out to sea where he would never find me, although I was reluctant to abandon my newly acquired pets.

I watched warily as the salamander settled to the car park, blackening the concrete and immolating a few dry twigs. He was close enough that I could feel his intense heat, and I had to narrow my eyes to cope with the brightness. A scorching smell wafted across the open car park.

In much the same way as I had done, he metamorphosed into human form. His fiery light dimmed as the flames wrapped in on themselves, going solid and dark. Clothes formed over rich chocolate skin and my breath caught as the transformation completed.

I was looking at the most stunning woman I could imagine.

"But you're *female*!" I protested.

It was centuries since I'd heard even rumour of a female Salamander. I fought to get my head around this new wrinkle as unexpected sensations coursed through me. My knees shook and my heart fluttered. I struggled to breathe. But for my years of practice, I'd have wondered if I'd fashioned a faulty body.

I knew I hadn't.

She was breathtaking. From the tips of her dainty red toenails in their golden peep-toe mules to the top of her dense cornrows plaited with shining gold beads and woven into an elaborate crown, she was gorgeous. I've had my fair share of lovers of both sexes, and of different species, but this salamander was different; I *had* to have her.

Yet I could never go within feet of her for fear of wiping a whole country off the map.

She smiled wickedly and my body threatened to melt. Drawing myself up to the fullest extent of my inadequate height, I checked that the clothes I'd produced, beige slacks and a black tunic with ethnic embroidery around the neckline, clung to my petite curves.

My eyes drank in the divine form before me, and I sighed. I could *never* hope to rival such voluptuousness. Taller than me by more than a hand span, this vision of my desire had clad her curvaceous figure in tight fitting black drainpipe jeans and a screaming red t-shirt edged with gold sequins to match the beads in her hair. Chocolate brown pupils set in gleaming whites studied me from above a broad nose. Her mouth opened to reveal startling white, perfect teeth surrounded by plump, red-brown lips that I yearned to kiss.

But I'll never be able to touch her.

"You tried to douse me," she accused. Her voice was sexily deep, and the scent of her breath carried the thrilling promise of warm sand and intimacy.

I struggled to order my thoughts. She believed I'd tried to extinguish her. Whatever I said would sound lame, but I needed to say *something*.

"I was trying to save the animals," I protested. My fiery friend raised an eyebrow.

Without taking my gaze from her—no matter my feelings I was not stupid enough to turn my back on her—I pointed behind me at the tumbled heap of cages and baskets. "They were going to burn to death. I couldn't let that happen."

She peered past me, eyes widening. I took that to mean she'd not noticed the tiny scraps of life before.

"What did he want with those?" she asked, sounding curious.

Curious was an improvement on accusatory, and I felt bolder. "More to the point, what did he want with *us*?"

She shrugged, spreading her long-fingered, expressive hands wide, her whole body moving sensuously with the motion. How could an ordinary shrug be so sexy?

I grappled again with concentration. Would my thoughts ever be coherent anywhere near this salamander? And, oh gods, would I see her again after we'd finished here?

I had to. I had to know that she was not going to vanish completely. I couldn't touch her, but I needed to see her, to smell her, to talk with her...

"What's your name?" I blurted. I don't think I've ever been so gauche, but then I don't ever remember being so instantly besotted either.

"Gloria Hammond," she answered, and I sighed. Perfect. *Glorious Gloria.* How could she be anything else?

She stared at me expectantly and I gulped, wondering if perhaps she thought me simple. I hadn't given her much cause to think otherwise yet.

"Cassiopeia Lake. Cassie. Had you been in there," I tilted my chin towards the old power station, "very long? I don't think he trapped me more than a day or so ago."

Gloria's brows drew down into a frown, and even that expression was sweet to my eyes.

"I'm not sure," she replied, uncertainty making her voice even huskier. "What's the date?"

"September 8th, I think. Sunday." I wondered what it must have been like inside that opaque thermos. At least I'd been able to see out of my bottle.

"Three months. That bastard had me squashed in there for THREE MONTHS!"

She was growing angry again, and I could see a hint of smoke wisping around her. I hurried to divert her attention.

"How did he catch you in the first place? He got me to visit a coven under false pretences, and then wham! He had me in that bottle like a novice witch with no defences. Damn, but he was quick!"

"He was waiting for me outside work one night," she said. "I wasn't paying attention because there are always guys hanging around." She planted her fists on her hips, and added, "I'm an exotic dancer."

Ooh, lovely. This I *had* to see.

"He put a hand on my arm. He must have been holding a charm because before I knew it, I was inside that damned thermos." She frowned. "Shit! He really knew what he was doing."

"Oh sure," I agreed with an edge of sarcasm I wasn't quick enough to smother. "He's smart enough to capture two opposing elementals and put us inside a magical shrinking bubble together. I'm not certain that qualifies him for the 'knows what he's doing' bracket."

I regretted my words before I'd finished uttering them, but that's me; open mouth first and regret later.

Gloria looked offended and I couldn't blame her so I rushed on, desperate to retrieve the situation. "Having said that, he must have had his motives. Do you have any idea what they were?"

She shook her head and the gold beads flashed in the rays of the lowering sun. "Not a clue. You must have seen more of him than me, and that's the way I want it to stay. I think I should be getting back now, and find out if I still have a job."

"Wait, please wait!" I shouted as flames started to wreath her around. I didn't even know where she lived and it might take me forever to find her again. I couldn't bear the thought. She hesitated and I cast frantically around for a reason to keep her talking. Out of the corner of my eye I spied a discarded basket.

"The animals," I said. "We can't leave them here and it'll be dark soon. It must be thirty miles to Inverness and there are too many for me to carry."

I *could* have drifted back to town via the river, or floated there on the air, but neither would be quick, especially the latter without even a gentle breeze to help me along. Then I'd have had to find my way back by road, and hope that in the meantime no wild life had decided to snack on the occupants of the cages.

Gloria regarded me as if I was a bit mad. Okay, a lot mad, but it got me a result.

"You want me to fetch a car?" she offered. I couldn't believe my luck.

"Yes please, that would be fantastic."

"Back in a bit," she said, the last word crackling as her voluptuous body condensed into a bright pillar of flame. She shot skyward and off into the distance in less time than it takes to say thank you.

Alone, and with the back of my neck prickling, I turned to scan the dense forest.

What if the magician was still around?

I'd made the snap assumption that he would flee the area, crediting him with enough intelligence to foresee the possible disastrous outcome of his experiment-gone-wrong.

But what if he hadn't? What if he was too stubborn, or too crazy? He might still be lurking in the vicinity, maybe planning to recapture us for another attempt.

My heart thudded and I made a swift choice. Dropping the bonds holding my human form together, I flung myself into the river. Guilt coiled through me at leaving the animals unprotected, but self-preservation topped it. I anchored myself near the water's edge and floated there, keeping watch over them from a distance. The magician would never be able to separate me from the copious flow.

I hoped.

Senses wide, I listened to the steady rumble of the waterfall, punctuated by the crackle of the burning building.

Time passed and the magician failed to materialise. Relaxing, I began to enjoy the sensation of frothy water bubbling through me, tickling and energising. My mind strayed into neutral, nostalgic with echoes of a simpler past.

The sound of a car engine roused me, and I rose from the water.

Perhaps when I'd agreed to Gloria fetching a car, I should have stated what *type* of car.

She arrived as dusk was falling. The last glowing embers inside the old power station were fading to golden flickers amidst the ruined remains of the building. Even in that light I could tell that her Mini Cooper was pillar-box red. Probably a perfect match for her t-shirt and nail varnish. A pair of racy go-faster stripes slid over the bonnet to lie like a set of white 'do-not-overtake' road markings along the roof, before slipping down over the rear bumper. I almost expected them to continue on the road behind, as if the car itself was painting the council's white lines.

My expression must have been a dead give-away and Gloria went on the defensive.

"What? It's my car and I love it!"

"I'm sure you do, but how are we going to fit this lot in?"

Not to mention me. I surely was not getting into the passenger seat beside her. *Far* too close for comfort.

With no alternative, I set about packing the car. Two of the wicker baskets went onto the miniscule rear seats, one into the passenger foot well, and the remaining baskets and cages in a stack on the front seat. I rearranged things three times while Gloria stood back and watched, saying nothing. In the end I was forced to admit that there was simply not enough room for the last cage. This left one solution: the occupants of the remaining baskets would have to double up. I hoped that Flopsy Bunny and Peter Rabbit would not get up to what rabbits usually get up to, but in no time at all the boisterous rocking of the precariously perched basket forced one more rearrangement, and the love bunnies ended up at the bottom of the heap.

I fastened the seat belt around the stack and stood back.

"I'll travel in the back," I volunteered. Gloria eyed me sceptically.

"It's a bit tight back there."

"Watch me."

So saying, I coalesced into a cloud of vapour and drifted in through the open driver's window. I settled as far back on the opposite side as the tiny car would allow, behind the rear headrest and tight up against the back window. It was still too close for safety, but it would have to do, and it wasn't as close as I'd expected; the new generation Minis are amazingly akin to Doctor Who's TARDIS—bigger inside than outside.

How *do* they do that?

Gloria bent over and peered in through the open door. "So where am I taking you and your menagerie?"

Damn! Hadn't thought of that. I extruded a hand from my vapour ball and Gloria backed prudently away. The fingers I constructed were long and elegant and tipped with perfectly manicured nails which glinted in the light of the SatNav as I tapped in my postcode. Gloria waited until I withdrew before getting in and starting the engine.

She turned cautiously out of the car park, eyeing the unsteady stack beside her. When nothing fell over, she started to pick up speed. Soon, we were zooming along the country lane in what I assumed was her normal driving style. I gritted mental teeth and refrained from commenting, unwilling to form a mouth only to put my foot in it. I wasn't concerned for myself so much as for the animals, and not just those inside the car; highland wildlife has little regard for traffic, and I'd noticed a sign warning of livestock on the road. When a Scottish sign says animals on the road, it means it; I've seen many a herd of cattle sleeping on sun-warmed tarmac.

My other concern was that a car wreck might accomplish what the magician had failed to do.

As if my fear took form, we rounded a corner and the headlight beams bounced off the prone length of a huge tree blocking the road. Gloria stamped on the brake, and we all lurched forward as the car screeched to a stop.

"What the fuck? That wasn't there before."

We stared at the trunk. It was almost full dark now, and the solid shape wavered as mist blew through the light cast by the headlamps.

Mist.

Really?

Right time of year, but I couldn't sense any water out there.

The mouth I'd refused to produce earlier sprouted from my little ball of vapour.

"Drive!" I screeched. "It's not real!"

The passenger door snicked open as Gloria hit the accelerator. It snapped shut again as the car jerked into motion, and something bumped against the side, falling away as we shot forward.

"Nooooo!" Gloria shrieked as we hit the tree. And passed right through it.

I could hear her harsh breaths pumping in and out for miles after we left the ambush behind.

I hadn't been wrong. The magician *had* tried to re-capture us.

He wasn't finished with us yet.

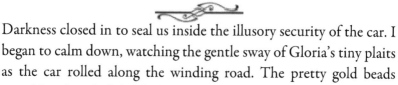

Darkness closed in to seal us inside the illusory security of the car. I began to calm down, watching the gentle sway of Gloria's tiny plaits as the car rolled along the winding road. The pretty gold beads sprinkling her dark head glinted each time we passed the light of a house, or caught in other cars' headlights.

Despite the emergency stop and our subsequent speedy departure, the ungainly stack of baskets had stayed in place. Soft rhythmic grunts from the bottom of the heap suggested that the rabbit population might increase soon, and my essence began to synchronise with their beat. My molecules started to pulse, rocking my little ball of moisture back and forth, growing warmer by the minute as I bounced gently against the back window. Gloria filled my mind, her beautiful round face, her dark eyes with their startling whites, luminous against her soft brown skin. I could almost *feel* the texture of her hair, imagine resting my cheek against her cornrows. Her unique, scorching smell wrapped my senses and—

"What are you doing, you crazy sprite?" Gloria's deep, sexy voice was raised and slightly panicked.

I came back to myself with a jolt to find I'd overheated, and expanded to fill the rear of the car. It was understandable, considering my thoughts, but oh, so dangerous. I pulled a mental blanket over my imaginings and shed energy, heating the surrounding air. Gloria opened the windows and cool air replaced hot. I shrank back to my tiny ball and pulled myself together even tighter than before. Huddling against the back window, I forced my mind to remain blank for the rest of the journey.

The moonlit countryside slipped by, the tall dark pines of the Caledonian Forest giving way to open farmland which rolled down to the edge of the Moray Firth, where the cold waters of the North Sea lapped at the grassy banks at the peak of a full tide. I am no great lover of salt water, but at that moment I would willingly have allowed the Firth to swallow me.

Gloria turned onto a small road leading away from the sea, and finally into the driveway to my house. I knew how impressive the façade appeared, with its huge, peaked panoramic windows, the fashionable cream walls and the towers at each end of the building. I worried what Gloria might think of me: too ostentatious? Too human? Or did she have something similar?

I *had* to find out where she lived.

Gloria followed the drive around to the rear of the house, wheels crunching on the gravel, and stopped smack in the centre of the square parking area. To the right stood a grey single storey converted steading. The big house was registered to an off-shore company with me to visit I take them to the steading. They don't need to know how much human wealth I've accumulated. Being a wee bit too ostentatious in the past has landed me in trouble and I like to think I've learned that lesson.

I waited until Gloria had exited the car and stepped back to a safe distance before easing myself out through the door she'd left open. As I shifted into human form I found it harder than usual to complete the transformation; I was seriously low on energy. I'd have to get a top up soon or I wouldn't be able to hold myself together.

Gloria went around to the passenger side and started to unload cages. She put them down a few feet away from the car, and I carried them into the steading. Even keeping my distance from her, she smelled hot, and I don't mean sexy; the scorching scent that had preceded her at the power station clung to her and, when I picked up one of the wicker baskets, I noticed slight burn marks where her fingers had rested.

If I was low on energy and struggling to hold a shape, how much more depleted must she be after three months stuck inside that thermos? And she was taking the time to help me out. It offered hope for our future relationship.

"Do you want me to light a wee fire for you?" I offered.

She shook her head, but smiled. "Thanks, but no thanks. There's a furnace I have in mind to visit as soon as we're done here. I hope you don't think I'm always this grouchy." Her apologetic smile made my knees tremble.

"No, no. Not at all! We're both tired, and that was a pretty scary experience."

Even as I said it, I realised for the first time how truly scared I had been. There's little that can threaten the existence of an elemental, but today I'd faced one full on, and I didn't feel I'd defeated it, merely postponed the outcome. At the time I'd allowed myself to be distracted by anger, using that to focus my wits. And afterward? Well. My ultimate distraction stood a scant few feet away from me, leaning against her Mini. I grabbed the opportunity to put our next meeting in place.

"We should talk about it and figure out how we can prevent it happening again, don't you think?" I rushed on, giving her no chance to answer. "Where shall we meet?"

Even in the gloom I saw her perfect eyebrows rise in surprise. Either she hadn't thought ahead, or it hadn't occurred to her to consider joining forces. If I hadn't been so besotted I might not have thought of it either, but a century of living and interacting with humans was having an effect on me.

I guess Gloria had been similarly influenced.

"Leakeys?" she suggested after a little hesitation.

"Great! When?"

"Give me a couple of day to see what shape my life is in. Three months' unexpected absence is going to take some explaining on a few fronts. 11 o'clock, Wednesday?"

"Grand! Just promise me you won't speak to any strange men in the meantime, or let them get close enough to touch you."

She gave me an odd look, and I wondered if I'd come across as over-protective. Of course I'd meant it that way, but Gloria had no reason to understand my concern for her safety.

"I'll do my best," she replied, sounding mildly offended.

But I was happy; our next meeting was arranged. I considered asking for her phone number, but I didn't want to sound desperate.

I studied every graceful, sinuous movement of her divine body as she slid into her car seat and closed the door, and then stood in the driveway watching as she drove around the side of the big house. The Mini Cooper disappeared behind the bulk of the building before its silhouette slipped briefly through the pool of light shed by the lanterns atop the gateway's substantial stone pillars. I continued to watch as she turned out of the drive and headed down the narrow lane, following her taillights until they vanished into the section of pine forest that yet survived the loggers, half a mile or so down the road.

I sighed then, building a vivid picture of her in my mind so that I would not forget any part of her face, her figure, or the way she moved. I stood there unmoving until I was distracted by the bumping sounds coming from the one basket that remained beside me on the drive.

Peter and Flopsy were at it again.

3. ENERGY

Feeding all the animals proved rather a trial, but fortunately I'd had guests to dinner a few nights before. Whilst I *can* eat, I don't actually need to, so I'm not in the habit of keeping food lying around. I raided the scraps bin and found some discarded cabbage leaves for the chickens, a few scraps of venison for the mink, and some left over slices of carrot from the pre-dinner dips for the guinea pigs and the loved up rabbits.

The latter pair was not interested; they had other things on their minds.

I knew I'd have to find proper homes for them all in the morning, but they were sorted for now and I *really* needed to fix my energy low before it became a crisis. I switched off the steading lights and headed over to the main house. As I trudged across the drive in the dark, my footsteps made barely any sound on the gravel, my weight so insubstantial that I was almost floating. I needed more mass as well as more energy, but the latter was more urgent.

I entered the pump house and checked that all the pumps and filters were fully functional, keeping the many systems in the house flowing with crystal clear, pure water. By the time I mounted the stairs that led up to the rear passageway I was almost gasping with anticipation.

At the top of the stairs I was met by what, on any other night, would have been a welcome sight—a handsome man wearing nothing but his boxer shorts.

Mid-brown hair hung straight to his shoulders, and I knew that if I touched it, it would feel as velvety as stroking one of the rabbits. He was masculine without being rugged, his face dominated by a pair of huge, liquid dark brown eyes that made him look far younger than I knew him truly to be. His apparent youthfulness was further implied by his washboard abs and narrow, tapering hips set above leanly muscled legs. His pleasure at seeing me jutted forward, making his boxers look like an over-sized codpiece.

"Euan?" I made a question of his name. "What are you doing here?"

His head tilted. "I need a reason? I don't recall ever needing one before."

I shook my head. He was right, he didn't need a reason. Euan was a free spirit, turning up when the mood took him and vanishing again without warning. The arrangement suited us both; pleasure without ties and sex without complication. If that makes me sound shallow, I hold my hands up. Commitment isn't integral to an elemental's makeup.

I smiled and ran a hand down his arm. "Sorry. I've had a bit of a day. I need an energy boost."

He shrugged. "Fine, go for it. I'll swim with you."

I held up a hand. "Whoa, slow down there sailor. It's rather more drastic than that. You can wait for me downstairs if you want."

"Okay," he agreed, and headed off towards the basement stairs. No argument, just straight acceptance: I loved him for it.

I made my way towards the front of the house, bypassing the rooms that were set up for human occupancy—bedrooms, living rooms, and the immaculate designer kitchen that never got dirty because it was never used. It was all for show in case anyone ever wandered around the house and wondered what sort of a freak lived there. I take care to guard the reality of my nature; as far as I can see, humans have enough to cope with in life without ever realising that the creatures of their dreams and nightmares live amongst them for real. The house was well equipped with a sophisticated burglar alarm, but that might not prevent someone from getting a good look before the police arrived. If the police had the time to respond to the silent alarm, that is.

I came into the grand entrance hall from the left. The dual, curved staircases swept up on either side of a large raised pool. I flicked a switch and a trio of chandeliers sparked the water to life with multihued glitter. From the centre of the pool rose an elegant marble fountain, its tall central spire sending a water jet high into the air. The spout reached almost to the level of the balcony where the two staircases met, before it cascaded down in fractured rainbows, creating a dome that made me shiver in recollection of the magician's trap.

This dome, however, was punctured in three places by the marble heads of huge trout that leaped upward from the base of the fountain. The fish had their jaws wide open, spewing water upward and outward, each one urged on to greater effort by the water nymphs that sat astride them. The sculptor might have intended the riders to be cherubs, but I was pretty sure that cherubs didn't appreciate getting wet; I've certainly never seen one riding a fish.

With a sigh of utter relief, I stepped over the low rim of the marble basin and dissolved into the water. I flowed through the choppy ripples at the edge of the pool, rejoicing in their slick caress. Like a salmon heading for the spawning grounds I rode the currents in reverse, travelling against the water flow towards the curtain of droplets cascading from the central fountain. The sensuous streamlined feeling of slicing head-on through the surge was intoxicating.

The undertow tugged at me and I surrendered, sucked down dizzyingly into the dark. Compressed by the narrow pipe, I was pumped through the filtration system. The sensation of being prickled all over with a light electric shock tickled deliciously.

Then I was speeding up the central column of the fountain, leaving behind the dark pipe work. White marble flashed past me until I whooshed back into the light and air, my atoms spread through the mist at the peak of the jet. Coruscating rainbows sparkled through me, lighting me from within. That moment at the apex of my flight lasted for an eternity and for a fraction of a second, and then I was falling, falling, gaining speed and energy as I cascaded back into the pool, drunk on light and power. Wonderfully refreshed and yet aching for more.

Replete for a short while, I floated luxuriantly. Then I went through the cycle again. And again.

Eventually I had enough energy spare to hold my illusion of human form for at least a week. I can live eternally in my true state without ever needing such reserves, but to shape-shift and hold a convincing human body—not to mention the wardrobe that goes with it—I need my regular fixes.

As I rose from the pool and coalesced my human body, I paused to study my reflection and compare myself with the voluptuous Gloria.

My eyes grew distinct first: grey-green, the colour of the North Sea on a sun-kissed day. Then my small, neat nose followed by my mouth: a perfect, kissable shape with plump lips that were just short of being a trout-pout. Straight blonde hair followed, reaching half way to my waist, cut square across the fringe to frame my elfin face. I've worn other faces but this was my current favourite, and I no longer had to concentrate to slip it on.

Even if the glorious Gloria removed her high heels, I would still be short beside her, no more than five feet five, and on some days a fraction less; it depended on how much mass I had to play with at any given time. And those curves of hers, mmm. I could almost feel her flesh beneath my hands as I mentally stroked her body, rising over her full breasts, dropping to trail over her tiny waist, spreading out with the swell of her hips and buttocks. Breath shuddered through me, my human self reacting with all the sensations such a body has to offer. My nipples tightened almost painfully, and the hot throbbing in my nether regions made me want to lie down on the cool marble and stroke myself to a climax.

I resisted, for the moment. Tempting though it was, I had a guest waiting for me; one who would pleasure me well, and who had a more important contribution to make to my body tonight.

I headed back along the passageway. Despite having just stepped from the pool I knew my bare feet left no damp footprints; every scrap of moisture was now locked into my human shape. I didn't bother with clothes as there was only Euan in the house and he preferred me naked.

Passing the door to the pump room, I continued along the corridor to the basement stairs. As I started down I could hear the shush of moving water, and I breathed deeply of the sharp, clean scent of mountain-fresh run off with its underlying peaty tang.

The stairs opened onto a huge cavern beneath the foundations, lit by enough daylight bulbs to evoke a bright summer's day. I remember when I commissioned the structure how the engineers had fought me, saying, "It can't be done." But there is always a way when you have money, and I had plenty, courtesy of all the trinkets that people had gifted me over the millennia, left as offerings at the shrines dedicated to me. I'm not sure when or why I started squirreling them away, but boy, did they turn out to be useful. Especially the solid gold ones.

I'd had the house built beside the burn, but once all was ready I had bisected the water flow, splitting off a branch to enter at one side of the house and drain out of the other, flowing in a steady rush across my own private river bed beneath the house. The rocky bed made the flow jump and swirl, while in places deep dark pools of almost still water were edged by frothy white bubbles. The water itself appeared peaty brown; one of the miracles of the Highlands, that water can be both sparklingly clear and yet peat-coloured at the same time.

I caught a flash of movement in one of the deeper pools and the domed head of a seal surfaced. He blew water from his nostrils and bobbed up and down a couple of times, deep brown eyes inviting me to join him. I dove into the icy water, keeping enough cohesion between my molecules to be visible. This is my natural element and the thrill of that fresh, cold force moving relentlessly over my fluid-self never fades.

I swam to the seal's side and stroked the curve of his head and neck, and down his shoulders where his mottled grey skin stretched taut over the thick layers of blubber, yet felt as soft to the touch as the plushest-coated cat. He preened, cat-like, under my liquid touch, and then dived, inviting a game of tag. I grinned and dived after him.

We chased in and out of the rocks and weeds. The vegetation wrapped itself around us, although in this I held a clear advantage, for there was nothing truly substantial about me whilst the seal, even with his slick hide, was quite solid. We played for some time, enjoying the water and the solitude of my private little world, but eventually with the help of the weed and the fact that he wanted to be caught, I snared him. Even as he tried to swim away I flowed over him, mounting to ride on his back, clinging onto his smooth curves with my long legs wrapped around his middle. Our twined bodies twisted in and out of the rocks, through the exhilarating rush of the fast-flowing current and the still of the deep pools. I rode him until his plunging became a soft undulation and the warmth of his plump body between my legs stirred desires that I was about ready to satisfy.

I leaned forward to put my arms around his neck and my nipples brushed against him, teasing a gasp of pleasure from my lips. The seal twisted around beneath me and swam the last few feet to the stream bank on his back with me resting on his broad belly.

As I left the water and re-clothed myself in solid flesh I kept my back turned. I heard nothing above the normal sound of running water, but was unsurprised when Euan's warm hand clasped my shoulder. I knew that no matter how hard I might search I would never locate his hidden sealskin, for a selkie depends on being able to hide his skin so well that no one will find it, or he may forever lose his ability to return to the sea. A selkie whose sealskin has been stolen or destroyed will become the most desolate of creatures, gaunt and hollow eyed, wandering aimless and uncaring through the remainder of a life no longer worth living. You may have seen one and not known it, thinking him a useless drifter, a drug addict or a homeless bum, all of which he may have become in fact, though not by choice.

Euan was a most cautious selkie. Even knowing that we were alone here in my private world he was careful, scrupulously maintaining the habits of his kind. I would have it no other way; I loved him as he was—ingenuous and wild. My sailor, who would arrive with the tide and leave again with as little fanfare.

He moved closer behind me and his arms slid around my shoulders, his warm hands cupping my breasts. His fingers began to stroke gentle circles round and around, without ever quite touching my aching nipples. I sucked in a sharp breath as every tiny muscle beneath my skin pulled taut.

Feather-light fingertips traced tingling lines down my ribcage, over my belly, then on down my legs before returning up the insides of my thighs. When his thumbs met, they brushed that nub of flesh that pulsed eagerly in demand, forcing a whimper from my throat.

His warm breath tickled against my cheek and brought with it the salty scent of ocean spray. I snuggled back against him, leaning my head to one side as his lips nuzzled the hollow at the base of my neck. I reached up with both arms, twining my fingers into his soft hair and pulled him tighter to me. My nails raked his scalp.

"Hai! You little shark!"

His teeth grazed my shoulder, ending with a swift nip that made my whole body jerk. I giggled and writhed inside his grip. Pressing back against him I could feel him long and straight and ready for me. My breathing quickened as he started to roll my nipples between each thumb and forefinger, sending streaks of lightning through my body. I twitched and moaned.

My body started to tremble as he tightened his grip, making my breath come in little gasps. I moaned again, willing him to get on with it, to slake my need. Heat built in my loins, fed by little runnels of flame. Was this how it would be with Gloria? Her fire would destroy me, and yet I would welcome it.

My trembling legs gave way and I sank to all fours, drawing Euan down with me.

"Please!"

The word burst from my throbbing lips and that was his signal. I was so ready for him, and yet as he slid into me the intense burst of sensation made me buck, almost tearing us apart. I pushed back and down hard, impaling myself upon the length of him and cried out, a shout of pure ecstasy.

We moved together in a harmony that is older than music and just as sweet. I could feel him growing inside me, expanding to fill every part of me as slowly, inexorably, we drew closer to that intense speck of promise.

I climaxed ahead of Euan, his voice echoing mine a few seconds later. For a short while we were creatures of pure sensation, our bodies lost to us in that molten moment when nothing and nobody matters, a moment that should last for eternity but is so brief it leaves you clinging to its fading echoes.

Euan bent over me, his smooth chest hot against my back and his breath rushing through my hair like wind through the treetops. The fresh smell of the sea filled my nostrils as his salty sweat dripped onto my skin, sinking in to become another part of me, as did his gift of semen with its precious load of DNA. Now I had the building blocks for the mass I needed to complete my illusion of humanity.

We clung together, twitching to the tune of diminishing spasms. Our breathing slowed and the languid feeling of satiation stole over us. I stretched out to lay full length on the artificial turf. Daylight bulbs are wonderful things, but if you grow grass, it needs cutting, and that's not my thing.

Euan reclined beside me, and I pulled one of his thighs between my legs, pressing him against me to prolong the aftershocks. He searched my eyes.

"You were ready for that, weren't you?"

I snorted and slapped his shoulder. "So were you, don't deny it!"

"Why would I?" His beautiful, clean-cut features drew into a puzzled frown, and I marvelled at how naïve of human ways he was, even more than me. Euan's contacts tended to be serious conservationists with devout passion for their beliefs. Casual teasing wasn't their style, so perhaps I shouldn't be surprised.

I drew a deep breath. By now my body had quieted and I was ready to enjoy the torpor earned by the thorough slaking of my lust.

"It's late and I'm tired," I said, not wanting to get into one of those confusing conversations that sometimes began with Euan on the back of one of my throw away comments. "Shall we?"

I rose fluidly and stepped off the bank into the water. We'd barely made it out of the stream in our haste, and I had to resist the urge to peek over my shoulder to try to spy Euan's—or indeed, any—hiding place this close to the water's edge, but even as I dissolved my human form there was an almighty splash, and the large seal hit the water as if from a running dive, swamping me. If

I'd still been human I'd have come up spluttering, but in the silence of my native form all I could do in return was to raise an unexpected swell that ducked the selkie. His smooth, sleek body flipped over and then bobbed to the surface, blowing water from his nostrils as he sneezed his laughter. We were like a pair of children in a candy store, and I'd eaten myself to a standstill.

Euan chose our favourite deep pool, and swam to the far edge where a large, flat slab of rock jutted from the bank below the surface. Turning onto his back, he manoeuvred his bulk until he rested on the ledge with his head clear of the water, and the rest of him submerged. He invited me to join him with just a look in those wonderful bottomless eyes, and I didn't hesitate, flowing onto his broad, soft belly and coming to rest with the peaceful water lapping gently, soporifically over me.

In truth, I don't sleep; I simply float without conscious thought, and that's what I did, supported by Euan's body. In the days before technology made my life so hazardous I would drift wherever the currents took me, gazing up at the ever-changing sky, watching day become night, rain give way to sun and back again, the seasons turn and the centuries float past. Sometimes I would stay that way for millennia. It's a useful skill during an ice age, when I would stay frozen into a glacier, creeping inexorably, piece by infinitesimal piece across the unchanging landscape until the warmth returned and unlocked the land from the beneath the ice. I *could* have escaped if I'd been bothered to store up the energy beforehand, and then moved south to warmer climes, but this was my home and I had no desire to leave it.

And besides, there's not much point being active during an ice age. Not a lot to do, is there?

4. WORK

In the morning it was raining.

Damn, but I hate the rain! Of course this can be a teensy problem as it rains rather a lot in the Scottish Highlands. In my natural state I never notice it one way or the other, but it makes holding a human shape far more of an effort.

It was one of those grey, blustery autumn days where the sky tries to press down and smother you, and you know that if only it would lift a little you'd see the first white caps of the season shining on the mountain peaks, like vanilla icing on cup cakes.

Big, fat droplets beat into the gravel between the big house and the steading, and with a resigned sigh I dashed across the open space, not worrying *too* much about the cohesion of my body but ready with an extra surge of energy should the postie arrive early. At this moment, the clothes I appeared to be wearing were no more than an extension of my adopted shape. It's a useful ability but clothing also takes energy to simulate, so once the steading door swung shut, I grabbed a peach-coloured t-shirt and a toning pair of joggers from the airing cupboard and slid into them.

I checked the clock: 08.45. Damn, but I was running late! It was Monday morning and my first client of the day was always punctual. The animal cages smelled ripe, but I had no time to stop and deal with them. With any luck I'd be able to re-home all the poor unfortunates by the end of the day. The mink might be more of a headache, but that would all have to wait for now. I tossed in the last of the scraps I'd salvaged from the bin last night and dashed out to the garage, throwing on a zip-up fleece to match the joggers.

I paused briefly to consider my choice of car for the day, and the VW Tiguan won hands down. I love my Golf, and the sleek little Audi Quattro, but I had miles of poorly maintained driveway to cope with later this afternoon, and the 4x4 Tiggi was far more suitable. Whilst deliberately not *too* grandiose, my collection of cars is the envy of my friends. Like the big house, they believe them to belong to the fictitious owner for whom I act as caretaker.

I climbed into the car and started the engine. As I glanced in the rear view mirror to reverse out, ghostly fingers invaded my ribcage, clutched my heart and squeezed. The sensation was fleeting, but it tore a gasp from my throat.

What if the magician knew where I lived?

I don't need a real heart, or blood, but the DNA I use to pattern my physical shell creates the whole package, inside and out, and I gulped several deep breaths to quell my panic.

Gods, it wasn't something I'd even considered! Not whilst I was re-energising last night, nor while I was fucking Euan, nor yet whilst dressing for work this morning. But he'd known so much about me it was something I needed to take seriously.

My throat closed up and I glanced again in the rear view mirror, half expecting to find him behind me, but all I saw was wet gravel. I backed out cautiously and vowed to keep a much warier eye on my surroundings until I found the little squirt and dealt with him.

My driving this morning was scarily reminiscent of Gloria's, and I made a mental note not to be critical another time. In truth, I didn't want to be critical about anything to do with Gloria; I just wanted to see her again. I wanted it so hard that I ached, in my chest and in places lower down in my body. I wasn't sure how I was going to survive until our meeting on Wednesday. At least I had plenty to do during the days. Nights might be more of an issue, depending on whether Euan stayed around or not. I knew there was a naval exercise scheduled for the Moray Firth sometime soon, and I guessed that was behind his sudden appearance; he would be masterminding the protests against their use of high-intensity active sonar.

Quite apart from enjoying Euan's unscheduled visits, I heartily approved of his activities. Why does the human race police noise pollution everywhere but in the oceans? How can the deafening of whales and dolphins and other sea dwellers be justified, or is it simply that none of the afflicted were ever going to represent themselves in a court of law? The seas around the Moray Firth are noisy enough as it is, what with heavy shipping, oil drilling and seismic surveys, not to mention underwater sonic alarms to keep seals away from the fish farms. The noise levels do not need adding to for the sake of an exercise. Protests such as Euan and his compatriots masterminded have produced concessions, moving these abominations into deeper water, further offshore from the fragile ecology of the Firth. But they still use them further out, still deafen, maim and kill hundreds of cetaceans every year, and it has to be stopped. Everyone has their soapbox, and for obvious reasons, this was Euan's.

"Whoa, watch it asshole!"

This, to the driver who had overtaken me through a huge puddle, spraying my windscreen with so much water that I was momentarily blinded. My wipers clicked onto high speed. I had just enough time to see the taillights at the back of the queue to the roundabout to stop without aquaplaning. It would have been ironic for me to have an accident caused by water, but I wasn't in an ironic mood today.

"I don't believe it!" I fumed as I realised I was only halfway across the Kessock bridge. It was going to take forever to get into the city today.

I was ten minutes late. I dashed across the puddle-infested car park with a raincoat clutched around me. Each of my cars carries at least one waterproof, and most carry several. I *really* don't like the rain.

I barged through the doors of the gym like a battering ram. Heads turned and turned away again. My moods have a reputation.

I dashed to the staff changing room, offloaded my waterproof and fleece and picked up my clipboard. When I first started working as a personal fitness trainer several decades (and appearances) ago, all I had to do was to teach people how to use the equipment, and then stand back and shout at them. Simple. Nowadays it's paperwork, paperwork, paperwork. Thank the gods for adult learning centres. I survived millennia without ever needing to read or write, but after a single century of human existence I've had to acquire a whole new skill set. You can't do this job today without filling out risk assessments, health assessments, record keeping, diet plans, etcetera and so on. Yawn. One day I might change my profession.

I've tried the rich party girl scene, and whilst DNA is easy to come by on that circuit, I bored of it fast. Hairdressing was another obvious choice, but the bitchiness and backstabbing put me off. The crowd at the gym have a positive approach to life that appeals to me, and for now it fulfils my needs.

Dylan, my first client of the day, was sitting astride a bench. He stared at the treadmill with that love/hate expression you see on the face of the guy who is attracted to the wrong type of girl; the one he adores but who he knows will let him down by cheating on him the moment his back is turned. Exercise and weight loss can be just so—short-lived and disappointing unless you keep on top of it one hundred percent of the time. At least it's not something I have to worry about.

"So, Dylan, let's start by getting you on the scales, shall we?"

Weigh in complete, heart monitor on, water bottle checked. Dylan complied with all my requests like a little boy eager to be teacher's pet. I know I look good in this body, but did he really think I could be attracted to a forty-something, overweight and balding salesman? Sorry, sales *executive*. He was a sweet man, but I wanted only one thing from him, and that was going to be on his towel when we'd finished this session.

I'd set his programme on the treadmill and watched his face close down to utter concentration as he focussed on striding along at a pace fast enough to make him sweat, when Alison bounced in. Alison bounces everywhere; she's a genuinely bouncy person. Her sleekly straightened shoulder-length red hair shone with the gleam of avocado shampoo, and her green eyes twinkled. There had been a time when I'd considered seducing Alison, but I'd decided to keep things on a friendly basis rather than risk changing our relationship so radically. Alison was fun, and I wanted to keep her that way.

"Cassie! Did you have a great time? You were gone all weekend, what did you and that guy get up to? I didn't think he was your type, but obviously I was wrong. I want to hear *all* the details!"

It took me a moment to realise she was talking about the magician. Ugh! Did Alison think I could be attracted to a nerd who wears his jeans below his boxers? Could she not credit me with a little more taste?

"Um, Cassie...?"

"Oh, sorry Dylan." I slowed the treadmill and switched it off. "Take a break for a moment and a drink of water. I'll be right with you."

I sauntered out to where Alison was starting to arrange things for her body balance class. I considered my approach. It's taken me a while to appreciate that direct questions are not always the best option, but I am learning. This time I reckoned that I might get more by playing along than by denial, even though I found the idea of taking up with the nerd offensive.

"Did you enjoy the meeting?" I asked. "Was it what you hoped for? I'm sorry I abandoned you."

"Hey, nae bother. I know you only came along to hold my hand. Witchy stuff doesn't really interest you, does it?"

There was bravado in her voice, and I realised the hand holding wasn't over yet. Well, it was the only way I was going to get a lead on Mr Magician anyway.

"Not true!" I protested. "I got sort of sidetracked, that's all."

Alison's grin revealed her wicked side. Just as well her interest was in white witchcraft, or else certain persons, such as her soon-to-be-ex-husband, might be in serious do-do.

"And I'm waiting for a full report on that. And I do mean full." She glanced across at Dylan. "But you'd better get back to work. Lunch? Or do you have to dash off?"

"I think I can spare a half hour. Tisos, half one?"

"Sure."

I went back to Dylan. By the time I'd finished with him he was sweating bucket-loads. I handed him a couple of towels in a plastic bag. While he trundled off to the male changing room for his shower, and to put lots of lovely skin cells all over my towels, I sat for a few moments to sign off on this session's paperwork and to mull over what to tell Alison. For someone who was quite reticent about her own private life, Alison wanted to know all the gory details of everyone else's, especially the steamy bits.

My musings were interrupted by Dylan's presentation of the plastic bag containing the used towels. Some of my clients thought it quaint that I provided them with towels and laundered them myself, but most of them went along with it to keep me happy. Which it did. They had no cause to suspect anything other than mild eccentricity, and besides, once they'd shed those skin cells they had no further use for them whilst I did. I viewed it as recycling a waste product.

Two more private clients filled the slots leading up to lunch, and by then I was ready to survive Alison's interrogation. When we emerged from the gym the rain had ceased and a watery sunshine was leaking through the cloud layer. A faint rainbow arched high above our heads. Alison wanted to walk, to enjoy the rain-refreshed air but I didn't trust the weather, so we hopped into my car for the couple of minutes it took to negotiate the busy roads around one of Inverness's main retail areas and park right in front of the glass-walled Tiso store.

Tiso is one of those stores where you find the most rugged of outdoorsy people buying all manner of camping, hiking, survival and outdoor pursuit gear. It also houses a superb café, always busy at lunchtime, upstairs on a mezzanine floor with an excellent view of the climbing wall. Today the wall was empty; plastic simulated rock that resembled an artist's oversized impression of human skin seen under a microscope. Now, *my* skin would never look so, even highly magnified, for I *truly* have a flawless complexion.

The bearded waiter flashed us a dazzling smile. We were regulars, and I was pretty sure he entertained hopes of getting to know Alison rather better. She appeared oblivious to his interest and I didn't feel any urgency to point it out to her. She'd been going through divorce for some time now, and it was messy in both the financial and emotional departments, so I doubted she would be letting any man get close to her again for some long while, even one as cute as this guy.

"Your usual, ladies?" He flashed the grin again.

Alison raised an eyebrow towards me and I nodded. "Thanks," she confirmed. "Same as ever." She smiled her dazzling smile in return and I could almost see the waiter's knees go weak. Oh, he had it bad, poor lad.

"So, now you can tell me *all* about it."

I produced the mildly embarrassed look I'd been practicing in front of the mirror during unnecessary comfort breaks.

"I'm sorry I skipped out on you that way. I don't know what came over me. As you say, he's not my usual type."

"Name?"

Had I heard his name? I remembered seeing him when we arrived at the coven meeting, but had we been introduced? I hesitated a moment too long.

"Cassie! You don't even know his name?"

Now I didn't have to feign embarrassment. I shook my head. "Can't remember it. Can you?"

"Me? Why should I?"

"I thought perhaps he'd been introduced by the group."

"Not that I can recall, but I'm not the one who sloped off with him. Did you go to his or yours?"

"Um, his. I think. It looked a bit derelict."

"Oooh, weren't you scared?" Alison wrapped her arms around herself and gave a dramatic shiver. "He could have been one of those weirdoes, you know, an axe murderer or something."

It was my turn to raise an eyebrow, Spock-style. "I'm pretty good at taking care of myself, you know that." I cocked my head on one side and put a finger to my chin. "No, I don't think axe murderer entered my mind."

"Stop it!" Alison punched me playfully on the arm just as our drinks arrived, almost causing a minor catastrophe as my shoulder knocked into our favourite waiter.

"Whoa, sorry!" Alison's hands flew up to cover her mouth and hide her mortified expression. For someone who was so outgoing, she had a massive vacuum where her confidence should be courtesy of her soon-to-be-ex, Simon.

"Nae bother," our waiter assured her, mopping up the spilled coffee with the dishcloth he plucked from his waistband. "Really, nae bother at all."

He beamed again and got a tentative twitch of Alison's lips in reward. Perhaps I was too hasty in assuming that nothing would happen here; true love might begin so gently and blossom with time. I'd seen it happen over and over in the human world, although I'd always been a mere observer. I wasn't sure that a sprite was capable of experiencing true love. Perhaps I was doomed to fall forever in lust with one person after another, although my obsessively strong feelings for Gloria were giving me grounds to reconsider.

"So when does the coven meet again?" I asked once the smiling and eyelash fluttering was over, and the waiter had moved on. "I have another friend who might want to join."

"Oh, who's that?"

"You won't know her; I met her recently, at a party."

Alison eyebrows lifted. "And you happened to get onto the subject of witchcraft? You usually have other things on your mind at parties. Don't think I haven't noticed!"

The twinkle in her eye made me wonder if I'd made a mistake, not seducing her. Then my mind's eye threw up a vision of Gloria as I'd first seen her, smouldering with righteous anger, and my body suffused with a heat that had nothing to do with the steaming mug of hot chocolate—topped with whipped cream, of course—that I was nursing between my hands. Alison was sweet, but Gloria? Gloria did something to me deep down that I wanted to keep right on feeling. If this was love as humans experienced it, then I could begin to understand why it was responsible for so many irrational and reckless actions.

"Cassie?"

I blinked and refocused on Alison. "Sorry, drifted off for a moment."

"No kidding. Was he worth it?"

He? Oh, of course; back to the nameless magician. As if.

I decided to make a bold statement, at the risk of shocking Alison. "You know, not only do I not know his name, but I don't even remember where he lives. The coven is the one way I have of trying to meet him again."

Truth, all of it.

"Cassie! Were you pissed?"

"Oh yes, indeed!" I agreed, though not in the context Alison meant.

"As it happens, they're having another meeting tomorrow afternoon. Can you make it? And your friend?"

I'd rather planned on seeing Gloria again before I went magician hunting, but I didn't want to miss the opportunity. Attack being the best form of defence, and all that.

"I've got a couple of classes in the morning but I'm finished by lunchtime. Pick you up on the way?" I offered. "I'm not seeing Gloria again until Wednesday, so just me this time."

"Okay, great." The big beaming Alison smile was so bright it threatened to eclipse the cheery painting of sunflowers on the wall beside our table. When Alison smiles, everyone feels compelled to smile right along with her, as if there is a little bit of magic escaping her soul and infecting those around her with goodwill.

Our meals arrived at that moment, preceded by the rich smell of cooked bacon and delivered by a different waiter. Alison's Brie and bacon toastie was a special, not on the standard menu, but always available to us. My minestrone soup was nice and liquid, and I could sip away at it without being too obvious that I wasn't consuming the floating bits. Eating does cause me one problem; namely what to do with it once I've ingested it. As I have no way of incorporating it into my body I prefer not to eat unless it's socially unavoidable. It's a shame because my taste buds work perfectly well but hey, abstinence is supposed to be good for you, isn't it? Or is that sex?

About half way through the meal I remembered the other reason I'd wanted to speak with Alison today.

"Oh, Alison, do you have any room for a few more pets at that wee croft of yours?"

"What sort?"

Alison was always up for homing waifs and strays, and although she had a fair sized garden that had once been crofting land, she had limited funds to support her ever-growing animal refuge.

"A couple of chickens, a pair of lop-eared rabbits—although I suspect there might be more of those on the way—three guinea pigs and a mink."

Alison barely hesitated. "I can take them all but the mink. I don't fancy the chances of most of my darlings if it got out. I know a family that will take the guinea pigs, and the others are welcome to join the throng. How on earth did you end up with that lot?"

"I found them abandoned in a car park," I answered truthfully. Alison was predictably scandalised, but I hurried on, not wishing to expound further. "I'll fetch them over when I pick you up tomorrow, okay?"

"Fine. I can get housing arranged tonight." She glanced at her watch. "Time I was getting back. I'll walk, then you can get away. See you tomorrow."

It was my turn to pay the bill, and as I waited for my change I watched the top of Alison's bright red head bobbing down the spiral staircase. I wasn't the only one to watch her go. Whilst our friendly waiter appeared charming and inoffensive, I was going to keep a close eye on things as they developed.

If he hurt my best friend he would have me to answer to.

5. MINKIE

Back home, I parked the Tiguan outside the steading.

I'd spent the afternoon driving around the area, visiting my wealthy private clients who were willing to pay extra for a home visit. I'd also spent much of that time looking over my shoulder, worried in case the magician had somehow gained access to my private files, and might be lying in wait for me at one of the secluded properties. My unease increased as I turned into my own drive, and I sat tensely inside the stationary car after turning the engine off. I scanned the gravel for signs that anyone might have been there while I was out. It would have been faster in my natural form with its all-round awareness, but I was unwilling to drop my pretence of being human until I was certain no one was there.

Perhaps it wasn't so important to keep my nature secret; I'm sure none of my human friends would intentionally out me. But humans in general are so inconsistent at keeping confidences that I was not inclined to test the theory. The potential public panic and media frenzy such a revelation would generate were things I had no wish to contemplate.

The gravel outside looked as grey and wet and static as ever; not the best material for harbouring clues. Letting go my tension with an audible sigh, I opened the car door and stepped out into the chill, damp air of late afternoon. Grabbing my shopping bags from the back seat, I dashed through the pelting rain to the steading, wincing as my boots crunched across the gravel. No one leapt out of the shadows to ambush me as I opened the door, and I forcibly reined in my paranoia. There was no evidence to suggest that the madman who had captured me had any idea of where I lived. No proof to the contrary either, but unless I decided to move out until this whole thing was sorted, I would just have to live with it.

A pungent odour, so strong that it almost made me retch, greeted me as the door swung open. Thank the gods I was going to be rid of most of my unwanted menagerie soon! A copy of the local newspaper, the *Press and Journal*, lay on the mat and I picked it up. The main headline was yet again about the power cuts plaguing London, but the lead local story was headed: 'VANDALS SET FIRE TO DISUSED POWER STATION'.

I closed the door behind me and stood on the mat, my wet coat dripping onto the coir as I read the article. Half the front page was taken up by a photograph of the burnt out carcass of the old power station, its charred roof trusses sticking up like the broken ribs of an ancient skeleton. The police were not speculating on the culprits, but the journalist writing the piece proposed the theory that a bunch of war-games freaks might be responsible. He cited the intensity of the fire as evidence of the use of some sort of flame thrower.

Flame thrower? Yup, I'm sure Gloria could be described as such, but I was equally sure that neither journalist nor police were going to get to the bottom of this perpetrator's identity. Between the flood and the fire, I was pretty certain there wasn't much evidence left and anything they did find would lead them to the architect of the whole sorry mess. The magician.

If only I had a friend in the local constabulary.

With a sigh, I stripped off my coat and boots and dropped them in a soggy heap on the mat. Images of Gloria in all her fiery splendour on the tarmac outside the blazing building drifted across my mind. My body responded with a tightening that verged on painful. I wasn't sure I could wait two more days to see her again. Why hadn't I asked for her address, or found out where she worked? I had not been thinking straight. Or indeed thinking at all.

Knowing there was nothing I could do to change how useless I'd been, I took a deep breath, resolved to be more intelligent at our next meeting, and almost choked on the smell from the utility room. Resigned to more immediate necessity, I peeked around the door, hoping that none of the animals would notice. A cacophony of cries greeted me and I sighed again. No peace for the wicked.

"Aha! Fooled you, didn't I. You thought I'd forgotten you. Well you were wrong!"

I emptied the contents of my hessian re-usable shopping bags onto the floor. Cat litter, guinea pig and rabbit food, chicken pellets and a pack of frozen tripe for the mink, now partially de-frosted. I was trying to figure out how to clean the baskets without losing their occupants when the doorbell rang. Icy shards sliced through me. I told myself that it would be nobody of import, that the magician would hardly ring the doorbell to announce himself. At the same time, I secretly hoped Gloria had decided she couldn't wait until Wednesday either. I slunk into the front room. Moving very slowly, I eased up to the window and peered out from behind the curtain.

My neighbour stood there. I breathed again in relief and went to let Morag in, kicking my sodden coat and boots behind the door as I opened it.

"Sorry to keep you, Morag; I'm dealing with an unusual problem."

"Och, do tell me more," encouraged the farmer's wife. Morag was a somewhat dumpy lady of around sixty. Her round face was capped with short but quite unruly greying brown curls, which today were crammed under a dripping waxed hat with a wide brim that sported a rather limp pheasant's feather. Her rosy cheeks were two high spots of pink against her pale complexion, resembling those on a porcelain doll. The rest of her was hidden beneath an oversized drover's jacket that hung to well below her knees, with a pair of formerly pink wellies sticking incongruously out from beneath the shapeless coat.

"Come and see for yourself."

Morag divested herself of her wet weather gear, dropping it on top of mine, and followed me into the crowded utility room. She stared in bemusement at the stacked cages and baskets.

"Well! Whatever are you doing with this lot, Cassie? Starting a rescue centre?"

"As if! I found them abandoned in a car park miles from anywhere, and I couldn't leave them there."

Morag looked as shocked as Alison had done. "Of course not, poor wee things. But what are you going to do with them?"

"Alison's volunteered to sort out homes for everything but the mink. Any idea what I can do with that?"

Morag's mouth twisted. "Nae. They dinna make good pets, not like ferrets. Give it to a mink farm?"

For some reason this sensible and practical suggestion shocked me. "And have it end up in a fur coat? I don't think I could do that. I guess I'll have to keep him."

"Well dear, if you want to give it a go, there's an old cage lurking around in the undergrowth back of our small barn. If you can drag it out you're welcome to it. And in the meanwhile, I think we'd best do something about these other poor wee dears."

"Morag, you're a star! I'll put the kettle on."

Together, we made short work of it. Unlike me, Morag handled animals every day, and in no time at all we'd cleaned all the filthy straw from each basket and replaced it with a layer of newspaper topped with cat litter. Each of the occupants was efficiently moved from its basket to a cardboard box for the duration.

As expected, the mink proved more of a challenge. The moment he was out of his cage he took off around the utility room, jumping first to the work surface beside the sink and from there, a prodigious leap landed him onto the top of the waste bin's flip top lid, which promptly flipped and dropped him inside. This didn't seem to bother him too much so we left him there, rootling through the rubbish until it was time to return him to his freshly littered cage.

"Careful now, dear, mink have fearsome teeth."

I shrugged my eyebrows; a mannerism I'd copied from an actor in one of my favourite TV shows. "If I'm going to keep him, I have to start somewhere."

Reaching into the bin, I discovered exactly how sharp the little bugger's teeth were. Fortunately for me, as I'm largely illusion no matter how solid I may seem to the touch, his needle-sharp gnashers found nothing to pierce, and I lifted him triumphantly from the bin with a rather stunned expression on his furry wee face.

"Bravo!" Morag enthused, as I bundled him back into his cage and shut the door. "Right you are, I'll make us a nice pot of tea."

The kettle was singing on the Aga, and Morag bustled about the kitchen making tea. She was so frequent a visitor, she knew where everything was. Bless the woman, she had such a good heart, and whilst there was nothing I was ever likely to need from her I knew that if there had been, Morag would have been around with whatever it was as soon as she was able.

We sat in the kitchen, which now smelled blessedly better than before the basket purge. I nursed my mug of tea and asked, "So what's on your mind?"

Morag blinked. "Och, I quite forgot! I came to see if you wanted some eggs; we've quite a surplus just now."

Morag and her husband Jock's little farm staggered from one financial crisis to the next, and I was always willing to help out where I could, even with something as simple as buying an extra box of eggs. These usually went to Alison, either for feeding herself or for some of her animals, but I realised that with a mink to feed I might now have a use for some too.

"I'll have a couple of dozen then, if you have them going spare."

"Right you are then, dear. I'd better be getting along," she said, but lingered indecisively in her chair.

"Morag? Was there something else?"

"Oh, Cassie, you always do know when I've something on my mind. It's Jock. His birthday is coming up and I dinnae know what to get him. You always have such good ideas; you've such a wise old head on young shoulders."

"What did you get him last year?" I asked, wondering how I'd gained this reputation for wisdom. Why in all the oceans would *I* have any idea what a human male would want? Apart from the obvious, that is, and I've long since learned the hard way that not *every* human problem can be solved with sex.

Most, maybe, but not all.

By the time Morag and I were waving goodbye I'd heard about Jock's last ten birthday presents. I doubt the one we'd settled on—a new waxed jacket and hat—was going to be any more exciting than the previous ones, but at least it was something he needed, and so could be justified as money well spent. And he'd look, not to mention smell, a bit better at the pub for at least a few weeks.

As I was about to close the door, Morag's voice wafted back to me through the drizzle. "If you're going to keep that mink you'd better give it a name. How about Jock?"

"I'll think about it," I promised, and shut out the night. But I didn't need to think about it. I'd already named him. Minkie. Not original, I know, but appropriate.

I popped Minkie's bowl of minced tripe into the microwave to finish defrosting, and picked up the clear plastic bags containing today's used towels. Their contents went into my specially prepared soaking bowls to remove all the flakes of dead skin that humans shed every day of their lives.

During the night my body had converted Euan's semen into the usable chains of DNA that make my human body tangible, but it wasn't as pure as it would have been if he'd been a real human, and so wouldn't last as long. The skin cells are my emergency backup. Whilst I can appear solid enough on energy alone, to *feel* the real deal I need the authentic building blocks—not in huge quantity, but without them my body is no more than illusion.

I was replete now for a while on both fronts, so it was time to concentrate on finding the audacious magician who dared to imprison not one, but two elementals and try to bend them to his will.

Hmm. Something wrong with that thought. I still had *no* idea what it was he'd been expecting to happen when he shrank that spell-sphere to force us together. It made no *sense!* He might have been insanely confident in his abilities, but he hadn't appeared truly mad, and no one but a madman would want to create an explosion of the size that one promised to be, and stand within a hundred miles of it.

The microwave binged and I removed the glass plate with Minkie's now defrosted supper on it. I reckoned a glass plate was the safest thing to give him, as I suspected the little plastic bowls I'd supplied the other animals with might not survive his teeth. He stayed respectfully at the back of the cage when I opened the door and slid the plate in. His beady black mink eyes regarded me warily. I think he'd been shocked by his inability to draw blood from me, and was treating me with respect. A good way to begin our new relationship, I felt.

With my pet chores complete, I switched off the utility lights and shut the door. Giving myself no time to hesitate, I flung open the front door and peered out into the rain. Nothing moved out there, and I bolted across the gravel to the main house, not caring if I melted a bit at the edges.

Inside, the house was dark. No Euan tonight. With the magician lurking constantly on the fringes of my thoughts, I went straight to my basement hideaway. For the first time ever, I locked the doors behind me. They were sufficient to keep out casual intruders, but a magician?

I put that disturbing notion aside and slid into the stream. Even if he found my hideaway, he was going to have trouble extracting me from thousands of gallons of moving water.

The next morning, thankfully bright and sunny, dragged past in a blur of training sessions and classes with nothing out of the ordinary to pique my interest. Frequent thoughts of Gloria distracted me and I ran on autopilot. I doubt most of my clients noticed. They were too busy panting and sweating.

Back home in the steading, I made the most of one of the biggest advantages of being a sprite: I have no need to spend time bathing or showering, which gives me more time for dressing.

Going to a coven meeting was hardly a high fashion outing, but I always enjoy looking my best whether my clothes are real or illusory. Bearing in mind that I had all the animals to deliver first, I picked over my extensive wardrobe, discarding garments that were either too dressy or too business-like. I settled on a pair of heavily embroidered blue jeans with geometric designs in red and gold. They fit snugly over my rear and upper legs, flaring out below the knee to fit over my favourite cowboy boots. I teamed them with a red and blue checked blouse with frilled cuffs on the three quarter length sleeves, and then added subtle colour changes to my eyelids and lips to blend with the hoedown country-girl look. I knotted my hair on top of my head, tweaking out a few stray blonde tips to form an artistically tatty bun. I don't understand the concept of vanity. Why would anyone not want to look good if they can? And I surely can.

After one more twirl in front of the mirror, I went outside and stacked all the animal baskets on top of plastic sheeting in the back of the Tiguan. I was ready too soon, so I filled up a bit of time preparing a meal for my new pet.

Minkie was still staying clear of me, lurking at the back of his cage when I put his food in, but I swear his expression was one of relief when I shut the utility door without taking him too.

I drove slowly to Alison's. Her croft lay out behind Drumnadrochit, a village on the banks of Loch Ness. As I drove along the windy road that hugs the edge of the loch I took frequent glances at the grey and choppy water, wondering when I might find a moment to once more visit its dark depths and well-kept secrets. At twenty three miles long, a mile and a half wide and up to 900 feet deep, Loch Ness has such capacity that if you were to drop the entirety of the planet's human population into it, they would all fit. No small wonder then, that after countless studies and oodles of so-called scientific research, this great loch yet retains its mysteries.

On reaching Drumnadrochit I drove past the Loch Ness Monster Exhibition before turning onto the road to Cannich. Alison's croft was half a mile up a narrow rutted drive. And I do mean, *up*. Considering the animals in the back, I crawled up the drive, arriving to my relief with everything still in place. I looked the place over with my customary bemusement.

The building was a traditional single storey croft, rectangular and white painted with a dark grey slate roof. The red paint on the windowsills and front door was peeling, and creepers climbed every drainpipe to invade the guttering. The waist-high wooden palisade fence was in somewhat better condition than the house, surrounding a bewildering hotchpotch of chicken houses, hutches and runs. There was just enough space to push a wheelbarrow between them, and the mud was kept at bay by the liberal use of wood chippings. At the farthest end, a chain-link fence penned in a pair of black and white nanny goats.

I parked behind Alison's ancient Peugeot and scowled when I saw Simon's BMW beside it. What did that git want now?

Raised voices issued from the open front door.

"Why did you have to go poking your nose in? Now you've ruined everything!"

I could hear Simon's voice long before I made it to the front door. As if it wasn't bad enough that the creep was breaking Alison's heart, he was also trying to lay the blame at her feet.

Bastard!

"*Me?*" shrieked Alison. "You're the one with a whole other life and whole other family! What did you think I was going to do, leave them in the dark so you could carry on fucking with their lives like you have with mine?"

Whoa, this was getting real heated, real fast. I hurried up the path and pushed the door open. "Alison? You okay?"

"I might have known you'd call the cavalry," Simon snarled. "Hello Cassie," he added without looking round as I entered the kitchen. "Come to poke your nose in where it's not wanted?"

"I'm here to support my friend," I said, "and speaking of being where you're not wanted, I thought you didn't live here anymore. Not happy being with your other wife either, eh?"

He stood up then, and turned to face me. If a man could be judged by looks alone, Simon would have been a winner. Providing you like the tall dark and handsome cliché. Sadly, his delectable surface hid some nasty surprises, one of which Alison had accidentally discovered: a second wife and two kids.

"I'll come back when we can get some privacy," he said, and stormed past me. "And don't think you're keeping the plasma screen either," he flung over his shoulder as he exited.

"As if I'd want that monstrosity!" Alison screamed at his back. She stood in the middle of the kitchen, hyperventilating. Outside, Simon's car door slammed and the engine started. I allowed myself a nasty wee smile then, picturing Simon's face as he discovered that he was sitting in a puddle. Fabric car seats can hold *so* much moisture, and I'd added a *teensy* bit to it when I passed his car. I'm not normally vindictive, but for Simon I was happy to make an exception.

"Oh, goddess, I hate that man!" Tears ran down Alison's cheeks and gathered in little rivulets that dripped off her chin. "Is that wrong of me?"

"Of course not," I said. "Come here." I wrapped her in my arms. Humans derive such comfort from touching, and whilst I wasn't human, she didn't know that.

"Oh Cassie, what did I do wrong? I really thought he was the one."

I'd heard about this 'one' before, but until Gloria I hadn't any idea what they were talking about. Gloria was the 'one' for me, I was two hundred percent certain. Thinking of her in another's arms made me rage inside, like a whirlpool or a tsunami.

Alison dissolved into weeping interspersed with stuttered little phrases, "How could he?" Snuffle. "No one deserves to be treated like this!" Sniff. "You'd never dream of doing anything like that, would you Cassie?"

"Of course not," I assured her, and hugged her close.

"How could he? He lied to everyone, even *her*! Promise me you'd never keep a secret like that, Cass? *Promise* me you wouldn't!"

"Shhh." I stroked her sleek ginger hair. "Of course I wouldn't, silly. I'd never keep a secret like that from my best friend."

I crossed my fingers behind my back. My secret wasn't quite the same as Simon's, was it? And besides, Alison would never know the truth. I've had many human friends down the centuries and none of them have ever known; why should this time be any different?

She looked up at me, tears making her eyes sparkle. "Promise?"

"Promise."

She grabbed a tea towel from the Aga rail and wiped her face. A fluffy white cat appeared from nowhere to twine about her ankles. Jemima, one of her pair of feline companions.

"It's okay, my darling," Alison reassured, and reached down to stroke the cat with a shaking hand. I waited while she regained her composure, and after a couple of minutes she straightened up.

"Right, we'd better get those animals in or we'll be late," she said, her voice almost stable. I followed her out of the house with Jemima trailing in our wake.

I duly carried baskets around the garden, saying goodbye to each of my temporary charges until the Tiguan was empty and we were ready to go. Alison closed the front door without locking it. Burglary is so very rare in the Highlands that locked doors are unusual.

Unless, like me, you have a crazy magician after you.

We set off down the track and turned right out of Alison's drive, heading further into the hills.

6. THE COVEN

"Well, hello again! We are *so* glad you could make it!"

Saffron, the larger than life High Priestess of the coven, always spoke with exclamation marks. Older than Alison by at least a generation, she was also taller than the pair of us and probably combined our waist measurements around her girth, hidden though it was beneath a voluminous midnight blue velvet dress. Her jet black hair was about as real as her inappropriate name.

She and the rest of the coven were standing on the lawn at the front of her house, a very grand eco-friendly log cabin set in a clearing deep inside the Caledonian Forest. The facade sported acres of glass—triple glazed, of course—and the wood was colour treated to match the bark of the surrounding Scots pines. The last meeting had been indoors, and I knew that the twee furnishings were very in-keeping with Saffron but revealed little about Gordon, her druid husband.

As thin as Saffron was wide, Gordon did nothing to try to hide his age, with his straggly grey hair reaching almost to his waist. On our last visit I'd gained the impression that he had far greater depth of knowledge and length of devotion to his calling than his partner, yet he was not counted as a member of the coven, choosing to watch quietly from the sidelines.

This evening, Gordon was deep in conversation with a middle-aged balding man whose paunch overshadowed his denim jeans and stretched the button holes on his pale pink, open-necked shirt.

Saffron swept across the lawn to greet us.

"Follow me, girls, you must come and meet our guest!"

Raising both arms expansively and wafting a strong musk perfume our way, Saffron ushered us across the lawn, hardly pausing to draw breath as we went.

"It's too exciting for words; this is such a coup! Brian Chivers is far more important than anyone Rhona's been able to get!"

"Rhona?" queried Alison.

Saffron waved a hand dismissively. "High Priestess of the Ullapool coven. She thinks she's such a big fish, always bragging about her contacts. Just you wait until she hears about this! Brian is Britain's *best* water diviner; probably the best in Europe, in fact, and he's agreed to give us a demonstration and then teach us all how to do it!"

At first mention of Brian Chivers' speciality, I balked. By the time Saffron got as far as the reason for this extra meeting I was back-pedalling as fast as I could go. Saffron turned round to watch me, compassion oozing from her over-made-up features.

"Oh Cassie, dear, don't be afraid! It won't hurt you, and if you're worried about not succeeding, please, don't be. Not everybody has this talent, and you don't *have* to try. I'm sure you'll find it fascinating anyway."

I raised both hands in a 'stop' gesture and shook my head. "Honestly, Saffron, it's nothing like that," I protested. "Don't worry. Just an urgent call of nature. Back in a minute."

With barely a glance at Alison's bemused expression, I turned and fled into the house, locking myself inside the bathroom.

How could this be happening to me? I couldn't leave and abandon Alison with no transport, nor could I go out there again. A *water diviner*! Was there a twisted god's sense of humour behind this? First, I'm captured by a magician at one of these little parties, and now this!

I closed the toilet lid—pale peach with embedded sea shells—and sat down on it. I *could* slip away and come back later. I didn't even need to leave the house: the plumbing right here in the bathroom offered me as good an escape as a wide open door. Not that I was too keen on the idea. You'd be horrified at what you find down some people's pipe work.

I jumped as knuckles rapped on the door.

"Cassie?" called Alison. "You alright in there?"

"Oh, I'm fine," I answered, aware of the heavy irony in my tone. I wasn't sure what Alison made of it because she went silent for a while. Then, "Do you want to go home?"

Offered the ideal get-out, I hesitated. I still needed to track down the magician, and this coven was my sole lead. Perhaps I should go away and come back some other time. But these meetings were not regular, and it might be too long before there was another; he might find me first. I stood up, closed my eyes and drew a deep breath. I really was getting carried away with this human emotion thing.

When I stepped out, Alison was leaning against the pale green wall along from the bathroom door. She searched my face.

"Are you sure you're okay? We can go if you want to."

And there it was. The final clincher. There was no way I was going to spoil Alison's evening. After that nasty scene with Simon, she deserved to have some fun.

"It's fine, but I'd rather not get too close to that guy; he creeps me out."

"I think we can arrange that," Alison said with a degree of confidence I was proud to hear from her. "You stay behind me."

Only too willing to go along with this idea, I linked arms with Alison and we exited the house via the forest-painted hallway with its green shag-pile carpet that I *think* was supposed to simulate grass. I preferred my artificial turf.

The coven, fifteen in number tonight including the two of us, was gathered in a semi-circle on the lawn around Brian Chivers, who was brandishing a split hazel rod rather in the vein of a blind man's cane. We arrived in time to hear the end of his explanation, and positioned ourselves behind the others. It was as far from Brian as we could arrange without looking suspicious.

"... you can dowse with almost anything, the most popular these days being plastic rods because they're light and long-lasting, but I prefer to use a natural material, and hazel has a particular affinity for water."

Staying behind Alison, I peeked over her shoulder as the diviner raised his rod to show it off better.

"I cut this one a couple of days ago. See," he ran his finger down one side, "how I've split it. A very delicate procedure on a branch as fine as this. And then," he pointed towards the end, which was bound with white tape, "I've taped the end to keep the split from extending. It won't last forever, but this will prolong it until the wood dries out completely, at which point it will need replacing."

He marched to the top of the sloping lawn. "And now I'll show you how it works." He held the split ends of the twig delicately and proceeded to walk very slowly down the lawn, with his arms extended in front of him. "I'm looking for underground water courses, of which there should be quite a few in this area. Aha!"

The end of the twig twitched downward.

"And here we have one."

He continued his stately dawdle. As he passed his rapt audience I edged further behind Alison, but as if sensing my movement the twig jerked sideways, almost ripping itself out of Brian's left hand.

"What the—?" Brian snatched his twig back into its correct position, looking flustered. I guessed it wasn't supposed to act that way. Mary, an older witch with a perfect Cleopatra bob in silver-grey and the eye makeup of an Egyptian maid, glanced over her shoulder, searching the ground behind us. Her eyes slid over me, searching for some other source to explain the twig's aberrant behaviour. Evidently she also knew it shouldn't do that sort of thing.

"Sorry ladies, I must have lost concentration for a moment. Just let me—aha! Here's another one."

He proceeded down the lawn to the bottom of the slope near to where the collection of cars was parked, marking out the sites of little underground rivulets, and in one case a quite large but deep water course that ran crosswise, narrowly missing one corner of the log cabin. And he was accurate, too. Fascinated to be for once so close to this human ability I'd done my best over the millennia to avoid, I checked his findings by opening up my senses and reaching down into the ground, *feeling* where the water ran, *seeing* the aquifers below our feet as a 3-dimensional image overlaid upon the human vision I was using at the time.

"What the..!"

The masculine bellow snapped me back to the surface in time to see Brian Chivers spinning in a circle, grappling with his dowsing rod as it yanked and twisted in his grip. Horrified, I withdrew my sprite senses and the thing ceased its errant actions. Brian glared wildly around, scanning the faces of the stunned coven.

"Whoever's messing with me, you can stop right now!" He glared at the stunned group of women. "I have *never* been treated like this!"

Saffron rushed to his side, visibly upset. She enveloped him in her ample arms.

"My dear Brian, I'm *so* sorry!" Saffron paused, looking thoughtful, and started to draw Brian away from the perplexed coven. "A quiet word, please."

Now what was going on? Had I unintentionally opened up the proverbial can of worms? I strained to hear, but the other members of the coven were eager to expound their own theories on this evening's bizarre events, and their mumblings and mutterings drowned out Saffron's tinkling tones. Frustrated, I turned my attentions to their speculations.

"...a spirit of some kind. Perhaps a poltergeist, they can be so playful..."

"...he's reading something else, not water. Perhaps he's picking up on some kind of energy. Maybe ley lines?"

"...perhaps Rhona's planted a mole in our midst. What that coven wouldn't do to get one up on us..."

I looked at Alison and shrugged. She had no idea what was going on, and we weren't insiders enough yet to be included into the discussions. Glancing away again, I met with a pair of deep green eyes, the type that are jewel-like in their quality, with the fathomless depths that betray their ability to see beneath the surface. Under a crown of frothy red-brown ringlets that tumbled to her waist, the eyes belonged to Dawn, a lass not long out of her teens and the one true-witch in the coven. Where the others were only humans scratching at the edges of magic, Dawn was something more.

The Scottish highlands have long been known for their fey women, but as the centuries have rolled by the blood of the true-witch has become ever-more dilute as a result of inter-breeding with the human clans. Some lines have remained more pure than others, and some have even been strengthened by careful inbreeding. I guessed Dawn to be a scion of such a bloodline. I had marked her out at our first meeting as the one member of the coven to smell strongly of magic, and her scent was all of pure things, of grass and trees and skies, of the snow that melts to feed the rivers, and of the earth. She was a witch of growing things who in the elder days would have been priestess to a fertility goddess. She neither scared me nor worried me. She had her own secrets to keep.

"It's Cassie, isn't it? And Alison?" Her voice was warm and friendly.

"Yes, and you're Dawn, aren't you?"

She nodded. "Yes, I am." She seemed pleased that I'd remembered, and flashed a shy smile. "Is this your second time here, or third?" she asked.

Oh, so politely we hedged around what she really wanted, which was to speak with me alone, but by this point Alison was clinging onto my arm and I wondered if this would be the end of my friend's aspirations to become a witch. I truly hoped not, as she had more potential in her little toe than most of these other trendy types and washed out hippies had collectively. True-witches used to be famed for their flame-coloured hair, and looking at Alison's sleek ginger head I suspected there was more than a hint of their DNA in her genes.

"Second," I confirmed, returning my attention to Dawn. "And to be quite honest, we're not sure what's going on."

The three of us drifted away from the gaggle of wanna-be witches. I'm sure they were all very sincere, but it was becoming ever clearer to me that they were in reality a bunch of new age hippies who'd taken a fancy to dabbling in witchcraft. Ah well, it wasn't a bad starting point from which to ease Alison into her abilities, and she could move on when she outgrew them, which I suspected would not take long. That then, begged the question of why Dawn was with them.

"How long have you been a member?" I asked her.

She shrugged. "Oh, from the beginning," she said, but as my eyebrows rose she explained, "I'm Gordon's daughter."

She must have seen the look of surprise on my face because she added, "Saffron's not my mother! Father would never re-marry, not after mum died, but he missed the company, and Saffron mothers him to within an inch of his life. She makes him happy, so I play along."

"And Saffron got the idea about becoming a witch after she met him?"

Dawn laughed. "You've got it. It's a fashionable thing to do for ladies who have time on their hands, and an easier choice than veganism or Kabbalah. Father indulges her shamefully, and nobody's coming to harm so," she shrugged, "we help them blend a few spells and lend a hand here and there."

Alison was starting to frown by now. She might have been scared, but she wasn't slow.

"So these women aren't real witches, then?" she asked, glancing back up the garden at the furiously debating group of women. Dawn matched her gaze.

"Well, by intent, they are. They all have a genuine desire to live in harmony with Nature and the spirit world. They're just a bit short on talent. Mary—" and she pointed at the ageing Cleopatra, "—probably has the most. She can see powers and spirits and auras, though she's not much good at doing anything with them. But they do try. I only wish they hadn't got into this rivalry with Rhona's coven; it's making them very competitive."

"And you?" asked Alison. "You're not like them, are you?"

Dawn smiled. "No, and nor are you two. I've waited a long time for some real talent to show up, and then along come two of you at once!"

Alison's face snapped round to me in surprise, but for me this was the moment I'd been seeking and I grabbed it.

"But what about the guy who was here the last time we came?"

Dawn bit her lip, looking very young. "You mean Liam." She shuddered, and it wasn't an affectation. "He's powerful alright, but I wouldn't trust him. He's dark-shrouded, and I don't care for anyone who hides what they are."

With her last words she raised her eyes and pinned me with a glare, and I knew I had to talk to her alone.

"What do you mean?" Alison asked.

Dawn shrugged and chewed some more on her lip. "He answered an ad Gordon put in the local shop, to help set up our website. He pretended to have no more than a vague idea of what we were doing, but some of the things he said; he knew far more than he was letting on. And that dark aura..." Her shiver ran right down to her toes and she went up in my estimation. She *really* didn't like him.

Liam. So I had a name to pin on him, at least. Now I needed an address.

"Do you know where he lives?" I asked, fully aware of Alison's knowing expression. But my hopes for a simple conclusion to my investigation were dashed as Dawn shook her head.

"Sorry, not a clue. He just turned up here to do the website, and to that one meeting you came to." She frowned. "Didn't you go off with him?"

I grimaced. "Not exactly."

"Oh come on, Cassie!" Alison butted in, and glanced sideways at Dawn with a wicked grin. "Cassie had wild sex with him in some place she can't remember and now she wants to find him again."

Trust Alison's confidence to choose this moment to take an upswing. Dawn's expression turned wary.

"Well I'm afraid we can't help you," she said in cool tones. "He hasn't been back since then, and I don't expect him to turn up again. I rather got the impression we bored him with our petty magic. But perhaps he got what he wanted after all?"

I was pretty certain Dawn had no idea what I was, but she knew for certain that I was hiding something.

"Ladies, we are being remiss in our hospitality," announced a deep, sincere voice from behind me. Turning, I found that the ladies of the coven had converged on us. The rich tones belonged to Mary who, in the continued absence of Saffron who had long since vanished inside the house with Gordon and Brian Chivers, was taking upon herself the role of hostess.

"I am sure you have many questions, which we will endeavour to answer. Do come and join us. There's tea and cakes, or alcohol if you prefer."

"Oh I think I could do with some of that," Alison said with feeling. "And I can, as you're driving!" She dug me in the ribs with an elbow.

"Go right ahead," I encouraged. "I'll be good."

Alison allowed herself to be led away, happier now that she knew the other ladies were relatively harmless. Mary glanced over her shoulder at me and, bearing in mind what Dawn had said about her being able to see auras, I wondered what she saw when she looked at me. It could not have been too startling as it had failed to distract her earlier, but she obviously saw something now. I didn't have long to wonder though, as Dawn's hand took my arm and steered me towards the head-high rhododendrons bordering the lawn. We followed a narrow path between the bushes until we were into the forest proper, and could no longer see or be seen from the house before Dawn drew us to a halt.

"Okay, time to come clean," she said.

I'd played this sport before, and chose the silent waiting game. I've found you can learn far more by not answering than by speaking, so I raised an eyebrow and kept my mouth shut.

"I know you're not what you seem, your aura's nothing I've ever seen before! It's clear and yet it shrouds you and permeates you and it's always moving. *What the hell are you?*"

Oh boy, I'd have to be more careful in future. Whilst I take great care with the illusion of my human body, I'd given no more than a cursory thought to my aura. Most human witches would see what I suspected Mary was seeing: something a little out of the ordinary, perhaps a little more pearlescent than the norm, but nothing that couldn't be explained away by being slightly goddess-touched.

What I hadn't bargained on was Dawn's blood being far more pure than any other true-witches I'd met in a long time. Damn! I should have anticipated this.

"You've got me cold, haven't you, little witch. Never seen a faery before, have you?"

Why did I choose to masquerade as a fey? No idea. It was the first thing that popped into my mind.

Dawn gasped and her hands flew up to cover her mouth. I breathed a sigh of relief. No, she'd never seen a faery and she probably wouldn't around here either. Most of them live in America these days. That's why Hollywood abounds with beautiful people, many of whom are rather too vain to be seen to be ageing as ordinary mortals. I hadn't *exactly* said that I was one, and I reckoned that a little misdirection was going to be less complicated than telling her what I truly was—a genuine force of Nature, that by many cultures would be considered a goddess.

"But what are you doing here?" she asked, with a slight tremor in her voice. I wondered how many non-humans she'd met before. Not too many, by her reaction. I decided to be honest at this point, or partly, at least.

"Alison is my friend. Human, it's true, but a good friend nonetheless, and she wants to become a witch. I'm trying to help her out."

"Really? So what were you doing with Liam? You *did* go off with him."

I injected my loathing for that event into my voice. "Trust me that was not of my choosing. I got away from him as fast as I could, but I didn't want to upset Alison with the truth. She's too new to all of this, and she scares easily. I just need to find the nasty little weasel to warn him off for good."

Dawn wanted to believe me, I could tell, but she wasn't certain I was being candid, so I added, "Alison has no idea what I am and I'll thank you to keep it that way. She has a lot to learn and I don't want to give her any shocks she's not ready to handle this early on."

True, all of it, just not quite the full story. I could see Dawn considering my 'revelations'.

"So you don't intend any mischief? There's nothing I should be warning Gordon about?"

Aha! If Gordon's sight was not as clear as his daughter's then he was not the sole source of Dawn's true-witch genes. I wished I'd met her mother.

It occurred to me to wonder if Gordon had prepped Dawn to keep an eye on new coven members, or if she was doing it off her own bat. In practice, it didn't make much difference either way; it was Dawn I had to reassure and Dawn I wanted to cultivate. One never knew when having a true-witch on-side might be useful. And it didn't hurt that I found myself liking the girl, either.

I smiled, putting as much genuineness into my expression as I could simulate. "None whatsoever. I just want Alison to develop herself and have fun. Looks as if I've found the right person for the job. Dawn, you're hired!"

7. AMBUSH

Once I'd finished filling Dawn in on her new role as Alison's mentor, I sent her off to commence work.

Pleased with myself, I stretched my arms wide and breathed in a deep lungful of fresh woodland air. A sweet, fruity aroma filled my nostrils, and I wandered towards it, curious to see what was growing out here so late in the season.

Any excuse to avoid Saffron and her pet water diviner for a bit longer.

Dawn was a perfect fit for Alison's situation. Now, if I could only sort out the magician as easily. I had his name but still faced a dead end. How to track him down? I didn't even have a clear memory of his face, just a distorted image through thick glass and a few glimpses while trying to avoid Gloria.

Oh, Gloria! My beautiful salamander's face hung painted in exquisite detail across my mind, and a great, aching heaviness settled inside my chest. Elementals are not made for human-style bonds, and yet for the first time in my long existence I felt isolated. No matter how much I wanted Gloria, even if I accepted that I could never touch her in the ways I wanted to—never, in fact, touch her at all—I knew deep down that *any* relationship would be doomed to failure.

Yet I still wanted to see her. The terrible, empty sensation inside me when I thought of never setting eyes on her again was so ghastly I couldn't bear the thought of embracing it for eternity.

Positive mental attitude, Cassie. Get a grip!

I would see her tomorrow. Think about that. What should I wear? Was Liam enough threat to convince her to join forces?

I paused. Was Liam the threat I was making him out to be? Thought of him made my stomach lurch south, down into my pointy-toed cowboy boots. Yet I'd seen no sign of him since that awful day.

The strong scent of strawberries washed over me, and I froze. Strawberries? In the forest, and at this time or year?

My breath caught, and a total absence of sound crashed against me. I scanned my surroundings and cursed the inconvenience of two forward-facing eyes. I felt very small; a rodent caught by the gaze of a hawk. The silent trees towered threateningly over me and my heart began to pound.

Into this void sneaked a tiny, repetitive sound—the shallow, quick breathing of an excited human.

Liam!

Stupid, stupid sprite!

I'd let my nose lead me into trouble. Again.

If the coven was my one means of tracing Liam, then the reverse might also be true.

I ducked, and started to run like hell.

Liam was between me and the house, but there lay safety. He wouldn't try to take me in front of so many witnesses. Would he?

I needed to circle around him, and chose speed over stealth, pretty certain he would find me with magic if I delayed. Pinning my hopes on catching him by surprise, I pounded towards my goal. My footfalls sounded hollow on the compressed heather and shed pine needles underfoot. Twisting and turning along faint animal tracks, my clothes snagged on gorse and broom, hair catching in trailing branches until I caught sight of the front gable of my sanctuary. Whereupon I smacked headfirst into a magical barrier.

With a loud squeak of shock, I bounced backward and hit the ground, measuring my length on the springy heather. The back of my head cracked against a protruding boulder and a shower of stars sparkled across my vision. I lay there for a moment, stunned. If I'd been human I might have been knocked out rather than just shocked, but the pain was real all the same. For the first time, I truly appreciated that I couldn't have the pleasure of which this body was capable without the converse too.

Liam crashed towards me. Despite the stilettos stabbing inside my head I found in that light-bulb moment yet another facet of human drive—the survival instinct. Almost of its own volition, my body scrambled to unsteady feet. I put a hand out to the nearest tree trunk and dropped some of the cohesion binding my human form. The pain lessened.

If Liam believed I was going to be easy to capture this time, he had another think coming.

"Ouch!"

A sizzling bolt of energy shot through the air where my body had been a fraction of a second earlier, passing almost without effect between my more widely spaced molecules. The same could not be said for my blouse, which now sported singed holes back and front. It stung, but my human body would have been stunned. I bolted in the opposite direction, zigzagging. I had no idea what Liam was capable of, and no wish to find out.

Another bolt zapped into a tree trunk, spitting splinters of wood in a shower that passed harmlessly through me, although some snagged in my clothes. Optimistic I would escape after all, I slammed into another of his barriers. Invisible but impenetrable, not even separate molecules were going to pass through. As I scrambled upright it nudged me, herding me towards wherever it was Liam wanted me. He couldn't be far away; I could hear him coming, reacting like a spider to vibrations in its web.

I dropped my remaining cohesion. My clothes fell into a heap on top of my favourite cowboy boots and I took a scant moment to shift them beneath a broom plant. Liam might spot them but with no better hiding place on offer, what choice did I have? Now I was no more than a blur to the human eye. Liam might know I was in the vicinity and he might even have spells that could find me, but I was going to make the bastard work for it.

I sidled away from his approach, floating a hand span above the ground. Even in this state I might have disturbed leaves and branches if we'd been in a deciduous forest, but the Caledonian is blessedly populated by tall pines. Almost all the lower branches had long since been nibbled down to nubs by red deer, and the dense canopy far, far above blocked much of the remaining light.

I hung motionless as Liam passed barely two feet in front of me, and I got my first clear look at him. Tall and slim with a mop of unruly brown hair, he appeared to be in his early twenties. His narrow face had close-set blue eyes and an elegant aquiline nose over a generous mouth. In a strange sort of way he was quite good looking, but the eagerness of the hunt etched an ugly cast on his features. I committed that face to my long, long memory.

As he vanished in the direction I had come from, I drifted off at a tangent, trying to think laterally. I studied the trees around me. Where was a Ghillie Dhu when you wanted one? I knew the tree spirits were more active after dark and it wasn't that late yet, but I could have done with some help about now. Looking up, I wondered if Liam's barrier arched overhead. I had to test it but, just in case, I wanted to investigate other options before setting his web jangling again.

"Come out, come out, wherever you are. There's nowhere for you to hide." Liam's voice drifted through the trees.

I reached out with those senses I'd kept under wraps since the debacle with Brian and the divining rods, and sought the nearest water. *There!* Little more than a trickle, a tiny burn, nigh on invisible where it undercut a nearby bank. Fed by a small spring that welled beyond the boundary Liam had set, it flowed back towards the house.

Turning my attention skyward, I floated up. Almost, I wished for Gloria's ability to rocket through the air at high speed, but at least I could move unseen.

This time I felt the barrier before blundering into it. My outermost fringes tingled with a mild electrical charge, and I aborted the let's-just-sail-out-of-here-and-he'll-be-none-the-wiser approach. The little stream was looking more and more like my only route, and that worried me. I was developing a grudging respect for Liam's intellect. Could he have failed to notice the little trickle of water?

At this point, I was forced to consider a more drastic option. The human body is around sixty percent water, but you don't have to remove anywhere near that amount to kill. I've done it twice before and I still find the memories distressing. I would far rather find another solution, but if cornered and threatened, I would do it. My biggest problem was deciding when we'd reached the point of no return.

If only I knew what Liam *wanted*.

The energy barrier prickled my surface. Running out of alternatives, I glided towards the little burn. Studying the small trickle of water bubbling cheerfully over its rocky bed, I could tell it had once been a far bigger underground stream, carving away the land both above and below in its shallow subterranean passage. Where it had once filled its rocky channel, now it merely oozed along the bottom, chattering happily to itself as it reminisced about days of greatness long past. Where I hovered before it, the ground had shifted at some time and cracked, such that a small stretch was open to the forest floor. At each end it plunged back into darkness, disappearing again into the earth's crust. The perfect escape route.

Maybe too perfect.

Studying the entire area in minute detail, I searched for magical triggers but found none. That didn't mean there *were* none, merely that I couldn't identify any. Liam had already proven himself to be an accomplished magician, whereas I was relying on instinct.

The barrier nudged me again and I decided to pin my hopes on the fact that the watercourse was *very* small, and that Liam might have missed it. I eased myself into the dribble of water, welcoming the shaded dark of the overhang, draped as it was with ferns and mosses that further hid the burn from view. Maybe I was going to get away with this after all.

Or not.

<*Shit!*> I yelped silently as the trap sprang shut, almost shaving a few molecules off my backside. <*Shit, shit, shit!*>

I'd taken the gamble and it hadn't paid off. I was out of options and it was way too late to backtrack.

"Gotcha!" Liam's triumphant shout came hot on the heels of the shimmering walls of force that sprang up to block each end of the channel. Above me, it glittered in a threatening arc that mimicked the rough underside of the cut-out and formed a fuzzy barrier between me and my already restricted view of the outside world. A pair of tattered jeans hove into view, and then a long-fingered hand swept aside the trailing undergrowth. Liam peered in.

"Beautiful!" he breathed.

Unless he had some visual super power that allowed him to see more of me than a vague outline, he wasn't complimenting me on my good looks.

<*Bastard!*>

I writhed within my prison, lashing out to test its limits. Liam flinched back as water sprayed towards him, but it hit his energy barrier and slid harmlessly down, like rain sluicing down a window.

"Now, now," he admonished, wagging a finger. "Be a good lassie and behave, or I might have to make things a wee bit less comfortable for you."

Less comfortable? What else could he do? I found I had no wish to know, and ceased my thrashing.

"Atta girl. Hang in there a mo and I'll be back."

The undergrowth swung back into place and Liam's legs vanished. I guessed he'd gone to fetch a rather more portable means of containing me.

Time was running out.

I probed the barrier at one end of my makeshift prison. The seal from floor to ceiling was tight as a plug in a bath. The water trapped inside this little pocket with me was staying put as securely as I was.

I ran feelers over every centimetre of the ceiling. Water-smoothed rock and rough stony earth were all perfectly coated by the energy field, as though someone had painted every last millimetre with infinite precision. Even where roots dangled through, the barrier slicked over them in a second skin leaving no chinks to exploit.

With increasing desperation I probed the barrier at the upstream end, aware that I was missing something important.

Think, dammit! What was I not seeing?

Realisation smote me: there wasn't enough water!

The spell prevented the water trapped inside with me from escaping, but equally well it should be stopping the fresh water from the spring side from entering. Even from such a tiny trickle there should have been a big enough build up by now for it to be far higher on the outside of the barrier than on the inside. But it wasn't.

So where was it going?

With panic beating at me, I forced myself to hold still and study the steady trickle on the upstream side of the barrier. After an eternity I spotted it: a minute crevice at the back of the channel. When the trap closed off its regular route the water had done what water does, and found an alternate path.

The water level inside the trap was constant, but when I explored the burn bed I realised there was no energy signature below me. I was trapped on three sides by Liam's force field and on the fourth by solid rock. Or was it solid? Extending my senses downward, I found the stream flowing inside a rock fault slightly to one side and below my jail. Could I reach it in time?

Firming my body up somewhat, I twisted around in the tight space, explored the streambed beneath me and came up with a hand-sized chunk of granite. Hefting it in my now solid hand, I attacked the weakest place above the subterranean stream. Pounding at the ground, spraying water with each blow, I dedicated my full attention to the task. If Liam arrived before I cracked it, I was lost, so I wasted neither time nor effort on keeping watch for him.

My knuckles smacked against the rock floor and I dropped the stone with a yelp. If I'd been human they would have bled. As it was, they hurt enough for me to stuff them into my mouth and suck.

Grabbing the lump of granite in my other hand, I resumed my assault. Bits of my makeshift chisel started to break off and despair gnawed at me.

And then, in a moment of inspiration, I reached into the ground and began to draw the underground water towards me. Erosion by water may be an infinitesimally slow process most of the time, but when there is already a weakness to be exploited it can be devastatingly swift. Loose shards of rock along the edge of the underground channel flaked away, and the aquifer shifted, working its way towards me. I carried on beating the ground, chipping into the stone bed.

And found the faintest fault in the rock. I redoubled my efforts both above ground and below. I could feel the aquifer mere centimetres away from me as it wore away at the weakest layer between us, until the rock groaned and cracked open.

With a loud gurgle the water trapped inside my prison rushed to join its parent stream with the whirlpool effect of bathwater down a plughole. My back tingled in terrified anticipation of being caught at the very last moment. I let go my body's cohesion and lunged towards the dark.

I heard Liam's angry bellow. Magic reached sticky fingers after me and for one terrifying moment it dragged at my trailing molecules. But there was not enough of me left within reach for Liam to get a solid grip, and I slipped from his grasp into the blessed silence of the underground waterway.

8. ADDRESS

Gordon's septic tank needed emptying.

I could say this with great certainty after skimming the top of the sludge layer inside it as I worked my way across from the drain field outlet.

Within seconds of my escape, I'd oriented myself within the ground and identified my saviour stream as one of those that Brian had tracked earlier, specifically the one that passed close to the south-eastern corner of Gordon's house. With the leisure to think, I recalled noticing the tell-tale manhole cover that marked out a septic tank, half hidden behind some bushes.

Although the change in water quality was tiny, as I was swept along with the blissfully fresh water in the stream towards the house, I began to taste the proximity of effluent percolating through the soil. Perhaps *'taste'* is not an accurate description for the sense I was using, but it approximates it near enough. The tang of nitrate and the tiny bodies of the microbes wriggling their last in the miniscule pockets of moisture within the drain field were my guide. With regret, I said goodbye to the stream and pushed my way laboriously through the moist soil, slipping from damp patch to damp patch.

The moisture in the soil increased as I neared the outlet pipe and my passage became easier. Fortunately for me, the Highlands are formed largely of granite, and I rarely end up slopping around in mud. Rather, I find myself squeezing between layers of stone. On the downside, water disperses quickly through the uppermost layers, making it harder to move without an external medium. More laborious, but not impossible.

Metaphorically speaking, I held my breath as I traversed the odious midden of the septic tank. This was precisely the sort of experience that had helped me make my decision to live in human form. This, and one sewage processing plant too many.

Reaching the house inlet was almost a relief. Almost, but not quite. The house was full of ladies partaking of various beverages, resulting in frequent trips to the bathroom. Every time someone flushed, I was forced to battle the current and, contrary to the exhilarating experience of swimming upstream against a gushing mountain river, I fancied I could feel the effort draining my energy rather than enhancing it. It was all in my imagination I expect, but with my anxiety rising over how to stage my reappearance, it felt real.

Someone flushed again and I clung to the edges of the waste pipe as water and unmentionables swept past me. Honestly, you'd think all the ladies would know that you don't flush sanitary products down the pan when it leads to a septic tank. Or perhaps that was why the tank was in such dire need of emptying.

I lurked just around the bend for a while, and then risked slipping up into the bowl. Success! The bathroom was empty. I rose from the water, wincing at the slight glugging sound and, coalescing as I went, glided swiftly across to the door which I shut and locked. Time to get to work.

It doesn't matter how much care a girl takes when dressing, trying to re-create every little detail from memory is plain short of impossible. What were the precise colours of my checked shirt? And which way did the criss-crossing lines lay? Were the patterns on my jeans on both back pockets, or just the one?

When I was finished, I studied myself in the mirror. I was a tad shorter than normal because mass that went into my clothes didn't go into my body, so I added another layer to the stacked heels of my favourite cowboy boots. Those were the one piece of clothing I didn't have to think too hard about to recreate—I knew every crease in the leather—but thinking about them made me angry. They'd better still be where I'd abandoned my clothes when I went to reclaim them, or Liam was going to pay, big time.

Someone turned the door handle, and then rattled it hard. I took one last look at myself in the mirror, hoping I had all the details correct before I turned the key and stepped out into the hallway.

Mary blinked at me in surprise, her Cleo bob swinging stylishly.

"So sorry, dear," she apologised. "I thought you'd gone home."

I smiled brightly and shook my head. "No, not yet. I was wandering around outside. Such a glorious evening, isn't it?"

"Indeed it is," Mary agreed before leaning in with a conspiratorial air. "And some of us are simply more comfortable out of doors, aren't we? I understand, dear." And she tapped the side of her nose with her forefinger before disappearing into the bathroom and shutting the door behind her with a quiet snick.

I remembered that Mary was the one who could see auras. Goodness alone knows what she thought I was.

First things first, though. I needed to find Alison and get away from here. I followed the babble of female voices, and found them standing in small groups in the main living room; a beautiful light and open space with floor to ceiling glass on three sides overlooking the garden and the forest beyond. Potted ferns and bougainvillea filled every corner of the room so that it resembled an indoor garden, and the faint whiff of incense lent it a hippy-era atmosphere. It wouldn't have surprised me to see the odd joint passing from hand to hand.

Alison stood on the farthest side of the room beside an open French window, in conversation with a pair of middle aged housewife types. She spotted me over their heads and sent a pleading look of the 'come and rescue me' variety.

I squeezed between groups of ladies, getting the odd puzzled look. When I was almost close enough to extricate Alison, I passed the open kitchen door. Saffron, still deep in shifty conversation with Brian Chivers, glanced at me and swiftly away again. A shiver ran up my spine.

Were they discussing me? Had they figured out that I was in some way responsible for what had happened earlier?

Gordon lounged against the dishwasher behind the conspirators and his steady regard was even more unnerving. Whatever they were up to, I vowed to keep as far away from them as I could. Liam was enough to contend with, without getting mixed up in any of their schemes to out-do their rival coven.

I shuddered, and moved on.

The two women holding Alison captive were holding forth on the shortcomings of the Ullapool coven.

"They're so far above themselves, it's laughable!"

The shorter of the pair smiled sagely, and wagged her head. "They've always been a pretentious bunch. It's not as if they've anything to brag about, is it? Rhona keeps hinting, but—"

"Oh, Cassie, there you are!" Alison's relief was all too audible.

"Sorry to drag you away," I said, "but I need to go." I beamed at the ladies and caught Alison by the elbow, leading her towards the door.

"Wow!" she exclaimed and shook off my hand as we exited the living room. "That was masterful. You'd better watch it or you'll be giving them something else to gossip about."

"Sorry?"

I can be a bit slow at times, especially when I'm thinking about how not to get caught by a maniac magician.

"Honestly, Cassie. They'll be thinking we're a couple."

"Oh."

I fell silent. The preoccupation of human beings with such labels has always been beyond my simple 'anything goes as long as it feels good and doesn't harm anyone' approach to life and love.

I paused outside the front door and took a quick glance around. No sign of Liam. The Tiguan was parked fifth car down the drive and I crunched nervously over the gravel alongside Alison, hoping that if the magician were hiding out there he would have second thoughts about attacking me in full view of a witness. Alison marched around to the near side of the car and pulled her door open. I cringed. I'd never thought to lock it. Whilst Alison settled herself into her seat, I opened my door and took a quick glance around the untidy interior, hoping I'd notice if anything had been disturbed.

My eyes locked on the back seat and my breath caught. It didn't look like anything had been disturbed, but lying innocently on top of a pile of assorted clothing was my client folder with, in case I should lose it, my address emblazoned across the cover.

***

The drive home passed in a blur of anxiety. *Why* had I left that stupid folder on the back seat? And had Liam seen it, or was I worrying needlessly?

Alison added to my stress levels when I dropped her outside her croft. As she turned to close the car door she frowned at me.

"I could have sworn your blouse had smaller checks than that. Must be my eyes."

Then she grinned and shook her head.

"Perhaps I need glasses! Oh well, see you tomorrow."

And she slammed the door with the gusto of someone accustomed to a much older car. As I bumped my way down the track, I watched in my rear view mirror as she scurried off down her garden, no doubt to check on the new inmates.

I took a quick glance down at my shirt. Alison was right: the checks should have been smaller. How did I manage to get that wrong? And had Alison been the only one to notice? It wasn't as if I'd stayed around for long after my re-creation in the bathroom, but such tiny details might be noticed by some, and that could spell trouble.

For the remainder of the journey, I daresay I'd have noticed if I'd hit something, but less than that was not going to break into the panicky scenarios running through my mind. Would Liam be there already, lying in ambush? Or would he wait until I'd satisfied myself that he wasn't coming, and then pounce? Perhaps I shouldn't go home at all. But I had to, because Minkie needed feeding. Whilst I could undoubtedly have asked Morag to do that for me, there was also the chance that Euan might resurface, and what might Liam do with a selkie?

I swung the car hard into the drive, scattering gravel. In the back of my mind I rationalised that the faster I got to the steading door, the more chance I had of beating Liam to it. In reality I think I was simply too nervous to go any slower. I floored the brake and slid to a stop outside the steading, spraying small stones all over the box hedge, and then sat there with a block of fragile ice filling my empty interior, too paralysed by fear to open the door.

What was happening to me? I'd experienced my first twinge of fear a mere thirty six hours earlier, and now I was in the grip of a full blown panic attack. I wasn't sure how humans survived these violent emotions, and this wasn't what I'd signed up for.

The steading door swung open and my body jerked as if I'd touched a live wire. A pathetic squeak escaped my lips before my brain caught up with my mouth and identified Euan. I drew a huge gasp of air that I didn't need, but which served to make me feel better.

"Are you coming in, or are you planning on sitting out there all night?" called Euan.

"I'm coming; just organising a few things in here," I answered. Now that my brain had begun working again, I wondered what I should tell him. As with all males, Euan could get more protective than might be good for him. Magical creature that he was, I was certain he would be no match for Liam.

My feet hit the gravel and I belatedly zapped the car to lock it. I'm not sure what good I thought it was going to do at this point, but it made me feel a bit more secure. I scrunched along the path, wincing at the sharp sound of every footfall, trying to get to the door as fast as I could without looking like I was hurrying. My surface prickled all over in anticipation of a magical strike that mercifully never came.

Euan backed into the hallway and I slipped inside, leaning back against the door to slam it shut without even slowing to turn. I took a deep, calming breath.

"So," I said brightly. "How did your protest go?"

"Quite well, I think," Euan replied with a small frown.

Nothing short of the total abandonment of the sea by human beings would count as complete success in the selkie's view.

"And you followed them out to sea to check they complied with the protocols?"

I wanted to keep Euan occupied while I decided what to tell him. If anything.

A loud splash came from the bathroom and I jumped clean off the floor. This would not be the first time Euan had brought a playmate home with him, but he'd always checked with me before doing so. Once my feet were firmly back on terra firma, I raised an eyebrow in enquiry. Euan returned my stare blankly.

Not a playmate then. Panic welled up. Was Liam already here, and was Euan's secret compromised like mine? In the faint hope that things were not yet that bad, I pushed past Euan and rushed to confront the magician. I had no plan, only a blind desire to protect a friend whose life was more fragile than my own. I flung the door open and stopped in confusion. The bathroom was empty.

Water slopped over the edge of the bath, followed by a whiskery nose and a set of beady black eyes.

Minkie.

"Oh sorry," Euan apologised. "I quite forgot. I let this poor fellow out of that tiny cage you had him in. What has he done to warrant such imprisonment?"

I ventured closer to the bath without answering. A contented-looking mink paddled around in ten inches of water in the bottom of the cast iron tub. The remains of a fish carcass floated near the tap end. I picked it out and held it up by the tail.

"Your supper, I presume?"

This time, Euan had the decency to look embarrassed.

"Well, yes. But I thought he needed it more than I did."

I snorted in disbelief. The contrast between the mundaneness of this situation and the terror of my earlier flight made our exchange feel surreal.

"Don't expect me to replace it for you," I warned him. "I'm not going fishing at this time of night."

"As if I would expect you to provide for me!"

Euan sounded indignant, and I had to remind myself again how literally he could take things.

The doorbell rang. Once more my feet involuntarily left the ground, this time accomplishing a one-eighty before landing. Despite the continued shocks, my brain started to work on a more logical level. Obviously, this would not be Liam. The magician was as unlikely to ring my doorbell and announce his arrival as Minkie was to morph into a handsome prince.

Morag stood on my doorstep, a large wire mesh cage by her feet.

"There you are, lass," she said, not waiting to be invited in. She dragged the rattling cage into the utility room and I hurriedly shut the door. It wouldn't do to have Minkie escape, now that Morag had gone to the effort of providing him with a more palatial home.

"I was clearing some of the old straw bales down by the bottom barn when I saw this disappearing into the weeds, so I thought I'd get it out and give it a cleanup for your new pet." She looked around and frowned. "Where is he? You haven't got rid of him, have you?"

"Not at all," I reassured her. "He's just having a bath."

"You're managing to handle him then? Good. I'd hate to think he might have escaped. Chicken is high on a mink's list of delicacies, you know, right after fish. And I do worry so about my girls."

"I'll be careful," I reassured her, glancing over my shoulder to see that Euan had closed the bathroom door. What a star. He might disapprove of any animal living in a cage, but he of all people knew what havoc a predator non-native to an environment could wreak.

Morag's face lit with a big smile as she caught sight of my house guest.

"Hello there, Euan! I didn't know you were around." Morag was almost blushing, and I recalled how she could get a tad flustered around the boyish-looking selkie.

"Hello, Morag. I pop in from time to time, when Cassie needs a bit of company."

"What a good wee lad ye are. Poor Cassie is here on her own so much. Those employers of hers never seem to be around and while Jock and I drop in when we can, well, we dinna have all that much time to spare, what with the farm and all."

My oh-so-kind neighbour drew a deep breath and before I could intervene, voiced the question I knew she'd been itching to ask for ages.

"So Euan, when are you going to make an honest woman of our Cassie? You make such a lovely couple, and Cassie could do with a man about the place on a more permanent basis." Her smile blossomed into a big, satisfied grin. "There. I've said it," she finished, plainly pleased with herself.

I cringed, waiting for Euan's confusion, wondering what he might make of Morag's very human ideas, but he chose that moment to surprise all hell out of me.

"You know, Morag, I've been thinking the self same thing," he said.

Morag's smile broadened as I blinked in surprise.

"But," Euan continued, "you know Cassie. Independent to a fault. I did try asking her once, but only once."

He smiled gently as Morag's face fell. Then he touched a finger to one of her perennially rosy cheeks, and winked. "Which means I'm still available."

Morag blushed and giggled like a schoolgirl. I studied Euan with fresh eyes. When had my selkie friend grown up? I'd blinked and missed it. Of course that happened a lot in my long, long life, but I'd thought I was pretty on the ball at the moment.

Then again, thinking back over the past few days, maybe not.

Morag took her leave, her colour still high and the smile lingering on her lips. I'm sure if she'd been unattached, Euan would have given her more to smile about, but there were some mores that selkies shared with humans.

Once the door closed behind my neighbour, I studied Euan quizzically.

"When did you ask me to marry you?"

Euan grinned. "It was a while ago. I think we'd just finished watching 'Pretty Woman', and it seemed like a good idea at the time."

Surprise and mirth bubbled up inside me. I laughed out loud at the memory and it felt great. The tensions of the day receded.

"That was years ago!" I protested.

Euan tilted his head on one side. "Indeed it was," he agreed. "And you said no. Have you changed your mind since then?"

"Of course not, you nitwit!"

"Well there you are; I did try."

"Oh Euan, sometimes I just love you," I said and wrapped my arms around him. He felt good. Warm and solid and dependable. I rested my cheek against his neck, breathing in his briny scent. A portion of my mind wondered where his seal skin was hidden, and if it was truly safe from the magician, but I decided that for now, at least, that worry would be mine alone.

"Only sometimes?" he asked.

9. MEETING

We spent a leisurely night over in the big house, most of it in my private stream beneath the building. I'd checked first that every door and window in the place was locked and bolted, and all the alarms turned on, which wasn't easy to do while trying not to arouse Euan's suspicions. Fortunately for me, other forms of arousal were occupying the larger part of his attention at the time.

In the morning, a clear, bright morning with a bracing, crisp breeze salty with sea tang, Euan took his leave, departing for Edinburgh and a government summit on alternative energy sources. Blackouts had been blighting the English capital more often of late, and the government was under severe pressure to solve the problem. I wasn't sure which way Euan's pressure group would lobby, wind or water power, but either would be better for the environment than their current nuclear programme.

He kissed me, standing on the doorstep with our hair whipping around our faces, and then marched off down the gravel drive. He never drove a car, and I never asked him how he got about. I would give him a lift once in a while, but every time he sat in the car I would experience pangs of guilt about the fossil fuel burning in the engine, so I rarely offered and he never asked.

I studied the selkie's rear view as he walked away, and a great rear it was. Encased in artfully shabby jeans, his long legs had a gorgeous lean grace to them, heightened by a few tantalising glimpses of bare skin showing through the rips. A black blazer and multicoloured skinny scarf knotted French style with its tail ends streaming in the breeze made him look suspiciously like a student. I determined to have a word with him one day soon about his dress sense. Attractive though it was, and well suited to his boyish image, if he wanted to be taken seriously at these high-brow summits then he needed to review his wardrobe.

As he vanished around the corner of the building, I gathered my cardigan close and jogged across to the steading. Slipping in carefully—we'd left Minkie with the run of the place last night—I locked the door behind myself and instantly dropped cohesion. My clothes slithered onto the doormat. I wanted to check the place for signs of intruders, and I wanted to be in my least vulnerable state while I did so.

Everything was as we'd left it; not a hint of anything out of place. I resumed my human shape, put the DVD of 'Pretty Woman' back in its case and returned it to the shelf, turned the TV off at the mains and rinsed out our wine glasses.

Minkie had spent most of the night curled around his stomach full of fish. I scooped him up from the sofa and deposited him into his new cage. He tried a playful nip, earning himself a quick tap on the nose. He looked mildly offended before curling up to continue his disturbed sleep in the cosy dog bed I'd bought for him the day before.

Now it was time to dress.

Bits of my body tightened in delight as I contemplated the day. I was going to see Gloria again! It seemed an age since we'd stood outside on the gravel and arranged to meet, yet it was only three days, barely a blink in the eternal lifespan of an elemental. I began to suspect that living as a human was rubbing off on me in more ways than I'd anticipated.

Back to clothes. What would Gloria wear? Unless I reduced my height to accommodate a redistribution of mass, I could never compete with those ravishing curves of hers. But I wanted to look my best. I felt like a giddy schoolgirl. Or at least how I assumed a schoolgirl felt, being guilty of reading a few teen novels.

I pulled clothes out of my wardrobe; jeans and sweaters, skirts and tops, even a causal suit. Each item went on at least once, and some of them several times in different combinations. In the end I settled on a tiered skirt in rich burgundy that swirled sensuously around my calves. I tried it with a frilly flowered top but changed it for a simple satin blouse, cinched at the waist with a broad leather belt.

Glancing at my bare calves in the mirror, I scowled. This type of boho outfit demanded my favourite cowboy boots. And where were they? Still somewhere in the woods behind Gordon and Saffron's house. At least, I hoped they were. I had every intention of going back to retrieve them as soon as I could.

I rummaged in the pile of shoes and boots stacked several layers deep on the wardrobe floor, coming up with a pair of elegant dark red courts, some snazzy short boots with chains around the ankles, and a pair of knee high leather riding boots. The chains won the day, and the hem of my skirt skimmed the boot tops showing a glimpse of flesh as I moved.

By now, I'd run out of patience with doing things the hard way, so makeup went on with a thought—subtle shadings that offset my blonde tresses. Those, I collected in a knot on the top of my head and teased out a few stray ends to trail across my face, completing the carefully created careless look.

I was ready to go.

I backed the Golf out of the garage, leaving the Tiguan sitting in the drive where I'd abandoned it the night before. Liam knew that car now and I wasn't about to make things easy for him.

The journey into the city passed in a haze; I was running on autopilot. Parking in the pay and display, I rummaged in the bottom of my purse and mercifully came up with the change for a ticket. Red lights held the traffic as I crossed the main road on foot and turned the corner into Church Street. Leakeys was a couple of shops along and I paused outside the tall blue doors, trying to settle myself ready for anything. Despite my earlier confidence, I couldn't help but worry that Gloria might have changed her mind.

But when I stepped through the door, I knew she hadn't. Her hot scent filled my nostrils, the scorched earth smell mingling with the dusty aroma of books and maps that crammed the tall shelves of the bookshop. I passed by the first alcove, the science fiction and fantasy section, and wondered how many of the books told true stories. Certainly there was plenty of solid research material in there for anyone who wanted to study paranormal beings like us.

At the rear of the shop I clanked my way up the wrought iron spiral staircase, ascending to the mezzanine floor coffee shop. Gloria's scent filled my nostrils, stronger even than the rich aroma of freshly ground coffee. I wondered if anyone else had noticed the distinctive odour. They'd probably attribute it to the wood-burning stove, whose chrome chimney rose up through the centre of the store.

Together with the quirky individuals found in a bookstore packed with second hand tomes, ranging from common to highly obscure, the large central stove and the wooden balustrades around the gallery level, Leakeys belonged in the Diagon Alley set of a Harry Potter film.

In the back corner of the cafe, Gloria was seated prudently at a four person table, enabling us to maintain a safe distance between us. I had a quick impression of a fitted red jacket displaying her plunging cleavage before I was falling into her deep, beautiful brown eyes. Everything external ceased to exist and if I'd actually needed to breathe I'd probably have fainted from lack of oxygen.

"Are you going to sit down or do you want to draw attention to us?" Gloria asked. Her rich, deep voice vibrated through me, setting up a resonance within my molecules that threatened to tear me apart. I dropped to the chair before I dissipated.

Gloria studied me, a half smile crinkling one corner of her lustrous lips. "What is it with you, sprite? I've never known one of your kind to be quite so odd."

Direct. I appreciated that. If only I could gather my wits and be my normal self. I opened my mouth to reply, but Gloria beat me to it.

"I've been thinking about your proposition and it appeals to me. I haven't had a good hunt since the middle ages, and barbecued magician sounds grand tae me!"

I found myself struggling for words again, this time for a very different reason. I'd forgotten how predatory salamanders could be; I don't think I've crossed paths with one in over a millennium.

"You tracked down any good leads yet, sprite?"

"It's Cassie," I reminded her, unable to keep a slightly nettled edge from my tone.

"Sorry, girlfriend, just eager to get the ball rolling. Well, sprite Cassie, do you know where to find him?"

There's direct, and then there's single minded.

<*This is what you asked her here for*> I reminded myself, but I was starting to wonder if it had been such a good idea after all. I shook my head. "No, but he found me again."

Shock blanked Gloria's lovely face for a moment. I reckoned that once she'd begun to consider Liam as prey, it hadn't occurred to her that we might not be the only hunters.

"You got away, though."

Was that approval? Or satisfaction that the magician had been thwarted again?

"It wasn't easy," I warned, worried that she might underestimate him. "I was lucky."

"Lucky or smart, you're here to tell the tale and that's what matters."

Oh, I positively glowed, basking in the warmth of Gloria's esteem. Funny how fast you can go from not being quite sure you like a person, to wanting to curl at their feet puppy-style and have your tummy tickled.

"I got a good look at him this time, though," I added, "and a first name. Liam."

Gloria smiled, showing a row of sharp, very white teeth. "That might or might not be useful, depending on whether my plan works. I propose a trap."

Wow, she *had* been thinking about this. Not that I was too keen on her idea, but at least it *was* an idea.

"Go on," I invited. Carried away with her enthusiasm, Gloria leaned eagerly forward.

I jerked back. "Woah! Not so close!"

"Can I get you anything?"

The voice right beside my shoulder made me jump half out of my chair. Gloria smiled sweetly at the waitress and ordered coffee. She must have seen the girl approaching, and neglected to react. If she was testing my awareness, I'd failed abysmally. I groaned inside; I'd just made it tougher to convince her that Liam was a real threat, when even a waitress could sneak up on me unnoticed.

"Make that two," I muttered.

"Anything to eat?"

"No thanks," we echoed each other. In accord on something, at least.

Scribbling on her pad, the girl sauntered away, and Gloria returned her hawk's attention to me.

"So, Cassie, are you up for a bit of bait-laying?"

I was intrigued, but my stomach stirred queasily. I wasn't sure I was going to like what she had in mind, so I hedged.

"Suppose we do catch him; what do you intend to do with him?"

Gloria raised her eyebrows. "What do you think?"

Just as I'd feared.

"Can't we, well, you know, *talk* to him?"

"And say what? He's dangerous, girl, we both know that. Do you think he's just going to be talked out of his plans, whatever they are?"

"I think we should try!" I protested. "We don't get involved in human affairs, do we? We'd risk upsetting the powers."

"Pah!" Gloria dismissed the unseen with a wave of her varnish-tipped fingernails. "Since when do *they* take any notice of what happens to individual humans?"

I shrugged. If I was truthful with myself, it wasn't the powers that troubled me. Yes, I'd contemplated murder when I was trapped inside the bottle, but in the cold glare of daylight I found myself loath to consider ending a life that was already so fleeting. If we could convince him we were not his to manipulate, then surely we could simply outlive him and forget about the embarrassing incident.

"We should find out what he wants, and convince him it isn't going to work."

"You think?" Scepticism dripped from Gloria's beautiful lips, but I stared her down, making it clear I would not back down on this point. It was her turn to shrug.

"Okay, we can always try. We have to catch him first, anyway. You up for that, at least?"

"Aye! That part of your plan I have no problem with." I cocked my head. "What precisely *is* your plan?"

Coffee arrived at that moment, the strong and rich aroma briefly overpowering the slight bonfire smell that clung to Gloria. I sipped appreciatively while Gloria outlined her plan.

"I told you that he found me at the club where I dance? Well, I still have my job, despite three months unexplained absence." She winked and my heart skipped a beat. "It turns out I'm very popular with the clientele. Anyway, I've been careful not to change my routine, so he should find it tempting to try for me again." She shrugged. "I dance, you lurk around and spot him, then wham! We trap him like he trapped us."

She sat back, clearly pleased with her proposal. My whole body tingled at the thought of seeing Gloria at work, but whilst she'd certainly devised a plan, from my perspective it lacked one important detail.

"*How*, exactly, are we going to capture him? I'm no witch, and nor are you, so how do you suggest we deal with his spells?"

Gloria sat back and flashed her pearly whites. "Don't you worry your head about that, sprite Cassie, my friend. That minor detail is all sewn up. Just come along tonight and do the watching. As soon as you spot him, sing out and it will all be over without need for you to get anywhere near him, I guarantee it."

I desperately wanted to show Gloria that I trusted her but, despite being totally smitten, I found that I didn't. Where I would have thought and planned and tried to see all angles of approach, she had one single vision—dive right in and assume it would all work out. Typical salamander. Perhaps she did have a way to control Liam's magic but, if she did, she wasn't about to share it with me. Which made me very uncomfortable.

So I was stunned to hear my voice asking, "And where do I find this club of yours?"

My jaw snapped shut, and I wondered if some alien being or higher power had taken over my body. But the simple answer was that I wanted to please Gloria at all costs, and my body was carrying right on with that intention despite the caution my brain counselled. Gloria's mouth split into that broad grin of flashing teeth, and my insides flip-flopped in response.

I half listened to her answer while picturing that gorgeous body of hers in a variety of revealing outfits. The place she described was a short car hop away, in the basement of a large Victorian property off the Old Edinburgh Road. Very discreet.

I could hardly wait.

"I start at ten. Meet you there fifteen minutes before?"

Chair legs scraped on the laminate floor as Gloria pushed back from the table. I scrambled to my feet, attempting to gather my wits.

"I can do that," I confirmed, "but how about I come to yours first and we can go over the details?"

"Girl, it's a simple plan. I'm sure you'll catch on. Later!"

This, thrown over her shoulder as she descended the stairs, and I swear that artful swing to her hips was exaggerated for my benefit alone.

Damn! I *still* hadn't got a home address out of her.

10. DAWN

I retrieved the Golf and drove the short distance around the corner to the gym. I could have walked but I had a couple of clients that afternoon and I resented the need to buy another ticket. I am a Scot, after all.

Frankly, I was surprised I arrived at all. My mind was anywhere but on my driving, and the two roundabouts I had to negotiate were notorious for the speed and aggression with which most drivers tackled them. I shot round both to the indignant blaring of horns, but pulled into the gym's private car park without a scratch. In general, I consider myself a safe driver but since Gloria showed up I'd definitely lacked in the due care and attention department.

After a quick change in the staff locker room, I dropped into the main hall to see if Alison was around. She was finishing up a spin class, and to my pleasure I saw that one of her clients was the young true-witch, Dawn. Delighted that my bid to encourage a friendship between them appeared to be paying off, I waved cheerily as they headed towards me. Dawn stiffened at sight of me, and I recalled that I was supposed to be a faery masquerading as a would-be witch.

When did life get so complicated?

Trying to keep things normal, I hailed them. "Hello there, ladies! Nice to see you here, Dawn. Did you enjoy that?"

Dawn's wary eyes studied me as she wiped a towel across her damp brow. She puffed a quick breath before replying. "I'm not sure *enjoy* is quite the term I'd use for it, but I certainly feel virtuous."

I laughed, hoping to put her at her ease, and Alison joined in, for once blissfully oblivious to the slight tension in the air. "If only we had a pound for every time someone said that!" wailed my red-headed friend.

"Oh hey, Alison, I have something for you." I dashed back to my locker and returned with a shopping bag stuffed full of rabbit food. I knew Alison would never take money from me, but rabbit food was something she could hardly refuse when I'd landed her with more mouths to feed. I intended to make this a regular donation, on a larger scale than was necessary to feed just the bunnies I'd re-homed with her.

She glanced into the bag. "Oh, Cassie, you didn't have to."

"You have quite enough animals up there without me adding to them, so I wanted to contribute." I put on my most stubborn expression and Alison had the sense to give up without further protest.

"You keep rabbits?" Dawn surmised.

I laughed again. "And the rest! I'm sure Alison will invite you over to view the zoo. You like animals?"

Relaxing a little, Dawn's emerald eyes twinkled. "I love them, but I can't have fluffy ones at home because Saffron's allergic."

"Oh, how sad," Alison sympathised. "For both of you. What's a home without animals? Even Cassie has a pet now, though I haven't met him yet."

"Oh, what do you have?" asked Dawn.

"A mink," I answered a bit reluctantly. I hadn't decided yet whether the arrangement was permanent. "It's early days and he's a bit wild."

"Interesting choice," Dawn observed. "Eminently suitable as a witch's familiar."

That hadn't occurred to me. Until now I'd done my best to keep my distance from those who might recognise me for what I truly was, so I was rather ignorant of the finer details of a witch's domestic arrangements. I shook my head. "I didn't know that."

"Oh aye," replied Dawn, warming to her subject. "Agile, intelligent, independent—"

"Sounds more like Alison's cats to me," I said, shifting the spotlight back onto Alison. "She has two of the smartest cats I've ever come across."

"I shall have to meet them," Dawn enthused, but then hesitated, as if worried about overstepping some invisible line. "If you don't mind, that is?"

I wondered who had spurned her friendship in the past. More fool them. I knew her type, and Dawn would make a good and steadfast friend.

Face alight with thoughts of her cats, Alison reassured Dawn. "They'd love to meet you. Jemima rules the house, but Horatio has the loudest voice—he's half Siamese. You could come back with me now, if you have time? It's on your way home. I have all sorts of questions for you." She glanced at me. "Are you busy right now, Cassie? We could all go back for a cup of coffee."

Damn. I wanted to; there was so much I needed to learn about magic, but the two clients I had scheduled were both steady customers, the sort you don't want to lose.

"I can't right now. I'm working the next couple of hours."

"Neither can I," said Dawn. "I have errands to run for Gordon, but I could drop by later if you're going to be there? About four?"

"Great! I'll have the kettle on. Take the wee turn past the road for Kiltarlity, and then third drive on the left. 'Tis a mite rough but just keep on driving. I'm right at the top. Cassie?"

"Aye, I'll be there."

I spent the time, while my clients worked up a sweat, wondering what sort of errands Gordon needed running. I couldn't shake the memory of how he'd looked at me when I passed the kitchen door on my way to rescue Alison. Not unfriendly, but calculating. Could he see past my surface veneer to the elemental force that lay beneath? What had he and Saffron been discussing with Brian, the water diviner?

I was feeling decidedly paranoid. Having someone kidnap and try to kill you can skew your outlook on even the most mundane. I determined to keep close to the coven leaders until I knew what they were up to, and Dawn was my way to do that. I felt pretty sure she had nothing to hide, although I could be mistaking youth for innocence.

"Okay, Doreen, that's your last set for today." My middle aged and somewhat overweight victim huffed with relief. I waited until she'd showered and changed, collecting my towel from her along with payment in crisp new bank notes. Once we'd booked her next session and said goodbye, I grabbed my things and headed out towards Alison's. I was a little calmer than earlier, and so was my driving. By the time I'd covered half the length of Loch Ness, I was in a relaxed and mellow mood.

Dawn had beaten me to it. She was climbing out of her little black Ford Ka as I pulled up beside her. I parked up and opened the car door, inhaling the rich aroma of animals and manure.

"You found me okay then?" called Alison as she leaned over the rusty iron gate. The sun chose that moment to punch through the cloud layer and illuminate the croft and its owner with a bright golden glow. The effect was pure chocolate box, all the imperfections of the dilapidated old property melting into the quintessential highland scene of the dream-perfect crofter's lifestyle—the neat little single storey dwelling surrounded by contented livestock.

Of course, that picture was nothing more than a dream. Poor highland crofters eked out a living from their meagre acreage of poor soil and tended to share their domestic arrangements with their animals. But modern romanticism flies defiantly in the face of recorded history.

On closer inspection it would be obvious to anyone with half a brain that Alison's property was no longer a working croft. Although the chickens and goats were potentially productive, too many of her animals were beyond their best years, living out their retirements in what comfort Alison could offer them, whilst the rabbit collection did nothing but expand. I knew she re-homed a few when the opportunity presented itself but, being as cautious as she was, few potential new owners came up to Alison's exacting standards.

"Come in, the kettle's on," Alison invited. I could see the astonishment on Dawn's face as she took in the extent of Alison's collection of waifs and strays, but she merely raised her eyebrows and followed our hostess into the croft.

"Oh, what a gorgeous cat!"

Jemima puffed up her white fur in delight at the attention, and twined herself around Dawn's ankles.

"Don't let her trip you up," Alison warned, but despite being disadvantaged by her lack of cat ownership, Dawn had no trouble pleasing the resident felines. She scooped Jemima off the floor and was soon wearing her around her neck like the Snow Queen's fur muffler. Horatio greeted her with one of his darkest brown meows as we entered the kitchen and Dawn's spare hand, the one that wasn't caressing Jemima, instantly became attached to his chin. A deep rumble vibrated through the room.

The kitchen was the most modernised part of the croft, with a red oil-fired twin oven Aga, and white cupboards bearing stencilled flowers. It was the one part of the property that Alison and Simon had spent any money on before their acrimonious split.

The deep Belfast sink was full of dirty dishes, and I guessed the dishwasher had packed up again.

Sitting down at the square table opposite Dawn, I rested my elbows on the red and yellow table cloth. Snuggled into the crook of Dawn's left elbow, Horatio eyed me from beneath lids half-closed in ecstasy, and I swear I could almost hear his thoughts: '*You* never do this to me'.

Liar.

"Tea?" Alison waved a couple of mugs at us.

I nodded.

"Do you have any herbal teas?" Dawn asked.

"Aye. Come and see if there's anything you fancy."

Dawn disentangled herself from Horatio and took Jemima with her, still wearing the cat around her neck. Horatio sat on the table and washed his paws, pausing now and again to glance at me from slitted blue eyes. For the first time I found myself wondering about the intelligence levels of cats; there was a calculating scrutiny to each pause.

The smell of lemon and ginger tea wafted my way and I accepted my mug gratefully. Anything to be diverted from the uncomfortable feeling of being like a bug under a microscope.

"So Dawn, tell us more about familiars," I asked, keen to keep the attention away from myself.

Alison sat down beside me and Dawn resettled herself opposite, almost in an echo of Gloria, keeping the width of the table between us as a barrier. She, too, nursed a mug of lemon and ginger tea between her cupped hands. The steam from the hot drink curled up in front of her face, for all the world Gipsy Rose Lee, come to tell my fortune.

"Not every witch has a familiar," Dawn explained, "but having one can be a great asset, because they enhance your psychic powers."

"Oh, I can believe that," commented Alison as Horatio arranged himself in a neat, purring circle on her lap. "I've always felt there was something magical about cats. How does it work?"

"Well, you see, no matter how hard we witches try to find communion with Nature, animals are always more in tune with Her than we are. But if you have a familiar, you can merge with its instincts and via that link you can interface with the intelligence of Nature. Animals' psychic senses are stronger than humans', so such a close rapport enhances the witch's own psychic abilities."

"And does the familiar get anything out of this relationship?" Alison queried, ever the one to stand up for animal rights.

Warming to her subject now, Dawn nodded. "Oh, it's not a one sided relationship, believe me. From linking with us, a familiar gains an expanded view of reality, which in turn augments their energy pattern. Together, a witch and her familiar can open portals to other realms, and perform magic in the material realm as well an on the astral plane."

"And can any cat be a familiar?" Alison wanted to know.

"I think it's rather more that the cat has to choose you as a partner. I think they may all have the potential, but they don't all choose to exercise it."

"Typical cat!" The words were out of my mouth before I could stop them. I cursed silently. I'd had every intention to sit quietly and listen, not participate.

"Absolutely!" Alison agreed, but the damage was done. Dawn's intense gaze eerily echoed the examination Horatio had subjected me to earlier.

"It isn't just cats," Dawn elaborated. "Lots of creatures can form familiar partnerships. You have a mink, Cassie, yes? They are notoriously picky, even more so than cats. But according to folklore, it's not only animals that can be familiars. It can also be one of the fey."

Alison's eyes went wide. "You mean, like a faery?"

Dawn nodded without taking her gaze from mine. "Yes, indeed. Exactly like a faery."

Shit! How had I managed to dig myself a hole of these proportions?

Jemima chose that moment to stretch mightily with a huge yawn, and stick her claws into Dawn's shoulder.

"Ouch!"

"Oh Dawn, I'm sorry!" Alison leaped to her feet, mortified, and tried to remove Jemima from around Dawn's neck. Jemima had other ideas, entangling her claws in Dawn's woolly sweater and clinging on as if her life depended upon it.

"Really, its nae bother! Leave her be; I'm sure she'll get down when she's ready."

Alison let go of the irate cat and Jemima settled back down, disentangled her claws and licked her front paws until she was satisfied that she was not about to be evicted. She then draped herself artistically back into fur collar mode with her chin lying alongside Dawn's cheek. Whereupon, she fixed her big green eyes upon me and blinked.

No! She *winked!*

Stupefied, I sat back and kept quiet as Alison and Dawn swapped stories about cat behaviour. Dawn's mother had kept cats when Dawn was a child; only since the advent of Saffron and her allergies had the poor girl been bereft of feline company.

I watched Jemima closely for any other non-typical feline behaviour, but apparently satisfied that she had disrupted Dawn's train of thought, she relapsed into sleep. The tip of her tail gave the occasional twitch to prove she was still aware.

Which begged my earlier question: how intelligent *were* cats?

The conversation drifted onto more mundane topics, such as Aga cook books and raised veg beds, neither of which invited any input from me. What use would I have for such things? Alison knew of my monumental lack of interest in most foods and, aside from the odd glance to make sure I wasn't looking bored, she didn't try to involve me. Much though I wanted to stay and watch things develop between Alison and Dawn, I had an engagement to prepare for, so I finished my tea and pushed back from the table.

"Sorry ladies, but I have to go."

Dawn glanced at her watch. "I ought to be getting on too. Thank you so much for the tea."

As if on cue, Jemima jumped down and stalked away without a backward glance.

"Well, there you go," Alison said. "Intelligent or what?"

Oh yeah.

As I trundled off down the drive in the Golf, I watched in my rear view mirror. Alison and Dawn continued to natter even as Dawn sat in her car, ready to leave. The friendship idea had been a good one all round.

I gave myself a pat on the back.

The croft vanished behind me and I allowed myself to think about what this evening promised. My body started to tense up in anticipation: I was going to see Gloria dance! I wasn't sure how I was going to endure the time that still stretched between now and then, even though I had plenty I could do to fill it up. I wanted to be there instantly, with everything done and nothing to distract me. In fact, I would be annoyed if Liam turned up; his presence would ruin the whole event. Catching him might be the purpose behind Gloria's plan but, at least for tonight, I would prefer his continued absence.

Let him come another night. Tonight was mine.

11. THE CLUB

Back at home, I assured myself that the steading had received no unwanted visitors, and then popped my head into the utility room to check on Minkie. He chattered at me in a friendly tone and I thought about what I'd learned regarding familiars.

Strictly speaking, an elemental can't become a witch. You'd need witch genes, and I hadn't harvested any of those to try yet, but I couldn't see any harm in exploring any natural skills I might have. I'd rarely felt as helpless as when Liam held me captive, and wished never to be subjected to such anguish again. I wondered if Minkie had come into my life for a reason.

"You want out, don't you?" I unclipped the latch on his cage. It couldn't hurt to try building a relationship. "There you go. I'll get your tea out of the fridge. Just give me a moment to warm it up."

He followed me through to the kitchen with obvious anticipation.

I sat at the kitchen table while the microwave buzzed to itself. Minkie hopped up onto the work surface with his nose twitching, testing the air. He jumped back a pace when the oven pinged, then surged forward as I retrieved the plastic container of tripe.

"Hang on a minute! Let me get it into your bowl!"

My prospective familiar hoovered up his supper at such speed I wondered if I was feeding him enough. I'd never had a pet before, so this was all new to me. However, once finished, Minkie seemed content. He followed me through to the room I use as a dressing room, climbed onto a pile of dirty laundry and proceeded to polish his whiskers.

"You seem to be making yourself at home. Next thing you'll be demanding your own river, like mine."

It occurred to me that perhaps I should think a bit about Minkie's future. Keeping him in a cage inside a small building didn't seem very fair to an animal designed to live and hunt in the wild.

Just not in the Scottish Highlands.

But that was a consideration for another time. Right now I had more immediate concerns. What to wear? Once again, I was in a dither about the right outfit to impress Gloria, although this time it would all need to be created rather than worn. I might need to turn invisible at any moment, in case Liam decided to ruin my evening by turning up after all.

"What do you think then, Minkie? Any fashion tips from one wild creature to another?" I caught the almost intelligent regard of his beady black eyes studying me as I preened in front of the mirror. "Not fur, I'm guessing."

I sighed and then wailed, "It's not *fair*. Gloria's so confident, and she has so much more mass to work with than I do! You'd think a salamander would burn it all up, wouldn't you?"

Minkie blinked.

"Yes, I'm going to see her again. Twice in one day! And this time I get to see her dance. Ooh, I can't wait!"

A little snort erupted from my laundry pile. Amusement or disgust? Or was I anthropomorphising, and it was really only a mink sneeze?

Why was I so taken with Gloria anyway? Our meeting earlier had reminded me of the fundamental incompatibility of our natures, the very reason opposing elementals tended to avoid each other.

Apart from the obvious danger.

Whatever the reason, she'd captivated me as surely as a human who falls blindly in love with an unsuitable partner. I might not possess a heart in the literal sense, but whatever I did have, it now belonged to Gloria.

On the flipside, our meeting had shown me that Gloria didn't reciprocate my feelings. So now it was up to me to convince her that she wanted me as much as I wanted her. Which led me right back to clothes.

After trying numerous looks, I settled on a short nude-coloured lace dress with plunging cleavage. I'd never fashioned myself with huge breasts, feeling that the adage 'more than a handful is a waste' was in general a good guideline, but tonight I sacrificed yet more of my height to go from a C-cup to a DD. I felt a touch top heavy, but was pretty sure they wouldn't look out of place where I was going. A pair of vertiginous killer heels replaced the height I'd lost to my bosom, and I thanked the gods that, unlike a human, I didn't have to suffer the discomfort of wearing such torture implements for real.

I matched the fabric of dress and shoes, added subtle make up and slicked my hair back into a short pony tail. I was ready.

"Good night, my son," I waved to Minkie as I left the room. "Don't wait up."

The drive into town seemed to take forever.

In truth, it took no longer than any other time, but I was impatient. I'd chosen the Audi Quattro this time—no point making things easy for Liam—and I was frustrated that I could not use all the power the sleek little beauty offered me. Every driver who delayed me by even a fraction of a second had me fuming at the wheel. By the time I turned into the club's paved driveway, I was as near boiling point as it is prudent for a sprite to reach. A discreet parking attendant, whom I suspected doubled as a bouncer, pointed me to an empty bay, and then directed me to the head of the stairs leading down to the basement club. Not wanting to arrive looking flustered, I paused to gather myself.

Hair still caught in pony tail band. Check. Dress neckline showing equal expanse of skin either side of cleavage. Check. Hem straight and not *quite* riding high enough to show that I hadn't wasted mass on fashioning underwear. Check.

Ready to go, I stepped one well-shod foot onto the first step down. And froze. Involuntarily, my body ceased to function. My mind blanked and a chill of fear iced my veins. I gazed numbly at the slender, dark figure lurking at the base of the stairs until he glanced away, freeing me, permitting life to return to the lifeless.

My paralysed brain shot back to working order. Recognition of the figure chilled me all over. *Vampire.*

Not something you see every day in downtown Inverness, but I'd encountered enough of them in the distant past to know one when I saw one. And to know the horror of being trapped by their gaze, unable to move or even to think.

This one, darkly handsome and with more than a passing resemblance to a youthful Bryan Ferry with his ever-present hint of a sneer, glanced at me again but without interest. Vampires prefer their blood more full bodied than the pseudo-stuff that runs through my counterfeit veins.

Somewhat troubled at finding his sort here, I was, however, still determined to continue with my evening's plans. I descended, brushing past the cold figure in his immaculate Armani suit. A body-wracking shiver ran down my spine, even though I knew I was in no danger from him.

I wondered what he was doing here. Perhaps it was simply a good place for him to get a carry-out meal.

Once past the heavy door, I took stock. A long, tiled corridor led in one direction to the Ladies and Gents and in the other to a small cubby that bristled with CCTV monitors. The bald man seated in front of the screens glanced round and sent a friendly smile winging my way. His expensive white teeth flashed in a face covered by swirling Celtic tattoos. I smiled back and he inclined his head before resuming work.

Ahead of me, a beaded curtain invited entry to the club proper.

Beyond the heavy strands it was hot, dark and loud. Semi-naked waitresses in frothy miniskirts strutted between tables, their hips swinging like pendulums. A gilded cage mounted on a platform dominated the centre of the room. Inside, a steel pole stretched from floor to ceiling. Three other podiums with bare metal poles were arranged around the perimeter, and curtained off alcoves suggested more intimate amusements were available if desired.

A room such as this would once have suffered a blue-grey fug of tobacco smoke. Now the air was clear to the eye, if slightly tainted by more exotic—and less legal—aromas. The subdued lighting failed to give the customers quite the same level of anonymity they had enjoyed pre-smoking ban, but the few bodies currently lolling at the tables seemed unconcerned.

I glanced around, wondering where I would find Gloria. It was early in the evening for this type of establishment. The clientele was still thin on the ground, but I was certain she would be here already, preparing for Liam's capture, should he turn up. Or did Gloria count Liam a priority? I wasn't convinced that she was taking this whole situation seriously.

I sashayed over to the bar, enjoying the admiring glances that tracked my progress. I've never gone out of my way to be the centre of attention, but when you've got what it takes, why not flaunt it? It certainly had the desired effect. Two of the less seedy patrons joined me and offered to buy me drinks. I accepted both, enjoying the confused and competitive expressions elicited by my refusal to choose one over the other.

Number one was a typical middle aged, overweight suit, sweat beading the rim of his balding hairline. Number two was younger but instantly forgettable, from his mid brown hair to his nondescript jeans and t-shirt. Nothing to recommend one over the other for any sort of lasting liaison, but fine for a quick drink while I tracked down my evening's entertainment.

Sadly, alcohol has no effect on me—I guess I dilute it—but I enjoy the taste. I ordered a mint julep, courtesy of Mr Suit, and a strawberry daiquiri paid for by Mr Forgettable. I sipped first one, and then the other, allowing the flavours to roll around my mouth. The icy sweet essence of the julep contrasted beautifully with the fruity zest of the daiquiri. My two companions leaned against the bar, one to either side of me, and avoided making eye contact with each other. Their efforts at small talk and chat up lines were frankly dismal and after a few minutes, first Mr Suit and then Mr Forgettable wandered away, leaving me to enjoy my drinks. I'm sure if Alison had been with me she would have told me how guilty I should be feeling, but guilt is one of those human emotions I still struggle to understand. Why should I feel guilty for bumming drinks off those guys when they had obvious ulterior motives? It would be tantamount to admitting they could buy sex with me, because that was plainly what they were after. Nice men didn't come to this sort of club.

Mind you, nor did nice girls.

I turned around to survey the club. A handful of new patrons had entered whilst I'd been engrossed in my drinks, and to my delight I saw Gloria wending her way between tables towards me.

She looked stunning, as ever. Not yet revealing her evening's outfit, she sported a deep blue knee-length wrap with spangles around the plunging neckline. She wore flip flops on her feet and dainty, blue tipped nails graced her elegant toes. Her gold bead-studded cornrows were piled high on her head and pinned in place with winking sapphire butterfly clips.

She stopped a few metres along from me and lounged against the bar. "I see you've made yourself welcome."

I raised a glass. "You want one?"

She shook her head. "Later. My boss doesn't care to see us drinking before we dance. Now, have you met Alistair yet?"

"Alistair?"

Gloria grinned and winked. A hot flush raced over my skin.

"My secret weapon," she said. "Our means of capturing this upstart who thinks he can use an elemental for his own ends."

"Another magician?"

A sharp negative jerk of her head set the ends of the cornrows swinging. "No. I've never much cared for magic users. Look over there."

She pointed to the darker recesses of a door half hidden by trailing curtains in heavy crimson velour. My heart, such as it was, sank. Alistair was the Bryan Ferry-lookalike vampire I had encountered on my way in.

"*That's* your idea to catch a powerful magician?" I forgot for a moment how much I longed for Gloria's approbation. Sarcasm and disappointment clouded my tone.

"What?" Gloria almost snarled. "You don't like it? You have a better idea?"

I recoiled slightly from the aggressive snap in her voice; I kept forgetting how volatile salamanders could be. I backtracked in a hurry, trying to flow smoothly around the situation.

"I rather suspect Liam might have wards against commonplace paranormals, and I don't want to risk us ending up in his clutches again." I shrugged. "But if you think a vamp can do it, we can but try."

Gloria's flash of temper was replaced with amusement. "Commonplace? I shouldn't let Alastair hear you call him that, although it might be too late already, with his hearing."

Indeed, the vampire was threading his way across the floor in our direction, and I shivered as my skin turned icy. He stopped a couple of steps away and regarded me as if I was a potentially tasty morsel. Frost crept through my veins.

Alastair raised one well groomed eyebrow and bestowed me with a sardonic nod of his head, his long fringe falling artistically over one eye.

"I am no youngster, sprite, to be offended by your ill-chosen words, but I advise you, have more faith in your companion's counsel. I am assuredly capable of the task ahead."

Mmm. Not local, from that speech pattern. Or maybe he was lingering a tad too far in the past. Whatever. If he believed he could do the job, who was I to argue? I consciously stifled my reservations.

Gloria beamed at him and a pang of jealousy cut through me. "Of course you are, my chilly friend." She shivered artistically, making her skin ripple. I wanted to reach out and caress her, to make my touch the source of that quivering, but her attention was all for the frigid vampire who stood stiffly before us, apparently uncertain whether he was being mocked or not.

"Until later then," he said in clipped tones and turned away, slipping from our awareness as only such a creature may.

"So you see, it's all sorted," Gloria announced.

12. POLE DANCER

Gloria's sinuous body wrapped around the pole as flame wreaths a wick, licking, caressing, writhing.

The club was packed by now, every table groaning beneath the weight of half empty glasses and sweaty hands and elbows leaning hard as every male in the audience craned forward to get the best possible view. The heavy air stank of cheap beer and testosterone, and the music was deafening.

Perched on my barstool I could see above most of their heads, and I was as captivated as they. Gloria undulated up and down the pole in a way I'm sure a less drunk audience would have realised wasn't strictly possible for a human. My salamander truly lived to dance. Had there been no spectators at all, I doubt her performance would have been any less spectacular.

No wonder her boss didn't want to lose her. If I read the situation right, Gloria's was the most popular routine of the evening, the clientele rolling in not long before, just to see her. And spending plenty at the bar as a bonus.

The music swelled to a crescendo, the roars of the spectators almost matching it in decibels. Gloria slithered headfirst down the pole, before somersaulting into splits at its base for her grand finale. She flung her head back in triumph. The gold beads scattered through her hair coruscated in the spotlights while she posed, panting artfully as if she really needed the air.

The throng of Scottish manhood surged to its feet in acclaim. Over their heads, her eyes met mine and they glittered with roiling emotion.

The world around me receded.

Dare I hope those sparks were for me? Shivers tingled down my spine.

Then she glanced away, and the moment was gone. I replayed it over and over in my mind as reassurance that I had not imagined it.

Gloria retrieved her wrap and draped it over her silver and sapphire corset. The depending tassels swung provocatively around her hips as she sauntered towards the dressing rooms. Once she was out of sight, most of the patrons settled back to their drinking.

Several men had tried to chat me up whilst I held my vantage point at the bar, and I was now happily the wrong side of several more exotic cocktails. I think the bartender was developing a soft spot for me; he appeared to enjoy the challenge of mixing rarely requested concoctions.

The latest no-hoper had not long departed when I breathed in Gloria's unmistakeable hot scent. She'd changed into a slinky red one-shouldered dress and high heeled strappy sandals. I was very glad to be perched up on my high stool, despite the heels I myself sported.

"Did you enjoy that?" she asked huskily, and sat down one stool over. Even at a safe distance, the heat radiating from her body raised my temperature.

"Divine, darling," I said without thinking. Gloria smiled, and for once her expression was totally without artifice. "Thank you," she said, sounding genuinely pleased. "Surely you dance too?"

"I do, but without your fire."

She laughed. Being what she was, I'm sure that the thrill of the dance itself was enough for her, but the adulation it brought with it was a happy by-product. I basked in the glow of pleasure that oozed from her, and wondered where this new phase of our relationship might lead.

Seizing the moment, I asked: "How did you first find out you could take human form?"

A shadow crossed her face. "I was a magician's toy, once. He had a habit of burning his enemies, and I was his tool. I've never liked being summoned, and one day I was particularly pissed off, so I dallied with his victim. Turned out that having sex without burning him up too badly was far more fun and hey presto! Amazing what semen can do, ain't it?"

I smiled, picturing the scene. "What happened to the magician?"

Gloria flashed her teeth. "Well, although I did kill my first lover, what I got from him made it easier with the next one, and once I'd burned that one's bonds, he ran the bastard through. Haven't been summoned since." She paused, eyes growing alarmed. "You don't suppose this magician knows how to summon, do you?"

I shuddered at the thought but shook my head. "If he did, he wouldn't have used such elaborate traps the first time, would he?"

"Of course. Silly me."

It was so nice, having a normal girly chat with a fellow elemental. Trust a human male to spoil it.

"Hey gorgeous! Ye wanna drink?"

I sighed. How many times had I heard that line already tonight?

But this time the words were not for me. The intruder took the vacant stool between us, presenting his back to me. Gloria beamed at him, and wasted no time requesting a wee dram. A Glenfiddich single malt, to be precise. Her admirer, a scrawny specimen with over-large ears and a weak chin, looked even more impressed, if that were possible. His chest puffed up and he thrust out his jaw, showing off his laughable attempt at designer stubble. To my dismay, Gloria simpered, murmuring encouragement.

My vision tunnelled. This pathetic excuse for a human being did not even belong in the same room as my glorious salamander. My mood rushed dangerously downhill.

Gloria's whisky arrived, along with a second glass of malt with water for him. I smiled then. Not a nice smile, but I couldn't help myself. How *dare* he take her attention away from me?

Fortuitously, he'd supplied a tool I could use to discourage him.

Wrapping a possessive arm around my intended, the odious little man planted a kiss on her cheek.

"Baby, you're *hot*!" he declared.

"Honey, you have no idea!" she whispered in his ear.

I gagged, and Gloria shot me a warning look. Perhaps she wanted some DNA tonight and wasn't about to be fussy. I've been there a few times myself, but I try not to let my standards slip.

Perhaps Gloria's standards were different.

Whatever, I found I couldn't let her do it. As the wretch raised his glass to his saggy lips, I reached into the water molecules floating amongst the whisky and shot them up his nose.

The tumbler crashed back onto the bar as he choked and snorted, struggling to remove the invading moisture from his lungs. He waved his hands helplessly around, and a passing waitress dropped her tray and rushed over, slapping him hard on the back.

Go on, harder! I thought uncharitably, as his eyes bulged and he gasped a ragged breath.

Patting himself on the chest, he waved the waitress away and pointed significantly towards the Gents, staggering in that direction, still whooping the odd wheeze of breath.

Gloria fixed me with a significant look.

"Oops!" I said, slipping off my stool, "I guess it's about time I vanished. If you want his malt too," I pointed at the abandoned glass on the bar, "it's now neat. See you later."

And I fled to the Ladies, half choking with laughter. Maybe this is what humans mean when they say immortals are cruel and unfeeling, but I'd done the guy no permanent harm, and I'd saved Gloria from compromising herself by harvesting DNA from such a low life.

I slipped into the Ladies and checked the cubicles for signs of life. Nada. I went back to the main door and propped it ajar with a small wad of hand towels for a wedge, before dropping cohesion and melting into total invisibility. I drifted through the gap that I'd left for myself and made my way back to the bar.

Unbelievable! In the infinitesimal time I'd been gone, Gloria had picked up another man and was openly canoodling. I hovered above his head like an angry raincloud. <*Fuck off!*> I screamed silently at him, but without the luxury to become visible, I made no impression.

I dripped the odd spot of water onto their heads. That did the trick, at least with Gloria. The drops that touched her skin hissed and evaporated instantly—boy, she was running hot! And her temper was starting to do the same. While she'd been indulgent with my treatment of her first catch, she wasn't going to be so charitable with her second. As he buried his lips into her throat, nuzzling her like an offspring searching for a teat, she tipped her head back and scowled up at me.

I took the hint and ceased dripping, but I was not going to float around and watch Gloria have sex with anyone else. If I couldn't have her, no one was going to. Certainly not while I was present. I knew I was being unreasonable; I could never have her under any circumstances, but that's jealousy for you. Such a perverse human trait.

Warned off from dampening their ardour, I investigated his glass. No luck there. Empty already. Rats! I wracked my mind for other possibilities, and then the sweet, darling little chap dropped himself so totally in my lap I couldn't believe my luck.

"Just goin' t' tak' a leak," he announced with all the sensitivity of an undertaker ogling a road crash. "Don't you be going nowhere, lassie."

Gloria smiled at him in a way she'd never smiled at me, and my temperature soared towards boiling point. I attached myself to the rear of his jeans and let him pull me along into the Gents; no point exerting energy when one doesn't have to. As he settled himself into position and undid his fly, I manoeuvred myself around to get a good view. I was starting to feel a touch guilty about the other guy, so I decided to be considerate with this one and let him finish his business before ruining his evening.

He had started to tuck himself away when the urinal flushed early and over-enthusiastically with a little help from me, soaking the would-be Casanova from navel to knees. He leapt back with a screech of horror and indignation sufficient to cover the bubbling hiss of mirth that escaped my overheated essence.

He dabbed frantically at his clothes with wads of paper towels. He even tried standing with the hot air dryer directed downward, but he was never going to dry himself sufficiently not to look as if he'd had an accident. Finally he gave up in disgust. Too embarrassed to go back into the club, he slunk out into the night and I snuck with him, attached to his sopping wet shirt. Once outside, he dashed up the steps, passing Alastair without noticing him, other than a quick shiver that he probably put down to the cool night air and his wet clothes.

Disconcertingly, the vampire seemed to sense me.

"Up to your elemental tricks, sprite?"

He sounded less than impressed—an adult dealing with the pranks of an annoying juvenile. I was comforted to note that his eyes cast around, apparently trying to spot me but unable to do so. On the other hand, I felt shamed by my behaviour and vowed to start concentrating on the evening's serious side.

Gloria's plan relied on Liam showing up to order. He had already proven to me that he was scarily capable of being unpredictable, and I saw no reason why he should meekly fall in line with Gloria's arrangements. I suppose I should have been pleased at the prospect of having to return night after night until he materialised, but considering how the last hour had gone I feared that at best it was going to turn into a rather uncomfortable experience. At worst, Gloria might end up murdering me.

I slipped back inside the club the next time someone opened the door, and made my way back to the bar. Gloria sat there, alone now and appearing rather grumpy. I shrank into a corner and stayed put for the rest of the evening, as the club gradually emptied and the staff started cleaning tables. Alastair dropped by from time to time, exchanged a few words with Gloria, and then vanished again. After the excitement of getting ready, all the anticipation, and then witnessing Gloria's thrilling performance, I was left feeling flat and bored. If this was going to go on for some time, until Liam decided to cooperate and show up, I could quite see myself indulging as shamelessly as Gloria had intended to earlier this evening, just for something to do.

When the last customer had gone and the staff started locking up, I followed Gloria out and up the steps, pulling myself back into human form by the time we reached the car park. Alastair met us there, briefly delaying the moment when I would have to apologise to Gloria for ruining her evening's entertainment.

"Are you certain there is no way to track this magician to his lair?" asked the vampire.

I shook my head. "Not unless you can come up with something we haven't thought of. We don't have a last name or any background to start from."

"So we assemble again tomorrow and continue to wait?"

"Not my favourite part of this plan," said Gloria, sounding glum. "I hope he's not going to keep us waiting too long."

"Fine," said Alastair, the quirk of his mouth hovering somewhere between smile and sneer. "I will be here, as arranged."

He crossed the car park, leaving Gloria and me standing together. Not knowing quite what to say, I watched as the vamp slid into the driver's seat of a sleek dark grey Ferrari parked in shadow by a wall, and closed the door with a quiet snick.

Out of distractions, I decided to grasp the nettle. "Gloria, I'm sorry," I said honestly, hoping I could repair some of the damage my insane jealousy had driven me to. To my astonishment she laughed—a deep, throaty chuckle.

"I'd often wondered what a sprite could do, given your species general lack of balls. Frankly, I'm impressed! The first one—that was inventive, and the second? Hilarious!"

I raised my eyebrows. "You saw him?"

"Och aye, I came to see what was taking him so long, and I had a fair idea you'd gone in there with him. When I heard the cursing and the dryer, I knew! He looked well embarrassed, slinking out like that!"

"I thought you were annoyed. You were pretty grumpy at the bar."

Gloria shook her head. "Just bored, waiting for this poxy magician to show up. I'm not that desperate, although I might have to top up tomorrow. You'll have to let me have one, but I'm looking forward to seeing what you can cook up for the others. So, until tomorrow?"

Somewhat bemused, and with the jury out regarding Gloria's dubious sense of humour, I nodded. We made our way across the almost empty car park, with just a smattering of employees' vehicles still dotted around. My Quattro and Gloria's Mini Cooper had ended up almost alongside each other, one to either side of a pool of yellow cast by a streetlight over the boundary wall. Gloria's strides were longer than mine and she slipped into her car as I opened my door. I noticed absently that Alastair had not yet driven away, but I couldn't see him behind his tinted windscreen. Perhaps he was on the phone.

I lowered myself into the leather seat of the Quattro and pulled the door shut. I stretched for a moment, luxuriating as I replayed my memories of a rather remarkable evening, and then settled myself for the drive home.

I pushed the red starter button. Nothing. I frowned. This was quite a new car, and Audis are reliable, as a rule. I tried again. Still nothing. My evening was not supposed to end so. With a sigh of disappointment I pulled out my phone and searched for the assistance number. Bizarrely, my phone showed no signal. At home on the Black Isle, I might have understood this; reception could be patchy out in the wilds. But here, within the city bounds, it was very odd.

With an even deeper sigh I pulled on the door latch, intending to wander around until I could locate a signal. The door refused to open.

For the second time that night, ice froze my veins. Suddenly, I knew the reason that Alastair hadn't driven away, and when I looked across at Gloria's Mini, I could see her wrestling with her car door, trying desperately to pry it open.

Liam's trap spells were so accomplished, you had to admire them even while you panicked. There had been no hint of this one until we, his intended targets, triggered them, and even then I hadn't noticed it happen.

I tried to think, to figure out where there might be a chink in the prison that my lovely car had become. I tried all the obvious things: the windows and the air vents. Damn it! Not even a keyhole these days, no little gaps to speak of in the modern car cabin. Wonderful for air conditioning, not so good for escape attempts.

Looking across to Gloria again, she was gesticulating wildly, pointing back towards the club. Twisting around, I could see a couple of the waitresses chatting beside a car that was parked right in the middle of the tarmac. I slammed my hand on the horn, and I could see Gloria trying the same, but Liam's spell was so well constructed not even sound got out.

My body started to shake and my heart raced. I slumped down in the comfortable leather bucket seat and wondered if this was it; out-foxed by a madman with major magical talent and an apparent suicide wish.

A flash of light snapped my head around. The inside of Gloria's Mini had erupted into flames. For an instant I thought Gloria's temper had bested her, but in my rear view mirror I saw the two waitresses running towards us. Good on Gloria!

From the girls' wide open mouths, I guessed they were also screaming. A couple more people sprang from the basement steps, and one—the security guy with the tattoos—started animatedly mouthing into his phone. Calling the fire brigade, I hoped.

I leaped out of my skin as my driver's door popped open and hands dragged me from my seat. I thrashed wildly, convinced that Liam had come to claim me, until I realised the voices in my ears were female. I recognised the waitress who had tried to help my first victim of the evening. Dropping my arms, I tried to make sense of what they were yelling at me.

"Is she inside? Did she get in it?"

What? My mind moved sluggishly, still gripped by the trauma of being trapped and facing impending annihilation. One of the girls grabbed my shoulder and shook me.

"Is Gloria in her car?"

My mind snapped back to clarity. Of course, they had no idea what was going on. I shook my head.

"No, no she isn't. She decided to walk."

"She's not in there!" yelled one of the girls to the bartender who appeared to be about to attempt to open the Mini's door.

"Walk?" repeated the other girl, sounding confused. I had no idea how far away Gloria lived, but guessed it wasn't within walking distance. "Why ever would she walk?"

I found myself on the wrong end of a pair of suspicious glares, and realised I needed to deflect scrutiny away from not only myself, but also Gloria, who was still doing a fine job of destroying her car's interior. We both needed to be away from here before Liam arrived to collect his prizes. I glanced uneasily around, wondering if he was nearby.

I also wondered when one of the small group of people gathered would notice that despite the intense flames, no smoke was escaping Gloria's car. But I could hear sirens approaching, so I concentrated on weaving a plausible story.

"She went to find a cab," I said. "Her car wouldn't start."

"Must have been an electrical fault," said a man's voice from behind me and I turned with my innards sinking towards my stilettos, but breathed again when I realised it was my friendly barkeep.

"Yes, that must have been what started the fire," I agreed. "It's so lucky she wasn't in it."

A big, red fire truck screeched into the car park and disgorged half a dozen fire fighters. We were all ushered back from the burning car and the professionals didn't wait around long enough to notice anything odd about the fire. High pressure jets of water hit the windows both sides, shattering the super heated glass and releasing huge gouts of flame to shoot skyward. We all rocked back as a wash of intense heat and stench of burning plastic rolled over us. I think everyone else was so busy blinking blurry eyes, that I was the only one to see the right hand pillar of flame shoot higher than the left. It condensed to a bright spot of light and shot away at a tangent, rapidly disappearing from view beyond the rooftops. I heaved a sigh of relief. Gloria was safely away. Now I needed to be gone too.

Edging my way to the outside of the group watching the fire crew foaming down the wrecked Mini, I peered suspiciously into all the dark corners. Surely Liam wouldn't be too far away?

Mercifully, there was no sign of him.

My eyes came to rest on Alastair's Ferrari. I'm not a vampire groupie, but this one had been prepared to help Gloria and so, by default, me. I had no idea if Liam had any interest in capturing such a creature, or what he might do with one if he did, but I wasn't about to leave anyone to the magician's dubious mercy.

I slipped across the car park, walking on tip toes to avoid drawing attention with my snickety-snick heels. With some trepidation I grasped the Ferrari's door handle and gave a quick jerk, releasing Alastair. He moved so fast, I saw him only as a blur before he stopped, half way across the car park in the shadow of the fire appliance. Gone was the urbane and slightly quaint, if somewhat cold, gentleman of earlier. Instead, a truly dangerous creature stood there radiating fury and blood lust, his perpetual sneer replaced by a predator's mask.

"Where is he?" it growled.

He couldn't hurt me but I shuddered at the rage in his tone.

"That's the whole point!" I said, marching over to join him. "We don't know!"

Alastair's gaze, eyes red-rimmed and wild, cast around the car park. They came to rest on the night club staff where they huddled behind the fire crew, still watching in morbid fascination. Perhaps they thought I'd lied and that a hideously burned corpse was about to tumble from the wreckage.

"Oh no, you don't!" I said as the vampire's stare locked on, and one of the hunky fire crew glanced uneasily over his shoulder. "He's not here, I tell you. If he was, do you think I'd be standing here right now?"

Alastair acknowledged my words with a slight shrug, but kept his vision boring into the back of his selected prey.

I lost it.

I'd been enthralled, annoyed, frustrated, bored and finally terrified this evening. I'd had enough. "Don't you *dare*!" I hissed and did what, for a human, would have been a truly stupid thing. I grabbed the vamp's arm and tugged, hard. He spun at an impossible speed, knocking me away so sharply I tottered on my high heels and lost my balance, crashing to my backside on the tarmac.

"Ouch!"

Damn, but that hurt! I'd never considered how *hard* a car park might be. I was also furious. I was only trying to keep an already tricky situation from getting worse.

"Sorry, I'm so sorry!"

I looked up to find an apologetic Alastair reaching to help me up. I shrank away and he stopped, holding his empty hands palms out towards me. He grimaced. "I'm afraid my nature still gets the better of me sometimes, even after five centuries. May I?"

I nodded and allowed him to help me up.

"We should get out of here," Alastair stated.

At last.

"Let's do that," I agreed, with one more inspection of the shadows for any sign of Liam.

One quick phone call later, and two cabs arrived, one for each of us. There was no way either of us was going to get back into our respective vehicles tonight. We'd need to get them thoroughly de-spelled before they were safe to drive again, and Alastair at least had a deadline: dawn was fast approaching.

"I believe you will have to re-think your strategy for capturing this magician," Alastair observed before getting into his cab.

My strategy?

"Sleep tight!" I wished him as he shut the cab door, not without a rather uneasy glance at the door latch.

I slid into the rear seat of the second cab as a police car with flashing blue lights turned in. My driver hesitated. "Nothing to do with me," I told him. "I'd like to get home now, thank you."

Sorting out the mess could wait until tomorrow. Right now, I was just relieved to be getting away from the place under my own steam. Of sorts.

As the club and the strobing blue lights dwindled behind us, I sat hunched in the back of the cab and pondered a further disquieting aspect of the night's events. Of all the evenings that Liam could have chosen to spring his trap, why this one? How had he known we would both be there tonight? Was it luck on his part, or sheer coincidence?

Or did he have some other means of monitoring our plans?

13. SECRETS

Brisk footsteps echoed down the entrance hall of the fitness studio.

"Hey, you! I want a word with you!"

I flinched, scratching an erratic blue line of ink across the open page of the gym's diary where I had been entering my bookings for the next few days. Since last night, every unexpected noise had me, as the saying goes, jumping out of my skin. In my case that might be a realistic possibility and I was increasingly worried that my paranoia might push me over the edge. I could imagine the headlines: 'Woman Dissolves in Gym'. Or worse, 'Spontaneous Human Liquefaction'.

The shrill voice broke through my musings.

"I'm talking to you, Lake."

Me? This woman was talking to me? Or rather, shouting at me. Baffled, I turned to see a brassy blonde bearing down on me with murder in her eyes. *Now* what had I done?

I put on a puzzled expression—not hard, under the circumstances—and asked, "I'm sorry, do I know you?"

"You know my husband, you slut! Keep your dirty hands off him or I'll rip your head off!"

A small crowd of spectators followed in the woman's wake, murmuring with excitement at the prospect of a cat fight.

I still had no idea what the deranged blonde was babbling about, but it wasn't hard to figure out what she was thinking. Funnily enough, if this had been a couple of years ago she could have been one of two women well within their rights to make such an accusation, but not right now.

"Hold it right there!"

To my utmost astonishment, my shy and retiring best friend was elbowing her way to the front of the mob, righteous indignation oozing from her every pore.

"How dare you accuse Cassie of such a thing: she'd no more sleep with your husband than with a fish!"

Oh, *bad* analogy. Not recently, perhaps, and not exactly a fish, but—

"I've seen how he looks at her," shrieked the wronged woman. "I know she's the one!"

Alison came to stand protectively in front of me. *Me!* Where had my timid friend's new-found confidence emerged from?

I cudgelled my brain into working order and succeeded in forming coherent words. "Alison, it's okay," I said, putting a hand on her shoulder to reassure her I could handle the situation myself. Power vibrated through that simple touch, and I recognised the wellspring from where she drew her self-assurance.

Perhaps Dawn's tutoring was going a little too well. I didn't want Alison to get into any trouble on my behalf, especially over a misunderstanding.

I stepped to one side of my voluntary shield-maiden.

"I'm sorry, but you're mistaken," I informed the angry woman. "Even if your husband does look at me that way, nothing has ever happened between us. I don't even know who he is or, in fact, who you are."

The poor woman's face crumpled and she sagged to the floor in tears. Two women, her friends I assumed, knelt down beside her, making comforting noises and rubbing her back and arms. Alison and I looked at each other in bemusement.

Then Alison glanced away. Following her line of sight I found Dawn leaning against the wall, staying aloof from the whole spectacle. She smiled warmly at Alison. My eyes swivelled from one to the other and back again. I was starting to wonder about this friendship, but hey, who was I to judge? If they were going to have a lesbian fling, good for them. Perhaps it would help Alison get over the odious Simon.

The mob that moments earlier had appeared eager to witness my anticipated humiliation, if not an outright punch up, was rapidly turning into a support group. Several of them regarded me with a suspicious air that said they wouldn't trust me with their own husbands for one second. One of those who had been first to comfort the distraught woman stood up.

"I should apologise for Hannah," she said in a cultured English accent. "We all knew her husband was playing away, but she refused to believe us until she opened his latest credit card bill. She jumped to the wrong conclusion because he's used it so much here, but this is where he's been meeting the woman. Several of us have seen them working out together."

"But why did she pick on me?" I asked.

"Oh, do be serious!" the woman snapped. "Take a look at yourself—what man wouldn't want you? You're almost too good to be true."

And with that, she turned her back on me and rejoined the comforting party.

Too good to be true? Hm. I'd never thought of myself in those terms, but perhaps I should make myself a little less attractive, at least around other women. To me, my lack of stature has always been a let-down, but maybe not everyone saw it that way.

Beside me, Alison trembled with rage. "You should demand an apology!"

Whoa! This was an entirely new Alison.

I flinched at a touch on my elbow, but turned to find myself gazing into Dawn's deep emerald, troubled eyes. She also had a hand on Alison's shoulder.

"Damp it down, Ali. Remember the centring exercise I showed you?"

Turning her attention to me, she asked in a low voice: "Can we go somewhere more private?"

"Sure, follow me."

I led the way to the tiny staff locker room. Once the coded lock had snapped shut between us and the crowd outside, Dawn and Alison started doing something with breathing that was lost on me. I stared through the small panel of glass in the side of the door, watching the mini-saga continue in the corridor. Finally it moved away towards the public changing rooms.

"Better now?" Dawn asked. I looked around to see Alison nod in confirmation, her usual sunny disposition reclaimed.

"What was that all about?" I queried. "And I don't mean the blonde. Since when did you become my advocate?"

Alison frowned. "I don't know. My head filled up with all the times you've stood up for me when I've had issues, like with Simon, and I thought it was about time I did the same for you, especially when the accusation was so outrageous."

Her brow wrinkled with anxiety; more the sort of expression I was used to seeing on her face.

"How did you know she wasn't right?" I asked.

"Because we're friends!" Alison stated, as if that was enough. And perhaps it should have been, if this had been a relationship between two normal human beings.

When I said nothing, Alison continued. "Friends don't keep secrets from each other; not big secrets like that, now do they?"

Oh goddess! I had no idea how to answer, so I gave her the only reply I could.

"Of course we don't. I'd never hide anything as important as that from my best friend."

Dawn's lowering brows boded ill for the favour I meant to ask of her, but what else could I say to Alison—that I was keeping the biggest secret she was ever likely to come across, and had been for all the years we'd been friends?

But since it was of no relevance to our relationship, and she was never going to learn the truth anyway, it didn't matter.

Or did it?

I squashed my unease, made all the more real by Dawn's glower, and moved on.

"I must admit I was impressed. This witchy thing suits you, but please don't go on the offensive on my behalf, will you? I'm sure this Hannah woman would look great with the head of a frog or the tail of an ass, but I think the idea is not to display that sort of thing in public. Back me up here, Dawn?"

Dawn seemed reluctant to come down on my side, but given the subject matter she had no choice.

"There's no danger of that, Cassie. But Ali, she's right. You need to be careful with your powers until you're sure of your control. And remember that whatever you do returns to you threefold."

"Okay, okay!" Alison held up her hands in mock defence. Catching sight of her watch, she gasped, "Is that the time already? I'm late!"

Grabbing her cardigan, she bolted for the door.

"See you later, D. Bye, Cassie."

And she was gone, leaving me alone with the true-witch.

Dawn's emerald eyes pinned me to the spot. "You do realise she's never going to forgive you don't you? She's going to find out some day."

I shook my head in denial. "Unless you plan on telling her, I don't see why she should. And she won't be any happier with you if you tell her either. It's secrets all round, but for the best possible reasons."

Dawn's brows drew down again, and I shivered. She could be quite menacing when her powers bubbled near the surface. "I don't think there should ever be a reason for lies, good intentions or not," she stated. Naively, in my opinion. "And truth has a way of getting out, like water from a leaky vessel."

Interesting analogy. Had Dawn made an intuitive leap? Or was her subconscious leading her towards the truth of which she spoke?

Right now I had other things on my mind. "Dawn, can I ask a favour of you?"

"Such as?" She sounded wary, and I didn't blame her considering she thought that I was fey. Things to do with fey often came with an unexpected kickback.

I decided to be honest, or at least as honest as I could be, under the circumstances.

"Some friends and I got into a bit of bother and our cars got spell-trapped. Would you help me de-spell them?"

She paused to consider, and then asked: "What sort of trouble? I don't want to find myself going up against one of my own if there was a good reason for the dispute."

So now the honesty bit started to get a *teensy* bit blurred.

"It was Liam. He seems to have a bit of an obsession with me, and he didn't appreciate that my friends and I weren't very welcoming towards him."

"*Liam!*" Dawn's distaste for the magician threaded her tone. "He's trouble, for sure. I'll help you de-spell, but Cassie, try to keep away from him—he's dangerous."

"You're telling me," I muttered. "Can we go do it now?"

Dawn paused to consider. "I'll need a few things from home. Do you have time to run me out there? My car is in for service, so I've nothing better to do."

"Sure thing," I agreed. "Let's get going."

A somewhat awkward silence prevailed for the first few miles. I think Dawn was over her awe of me and her suspicions had never gone away. She must have wondered why I needed her help with something as simple as a de-spelling, but she refrained from asking. There were all sorts of possibilities in the muddled world of human/non-human relationships that might have applied here, but as she didn't ask, I didn't volunteer any reason. Inter-species protocol is not my field.

Dawn broke the ice with the sort of question I could have predicted if I'd been bothered to think about it.

"So what's it like, being immortal?"

Now that was a question that was easy to answer with honesty.

"You know, it's not something I think about. Any more than you think about something you take for granted, like the colour of your eyes."

She canted a sceptical glance at me.

"But what about the practicalities? Do you pretend to age, or do you just drop your friends and move away?"

Oh, so *that* was where this was leading. I was a bit miffed that she thought so badly of me without making the effort to get to know me better first.

"No, Dawn, I would *never* just drop my friends. True friendship is hard to find, and I value it as much as you do, believe me."

"So how do you handle it?" she persisted.

I shrugged. "I can age if I choose, no problem, but I don't often need to; Alison is the first close friend I've had in a long time."

"Really? How come?"

I considered my answer with care. I didn't want Dawn to catch me out in a blatant lie, and I'd rather contaminated the spring by trying to keep things simple when I'd first met her. Whatever had possessed me to impersonate a faery? I seriously doubted that modern day humans would fall down and worship me, not like their predecessors had a few centuries ago. But to me the memories were still too fresh—one of the downsides of immortality—and I wasn't prepared to risk the embarrassment.

"Frankly, Dawn, I've made a point of not getting involved with humans unless I have to. I have had a few friends over the millennia, but by my scale people don't live long, so I have to really like them to make the effort worthwhile. Add superstition to the mix, and you might understand why I haven't done it often; the chance of being burned at the stake is a great incentive not to mingle."

I glanced aside and caught a grudging belief on Dawn's features. That I'd glossed over thousands of years before anyone even thought to consider magic evil rather bypassed her notice once I'd mentioned the burnings. It's the sort of thing witches got a bit obsessive over. I've witnessed a few pyres, so I do understand.

I believed that Dawn would be a smart woman once she'd grown up, but she was still hopelessly easy to manipulate. Not so her father, I deemed. I hoped he wouldn't be at home when we got there.

The grey waters of Loch Ness flashed past, weak sunlight glittering on the foamy tops of the little breakers that endlessly ruffled the restless water. No wonder so many people thought they saw movement out there.

Undoubtedly some of them did.

As we turned off the main road past the Loch Ness Monster Exhibition, Dawn announced, "You know it's quite useful, you coming out here today. Saffron wants a word with you."

I fumbled the gears. Not an easy thing to do in a car as wonderful to drive as the Golf.

"Oh?" I queried, trying to sound casual. "Any idea what about?"

"Some sort of meeting that she and Gordon have been cooking up between them. I think it's a surprise party, but don't quote me."

"And she wants to talk to me about it?"

"Mmm."

Shit! What was I getting into now? I resolved to have an urgent meeting that day, somewhere far, far away. Whenever it was.

My stomach was churning as we pulled up outside Dawn's house. I had quite enough going on in my life right now without having to add Gordon and Saffron's machinations. I got out of the car and zapped it, getting a startled glance from Dawn as the locks snicked shut and the indicators blinked. I doubt she ever locked her car at their isolated home.

"Everything I need is in the workshop out back," she said, leading off along a gravel path that vanished behind the house. Following her, I dared to hope I might escape the proposed invitation after all.

Silly me.

"Who's that?" called Saffron's plummy tones through an open window.

"Only me," said Dawn. "I came back for a few things, and I brought Cassie with me."

"Oh!"

Saffron's squeak of surprise held a hint of alarm and I wondered what I'd done to cause that. Unless I was reading too much into an inarticulate syllable. Even after all this time, I wouldn't describe myself as a good judge of human emotions.

The workshop turned out to be a wooden summer house set into the bank behind the house. It was so artfully blended into the cut away hillside and surrounding trees that I wouldn't have noticed it without the invite. I daresay that was the point.

Dawn mouthed something and her fingers flicked in a tiny motion before she set her hand on the latch. Very sensible, warding the door to such a treasure trove.

Curious to see inside, I was about to follow Dawn when the kitchen door behind me swung open.

"Cassie! My dear, how good to see you!"

"Hello Saffron," I answered, turning reluctantly to face her. "How are you doing?"

"Very well, dear. And you?"

I've never seen much point to the human predilection for greeting one another with questions to which you don't expect an honest answer, but I've become adept at copying the behaviour.

"Grand, thank you," I assured her and started to turn back towards the summer house door in the vain hope that nothing further would be said. Evidently optimism was one of those behaviours I'd assimilated rather too well.

"I shouldn't go in there if I were you, dear; it's such a mess. Gordon and Dawn know precisely where everything is, and they don't take kindly to anyone disturbing it. Come indoors and have a nice cup of tea with me while she finds what she needs."

Unable to produce a suitable excuse, I obediently followed Saffron's broad back into the large, airy kitchen, where a divine melange of scents enveloped me. Herbs, dried flowers and bunches of lavender hung from pan racks and antique Edwardian clothes airers hanging from the ceiling. Plant pots smothered the window sills and shelves until the purpose of the room almost vanished, but for the Belfast sink in one corner and the rather modern aluminium range on the opposite wall.

Saffron popped a kettle onto a hotplate and good-naturedly shooed me towards a rattan sofa. The rather garish lime and fuchsia flowered cushions were, I suspected, Saffron's touch in a room that owed more to Dawn's deceased mother than to her new age step-mum.

"What a perfect opportunity for a cosy chat," said Saffron, and perched on a stool beside the range. I waited for her to continue, apprehension roiling queasily around my guts.

"Gordon and I are planning a special event for the coven on Sunday, and we are very keen to include you."

"I'm sorry, Saffron, I have rather a busy weekend coming up and I'm not sure I'll have time to spare."

I was taken aback by the stubborn set that temporarily firmed up Saffron's well-padded jaw line.

"Oh, I think you should make the time, dear. Gordon would be *most* disappointed if you failed to materialise. In a manner of speaking, of course."

I sat mute while my hostess busied herself making tea. Was that a *threat*? How much did they know about me and what did they want? I knew it had been a bad idea getting involved with the coven.

"Indian or China?"

I blinked. "Pardon me?"

"Tea," said Saffron holding up two pots, her usual saccharine expression back in place. "Indian or China?" she repeated. "Or a blend?"

"Blended would be grand, thank you," I answered on autopilot, and watched as she poured from both pots into delicate porcelain cups decorated with finely painted birds and insects.

"I don't mean to be pushy," she announced.

Not half.

"But it's Dawn's twenty first and we want all her friends to come. She seems to have taken a shine to you and Alison, and Gordon doesn't want it to be just the old fogies."

"Oh," I uttered intelligently. Was I seeing conspiracies where there were none? Damn Liam, he was making me suspicious of everybody around me.

"Well, I could try," I heard my mouth offering. Why was it so rarely connected to my brain?

"That's good, dear. This Sunday, midday. We'll meet in the car park above Plodda Falls. You know it?"

Yes, I knew it well. From the car park, the path led sharply downhill past a stunning series of rapids that formed a gentle waterfall, before the stream took a sudden spectacular dive off the edge of a cliff, vertically down for over a hundred feet. The Victorians had built an iron bridge right over the top of the cascade, but in recent years it had been replaced by a wooden viewing platform that jutted out apparently unsupported into mid air.

Of course, I'd known it long before humanity began to appreciate the beauty of the power of water. A favourite haunt of mine for thousands of years, I'd not visited it in some time and although I was certain there was a good reason, I couldn't recall it offhand. Perhaps this would be a good opportunity to get reacquainted.

With a little more enthusiasm than I'd expected, I found myself agreeing to the meet as Dawn put her head into the kitchen.

"Ready when you are," she said cheerfully, and I smiled. It would be churlish to avoid the girl's birthday celebration when she was going out of her way to help me today.

"Coming," I answered, and put down my tea cup.

As we drove away I remembered that I *still* hadn't retrieved my cowboy boots from their hiding place out in the forest.

Damn!

14. CAR WASH

"So what's involved in this de-spelling?" I asked as we turned into the club's car park.

Dawn blinked. "You must have done it before, surely?"

"Well, of course I have," I blustered. "But not on this scale."

"Oh, I see. Well, it's not going to be any different, though it might take a bit longer than usual. You can hardly dip a car in a bucket, now can you?"

"My thoughts exactly," I agreed. I had no idea what we were about to do, but I wasn't going to let that slip.

"Sweet goddess! What happened here?"

Dawn's face had gone pale at sight of the burned out wreckage of Gloria's Mini.

"Was that Liam too?" Her voice was small, and the smell of fear burst from her. I couldn't blame her; Liam scared me witless.

But I wanted my car back so I did my best to reassure her. "No, it was an accident. The electrics shorted."

Dawn turned horrified, wide eyes toward me. "But was someone trapped *inside* it?"

I didn't want to lie to her again. Things were complicated enough between us as it was, and I had a feeling she might sense it if I tried to mislead her this time.

"Well, my friend Gloria *was* trapped, but someone let her out when the fire started."

"Liam?"

I shook my head. "No. I don't think he was anywhere close by at the time. It was one of the staff."

Dawn shivered; a deep, bone-shaking tremor. "That man is truly *evil*! Your friend might have been *killed*!"

"True, if she'd been human. Thankfully she's not."

I didn't offer any further information, and to her credit Dawn chose not to pry.

I parked beside the Audi and we got out. Dawn extracted a couple of buckets and some packets of what appeared to be herbs from the rear of the Golf.

"Water?" she asked.

Well, yes. Ironic question to ask a sprite.

"I'll see what I can find," I said.

Under the pretence of looking for a tap, I cast around for a nearby water source, and found an outdoor tap with my senses before my eyes.

"Over there." I pointed in the vague direction.

"Right then. Let's get on with it!"

De-spelling turned out to consist of washing the offending object with a dilute concoction of herbs and salt. So simple, it was an anticlimax.

By fortune the sun had come out and it wasn't long before we got into the swing of things. Once the door locks and dashboard were clean we switched the radio on, and pretty soon we were giggling like a pair of schoolgirls, slopping water over every surface and be-damned with worrying about wet upholstery.

Radio Scotland dug into its archives and obligingly played the most appropriate song we could have requested: '*Car Wash*', by Rose Royce. We sang along to the lyrics with enthusiasm, pausing every so often to punch the air.

"*Yeah!*" we chorused.

"What's going on here?"

I spun round, gripped with sudden terror at the male voice close behind me, and almost collapsed with relief at finding myself face to face with the security guard I'd seen monitoring the club's CCTV last night. There could be no mistaking those Celtic tattoos curling across his face.

"You startled me!" I gasped, clutching my middle for effect. The poor guy looked mortified.

"Sorry, miss! I didnae recognise you. Not quite the same outfit as last night," he observed, looking at my grey sweats. No, indeed.

"Are you trying to clean off the smoke damage?"

"Aye, indeed we are."

I do so love it when someone offers their own suggestion, and saves me from finding yet another excuse for whatever it is I'm doing.

"Grand. Well I have things tae do inside. Anything you lassies need?"

"No thanks," I began before a devious thought occurred to me. "Oh, actually yes, there is. I lost my phone last night; do you happen to have Gloria's number?"

"Nae bother," assured my helpful new friend. "It'll be in the records. Drop in before you leave and I'll have it for you."

He sauntered off towards the club entrance and I rejoined Dawn. We'd moved on to Robbie Williams by now. "*Let's entertain us!*" Dawn trilled, paraphrasing the chorus as she swung her hips and punched the air. I decided I was enjoying this de-spelling routine, and threw myself back into it.

By the time we finished, the Quattro was sparkling. Not a nanometre of its surface had escaped our attention, even the wheels, in case Liam could spell it to take me somewhere I didn't want to go. Dawn and I stood back to admire our handiwork at the same moment as the sun vanished behind a big black cloud.

"That's not fair!" Dawn protested. "I wanted to see it shine after all that work."

"Me, too," I agreed, "but this is Scotland."

"Too true, and where would we be without all our water? Basking in over-hot summers and power cuts, like the south!"

I almost preened. There were few times when my element was given the recognition it deserved. Of course Dawn didn't recognise the compliment for what it was; she still thought I was a faery.

"Damn!"

"What's the matter?" I asked.

"I forgot to fetch towels, and we're soaking."

With the clouds over the sun, the temperature had dropped appreciably and Dawn was starting to shiver.

"Nae bother!" I said, and popped the boot of the Golf. I handed one of the clean towels destined for the gym to Dawn and, taking another for myself, joined her in a vigorous rub down. I even allowed a little moisture to dampen the towel for authenticity.

When we were finished I bundled the towels together and sealed them up in one of the plastic bags I kept for that purpose, before tossing them onto the freshly cleaned leather of the Audi's passenger seat.

"Ah!" A thought occurred to me, rather late. "Perhaps we should do my friend's car as well." I looked across the car park to Alastair's sleek grey Ferrari.

"What, another one?"

Dawn sounded less than enthusiastic. One car was fun; two would be a chore. I took a couple of steps towards it with Dawn trailing me before she balked. When I glanced back she'd stopped with one foot raised, looking for all the world like a deer caught in the headlights.

"I'm not de-spelling that car," she announced, placing her errant foot to the ground with care. "I'm not even going anywhere near it."

When she dragged her eyes away from the quiescent Ferrari and turned them towards me, they were wide with shock and revulsion.

"You call the owner of that car a *friend*? Do you have any idea what sort of creature drives it?"

Okay, so Dawn's witchy senses were working well today. But did she have to look at me with such disgust?

"I only met him last night," I protested. "He's a friend of a friend and he was trying to help out with the Liam situation, which is why he got his car spelled too. So he's a vampire. Are you prejudiced against other supernaturals as well? If so, I think I'd better know now before any of my other friends offend you."

Sometimes attack is the best way to knock someone off guard, and I was a teensy bit piqued that a witch would be so judgemental.

Dawn's expression told me she hadn't thought of things in that light, but she wasn't about to back down.

"Vampires are evil, cold-blooded killers and I object to anyone who exploits others, whether they're supernatural or not."

Dear gods, was she truly that ignorant? I drew a deep breath, and released it slowly before correcting her.

"Only a newborn vampire would misjudge things enough to kill. And they're as liable to kill a sheep as a human. Once they get over their first bloodlust they soon learn how stupid it is to leave bodies lying around. If they don't, their own kind deals with them. And anyway, I've seen lots of humans who were more than willing to trade blood for the aphrodisiac in vamp saliva."

Dawn was visibly shocked. "That's disgusting!"

Children! The young regard life in such monochrome absolutes. Thankfully I've never been young. Not that I can remember, anyway.

"Dawn, I'm grateful to you for helping me out here, but I think perhaps it would be better all round if we keep my friends and you at a healthy distance; some of them might not be so tolerant of your prejudices."

"Oh."

There, that would make her think twice. I was fond of Dawn, but she needed to get out more.

"I'm prepared to leave him the ingredients, if you think he'll deal with it himself?" she offered in a small voice.

"That would be a nice gesture, thank you. If you hang on a minute I'll ask the security guard to put them somewhere safe. I need to go get my friend's number."

Leaving Dawn beside my sparkling clean car, I descended the steps to the front door of the nightclub. At this hour of the day it was shut, but when I pressed the bell something buzzed inside and it sprang open, emitting a waft of stale beer and sweat. There was no one there, so I stepped into the gloomy corridor. A warm light invited me to turn left into the pocket-sized security office. My tattooed friend was seated at his desk.

"Here you go, lass," he said, handing me a small card with a telephone number printed in neat handwriting. "I had to look it up anyway, to arrange getting the wreckage cleared away. Bad for business having it sitting out there."

"I'm sure it is. So the police didn't want to take it away then?"

He shook his head and the Celtic patterns adorning his head appeared to come alive with the movement.

"Nae. They were happy it was an accident."

Good. That meant I didn't need to come up with any excuses for the law.

"Thanks for this. I'll take my car away now. Oh, and do you think you'll be seeing Alastair, the guy with the grey Ferrari?"

"Aye. Odd that; I've never known him tae leave it behind before. Weird sort of evening altogether, last night. Did you want me tae gi' him a message? He's a regular; you could always come back if you wanted tae see him."

His mouth had curled into a rather knowing smile that subtly altered his facial decorations to something more edgy. I wondered if he knew more about Alastair than he was letting on.

I shook my head. "No, I don't think I have the time spare tonight. I just wanted to leave him something." I handed over the plastic bag of herbs. "If you'd tell him that these will deal with the smoke damage? Mix them with water and wash the affected areas."

"I'll do that. Hope we'll see you back again some time?"

"Maybe," I replied vaguely. With a wave of my fingers I bade him goodbye and walked back up the steps, adding *sotto voce*, "and then again, maybe not."

I got Dawn to drive the Golf. I was a bit nervous about getting back into the Audi but once the engine roared to life I felt happier, and by the time we pulled up at the gym I was enjoying it again. I was almost pathetically pleased with myself for getting back behind the wheel; Liam was not doing my self-confidence any good.

Dawn took herself off to do the shopping she'd planned before I hijacked her afternoon, and Alison was already gone, so I left the Golf in the car park and drove home in the Audi. I made my now customary survey of home and surroundings before relaxing, but with nothing out of place I was finally ready to reclaim some normality to my life and get on with my chores.

First, I had Gloria's number and I was going to use it! My fingers trembled ever so slightly as I tapped the keypad, and my insides wrestled with themselves as I listened to the ringing tone.

"Hello?" answered a suspicious voice, so rich I could almost taste it.

"Hello Gloria, its Cassie," I informed her, determined to keep my brain engaged for this conversation without her physical presence to distract me. Unfortunate then that her voice was enough to make deep parts of my body spring to attention.

"Cassie? How did you get my number? No, wait; the club gave it to you. Probably for the best; we need to talk about where we go from here with trapping that little bastard. I, for one, have no intention of letting him catch me a third time, and Alastair is positively spitting fangs."

Now *there* was an image.

Giving me no time to get a word in edgeways, she continued. "I hope by now you've lost your qualms about what we need to do with him once we have him."

An afternoon spent cleaning spells off my car alongside the burned out wreck of Gloria's Mini had gone a long way towards changing my mind.

"I'm starting to think you might be right."

"Thank the powers for that! You water types always try to go around a problem where sometimes what you need is the direct approach."

Hm. Correct in principle, but over time we 'water types' will grind down any issue, until eventually we get where we're going without need for a head on confrontation.

Not so my fiery friend.

"We can't afford to be soft with humans who think they can mess around with us. It's an open invitation to others to try," Gloria stated.

I recalled what she'd told me of the first magician who'd used her to burn his victims, and realised it wasn't her salamander hot-headedness alone inflaming her desire to kill Liam.

"I'd always rather find another option—" I started.

"You s—"

I hurried on, cutting off her indignant splutter. "But in this case I'm not seeing one. Do you have any other plans for finding and catching him, because I want this finished."

Guilt twisted inside me, discussing the cutting short of a human being's already miniscule quota of days in so casual a manner. But Liam was making my life a living hell. Since his arrival I'd experienced emotions I had no wish to be so closely acquainted with, and I wanted to go back to my quiet, private and continued existence.

"Good on you, girl." Gloria's approbation made me glow all over. "I have an idea or two, and Alastair is *very* keen to be included. How about you?"

"None," I admitted. "I spent this afternoon getting access to my car again, and I haven't thought about much else. Oh, and by the way, you were truly awesome getting out of your car that way!"

"My poor car," Gloria groaned. "I did love it. He's so going to pay for that."

No mistaking who '*he*' was.

"I'm sorry I had to leave you there like that," she said. To my astonishment she sounded almost guilty. "You didn't have any problems with *him*, did you?"

I almost swooned. Gloria was concerned for me! Perhaps our relationship was taking a step forward.

"No, no problems," I reassured her. "Liam never showed. Once someone opened my door from the outside, it was all over. What worries me is how he knew about our plans in the first place."

"Well at least we know it's not a phone tap," Gloria observed. "I'm guessing some sort of magical spying device. We need to figure out what it is and use it against him."

"I like your style," I said. "Let me know if you have any ideas."

"Ditto."

"So when shall we meet again?"

It was still me asking the question, but this time Gloria didn't hesitate.

"Tomorrow," she said firmly. "I have work tonight and the boss is not thrilled with me over last night's events, so I'm planning a grand performance."

I'd told Mr Tattoos that I was busy tonight. Now I was having second thoughts, but suppose Liam showed up? Best we were not caught together again. I had the feeling he might try to take us off guard if we assumed he wouldn't strike two nights in a row.

"Okay, tomorrow it is. Same place?"

"No, I'll come to your gym. You've seen my place of work, now I plan on seeing yours."

It wasn't until after we'd finalised arrangements and I'd closed my phone that it occurred to me I'd never told Gloria where I worked. She'd been checking up on me; I was thrilled. I didn't care about her motives; her interest was all I desired.

Ridiculously happy, I wandered back out to the car to collect the laundry.

"Damn!"

I heaved a sigh. I'd left the pile of used towels in the Golf, which was back in the gym car park. I scooped up the single plastic bag from the front seat of the Audi. At least I had the one Dawn had used. I hummed tunelessly to myself as I poured water into a bowl and put it on the work surface in the utility room. Minkie watched from his cage with dark, patient eyes until guilt overcame me.

"Alright, already," I chided him and leaned over to unlatch his door. "If I let you out, no getting into mischief, you hear? I need this bowl upright with the water still in it."

Those black, beady eyes regarded me with reproach, as if I'd accused him in advance of some heinous crime, making me feel guilty all over again.

Comes to something when even your pet can make you feel as if you're in the wrong.

I left the towel soaking and ran a vacuum around the rest of the steading. Minkie appeared randomly at high speed from behind the furniture to attack the dangerous appliance, leaping aboard before abandoning his perch with acrobatic leaps into mid air, and then vanishing into hiding once more. He soon had me in fits of giggles and I was almost disappointed when I finished.

Going back to the utility, he followed me in and stretched out on top of his cage to watch as I first agitated and then wrung the towel to dislodge as many skin cells as possible. I strained the water through fine muslin and stretched it out to dry. There was enough DNA there to give me two or three fixes in case I decided to forego my other source option. Having seen the standard of what I assumed was Gloria's regular catch, I was even more determined not to get desperate.

Next on my cleaning list was the bathroom, but that resulted in me filling the tub and watching Minkie swim. I was tempted to join him, but decided it might be a bit cramped.

I was cleaning the bath of his silky fine hairs when the front door opened. Minkie chittered in an alarmed manner and vanished behind the towel stand. My heart shot up into my throat, threatening to choke me. Does that happen in a human body? Perhaps my pseudo anatomy is rather more loosely fixed in place than the real thing.

"Only me," came Euan's voice, and my insides returned bit by bit to their regular positions. Tension drained from me along with the last dregs of water from the bath.

"Be with you in a mo," I replied, smiling at the prospect of a warm body to snuggle with tonight.

"Come on in," I heard him say, and it took me a confused moment to realise he was talking to someone else. Before I could ask, he called through.

"Hope you don't mind, Cassie, I brought a friend back with me from the conference. Well, technically, he brought me. He lives locally so we shared the journey."

"Oh, okay."

What else could I say? Euan didn't make many human friends, so whoever it was must have made quite an impression on him. Presumably they shared views on energy issues, and perhaps his guest was an activist too. But it was downright weird of Euan to bring him into my home without asking first. Euan knew how I felt about strangers.

"Will you come on out of there?" I urged Minkie, reaching around behind the towel stand to try and grab him. I thought it best to pop him back into his cage in case he decided to take a nip out of our visitor. He had other ideas. My grasping fingers slid through empty air as he whisked his bushy tail out of my reach and slid beneath the bath tub.

I considered lying on the floor and trying to drag him out, but frankly it didn't seem that urgent, so I opted for shutting the bathroom door and hoping that our guest would not want to use the facilities.

I hadn't met this person yet, and already I wanted him gone; I really don't do strangers.

On the other hand, a girl needs to keep up appearances. A quick thought smoothed my hair and touched up my colour. Not wanting to seem too hospitable, I decided against changing out of the jeans I'd donned for housework. I was presentable enough for the short time this person would be with us.

I paused outside the bathroom door, distracted by a lingering scent—something sweet and fruity. Must be from our guest, I decided. One of those aftershaves that human males sometimes wear. Odd choice, I thought, with a shrug. Following the soft murmur of masculine voices, I stepped through the kitchen door and stopped dead. My knees turned liquid and I wasn't certain if I should dissolve or flee. In the end, I was too scared to do either.

"There you are, Cassie," said Euan, as if nothing was wrong.

How could anything ever be right again? I stared in horror at the straggly specimen of a human being who stood in my kitchen as if he had a right to be there. In his Led Zeppelin t-shirt and his saggy jeans.

"This is—"

I cut Euan off with a sharp nod.

"Liam," I finished.

15. MOTIVES

Why does fear cause immobility? I've never understood that as a survival trait, and I didn't appreciate it now, with my limbs frozen and my mind in a gibbering state of indecision.

At a deeper level, the urge to extract every last drop of water from Liam's body wrestled with my fear for Euan; the selkie reeked of strawberry essence. What spell had Liam laid upon him? Could I kill Liam without hurting or—oh gods, don't even think it—killing Euan?

"You two already know each other? That's great," said Euan, innocent to his peril. "I know how Cassie feels about strangers in her home."

My unspoken, <*So why did you bring him here?*> went right over Euan's head. And besides, it was a fair assumption that the idea hadn't been his.

Liam smiled. He looked me up and down, making me feel raw as a prime cut hanging on a hook. I forgot to breathe.

"Yeah," he said. "We've bumped into each other a couple of times, haven't we, Cassie?"

Hearing his voice here, inside my own home, made me quake. I wanted nothing more than to run away as fast as I could. But I couldn't abandon Euan.

I clenched my fists until my fingernails bit into my palms. If Liam was going to play this cool, then I could do the same.

I hoped.

"Sure," I said, marvelling at how steadily my voice came out when the rest of me was shaking fit to bust. "We've seen each other at a couple of meetings I went to with Alison, although we've never been formally introduced."

"We can remedy that easily enough," Euan offered. "Liam Oldman, meet Cassie Lake. Cassie, Liam."

The magician stuck a hand out towards me. Gritting my teeth and trying to still the traitor tremors that ran down my arms, I took the proffered fingers. I reasoned that if he had been going to do anything underhand, he would have done it by now. That didn't stop me from cringing as his fist clasped mine; I half expected to be liquefied and poured into a bottle again.

Nothing dramatic happened, and that was almost worse. I was going to remain on edge, waiting for it to come. Whatever *it* might be.

"So, Euan, tell me how you guys met," I invited through gritted teeth, then watched in dismay as the fevered light of passion set Euan's features aglow. He set to with gusto, describing the government summit. Arguing the case for sustainable, natural energy sources was to the selkie as preaching the bible was to an evangelist.

"It was uncanny," he enthused. "Liam shares all my views and he has a powerful voice in the scientific community. He's a nuclear physicist. Did you know that?"

I shook my head. I'd had no idea, but things started to click together inside my head.

"I can't believe we haven't met before," Euan continued, "when we live no more than a few miles apart. Liam, where have you been hiding all this time?"

"I've been a bit buried in my work," Liam replied, and his eyes pinned me in place, like an insect mounted on a block of wood. "I'm a bit of a mad scientist you see, always trying to find the answer to free energy production."

There it was. The answer to the perplexing question of what Liam wanted with a pair of opposing elementals.

Energy.

He believed the energy that would be released by forcing Gloria and me together inside his tailor-made magically-enhanced electromagnetic orb could be controlled and utilized as a source of free energy.

As long as you were prepared to sacrifice the lives of the two elemental participants.

Horrific possibilities played through my head. From instant oblivion to eternal torment, caught at the moment of explosion forever. My whole body shook as I realised how close to that moment we had been in the power station, and I found myself battling the urge to run screaming from the room, but the cloying scent of magic clinging to Euan stopped me.

"Any luck with that?" I asked in my best caustic tone. Euan frowned at me.

"Not yet," said Liam, "but I feel I'm getting close."

Yeah, right.

Anger at his cavalier attitude towards my kind started to outstrip my caution. "What about potential side effects? Your sort of science has a lousy record when it comes to predicting consequences; you don't have to look further than nuclear power stations to see that!"

"Cassie!" Euan sounded shocked.

Liam held up a hand. "No, Euan, she's right. But I think I'm on the track of something that will produce totally clean energy. Surely that has to be the ultimate prize for the planet?"

My stomach quivered. I could not condemn Liam's goals, only his means.

My voice wobbled as I asked, "Is there such a thing? Aren't there always consequences? Wind turbines were once hailed as the ultimate free energy source, but they blight the landscape and drive away wildlife. Hydro-electric dams sound wonderful, but they disrupt fish migration and cause sedimentation and flooding. Not to mention the odd disaster when a damn breaches. Even tidal power plants play havoc with ecosystems. And as for solar power? In Scotland? Don't get me wrong they each have their place, but none of them are *the* answer, are they?"

Euan, bless him, was full of pride for my speech. "Cassie's not one to ignore the world's plight," he said. "She's as concerned about it as we are."

"Ah, but is she as willing to *do* something about it?" said Liam.

I all but groaned aloud. Walked into that one, hadn't I?

It appeared Liam's new tactic was to get my willing co-operation by appealing to my community spirit. To sacrifice myself for the good of the planet, because my kind held the key to genuine free and clean energy production.

My head started to hurt.

"I'd do whatever it took," I said, "as long as it didn't hurt anyone. Can you say the same?"

Euan shot me a puzzled glance.

"Of course! I wouldn't dream of doing anything that might endanger a human life," said Liam, before picking up the leather bomber jacket he'd draped over one of my kitchen chairs and shrugging into it. "I'd better be getting along. Cassie, good to meet you properly at last. Euan, we should get together. How about Saturday? I want to hear more about your action group."

"Great!" Euan enthused, and the pair of them headed towards the front door without a backward glance, making arrangements as they went. I was left standing in the middle of my kitchen, my whole body shaking with reaction and fury. Fury with Euan for bringing the magician into my home. Fury with Liam for be-spelling Euan and for his ability to scare the shit out of me. Fury with myself for allowing him to have that power over me.

Queasiness roiled in my stomach. I licked my lips, tasting fruit. My brow crinkled into a frown—when had I used flavoured lip gloss? I had the nagging feeling that I was missing something but as I tried to grasp the thought, it slipped away from me.

Guilt hit me like a blow to the gut. I'd just sanctioned the murder of this human being whose one crime was a desire to better the lot of humanity.

Anger bubbled up again. Liam might have a laudable motive, but he also had a callous disregard for the consequences to my kind, and he was threatening Euan's safety. How dare he?

I opened my mouth to vent my wrath, and inhaled sweetness. My anger evaporated. What was I thinking?

I had to stop Gloria and Alastair.

No! I agreed with Gloria that Liam was too dangerous to be allowed to live.

Didn't I?

A perfectly rational thought, or so it seemed, popped into my head. I had to protect Euan. I had no idea how Liam's magic worked, and I couldn't take the risk that killing him might have terrible consequences for the innocent selkie. I had to keep Liam safe, at least for the moment.

A small creaking sound cut through the welter of conflicting thoughts ping-ponging back and forth inside my head: the bathroom door opening and closing. It was a moment before I registered its implication.

"Shit!"

I dashed out of the kitchen in time to see Euan step out through the front door alone. It was Liam in the bathroom.

I raised my hand to knock on the door, intending to warn him before he had a nasty surprise. My fist froze in mid air scant millimetres off the wood panelling when I heard his voice murmuring on the other side of the closed door, a weird sort of crooning noise.

"Come on out from under there, Minkus. No need to look so guilty; you've done an excellent job!"

Comprehension smote me like a blow from Thor's hammer. So *that* was how Liam had known Gloria and I were at the club last night—I had a weasel in the nest.

Far from being my prospective guide to all things witchy, Minkie was *Liam's* familiar!

Well Liam could take the treacherous little beast with him when he left.

Scuffling sounds came from behind the closed door, and then Liam's voice uttered a wordless yelp. "You bit me!" he said in what sounded like disbelief.

Good for Minkie. I needed Liam to live for now, but I didn't mind him getting a bit chewed.

The bathroom door key turned, and I melted back into the kitchen, my feelings all muddled. I wanted the traitor mink gone, and yet I didn't want to see him leave; he'd been good company. And Liam *had* abandoned him at the power station.

I could hear Liam talking with Euan outside, yet still I hid in the kitchen. I wanted our unwelcome guest gone and life to go back to how it had been before he ever appeared.

As if.

A car door slammed, but still they carried on chatting. I sighed in irritation and slipped into the bathroom. At least I could remove any remaining traces of Minkie's hairs to remind me of my short spell as a pet owner.

A pair of dark beady eyes watched me furtively from beneath the bath tub.

"Oh no, he's not leaving you here. You're a *spy!*"

If a mink could produce an expression of misery, then that was what Minkie did now. He cowered down, edging backward away from me, head lowered in submission. If this was an act, it was a bloody good one. When I reached for him he cringed, as if he thought I might strike him, or at least handle him roughly.

That was enough for me. Whatever hold Liam had over his familiar, it was clear the relationship was not enjoyed by both parties. I paused with my hand outstretched. Minkie crawled forward on his belly to sniff my fingers but made no attempt to bite as he had in the past. A troubling memory surfaced, of Dawn explaining how familiars chose their partners and not the other way around.

Perhaps that was not always the case. Or could a familiar make a mistake?

I shut the toilet lid and sat down, regarding my dilemma. "You don't want to go with Liam, is that it?" I asked, not finding it at all odd to be talking to a small furry animal. To me, Minkie's character was far bigger than that of a mere pet.

At sound of Liam's name, Minkie's lips drew back and bared his teeth, a glare of hatred sheening his dark eyes. I gave in.

"Okay, okay! You don't have to go," I assured him. "Just don't expect me to trust you, alright?"

The sound of tyres crunching the gravel announced Liam's departure, and Minkie slunk out from under the bathtub. Before I knew it, he'd sprung into my lap.

I had the oddest sensation then, as if someone had enveloped me lovingly in their arms. But there was no one there. I shrugged it off as a manifestation of the thing that humans call imagination, and stroked what was now my resident pet.

That's how Euan found us.

"Getting rather familiar with your new playmate, aren't you? As I recall, our relationship had a similar start."

I smiled at the memory. "True, but you never fitted into my lap."

"I could try, if you want?"

The easy banter between us came as naturally as ever, yet for me it had moved to a superficial level. Beneath my surface spun a whole set of conflicting emotions, and I needed time to sort them out.

Besides, I could still smell strawberries.

"Perhaps later. Why don't you go on over to the house and I'll meet you there in a bit."

"Okay."

As ever. My dependable selkie who took all things at face value. How did he survive amongst humans? I wasn't happy with him for what he'd done this evening, but I wasn't surprised. Liam must have found him easy to influence.

It was one more grudge to hold against the magician, even as I found myself in unexpected sympathy with his goals. Somehow I had to unravel the puzzle of how to convince Liam that Gloria and I were not the answer to his worthy ambition, while simultaneously keeping him from getting killed by an angry salamander and a predatory vampire.

All the while staying in Gloria's good books, of course.

I sighed, at last comprehending the human desire to tear out their hair.

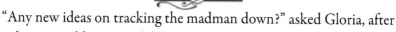

"Any new ideas on tracking the madman down?" asked Gloria, after gulping a scalding mouthful of her espresso.

I sipped my sparkling water, enjoying the fizzing sensation as it diffused through me. "Well I *might* have a lead."

"Grand! Let's hear it."

Gloria had shown up at the gym mid-morning as I was getting a spin class under way. She'd watched for a bit, and then wandered off outside. Salamanders aren't built for patience. Once I'd finished, we walked through the autumn sunshine to Tiso's cafe to sit on comfy sofas with a low table between us. The place would be filling up for lunch soon, but we were lucky enough to stake our claim before a business group arrived brandishing their laptops. Looking somewhat put out, they took a regular table instead.

"I have this friend, Euan, and he got introduced to Liam a few days ago." I didn't feel like going into details about last night; I was still working through my reactions and I didn't need Gloria's input. I felt like I was wading through muddy floodwaters, unable to see where I was going or what lay beneath the surface, and it had me on edge. I'd almost blanked Euan last night when I joined him in the basement, and despite the confusion and hurt that radiated from him, I'd found myself unwilling to talk. We'd spent a rather awkward night floating side by side in the shallows.

"So does this Euan know where he lives?"

I shook my head. "I'm not certain, but Liam's invited him to visit tomorrow. I thought I might tag along."

"Discreetly, I presume?"

"But of course! I have no intention of walking willingly into that spider's web."

"Hmm." Gloria laced her hands behind her head and leaned back into the leather sofa. "I think I like you, sprite Cassie. You're most unusual for your type; not as drippy as those I've encountered before."

She liked me. If she'd said that a couple of nights earlier I'd have been unconditionally thrilled. Now I wanted more.

"How much do you like me?" I asked. "Enough to deal with this guy in my way instead of yours?"

Gloria was apparently unused to being challenged. I could see a tiny hint of smoke wisping around her hair and a slight smell of singed leather rose from beneath her.

"Careful," I cautioned. "You wouldn't want to set off the sprinklers, would you?"

Momentary panic arced across Gloria's eyes, like lightning in a night sky. Then she laughed aloud.

"You got me there! I seem to keep losing attention when you're around, girl; you're quite distracting."

It was mutual then. That sounded promising.

"I meant it though," I pushed. "Will you let me try first?"

The look she gave made my heart skip. Anger at my opposition, yes, but also worry. Was that about me, or about the magician?

"The longer we leave him be, the more probable it is he'll try again," she said. "Can't you just accept that my way is quickest and safest?"

I shook my head. "Safest for us, yes. But we are talking," I lowered my voice, "of depriving a human being of his *life*, and that's not something I take lightly. You and me, we'll continue, but humans don't."

I wasn't about to bring my worries for Euan's safety into this. They weren't going to influence Gloria, and I didn't want to complicate things further by raising the whole boyfriend thing.

Gloria huffed. "I don't see why that's our concern; they're designed with short life spans. If this one wants to meddle with us, he's just going to find his shorter than most."

I sighed. Another human idiom—beating one's head against a brick wall—sprang to mind.

"Okay, okay!" Gloria raised her hands in mock surrender. "I won't incinerate him at first sight, but you'd better get on with whatever you're thinking of doing because I'm not hanging around waiting to be stuck back into a thermos. And I can't answer for Alastair; that vamp has a short fuse and Liam seriously pissed him off."

Victory of sorts. Now all I had to figure out what it was I *did* plan on doing.

"Let me know when your friend leaves. I'm coming with you," Gloria announced.

"You are?"

"What, don't you trust me?"

Truth was, I didn't. Impulsive as she was, I suspected Gloria's temper would flare once she got within a hundred paces of Liam, and the possibility of a direct confrontation terrified me. Traitor though it made me feel, I wasn't convinced Gloria would have the upper hand.

"It's not a matter of trust," I said. "I'm just not sure it's a good idea for the pair of us to get too close to him together. Sort of an easy target, if you see what I mean."

"Typical water type! Too cautious by half. I'm coming, that's all there is to it. Why should you have all the fun?"

She thought this was *fun*?

16. LIAM'S LAIR

I clung to the car's bumper in the form of a tiny ball of water vapour damping the paintwork. A little way from me, a flickering spark nestled in the end of the exhaust pipe.

Euan rated visiting Liam important enough to call a taxi and use up precious natural resources. The taxi wound its way through the centre of Inverness city and out along the route to Dores, thence along the winding road that traversed what could be considered the back side of Loch Ness. That stretch of road is dotted with odd houses, some of which lurk at the end of rutted paths leading into the hills overlooking those enigmatic depths. We turned down one of these, and bumped along for an inordinate time, causing me to wonder if the address was fictitious. Finally, however, we arrived.

In the middle of nowhere, with no cover bar a few scrubby bits of broom and gorse amidst the low, dense heather that was in full autumn bloom, squatted the lair of the most dangerous magician in the Highlands. A dilapidated old mobile home on an isolated strip of concrete.

With no warning, I was swept clear of my perch. Stunned, I fell to the ground and rolled aside, resuming my human shape, though without the solidity to render me visible. As my mind began to function again, I realised that a magical barrier surrounded and protected Liam's hideaway. As if the remote location was not enough to keep unwanted visitors at bay.

I glanced behind me to find Gloria lying full length on the heather, resplendent in full human manifestation and garbed in figure-hugging jeans and sweater. Once I got over my shock at what I initially assumed was her arrogance, I realised that she'd been obliged to complete her transformation or risk setting the brush alight. Unusual for the Highlands, we'd had a relatively rain-free autumn and the heather was dry. Not a good combination with Gloria's propensity for smouldering.

At least she'd had the presence of mind to synthesise clothes that toned with the pale purple of the tiny heather flowers. It wasn't a colour I'd seen her wear before, but it complemented her dark chocolate skin beautifully.

She started to raise a hand.

"Keep low," I hissed at her.

She glowered back. "What do you think I'm going to do; stand up and wave?"

Duh. That *had* been a rather inane thing to say, but I still found myself lacking in sense whenever I was in her presence.

"Look!"

Gloria's stage whisper snapped my head around in time to see Liam jump down the step from the caravan which sat propped on concrete blocks, its wheels long since rusted away. Liam greeted Euan with enthusiasm. Out here in the cold light of day and at, we hoped, a safe distance, the magician looked nothing special. How deceiving appearances can be.

I should know.

"Come on in," Liam invited. His voice carried across the open muir, and we watched in silence as Euan followed him inside. The door swung shut behind them and my chest tightened with the fear that I'd betrayed my friend, letting him walk into a trap designed for me. Nonsense, of course. I could no more walk past Liam's spell barrier than I could touch Gloria, but the sick feeling persisted. I tried to comfort myself by repeating inside my head that Liam had no reason to harm Euan.

I wasn't very convincing.

"Well I don't think the direct approach is going to work," Gloria observed as she plastered one hand against the invisible barrier and pushed without effect.

At least this one didn't sting when you touched it. I stroked the icy slick magic, wishing I had a clue what to do about it.

Something brushed my heel and I almost shot upward into the sky. Clamping a firm control on my nerves, I turned to find a large red grouse pecking at my foot. I guess he either couldn't see me or he didn't find me threatening, merely an inconvenience between him and the seeds he was intent upon eating.

"What—?" Gloria began, cut off by the startled squawk of a grouse that suddenly realised it had walked too close to an ambulatory oven. It shot into the sky, squalling its panic and setting off a chain reaction. Grouse after grouse became airborne in the noisy, flappy way that only such stupid game birds do.

"Shit!"

The caravan door swung open and Liam stared out. His eyes were drawn first upward to the fleeing birds, before travelling an unerring line back to the origin of the rout. He scanned the area where Gloria laid hopelessly exposed, face flat into the undergrowth. Perhaps her heather-coloured clothing was good enough camouflage, or else Liam chose not to do anything about his observer at that moment because he withdrew, slamming the door behind him.

A frisson of fear oscillated through my rather widely spaced molecules. I was pretty sure I'd seen a smile on his face as he backed away.

Quiet settled over the landscape with just the distant bellow of rutting stags to break the hush, and we stayed frozen in place, waiting.

Eventually Gloria dared to raise her head enough for a real study of the mobile home.

"He's self-sufficient, damn him! Not a power cable or a pipe in sight; not even a drain."

"No getting in by the usual devious means, then," I agreed. From where we lay I could even see the sealed water containers he used to fetch his own supply; nothing I could utilise to smuggle myself in there.

"What we need is someone who can take down this barrier," said Gloria. "We need to find us a witch. You know any?"

"Are you sure that would work?" I answered evasively. Gloria's propensity for using people was one of her less attractive traits, and I had no intention of involving Dawn or her father, Gordon—the only people I thought might be strong enough to help us.

"He's already proven he's more than we can handle, and frankly Alastair didn't cover himself in glory last time either. I'm thinking that to catch a magician we need someone who can go up against him with the same tools as he has. Preferably someone stronger, or else more of them. Didn't you say you met him at a coven? Should be enough witches in a coven to deal with one magician, surely?"

Wow. I was gobsmacked to hear Gloria admit we couldn't deal with this situation on our own. It goes against our nature to involve others in our business, and it made Gloria seem almost more human. Until she opened her mouth again, that is.

"We need them as bait, or a diversion."

That decided me.

"I'm afraid they turned out to be a bunch of middle aged ladies playing at it," I said, putting all the regret I could muster into my tone. "Not a jot of power amongst them. I'm afraid we'll have to come up with some other solution."

"That's too bad. Ah well, maybe Alastair knows someone we could use. Think we've seen all we can here. Let's go."

Without waiting for my opinion, Gloria started to slither backward, but before she'd gone more than a few metres the caravan door popped open again and both Liam and Euan emerged. I was so relieved to see Euan unscathed and unfettered, I almost dissipated with relief. Gloria ceased moving.

"I think that's an excellent tactic," Euan enthused.

"So we'll do this again, then, and take our plans to the next level," said Liam. "And you could bring your girlfriend too; she seems to have an interest in such things."

Wheels crunched up the rough track. Euan's taxi returning.

I began to drift away from Gloria. Two targets had to be more challenging than one, and I was certain he know we were out here.

"I'll ask her," Euan assured Liam as he climbed into the car, "but she's more pacifist than activist."

"Do try. It would be great to have her involved too."

Yeah, right! The involvement Liam had in mind for me was a bit *too* committed to figure in my life plan.

Waving cheerily as the taxi took Euan away, Liam kept eyes front until the car disappeared from sight. Then he turned with unerring precision to where I hovered. I'd thought I was invisible to the naked eye, but apparently he'd found some magical spell to alter his eyesight. Thank the gods he hadn't had it during our previous encounters.

"Do you hear that, Cassie? Euan would love to have you work along with us. And so would I. Can you forgive my earlier rudeness? I'd really appreciate it if you'd join me of your own free will; it would make things so much simpler. What do you say?"

The vaguest hint of strawberry essence tickled my senses and my molecules vibrated with fear. This close, if he sprang another of his traps I was never going to evade it. With nothing else left to me, I gathered myself defiantly into a more solid form and hissed my answer back at him.

"Never! I know what you're up to now, and I don't think you've thought it through. Unless you don't *care* what happens to my kind?"

On the edge of my awareness, I could hear Gloria creeping away. If I could keep Liam's attention a little longer she would be beyond his reach. With a barrier of Liam's own making between us, I began to feel a little bolder.

The magician shrugged his shoulders, showing empty hands in a placating gesture. "I'm sorry, okay? Perhaps I got it wrong. Now I've met you and I've heard what Euan has to say about you, I realise I made a terrible mistake trying to force you against your will. But you must be able to see the potential for the planet? Sooner rather than later, we are going to run out of fuel and here you are, with endless power all to yourself. Has it ever occurred to you that perhaps this is your destiny—to be the ongoing light of the world? You've had aeons of existence. Is it too much to ask you to give something back?"

Horrifyingly, I could see his point. Elementals have been around since the beginning of the planet; perhaps the time was coming when we would have to give ourselves up to help her continue. Maybe that's all we were, storage batteries that were in line for use after all other power sources had been exhausted. No one had ever explained *why* we existed.

My mouth opened to express agreement, and fruit flavouring coated my tongue. Coherent thought slithered away from me, but emotion welled up to take its place. I tossed my hair and glared at Liam, both furious and terrified by the subtlety of his spell casting.

"I don't think I'm ready for that kind of altruistic sacrifice just yet," I snarled.

"Give it some thought, Cassie. It makes sense, you'll see."

A flicker of light caught the edge of my eye, and Liam's head snapped to one side.

"You brought the fire lizard with you?"

He sounded shocked. I guess he hadn't expected Gloria and me to continue our alliance past the debacle at the club. His gaze spun back to me and his eyes glittered, reflecting the distant sparkle that was Gloria withdrawing to a safer distance.

"Don't get any funny ideas about using her against me, Cassiopeia Lake. Salamanders are devious creatures, as you should well know. I want what's best for the future and I'm willing to fight dirty to get it. Euan's a nice guy, but he has a weakness, and I can *see* it, no matter what he makes it look like. You keep that lizard under control or something might happen to that precious sealskin of his."

So *that* was how Euan did it. He concealed his skin right out in the open. It could be a rock, a shrub or a cushion for all I'd know, and as I had no magic I'd never see it for what it truly was. Unlike Liam.

A deep, deep chill penetrated every layer of my body.

"You'd threaten Euan?"

Liam shrugged. "I don't want to, I like the guy. But my safety will always come first. I'm the one who's figured out the answer to the global energy crisis, and I don't intend to let anyone stop me from completing my invention. It could mean the difference between human life continuing on this planet or not. Surely you can see that some sacrifices are worth that goal?"

Certain words sprang to mind, including deluded and egomaniac, but there was no denying, he might be right. For all their forward planning and attempts to limit the use of natural resources, the human race was without doubt entering a fight for survival in the not-too-distant future. Suppose he was right and he did have the answer?

Liam turned and walked back to his dingy little mobile home, with its gas cylinders and petrol-driven generator, power sources that would be useless once their fuel ran out for good.

Before shutting the door, he glanced round at me. "I'll let you think on it, Cassie. You know I'm right, I can see it on your face. When you're ready, I'll be waiting."

Did I believe him, or was his spell still affecting me? I couldn't taste strawberries any more, but I had no idea if that meant the spell was gone or not.

For the first time in my life, I felt sick.

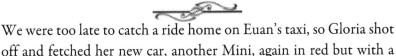

We were too late to catch a ride home on Euan's taxi, so Gloria shot off and fetched her new car, another Mini, again in red but with a Union Flag roof and wing mirrors. Once more I rode on the rear parcel shelf and half listened while she talked on her mobile to Alastair, describing to him where to find the caravan and arranging for him to keep watch that night. It appeared they'd already formulated some plans of their own, and I felt worryingly out of the loop. Without knowing any details, I didn't want to screw things up by warning Liam about the bloodsucker that would stake out his home. I paused, mid-thought. A vampire on a stakeout? There was something very wrong with that idea. But equally I didn't want Alastair killing him.

My immediate concern was Euan. If Liam considered threatening the gentle selkie to be an acceptable gambit, then I suspected the magic was already in place to carry out those threats. I *had* to put Euan beyond his reach.

I wasn't sure how I was going to accomplish this and I fretted over it for the entire journey. As a consequence, by the time Gloria deposited me in the gym car park where my Golf still languished, I realised that I'd missed most of her conversation with Alastair.

"So what's the plan now?" I asked before she could roar off into the gathering dusk.

"Alastair will watch him at night in case he makes a move, and one of us will take over for the day shift. I intend to know exactly where he is and what he's doing from now until we finish him."

"But we're going to try talking with him first, yes?" I said.

"Yeah, yeah. Whatever. Think I'll take tomorrow's early watch. You never know what opportunities might present now we have him in our sights."

I smothered a groan. She was as determined as ever to kill Liam without trying to defuse the situation first, and no doubt Alastair had the same intention.

Two against one. Not good odds, but for the moment Liam was going to have to take his chances; I had a selkie's safety to secure.

"Okay, I'll be over later in the day. What time do you want relieving?"

"You know what," said Gloria, "don't bother. I've nothing else to do tomorrow and it's dark by about five, so I've plenty of time to get ready for work. You take the next day."

"That's Monday. I'll have clients all day and it's a bit late to re-organise them."

"You want to do tomorrow instead?"

"Makes sense—oh! I've promised to be somewhere in the afternoon."

Gloria shrugged. "Back to plan A then. I'll let you know how it goes."

And she was gone, zooming out of the car park as if it was the pit lane of a race-track, and still without resolving the question over who would do the watching on Monday.

Fire signs!

17. UNRAVELLING

The whole drive home, I debated with myself over how to warn Euan off Liam.

For the first time in my long, long life, I was responsible for the safety of people other than myself and this troubled me greatly. An unyielding chunk of granite took up residence where my stomach should be, and I found myself reciting one of those pointless human phrases: why me?

I parked the Golf in the garage, but lingered in the shadows. This time I knew with certainty that Liam wasn't inside, and yet I hesitated. Euan's life might depend on what I said next, but my wits refused to come to heel.

When I could delay no longer, I drew a deep, steadying breath and marvelled at the impact such a simple action could have on a human body. The front door swung open as I ambled across the gravel.

"There you are," called Euan. Although his face was in shadow, I could hear his smile. Gods, this was going to be hard.

"Euan, we have to talk."

"Don't we always?"

"This is serious," I told him, and winced to hear the inane words pour out of my mouth. Not a good start.

Euan backed into the hallway and I sensed his confusion. 'Serious' didn't happen around us. Our lives were too independent of human needs to ever be truly serious. The only important thing in Euan's life was his quest to save the planet from profligate governments and businesses. How was I going to get him to understand the gravity of a situation he didn't even know existed?

"This new friend of yours, Liam—"

"Yes, I want to talk to you about some great ideas he has," Euan enthused as I shut the door behind me. I groaned as I passed him, going into the utility room to let Minkie out of his cage.

"What?" said Euan as the mink bounded past him, en route for the kitchen and food. "He's going to be a great asset to us. To the whole eco community. He has loads of ideas and the science to back them up, and with his qualifications they'll have to take him seriously."

Somehow I had to break through this hero-worship because, to my horror, that's what I detected in Euan's voice.

"Euan, Liam's dangerous," I blurted, and then wished I could take it back. This was not the way to get Euan to see sense, but I was shaking with fear and so scared that I wouldn't be able to convince him, that I was struggling to force my thoughts into any sort of rational order.

Euan looked at me as if I'd sprouted a second head.

"Cassie, what on earth are you talking about? If you don't *like* Liam, come right out and say it. Why make such a ridiculous accusation?"

Yes, that had been a truly stupid thing to say. As far as Euan was concerned anyone who could help his cause was an okay person, and my bald statement to the contrary would do nothing to change his opinion. Might, in fact, damage his regard for me and lessen my chances of persuading him to remove himself from danger.

And without doubt, Liam had reinforced Euan's idolisation with magic.

"I just know he is," I said hopelessly, and tried to appeal to Euan's sense of loyalty to our long-standing relationship. "Can't you trust me on this?"

Euan's face took on a stubborn cast that I'd rarely seen before, and I knew I was in deep trouble. My innards sank towards the floor.

"I'm sorry," he said, "I can't. Liam could be the one to make all the difference to our efforts, and I'm not willing to jeopardise his involvement because of your personal feelings. What's got into you Cassie? I thought you felt the same way about the cause as I do."

I was losing him, I could feel it. Give a man a weapon he can use in his personal crusade and no woman is going to separate him from it.

There was nothing for it; I was going to have to tell him the whole story. I so didn't want to. I was terrified that if Euan knew what Liam had tried to do to me—and to him—he might take some terminally stupid action. But I had clumsily talked myself into a position where nothing but the truth was going to convince Euan of the magician's untrustworthiness.

Perhaps Dawn had been right when she'd said that truth has a way of getting out. I took another of those deep, calming breaths.

"Euan, do you remember the state I was in when I came home last Sunday?"

He frowned. "Yes. Very tired, in need of energy. And sex."

"That was all down to Liam. We didn't just 'meet' before. He hunted me and he kidnapped me. He wanted to experiment on me and he didn't give a damn if he hurt me or killed me in the process."

Euan's face was a blank mask of shock. I guessed he didn't know what to think, what to say. I waited anxiously for him to say something, but when he did it wasn't what I'd hoped for.

"Cassie, you must have got it wrong. Liam is all about *saving* things—people, animals, the planet. He wouldn't hurt anyone."

Why are some people so blind? But perhaps that was unfair of me; Euan's trusting nature was one of the things about him that I treasured. It made me furious to realise how easy it had been for Liam to use that trust to turn Euan against me.

"You must be imagining things," Euan continued, looking worried now, but for all the wrong reasons. "Are you sure you're okay? I didn't think human illnesses could affect you, but perhaps they can in some way we haven't come across before. You must be having delusions. Did you hit your head, or zap yourself with electricity or something? You know how you and electrical gadgets don't get on."

I spluttered with frustration. "Euan, you're not listening to me! There's nothing wrong with me. Liam is a *magician*! He used spells to trap me, and he put me in a magical container with a *salamander*. Does that sound sane to you?"

The first cracks began to appear. "A salamander? Why would he do such a crazy thing? Cassie, are you *sure*?"

"I was there! It happened. And now I know why. He wanted to bring us together to cause a massive explosion so he could harness our energy, but he didn't care what happened to us!"

Euan's expression had gone from shock to bewilderment. "Why didn't you tell me about this before? And why didn't you say something when I brought him here?"

I drew a deep sigh then, spying a glimmer of hope. It sounded as if he was starting to believe me. Maybe I could win after all. Perhaps this truth thing had something going for it after all.

"Because I didn't want you to get hurt," I said, and my voice trembled ever so slightly. "You might have tried to protect me by confronting him, and I couldn't bear it if he hurt you. You're not immortal like me."

Euan ceased breathing for a moment, and his face was closed in a way I'd never seen before. It scared me witless.

And then I smelled strawberries.

"I'm sorry, Cassie," he said, but it didn't matter. Nothing about this conversation mattered anymore. Liam's glamour coated Euan and hung in a fruity miasma between us. Anything coming out of Euan's mouth now might as well have been scripted by the magician.

Euan took my limp hands in his. "I'm struggling to get my head around this," he said. "You think I'm too weak or too stupid to protect you, so you decided to hide this from me instead of talking it through and letting me make my own decisions?" He shook his head.

I tried to find something to say, some justification beyond my desire to keep him safe, but for once I was struck dumb. Nothing I could say would make any difference.

"Believe me, Cassie," he continued, "the only person you need protecting from is yourself. Did it never occur to you that I might have been able to help without acting the he-man and landing myself in trouble?" He dropped my hands and stepped back. "Fuck it, sprite, do you really think I'm that stupid?"

The hurt in his big puppy-dog eyes was like a red hot poker thrust into my side. I'd only tried to keep it from him so he wouldn't worry, so he wouldn't try to get involved and put himself in harms' way. But now, with a little help from Liam, that was all going to backfire on me in spectacular fashion.

Euan shook his head. "I never thought I'd find myself saying this, but perhaps your kind is as self-centred as legends say. I can't believe you think so little of me. That hurts, Cassie, it really hurts. I'm not sure how to deal with this."

"Please Euan, think about this logically!" Desperation forced words from me, even in the knowledge that Liam's spell made them pointless. "There was nothing you could have done. If I'd managed to deal with it you'd never have known and you'd never have had to worry about me. Wouldn't that have been better than fretting about something you could do nothing about?"

He studied me as though he'd never seen me before. I found hot, fat tears rolling down my cheeks. *Tears!* From a *sprite.* To leak water unbidden from any part of me was beyond unnatural, but for some perverse reason I clung to my human body and all its hideous unwanted emotions. As if to do otherwise would be to admit that he was right, that I was a self-obsessed elemental with no respect for other forms of life.

"And you think that would have made your omission any better, if I'd never found out about it?" Euan said quietly. "Cassie, friends are supposed to share their problems. Isn't that what friendship is all about? And weren't we something closer than friends anyway?"

'*Weren't we.*' Past tense. My whole body cringed.

"Forgive me, please?" I begged. "I made a mistake. I'm not good at this whole emotion thing."

He shook his head again, and in his eyes I could see a terrible, deep sadness. And pity.

That was the moment I knew it was over. Our lovely, carefree relationship could never be recovered. Even without Liam's interference, the damage I'd done was irrevocable. With all the right motives, I'd nonetheless ruined our friendship. More tears streaked my face and I allowed them to fall, allowed part of myself to fall away as I'd allowed our friendship to fall. It was too late, too late for tears, too late to backtrack and wish I'd entrusted him with the whole sorry story right from the outset.

Too late for us.

"I'm sorry, Cass," he said softly. "I've loved you, and I've tried so hard to be what you wanted me to be, but I can't do it anymore. I'm going to leave now. I'm not sure if I'll be back."

"Please!" I cried, clinging onto his arm. "Please Euan, don't do this!"

"I'm sorry, Cass; I can't stay."

"At least promise me you won't go near Liam? Promise me you'll stay away from him!"

"I need to think," he said, gently peeling my fingers from his arm. "I'm truly sorry."

And he left. Without answer or promise. Trailing the scent of strawberries behind him.

I stood alone in the hallway. So very alone. I had no assurance that he wouldn't go to Liam, no guarantee that he would stay safe.

All my fault.

Some while later, when the remaining light had faded from the sky and a strong wind had risen to howl around the steading and rattle the windows, I found myself sitting on the hallway floor, staring at a blank wall. Something rasped softly at my fingers, rousing me from my numb stupor. Minkie, licking me with his rough pink tongue.

"You want feeding. I get it."

I hauled myself off the floor, my body moving as if it was weighed down by twice the mass I usually carried. I trudged through to the kitchen and fetched Minkie's tripe from the fridge. My mind refused to function.

Euan was gone, that was all it could comprehend. I became aware of a sharp pain somewhere deep inside me. It ached and yet also clawed at me, raking me with talons sharp enough to rend my pitiful soul. If I'd possessed one.

"Oh Minkie, what do I do now?"

More tears trickled down my face and dripped into Minkie's tripe. I scrubbed at my eyes with balled fists.

"I don't understand. I thought telling the truth was supposed to be the right thing to do," I wailed, utterly bewildered. Minkie licked tears from my fingers, and then dived into the food bowl before I had a chance to put it down on the floor. I let him stay up on the work surface and absently stroked his soft back while he ate.

I needed to speak with someone who could actually answer me. I reached for the phone and speed-dialled Alison's mobile number.

"Hello?"

Her voice sounded strangely distant, as if it was coming from inside a wind tunnel.

"Alison? It's Cassie. I need to talk."

"Sorry Cass, you'll have to speak up. I can hardly hear you."

"Where on earth are you?" I asked, somewhat vexed that this was not going the way I needed it to.

"We're up in Boblainy Forest, and oh, Cassie, we should have invited you along too!"

I had a shrewd idea about the probable identity of Alison's companion, but I had to ask.

"Who are you up there with? It might not be the safest place at night, Alison. Remember not so long ago there were some wildcat sightings? And some of them sounded more like big cats than the local version."

"Don't worry, I'm with Dawn, and she's showing me all sorts of things. Cassie it's magical! There are things out here that I would never have believed existed. You'll have to come another time. You won't believe me if I tell you."

You might be surprised, I muttered beneath my breath, but asked, "Such as?"

"Ooooh!" she squealed. "There's another one!"

I heard Dawn shushing her. I could picture the cosy little scene. Dawn coaxing out Ghillie Dhu from the trees, or wild Bodach from their burrows; Alison's entranced face as she realised there were more creatures in existence than she'd ever imagined.

Magical creatures like me.

And I wanted to talk with her about busting up with my boyfriend. There really was no contest.

"Sorry Cass, you simply won't believe what I'm seeing. Was it something urgent you wanted?"

It was, but it was just my selfish side demanding attention. I smothered my feelings deep enough that she wouldn't hear them.

"Never mind right now, dear heart. We can chat when you have time. Enjoy your field trip; I look forward to hearing all about it."

"Okay," she whispered, evidently enthralled by something happening before her. "We can catch up tomorrow, on the walk."

Walk? What walk? Ah, the coven outing. I *so* didn't want to go, particularly after what had just happened.

"I'm not sure I'm going to make it," I told her.

"Hold on a mo." Clearly an aside to Dawn, followed by sounds of creeping through undergrowth, complete with a muffled, *'ouch!'* and the sound of ripping cloth.

"Cassie, you still there?"

"Aye," I said. Nothing more.

Alison continued in a stage whisper that must have been heard by every one of the magical creatures she was being introduced to. And probably also by Dawn. Not that I cared. "You *have* to come, Cass. It's Dawn's birthday and Gordon has some sort of special surprise for her. He wants us all to be there. *Please* say you'll come. I'm not sure why, but I get the impression that the surprise won't be complete without the whole coven there, and they're counting us as members now."

<*Well they shouldn't*> was my first reaction. We'd undergone none of the rituals I understood to be necessary for joining a coven. But Alison wanted to belong, and I couldn't bring myself to disappoint her.

"Oh, alright. There's something else I ought to be doing, but I suppose I can get out of it."

Already had, if I was being honest. Gloria was covering tomorrow's magician-watching shift and I'd already told her I was too busy to take over. Damn! I should have said I'd do it, and then I'd have a real excuse to avoid Gordon's 'surprise'. Whatever that was.

"Great! See you tomorrow then. Bye!"

The phone went dead. Aside from the wind howling round the walls, there was hush in the steading. Living with nothing but the sounds of nature is the norm for a sprite, but I no longer found it comfortable. I'd become accustomed to the sound of another voice, or even the quiet breathing of a mortal creature, and I missed it.

Tears welled up again. When I'd suggested Dawn tutor Alison, I'd never imagined the new relationship would draw my best friend away from me.

And I'd driven Euan away by my own naivety, thinking I could control the situation. I might even have put him in more danger than before, if he ran to Liam. <*Please, Euan, don't do that!*> I pleaded into empty air. I was so frightened, my body shook. The world spun around me and I slithered to the kitchen floor. Minkie jumped down from the work surface and climbed into my lap where he proceeded to wash himself, cat-style, accompanied by slurping licks. It wasn't quite the sound I'd have preferred to hear, but at least it intruded on the unwanted quiet.

"Oh, Minkie. What should I do now?" I repeated.

He paused in his washing and fixed me with one beady eye. I had the distinct impression that he was considering my words with care.

The feeling I'd had before, when I'd first allowed Minkie to stay despite his treachery, came again. The comforting warmth of illusory arms around my shoulders, enfolding me in tenderness. A comfort I had done nothing to deserve.

Tears spilled over, trickling down my cheeks and I clutched Minkie to my chest, sobbing into his thick fur. I had no idea what was happening to me, except that I was sure with a frighteningly cold clarity that my cosy, unexciting and stable life was starting to unravel.

18. SHRINE

I walked in a daze. Roots and stones tripped me. I barely noticed. The world around me was fuzzy, out of focus.

Euan was gone.

He'd come and gone for years, never guaranteeing his return. The way I liked it. No ties. Yet now there was a gaping hole where he'd been, and it hurt.

A line from an old song played through my mind, about not knowing what you've got until it's gone. Oh, how true was that.

And beneath the pain lurked bone-chilling fear. Please let him not have gone to Liam. Please let him be safe.

I stumbled again, and began to pay some attention to my surroundings. We trekked along the broad logging track in little clusters. Me, Saffron's coven and, for some reason unknown to me, Rhona's coven also. I ran a jaundiced eye over the strangers.

Going by the snide comments at previous meetings I'd expected Rhona to be an ancient wizened crone. She was, instead, a young woman with garish pumpkin orange hair that stood out in gelled spikes. The rest of her coven, in their ubiquitous black garb enlivened only by the odd silver chain, wouldn't have looked out of place at a heavy metal rock concert. Perhaps some of the rivalry between the groups was an age thing, but I suspected that the social divide was simply too great between ladies-who-lunch and Goths.

In a rather disinterested way, I wondered why Saffron had invited them.

Saffron and Gordon led the way along the forest track, followed by Mary and a gaggle of gossiping ladies. Next, Rhona and her cohorts, clustered together in a rather defensive group. Alison, Dawn and I brought up the rear.

Even in the knowledge that Gloria had Liam under constant surveillance, I wasn't comfortable with this position. I felt vulnerable without a rear guard, and kept glancing over my shoulder to scan the empty path behind us. If either Dawn or Alison found my behaviour odd, neither of them chose to comment. They chattered brightly as they walked, their voices accompanied by the rustle of high-tech waterproof fabrics and the stomp of hiking boots. Low cloud misted through the tall trees and the fresh scent of pine washed over us. An idyllic morning in the Highlands.

Yeah, right.

"Cassie, I'm sorry about last night," said Alison. "What did you call about?"

"Don't worry, it was nothing. I had a row with Euan."

Last night, I'd needed to talk. Now, in the amber glow of this autumn morning, I didn't. It had happened. I would deal with it.

"Oh, Cassie, I'm so sorry! You've been there for me all those times when Simon was such a bastard, and I let you down when you need me. Goddess, I feel awful!"

"Don't." I wanted to reassure her, to put her off the topic. "I'm sure it'll all blow over."

"Of course it will," she pronounced. "You two have such a solid history, even if he's not around that often. I'm sure it'll work itself out. It's not as if the pair of you are serious or anything, is it?"

No, we'd never been serious. At least, I hadn't. Not until last night. What was it Euan had said? *'I've loved you, and I've tried so hard to be what you wanted me to be.'* When had I asked him to do that? I'd never asked any such thing of him.

Had I?

I wanted to be anywhere but here, held captive by my promise, and because I didn't want to disappoint my friends. I realised I was counting Dawn in the 'friend' category. I wasn't sure it was mutual but perhaps we could work on that; I was feeling short of friends right now.

"Actually, Cass, I'm feeling rather guilty anyway," said Alison. "I've been so wrapped up in learning stuff from Dawn that I've been ignoring you. That stops right now. If you don't want to get more involved with the coven, then we'll make special time just for us. What do you say?"

I couldn't help it. "And what does Dawn say about this?"

The two of us had slipped back, and Dawn was up ahead trying to make conversation with Rhona. I got the impression Dawn found the coven rivalry somewhat silly.

"She's cool with it—says I should take care of those closest to me."

Yeah, as in, '*Keep your friends close and your enemies closer.*'

Cynic.

"How about we make it the three of us?" I suggested.

"Are you sure? That would be grand! Dawn's great fun and she wants to get to know both of us better. Let's go out for a meal sometime this week. How about Thursday?"

Without waiting for an answer, Alison lengthened her strides and caught up to the pack. "Hey, Dawn, how about supper this Thursday? The three of us?" she asked.

Dawn glanced round at me, her deep green eyes coolly appraising. She tilted her head to one side. "If you like," she said.

I took that as an olive branch. Our last escapade together hadn't ended so well, with me lecturing her about prejudice. Perhaps she'd thought it through, and acknowledged that I had a point. Or not. I was sure I'd find out soon enough.

"It's a date!" Alison declared, and started chattering to the Goths. I'd never met anyone who could be so effervescent when life was going well; it was a delight to see.

Euan's gone.

The thought struck me out of nowhere. I went cold all over.

For a few seconds life had seemed almost normal. I dragged my feet and dropped further behind. The path, which had led steadily downward, did a sudden hairpin turn onto level ground. An isolated house had once stood there, pincered between the two arms of the track. Now all that remained was rubble and a ramshackle fence surrounded the plot. An ancient showman's caravan was parked on the drive beside the ruin, hitched up to a decrepit Land Rover. Smoke drifted from the caravan chimney, adding the sweet smell of burning logs to the pervasive aroma of the trees. There was no movement inside.

When we'd first left the remote car park dedicated to Plodda Falls, I'd been surprised we didn't take the footpath to the left, which led straight down to the falls. Then I'd considered the older ladies in the group. Several of them would probably not be capable of the rough, steep descent. The track we followed took a much longer route, but was far gentler on rickety knees and hips. It had been so long since I'd been down this way, I'd forgotten it existed. That someone *lived* down here was a revelation.

"I wouldn't hang around here if I were you." Dawn's voice beside my shoulder made me jump.

"Sorry?"

She nodded towards the track, and I realised I'd been stationary, lost in thought. Our party was small in the distance.

"You don't want to be seen here," said Dawn, starting to walk away. I frowned after her, and then back at the disreputable old caravan.

"Why?" I asked, but hurried after her.

"Because the hedge witch who lives there can likely see you for what you are. You don't want that, do you?"

"Hedge witch? They still exist?"

I hadn't come across one in a couple of centuries. Hedge witches practice alone, and most specialise in healing. Not something I would ever need.

"Of course they do," said Dawn. "Where have you been hiding?"

"You know this one?"

"No, but I know what she is. We respect each other and keep our distances."

Which was my intention too.

"Thank you," I said, and meant it. Dawn dipped her head in acknowledgement.

We walked faster until we'd caught up with our party. The path now followed a fast-flowing stream and the rushing bubble of water filled our ears. There was a palpable feeling of excitement from the ladies, as if we were nearing some thrilling goal.

Plodda Falls are spectacular, but that surely couldn't account for this air of anticipation. I began to think that some piece of vital information was being withheld. From me alone? Or were Alison and Dawn as much in the dark?

"Nearly there, ladies!" rang out Saffron's voice.

Rhona's girls clustered even tighter.

As the music of the stream changed subtly from babbling brook to gushing rapids, the rough track widened out to terminate in an oval turning area. Not all the vehicles that came here turned around; there were tyre marks in the sandy bank, testament to quad bikes, or similar, fording the stream. Across the turbulent water a pair of deep, muddy grooves disappeared into the foliage on the opposite bank.

We turned left, upstream, taking a small trail along the riverbank beneath towering Scots pines. The waterfall's thunder dominated. As the trail petered out and we started to make our way across uneven ground, some of the older ladies began to struggle. I was wondering why we weren't following the tourist path when Saffron called a halt. The two covens drew into separate clusters on the riverbank, and I came face to face with the 'surprise'.

A pile of rocks topped with a flat boulder stood in a small clearing, right by the water's edge. It would have been an easy task to build; there was no shortage of rocks hereabouts. It might have been thrown together by some kids, or by campers using it for a barbeque.

But I knew that wasn't so. Placed neatly on top was a brass cauldron, a bowl of water and a seashell.

A shrine.

More specifically, a shrine to a water elemental.

Icy fingers clutched my spine. I hadn't seen one in decades, and to my knowledge such an object wasn't integral to a birthday party. I started to back away, dropping cohesion as much as I could to keep my progress quiet, yet still keep my clothes on.

Was *this* what Gordon and Saffron had been cooking up with Brian, the water diviner?

Had my secret been rumbled?

And why, oh why, was Rhona's coven here as well?

Saffron began speaking, her tone one of reverence, oddly laced with triumph. I was too agitated to listen to her actual words, but they were producing two distinct effects. The older ladies of Saffron's clique shifted with nervous excitement, while the Goths gathered in a sullen huddle.

Sure as hell, I was not going to hang around to find out what was going on. I would manufacture an excuse for my behaviour later. Right now, I needed to be as far away from here as possible.

I'd made it back almost to the turning circle when an inexorable force started to tug at me. My heart lurched—Liam must have found me!

But then I realised this was different. I could neither sense Liam nor smell his magic. No, this was something else altogether.

I stumbled doggedly on. The insistent pull dragged at me, like struggling through treacle. A few more steps and it became impossible to ignore. My body was threatening to come apart without my permission.

A groan of recognition crawled up my throat. Someone was performing a summoning, and that someone was powerful beyond anything I could resist. I could not be certain about the identity of my summoner, but I had a shrewd suspicion.

"Shit!"

It became painful. I was being pulled apart, little piece by little piece, and I wouldn't be able to resist much longer. I kicked off my boots, remembering with a thrill of fear the last time I'd been forced to abandon my footwear. My poor cowboy boots were still out in the forest by Dawn's home, waiting to be rescued. I tucked this pair behind a tree and added my sweatshirt and jeans. Abruptly, my corporeal form disintegrated. My underwear dropped.

In my native form, colourless and almost invisible, I was drawn by the siren call that vibrated my essence and imparted pleasure and pain in equal measure. I've been summoned a fair few times in the long distant past, and each experience has its own signature, wrought by the individual summoner. I got a strong impression that this one wanted to make a point, and it wasn't just that he could summon me at any time he chose.

Knowing that resistance was, indeed, futile, I ceased to struggle and allowed him to reel me in.

I came to the altar via the river, so it was unlikely the enthralled ladies would make a connection between the sprite manifesting before them and an erstwhile member of their group. It helped that in my native form I look nothing like my human self.

Rising from the water in all my naked glory, with my long hair writhing about my body, I scowled at my summoner.

Gordon, the druid priest.

It was what I'd suspected. Druids were the guardians of the old ways. The aromatic scent of thyme bathed me—the fragrance of his ancient magic.

A sudden thought shocked me, sending fluid ripples down my length. Thank the gods Liam hadn't suspected Gordon's skill! If he had, Liam would undoubtedly have found a way to steal the knowledge, and then no elemental would be safe.

I had to keep Liam ignorant. But how? Killing Gordon was out of the question. For one thing, he wasn't the only druid around. And for another, I respected the guy. Anyone who could put up with Saffron on an ongoing basis had to be a saint. And I didn't think that choice would go down well with Dawn, either. I needed to give the question some serious consideration, but first I needed to deal with the immediate situation.

"Behold!" cried Saffron, her round face alight with an almost religious fervour. "Our goddess is come to us!"

And the triumphant smile she bestowed upon Rhona's group said it all. That's why they'd been invited—to witness the ultimate in coven one-upmanship!

I'd just become Saffron's status symbol.

If I could have groaned, I would have. Damn my natural shape for having no vocal ability. I could think of all sorts of things I wanted to say, none of which she'd have enjoyed hearing.

As it was, all I could do was to hang there with my feet anchored to the stream at the base of Gordon's altar. Until he chose to release me, I was stuck.

I glanced at Saffron's ladies, peering through my twisting locks. Mary had a knowing smile on her face, while Dawn and Alison were as shocked as the rest of them, jaws gaping and eyes wide. I suspected that a couple of the more staid members would have bolted if their shaking limbs could have been persuaded to carry them.

Rhona's girls were plain stunned.

"We are honoured by your presence, divine one," Saffron intoned. "How may we serve you?"

<By cutting the crap and letting me leave?>

I've never been 'divine'. The coven had nothing I wanted, nor did I have anything to offer them other than scathing words—if I could have uttered them. This silly woman was making an ass of herself. I spun round to glare at Gordon. He purported to love Saffron; how could he let her make such an idiot of herself in front of all these people?

Gordon stared impassively back in the face of my anger, and revelation rocked me: the only person who thought Saffron daft was me. Both sets of coven members were impressed beyond measure, even if Rhona's were sour about it.

Looking across at Dawn, I could see that even she was amazed, although I'm sure she realised that the power behind the summoning was her father's. Not a one of them appreciated how crass this all seemed to me, because none of them had ever been in this situation before.

I had.

Back then I'd let it go to my head, and believed my worshippers when they told me I was beautiful and wonderful and divine. Some of them had paid the ultimate price in the pyres of Christianity, and I'd been powerless to save them.

That wasn't going to happen these days, but I didn't want to be worshipped; I wasn't worth it. Yesterday had proven that. I'd failed Euan in an unforgivable way that I had yet to fully comprehend. If I couldn't manage my own affairs, what use was I to anyone else?

"Speak to us, heavenly one. Grace us with your wisdom."

Saffron's voice nagged at me. I tried shrugging at Gordon, opening and closing my voiceless mouth and shaking my head in the hope he could be persuaded to let me go.

Saffron had the glory and approbation of her own coven, and her victory over Rhona. Wasn't that enough?

Gordon wagged his head, a stubborn smile etched onto his face. He wasn't going to give in.

Impasse. If I didn't give Saffron what she wanted, I was going nowhere.

How long could we play this game, I wondered. Although the summoning spell could hold me indefinitely, at some point the ladies would grow cold, hungry, or plain bored if I did nothing. Then he would let me go.

Wouldn't he?

"Time for lunch I think, my dear," Gordon announced. "It seems our esteemed spirit requires time to ponder her answer."

And without further ado, he set about unpacking a small camping stove from his backpack.

Keeping half a wary eye on me, Saffron and some of the other ladies took out wrapped bundles and proceeded to put together the birthday feast, complete with cake and napkins. I watched in astonishment.

Hunger wasn't going to be an issue, then.

Both covens settled down then to their jolly little revel, with me presiding like a life-size blow up doll at a sex party. A few untrusting glances came my way, but after a while they started to ignore me. I guess that after the first shock, I wasn't that exciting.

I did notice Dawn and Alison backtrack through the woods for a bit. Searching for me, I assumed, but they didn't try very hard and returned quite soon. I was both relieved and miffed.

As lunch wore on, my thoughts ranged ahead. I needed to be out of here before dark, to keep an eye on Alastair. The vampire struck me as quite resourceful, and if he found a way to get to Liam, I wasn't certain who would survive the encounter. I was also worried about Euan's whereabouts. If he threw his lot in with Liam, he might get himself killed right along with the magician.

I had to get out of here.

"All you have to do is say a few words."

For a moment I thought it was my conscience speaking, but I turned my head to find Gordon beside me, watching indulgently as his wife held court over the picnic. She was visibly high on the adoration of her own ladies, and positively preening under the resentful Gothic glares.

I screwed my face into what I hoped was a pleading look. I must have been successful, I think, but it wasn't enough to sway Gordon. He shook his head.

"Sorry, but that's the deal. You only need to say a few words, and I'd take it as a favour if you were polite. Saffron's been dreaming of this day ever since Rhona split away from us to form her own coven, and I'd hate for you to spoil it. Remember, good manners cost nothing, and until you make her happy—" He shrugged. "I don't mind how long we stay here."

Hm. Finding a way out was looking less promising by the minute. Perhaps I should give him what he wanted. What harm could it do?

I nodded grudgingly.

"Ladies!" Gordon called for attention. "It seems our guest has found her voice."

Wondering what on earth I was going to say, I drew myself into a more solid form and concentrated on creating the features of a woman I'd been a couple of centuries earlier.

As I opened my mouth to proclaim a benediction upon Saffron's coven, the smell of thyme wove itself through me. My carefully chosen words died before birth as disbelief blanked every face before me. What had Gordon's spell done?

I stared uncomprehending for an icy moment. And then I saw the answer reflected in the wide, shocked eyes before me.

Cassie Lake's mortified features sat upon a disembodied head, framed by translucent floating hair.

19. LOSS

"Cassie?"

Alison's voice squeaked into the silence. Our eyes met, and I knew I'd lost another friend. With one last anguished look, she turned and bolted.

Dawn, in turn, cast me such a glance as would have flayed me to the bone, if that had been a physical possibility. Holding my gaze long enough to be certain she'd made her point, she spun away to follow my distraught former best friend.

I turned on Gordon.

"Why?" I hissed. It came out a bit like a kettle reaching the boil, and that suited my mood to a tee. "I was doing what you asked. Wasn't that enough?"

The druid priest met my anger with calm rationality.

"What I asked, yes. But still with deceitful intent."

"What did it matter if I used another face?" I raged, not caring what the ladies thought of me. Maybe Rhona's coven wouldn't be quite so in awe of Saffron's coup now. "You have no idea what you've done to me!"

Gordon scowled. His usual bland, easy-going features transformed into something far more awesome. "I've given you a taste of honesty, sprite. Something apparently lacking in your concept of humanity." His deep voice resonated with the rumble of the nearby waterfall. "You deliberately misled my daughter as to your true nature. That was unnecessary and unkind."

I couldn't disagree with him.

"I didn't think it would matter," I pleaded. "I never expected her to find out."

Gordon gazed at me with disgust-tinged compassion—expressions that mixed about as well as oil and water.

"In all your millennia, sprite, have you *still* not worked it out? Truth *matters*."

<*So everyone keeps telling me*>

It didn't seem to have done me much good yet.

"I knew there was something strange about you!"

I turned to face my latest accuser. Mary, the bob-haired Cleopatra-lookalike. Her face was flushed with success. So she'd noticed something strange. Bully for her.

It was the final droplet that burst the dam. I ditched my human restraints and hissed at her. A spout of water shot from my lips and knocked her to the ground. My version of a water cannon. She sat there, soaked to the skin and gasping with shock.

"Enough!" Gordon commanded. I found myself encased in a force bubble that was scarily like the one Liam had used to contain me. Shaking with fear and anger, I subsided.

"Sprite, I know you aren't evil," said Gordon for my ears alone; the others were helping Mary back to her feet. "On the other hand, you still have a long way to go to understand and truly pass for human. Is that your desire?"

Right now, I wasn't so sure. Humans can be such complicated and contradictory creatures. Did I want to be like that?

Trouble was, I did. Humans experience the world in much richer texture than elementals. I didn't think I could go back now to what I'd been before. Pouting, I nodded.

"Then make a start, and apologise to Mary."

Shame-faced, I nodded. "Would you let me down, please?"

"Of course. You only had to ask nicely."

My container vanished, and with it the spell that held me chained to the altar. I stepped onto dry land and pulled myself into full human form, complete with clothing so as not to shock the ladies any further. Both covens turned as one to face me. They all looked a trifle nervous.

I hung my head. "Mary, I'm sorry. That was unforgivably rude."

Dripping as she was, it was hard for Mary to look dignified, and yet she did. I wasn't sure I could have done as well.

"Apology accepted," she said. "On one condition."

"Name it."

She shivered. "Find a way to make me dry again, please?"

"Of course."

I stepped towards her, noticing with sadness how the others shrank away. I'd never set out with the intention of scaring anyone.

Saffron stepped between us, eyes a touch wild but her chin raised defiantly. "Are you sure this is safe?" she asked, looking at Gordon.

"Yes, my dear, I am. Cassie's not a malicious spirit, just an unwise one."

Unwise. Yes, that described me well.

Saffron stepped aside, and I reached a hand out to touch Mary, withdrawing the excess water from her skin and clothing. She held herself rigid, and it was a second or two before she realised that she was no longer wet.

"Well!" she said. "That's much better."

"I'm sorry," I muttered again, before turning my back and walking away.

No one made a move to follow me.

***

I trudged back to where I'd left my clothes. Now I'd so royally screwed things up with Dawn and the coven, I doubted I'd get the chance to claim back my favourite cowboy boots and I wasn't about to lose another pair.

What I hadn't reckoned on was coming face to face with Alison and Dawn. They must have found my not-so-secretly hidden garments and decided to make a stand there.

I hesitated, not sure what to say.

"Why?" said Alison. Just the one word.

That was one word more than I had for answer. Excuses and explanations didn't seem to be working for me, so I fell back on my old habit of waiting for the other party to speak first. It occurred to me that silence might reflect as badly on me as trying to talk my way out of things, but I felt so battered that I couldn't seem to force myself into action.

Dawn stood mutely beside Alison, much as I had during some of Alison's more heated exchanges with Simon. Dawn had known I was hiding the truth of my nature from my best friend, and I could have dropped her in it with Alison if I'd been the vindictive type. I'm not, though, so that secret would remain between us.

"Why did you do it, Cassie? I thought I was your friend!"

"You *are* my friend," I tried.

Alison shook her head, strands of red hair whipping about her face like autumn leaves in a gale. "Friends don't keep secrets like that!" she yelled at me. "You promised me! You swore you'd never keep secrets from me. You're no different to Simon!"

Ouch. That was as bad as it could get in Alison's books.

I made one last attempt to save things. "Ali, I'm sorry! I was scared that if you knew what I really was, it would frighten you away! Please believe me, I never meant to hurt you."

"You never meant to tell me either, did you? You know, I might not understand it, but I can accept *what* you are. What I can't forgive are your lies! True friends don't treat each other like that." She shook her head again.

"I don't know you," she said. "I've *never* known you."

Eyes shining with tears, Alison strode past me, returning to the coven. I made no move to stop her. Dawn followed a few steps behind. She said nothing; she didn't need to.

My deception, no matter how well intentioned, had indeed caught up with me as Dawn had predicted.

Numbly, I picked up my clothes and walked away, heading back to the car park by the long route.

I don't remember anything about the drive home. It was starting to be a habit, driving on autopilot. As well the Scottish back roads are so devoid of traffic.

I do remember slamming the door and throwing my discarded pile of clothes into the dressing room laundry basket, which erupted with furious chattering.

"Oh Minkie, I'm sorry. Perhaps you should try sleeping somewhere else."

I plonked morosely down on a kitchen chair, and wondered what to do. It didn't look like I'd be talking with Alison any time soon, if ever, and Euan wasn't likely to appear again if I'd read things right. I fretted over that, hating the uncertainty of not knowing if he was safe. Before the advent of Liam it had never occurred to me to even question where Euan was, but now everything was different.

Minkie hopped onto my lap and curled up like a cat. I stroked his plush fur absently while considering what to do with my sorry self. Burnt out on the emotions thing, I found myself considering practicalities. I was starting to run low on DNA and there were no more selkie donations in the offing. Before, if Euan had been a no-show for any length of time, I would go out and find a willing contributor. Now, for some reason I failed to fathom, I couldn't bring myself to do it; it would feel like betrayal. Stupid, untrue and totally impractical, but there it was.

My human learning curve was arcing faster than I could assimilate.

Minkie slid out from beneath my fingers and dropped to the floor.

"You don't want my company either, is that it?"

His beady eyes peered up at me, and I swear there was an admonishment in that gaze. He turned and stalked out of the kitchen.

I heaved a very human sigh and stood up to follow. I'd noticed earlier that the utility door was shut, and if Minkie needed the litter tray I figured I'd better let him in. He stalked down the hallway ahead of me and stopped outside the closed door.

"How did you manage to get yourself shut out?"

The answer presented itself immediately I opened the door. The room was in utter disarray. Clean laundry and towels were jumbled with dirty. The ironing board, brooms and vacuum lay on their sides. And my precious packets of skin cells—my reserve DNA—which I'd taken such care to order by date, were scattered throughout the chaos.

"What did you *do*?"

For the first time I wondered what had possessed me to offer Minkie a home. Memory of his arrival surfaced, and I pictured him bouncing around the room. He probably hadn't fallen into the flip top bin this time, just contented himself with trashing the place. Heaving another one of those sighs, I set about clearing up the mess. Minkie ignored me, sitting on the work surface, preening his fur.

Finally it was done. Ticking myself off for not taking time to label the packets of skin cells, I tossed them wholesale into a box. It wasn't crucial, but the quality did deteriorate over time, and I liked to use the oldest first. I'd probably utilize most of them in the next few weeks, and I could start afresh with a more sensible system in case Minkie decided to pull this little stunt again.

He chose that moment to stand up and stretch, revealing a stray packet he'd been using as a seat warmer.

"Are you quite finished with creating work for me?"

Oh well, I needed to top up; his pre-warmed packet would do. I unsealed the top and tipped the contents down my throat. I daresay a real human would have choked, but I have no problem with lubrication. Ever.

For some reason Minkie looked inordinately pleased with himself, and marched back out of the utility without using the tray. I took care to wedge the door open, in case he should change his mind, and composed myself again to face that 'what should I do now' moment.

I was saved by my phone.

"Alastair's found us a witch."

"Gloria? What, where?" I went cold, wondering who the vampire had enlisted.

"Meet us at the old power station just after sundown."

"Okay. But what about Liam-watching?"

"He's in his workshop—did I tell you we'd found it? I guess I didn't get round to that. Anyway, once he's there he always stays at least six hours, so we have time."

"You can't be certain—" I began. I had serious misgivings about Gloria's judgement, but she never gave me a chance to finish.

"See you there," she said, and the phone went dead. I stared at it stupidly for a moment. Should I call her back and point out the folly of making assumptions about Liam's behaviour patterns?

Perhaps not.

With Liam in mind, I had a sudden brainwave. I knew his full name. I could do some speedy research. Perhaps I'd find something that might help me convince Euan of Liam's untrustworthiness, although I'd have to find the selkie first. I gulped down the rush of emotions that threatened to overwhelm me at thought of Euan, and sat down at my desk.

It had been a while since I'd fired up the laptop. As Euan had observed, electrical items and water sprites don't mix well. By fortune it booted fine and I typed Liam's name into Google.

Pages of references flashed onto my screen. Writers, newscasters, artists; Liam shared his name with a whole range of humanity. I added 'nuclear physicist' to his name and searched again.

There were several references to his appearances at energy summits. He had plenty to say and was quoted in several magazine and news articles. His qualifications were impressive, as was the fact that he'd graduated several years early from Surrey University. His graduate thesis was quoted numerous times.

Of more interest was an older feature I found three pages down; a news story that had run in several national papers. Aged thirteen, one of 'boy genius' Liam Oldman's experiments had blown up his house, killing his parents.

Apparently he hadn't learned his lesson.

I closed the laptop and headed off to meet Gloria and Alastair, my anxiety regarding Liam riding uncomfortably on my twitchy shoulders.

20. WYNTER

"What kept you?"

Gloria. Impatient as ever.

"It's only been dark a short while," I pointed out.

"Can we go now?" said Alastair. His ever-present hint of a sneer was more pronounced than usual, and he sounded on edge.

We climbed into our respective cars—Alastair was driving a Freelander this evening—and set out in a mini convoy. I became even more uneasy about this whole witch thing when I realised we were headed in the same direction I'd gone this morning. I had a sinking feeling about our destination, and I wasn't wrong.

We bumped along the rough road to the Plodda Falls car park, and then continued on down the logging track, pulling up at last by the ancient showman's caravan. Light spilled from the open door. A slender figure stood on the top step, outlined against the glow. Her features were garishly lit from beneath by a pile of flaming logs on the open ground in front of the van; a cook fire, I realised, by the spit suspended across the flames.

Tousled hair of indeterminate colour stood out from her head in a messy shock. I couldn't tell if she was young or old, but she looked haggard.

So this was the hedge witch. Looking at that hair I could understand where the 'hedge' part came from.

Alastair was first out of his car, moving a bit jerkily. I thought at first it might be an illusion brought about by the flickering light, but I had my doubts. Something wasn't quite right here.

I waited until Gloria had joined the vampire beside the camp fire before alighting from the Tiguan. I was glad I'd chosen the off-roader. If I needed to beat a hasty retreat up the rough track it was definitely the best option. I stopped short of the fire, maintaining a cautious distance. The witch stayed at the top of her steps.

"Cassie, meet WynterRain," said Gloria.

WynterRain. Yeah, right.

"Pleased to meet you, I'm sure," said the witch. Despite its lyrical Irish lilt, her voice was as rough as the rest of her. "I believe we almost met earlier today."

She'd noticed. I was under no illusion; she could see right through my human shape to the sprite beneath.

"Likewise." I kept it short, not confirming her supposition. Gloria already looked too interested for my liking, and I had no intention of relating my earlier humiliation.

"Wynter is going to help us with our little problem," said Gloria. "Aren't you, Wynter?"

Wynter glanced nervously towards Alastair, and I wondered what hold the vamp had over her.

Alastair maintained his silence. I stared at him in suspicion. He was quivering, the minute, rhythmic clenching of his fists visible in the firelight, and I wondered when he'd last fed.

Alarmed, I turned back to Wynter and found my answer. Even in the half light, the peculiar mixture of fear and desperate longing that twisted her face was unmistakeable.

Wynter was a vampire junkie.

"Oh, do get on with it," snapped Gloria. "We'll wait out here."

Neither of them needed a second invitation. Wynter started to turn back into her van, but Alastair was on her before she completed the move. He buried one fist in her untidy thatch of hair and yanked her head back. She uttered a little scream as his fangs sank into her neck, but there was no real protest in the sound, or fear.

Wynter moaned and squirmed in Alastair's arms. The vampire's body jerked sporadically, and loud suckling noises interrupted the quiet of the forest. It felt obscenely like watching someone being raped, yet their enjoyment was all too apparent.

I wondered what it must be like, to be so desperate for something that you were willing to surrender your whole self, mind, body and purpose to another's control. Was the pain worth the adrenalin rush and the aphrodisiac in the vamp saliva? Or was pain an integral part of the whole thing?

Wynter uttered a groan that rose to a shriek. Consumed by a bizarre envy for an experience I was never going to have, I averted my face.

To be stopped cold by the sight of Gloria, her eyes riveted to the unfolding performance. Flames reflected in glittering splendour across the surface of her eyes, and something even hotter writhed in their depths. Her perennial scorching scent over-rode even the smell of the burning logs.

It was my turn to gasp. This time in recognition of my utter blindness.

Alastair was Gloria's lover. It was so plain I couldn't believe I'd missed it before. Pain stabbed through me. It had never occurred to me that she might have a regular lover. How stupid was that? I'd been jealous watching her reel in those bums in the club, but this—this pierced me like betrayal.

Totally unreasonable, of course. Gloria had never said she was free, and if I was honest, I'd never asked. I wanted to think her relationship with Alastair was akin to mine with Euan—open and convenient. But I'd just had it proven to me that what I thought I'd had wasn't what I'd really had.

And now here I was facing reality yet again. Gloria loved Alastair. It was obvious, from the inferno seething inside her to the smoke now rising in a curtain around her. I wondered if she knew, any more than I had. Perhaps we elementals have become too good at deceiving ourselves.

It was too much; I had to get away. I spun around, reaching for the Tiguan's door handle, only to find myself confronting Gloria. I hadn't known she could move that fast.

"Going somewhere?" she asked. My hand dropped, and I shook my head. She stood dangerously close.

"Don't worry, they'll be finished soon," she assured me. "It's a very convenient arrangement for us all, and I don't mind watching; I find it quite a turn on. I had thought you might too."

She misunderstood my reason for leaving. Or did she? I was starting to realise that Gloria was quite the manipulator.

But I wanted things in the open.

"It's not that," I said, jerking my chin towards the clinch in the doorway. "I saw how you looked at Alastair."

"Oh." She sounded surprised. "That. You know, salamanders burn up DNA much faster than other elementals, and I found out some time ago that vampire DNA lasts longer than human. As I said, it's a convenient arrangement."

She wanted to shrug it off, but I wasn't so willing to let things go.

"And how long has this *arrangement* been going on?"

Gloria shrugged. "A couple of centuries, on and off. There were others before Alastair, but humans have an annoying tendency to stake them just when I get things organised, and then I have to find another. Alastair is the latest and before you ask, yes, he knows."

Somewhat mollified, I wondered if I'd misinterpreted what I'd seen, jumping to conclusions that paralleled my own miserable mistakes. I couldn't be sure.

I moved closer to the camp fire, opening up a safer distance between us. All I really wanted to do was take her in my arms and show her how much I wanted her, despite everything.

"So you don't actually need those low-life bums from the club?" I asked.

She shook her head, gold beads glittering in her hair like precious raindrops. "I don't need them, but I like to keep in practice."

"And she is good at it," Alastair spoke from right beside me. I jumped. His intention, I was sure.

"Wynter will be with us in a moment," he continued. "She's gone to clean up."

We settled into an awkward silence, waiting. In truth, Wynter didn't take too long, but now I was aware of the true relationship between my companions, even that short time felt too long.

"Sorry to keep you waiting," Wynter said, descending the van steps. As she moved into the firelight I got my first clear view of her. She wasn't young, but neither was she old. In her forties, I reckoned, but gaunt as a crone. I suspected that somewhere back in her distant past she'd been quite a beauty, but not for a long time now. Probably not since she'd discovered the dubious delights of being a vampire's snack.

"So, to business," said Alastair.

We settled around the fire, perching on some plastic barrels and the odd tree stump.

"You want me to get you past this magician's spell barrier, yes?" stated Wynter.

"That's the gist of it," Gloria confirmed. "Once we're past that, I think we can deal with him between the three of us."

"You may be right," said Wynter. "But you may also be wrong."

Alastair leaned forward. "You have another suggestion?"

Wynter shook her head. "No, but I want to make sure you know that once inside, you're on your own; nothing more I can do for you. Okay?"

"But you *can* get us in?" I asked, wanting to be clear.

"I think so, from what I've seen and smelled so far. It's going to take a bit of manipulation from the otherworld, but with you two to power the spell, it should be possible, for sure."

I liked the sound of this even less. "What do you mean?"

"Don't play coy, Cassie," said Gloria. "She knows what we are."

Nettled, I snapped back: "I never doubted that. It was the 'powering the spell' bit I want explaining before I agree to this plan of yours. And what's the 'otherworld'?"

"It's quite simple," said Wynter, ignoring the obvious tension between us. "You two are basically raw power, yes? Wild and nobody's to command, unless you agree to it. That's what's at the root of this whole mess, isn't it?"

Someone had explained rather more to Wynter about our situation than I was comfortable with. Had it been Alastair or Gloria, or even both of them?

Too late to worry about now.

"What exactly will this entail?" I plunged on.

Wynter shrugged. "Nothing that will affect you adversely, for sure, but I need to view things from the otherworld first, before I can work out the details."

"And the otherworld is—?"

"Another name for the astral plane. You understand what that is, yes?"

Somewhere I couldn't go, I knew that much. You had to be able to separate your spirit from your body, and I was all spirit, so I was stymied.

"I have a general idea."

Alastair stood. "Then all we need is to agree a time for this event to happen."

"Give me a day or so for research," said Wynter. "Tuesday night. Okay?"

"The sooner the better," said Gloria. I could feel the impatience radiating off her. Or perhaps it was waves of heat. As we both joined Alastair on our feet, I edged away from her. We were becoming hazardously familiar with physical proximity.

"Alastair?" Wynter made a question of his name.

"Tomorrow, ma Cherie. I promise."

I didn't need to ask.

As the last to arrive, my car was parked behind the others, blocking them in.

"I'll see you back, yes?" Wynter offered, and walked to my car with me. I climbed in. As I leaned over to shut the door, Wynter pressed a small piece of paper into my hand. Startled, I hesitated, but Wynter slammed the door, whacking the elbow I was too slow to retrieve. She gave a minute shake of her head before going to the back of the car to guide me out.

I drove home, picking obsessively at a tiny piece of loose leather trim on the steering wheel. What was on the paper?

Once our routes diverged, and I'd watched Gloria's and Alastair's headlights slip away into the distance, I stopped. By the light of my sat nav, I read Wynter's note.

'Something we should discuss in private. Come back tomorrow, alone.'

I crumpled the paper and stuffed it in a pocket.

What did the witch want? Something to do with today's earlier event? But why alone? Could it be something about Alastair? Or Gloria? My mind was in turmoil by the time I got home.

Home. Not much to come home to. I've always loved my home; the solitude, the way everything is arranged to my liking. Now it was a house without a heart.

Very poetic. Not.

Of course Minkie was still there, and he greeted me as boisterously as ever. But I missed Euan, and I was going to miss the long evening chats I often had with Alison on the phone. So much had changed and in so short a time.

I went over to the big house and cycled through the fountain a few times, then returned to the steading. Now what to do with myself?

The knock on my door was so unexpected I jumped right off the kitchen chair. Turning lights on as I went, I flung the front door open, hoping beyond hope it would be Euan come back to me.

Jock stood there. My neighbour Morag's husband. At first it crossed my mind that he was here with the eggs I'd asked for, but then I remembered that I'd already collected them. And one look at his face told me this wasn't a social call.

"What? Is it Morag? Is she alright?" I gabbled. People other than me could have misfortunes, I realised.

"D'ya still ha' tha' mink in a cage?" demanded Jock. Confused, I glanced over my shoulder, wondering where Minkie might be. Then I recalled I'd left him in the kitchen, tucking into a supper of fresh steak.

I looked back at Jock's glowering face, and decided this was one of those occasions when truth would be the worst possible option.

"Indeed I do," I said. "Is there a problem?"

"Aye, there's a problem. Chickens are all dead. Two eaten, rest ha' their necks bit through. Typical mink signs. Morag's outa her mind. Are ye sure it's still in there?"

"Jock!" I wasn't sure what shocked me more—that Morag's lovely 'girls' were all dead, or that Jock was accusing me of letting a mink loose this close to the chicken coops.

Minkie hadn't been out of the house since the day I'd fetched him home. Of that I was certain.

"Tha' critter's not a pet, lassie. It oughta be shot."

While I was sorry for their loss, I wasn't in the mood to be pushed around.

"I'm very sorry your chickens are dead, Jock, but my mink had nothing to do with it."

His shoulders drooped beneath his new waxed jacket; the birthday present I'd advised Morag to buy for him. I got the distinct impression he didn't believe me. He muttered beneath his breath and stomped away, not bothering to be courteous.

Even knowing I was right, I didn't blame him.

Now I was truly friendless.

21. OTHERWORLD

At first light, I climbed into the Tiguan and drove back to Wynter's caravan.

I called my clients and the gym en route, and left messages pleading sickness. It was the first time I'd ever done that, so I reckoned I was due. I simply couldn't wait any longer to find out what the hedge witch wanted.

She didn't look surprised when I knocked on her door.

"Come on in," she invited, shivering in the chill early morning air. Sleep hadn't improved her dishevelled look, and the brown striped blanket wrapped around her shoulders did nothing to disguise how thin she was.

The interior of the caravan was cluttered. Mostly the normal sort of ephemera that humans accumulate but, here and there, items defining Wynter's calling peeped out from under mundane things. A simple clay chalice rested on the table amid scattered magazines, a tall walking stick balanced precariously beside it. Bunches of drying herbs hung from the curtain rail, imparting a faint medicinal odour.

"Coffee?" she offered.

"No, thank you. Caffeine doesn't do anything for me."

"No," she said, walking the few steps to the kitchen area to put the kettle onto the gas hob. "I don't suppose it does. I, on the other hand, don't function without it."

I wasn't going to disagree with that. In the harsh morning light she looked even more worn-down than she had the night before. I daresay having pints of blood extracted on a regular basis didn't help. I wondered how she'd come to this, but didn't feel it would be polite to enquire.

Could I be learning some tact, at last?

Anyway, to business. "So, Wynter, what did you want to say to me?"

She turned and scrutinised me in silence, eyeing me up and down as if searching for something.

"You use human DNA to pattern your body, yes?"

I nodded. She knew rather more about elementals than the average human.

"Have you used anything different, recently?"

Was it prudent to answer her questions? I found myself too curious not to.

"I've used selkie DNA for some time; it seems to work as well."

The kettle whistled and she turned away, shaking her head.

"No, that's not it. I'm seeing something different, something I wouldn't expect."

"Can you give me a clue?"

To the best of my knowledge all of my skin cell donors were straightforward humans, and I hadn't taken any lovers other than Euan for a while.

<Oh Euan. Where are you?>

Tears threatened to fill my eyes. I tried to reabsorb them, but to my astonishment they trickled down my cheeks. They shouldn't *do* that, not without my permission. Whatever it was I'd taken in, presumably that 'something different' that Wynter was seeing, it was affecting my ability to control my human form.

My fists clenched, fingers digging claw-like into the cushion beneath me. If I didn't know how my body was going to behave, I might make a fatal miscalculation next time I faced Liam. And I was convinced that confrontation was inevitable, regardless of whatever Gloria and Alastair had in mind.

I found Wynter staring at me again, cup of coffee forgotten in her hands.

"Are you alright?" she asked, her voice full of compassion. I hardly knew this witch, but I did know she was a healer. It seemed she couldn't switch off her empathy, even when faced with a non-human.

"Fine," I lied. I wasn't *quite* ready to open up to a stranger.

She knew it too but didn't push. She went up in my estimation.

"Can we try an experiment?" she asked instead.

"What sort?" Experiments were seriously off my agenda right now.

Instead of giving a direct answer, Wynter made a soft cheeping noise. Along from where I sat, a large fur hat uncoiled itself and stretched out, displaying ferocious sets of teeth and claws. A huge pair of deep amber eyes stared me up and down lazily from the depths of plush tabby fur.

Not a hat at all. A Scottish wildcat.

"Meet Keeva, my familiar."

I was impressed. Wildcats are notoriously independent. For Wynter to have one living in her caravan, she must be of worth in Keeva's eyes.

"She's beautiful," I said. Keeva rewarded me with a deep rumble which emanated from the depths of her belly.

Wynter smiled. "She likes you. That's good, because we need her help."

"We do?"

This was getting weirder by the minute.

Wynter sat down beside Keeva and absently stroked her fur. "Cassie, you remember I talked about the Otherworld?"

I nodded.

"Well, I want to try taking you there."

"What?" It came out as a squeak.

Wynter transferred her touch from Keeva to my hand. I flinched at the feel of her warm flesh, and glanced away, embarrassed by my obvious fear in the face of magic.

Magic. I honestly don't understand it. People think of elementals as magical creatures, but we're not. Not really. We are as natural as, say, a Scottish wildcat. What we can do with our element, that's not magic; it's an integral part of *being* an elemental.

"Don't be scared, please?" said Wynter. "If we can do this, it'll prove my point, and if not, nothing will happen and no harm done."

"What point?" I asked. Pointedly.

Wynter leaned forward, so close now I could smell the scent of her gathering magic, herbs and pine, sweet and sharp all together.

"When I look at you, I see two beings, one inside the other, as if you're wearing a human skin. I've never seen anything like it."

I leaned back, away from her. "I don't understand."

She shook her head. "Nor do I, but I want to know if what I'm seeing is real, so I do."

"And if it is?"

"Then it means you have something no other elemental has: a soul."

Weirder and weirder. What would I be doing with a soul? Where on earth might I have acquired such a thing? And more to the point, what would I do with one?

I started to have serious doubts about Wynter's sanity.

"Now hold on a minute. Whilst I doubt I have a soul, why should I care anyway? It's not as if I could do anything with one, is it? I'm immortal already."

Wynter's brow drew down, hooding her eyes. "Good point. But that's not what I'm getting at." She sat down opposite me and took a deep gulp of coffee. "I'm really not getting things straight this morning. Too much buzzing through my mind, I suppose." She leaned closer. "Cassie. I know what happened to you yesterday. I *felt* it."

I didn't need to ask which of the many things that had happened yesterday she was referring to. Gordon's summoning had probably deafened the hedge witch.

"And?"

"If I'm right, I can help you do something unique; I can show you how to prevent it from ever happening again. You'd like that, wouldn't you?"

I blinked. Prevent a summoning? That was like suggesting you could prevent rain from falling, or the wind from blowing. Crazy. Crackpot.

But if Wynter *was* right, this might be the most valuable lesson I'd ever learn.

"How?"

"By going to the one place it can be blocked. The otherworld. Which, of course, is a place no elemental ought to be able to access, mm?"

Did I believe her? I wasn't convinced, but with the demoralising memory of Gordon's summoning fresh in my mind, it was tempting.

"Okaaaay," I said. "What, exactly, are you proposing?"

Wynter's face lit up. The true vocation of the hedge witch shone through her. She really, truly, wanted to help me. I could feel the eagerness radiating off her. Perhaps a bit too eager.

"First, let's see if you can get there. If you can, then I'll show you what to do. Ready?"

"I don't think—"

"Just look into Keeva's eyes."

Involuntarily, I glanced at the cat. Too late, I found I couldn't look away.

"That's it. Let her draw you in."

"I don't—"

"Relax. It won't hurt a bit."

I was drowning in Keeva's eyes. *Me!* A sprite. Drowning.

The wildcat's gaze held me, sucking me deeper and deeper until I was submerged in a rich amber glow. The cramped caravan disappeared. I swam in a tawny sea, striped with veins of deep orange. The striations aligned, hurtling towards a pinpoint in the distance. I slid along them without friction, moving ever faster until I was giddy with the motion.

Amber gave way to grey, and I came to rest on a rocky grey plain, shrouded in grey mist. I couldn't see more than two feet in front of me, but overhead, silver stars glittered in such profusion that the sky glowed.

A figure materialised beside me.

"Feck!" said Wynter's voice. "Oh feck!"

It took my stunned mind several moments to shudder into action. From her voice, I was forced to surmise that the figure beside me was Wynter. Nothing else would have given that away as this person claimed no more than the vaguest of similarities to the Wynter I knew.

Against the ubiquitous grey, she blazed a riot of colours. Hair of deepest russet, big green eyes, clad in purple and jade in a fashion that belonged to sixties flower power. Petite still, but rounded and shapely. I wondered if I was seeing her as she once was, or if this was how she imagined herself.

Curious at her stunned expression, I looked down. Even if I say so myself, I was quite something to behold. With floating, blurred edges and frothing blue, green and white ripples, I towered over Wynter, a colossal wave at the peak of breaking, ready to crash down at any instant and drown the insignificant human before me.

I'd made it to the otherworld in my truest, most primal form.

"Um, Cassie?" said the tiny human witch. "Can you make yourself a wee bit more normal? Please?"

Normal? To me, this was normal, but I could see her point.

"I can do that?" I queried, wondering how. The words came out a bit bubbly, but she got the gist.

"You can be anything you want here, just picture it inside your head. Or, um, wherever it is you do your thinking."

I considered for a moment, and when I opened my eyes—yes, this time I had eyes—Wynter's were on a level. Expecting to see Cassie Lake's figure I was somewhat bemused when I investigated to find I'd reverted to an earlier persona. Morven Uisce was my earliest attempt at presenting a human face to the world. Perhaps she was more truly me than any that came after. I knew that her wavy hair was pale, almost colourless, and that her figure was more willowy than Cassie's, but it occurred to me that she was the template for many of my incarnations.

Wynter didn't seem to find the change too startling. Morven looked more like Cassie than did the real world Wynter and the vivacious girl before me.

"Thanks," she said. "I was going to get a crick in the neck looking up at you, so I was."

"So does this mean you were right?"

She chewed on her bottom lip before answering. "I don't think so, no. Your natural form is nothing like I was expecting, and it didn't look like any soul I've ever seen. I'm not sure *what* you are."

I'm a *sprite*, was what I wanted to say. State the obvious. But I sort of understood what she meant. She'd seen something different in me, and we still hadn't pinned down what it was.

Something else for me to worry about.

I gazed around. "Why do you come here?" I asked, curious why anyone would want to visit such an uninviting place.

A faraway look misted Wynter's eyes. "To learn. To journey, and to meet people I will never meet in the flesh. From here you can connect with anywhere in the physical world, with anyone. I can join with others of my calling, drawn here from the farthest reaches of the globe."

Not much incentive for me; there would never be others of my kind here. Back then, to the only thing of interest to me in this drab place.

"So show me how to prevent a summoning."

"Okay, but I think you'll need a little practice at manipulating the ether first. Take a look around. What do you see?"

"Not much," I observed, casting my eyes around at the greyness. But even as I watched, the world transformed. Grass grew from the dusty soil. Emerald twinkling blades poked their tips between the grey rocks and then surpassed them, covering them until we stood in a brilliant meadow. Sunflower heads blossomed around us and tiny orchids peeked from between their stems. Wildflower pollen drifted around us, honey sweet, and tiny birds chirped in the distance.

The grey walls of mist receded and a bright ball of orange fire burst into light amidst the still-twinkling stars overhead. As far as I could see, the meadow stretched.

"Did you do that?" I asked Wynter in awe.

"No. She did." Wynter pointed to a sinuous low-slung form making its way across the meadow to join us. Keeva, the wildcat. Her tabby fur rippled in the strange light and she appeared even bigger than before.

Suddenly she pounced, like a kitten with a mouse. When her head lifted from the deep sward, a rabbit dangled from her jaws.

"Is that real?" I asked.

"What's real?" Wynter countered.

Good point.

"Try it for yourself," she suggested.

"What?"

"Patterning your world. Just use your imagination."

Did I have one? I wasn't too sure about that, but this seemed like a good time to find out. I shut my eyes and drew up a favourite memory. When I reopened them, we stood at the bottom of a loch with water swirling overhead, ruffled by an unseen breeze. Fish brushed past us, trout and salmon, and a pike glared at us from beneath the nearby overhanging bank. Perfect.

Wynter smiled with delight. It appeared she had no more need to breathe here than I did back in the real world. Keeva leapt after one of my fish, catching a juicy fat rainbow trout. Her deep rumble of pleasure stirred little eddies that tickled the underbellies of the still placid fish above her head.

A shadow fell across the surface.

Keeva flattened herself to the ground, ears plastered to her skull, fish forgotten in her mouth.

"Keep still!" Wynter hissed.

I didn't need urging. The shape up there was like nothing I'd ever seen, or ever wanted to see again. Bulky and amorphous, it bulged obscenely in places and dwindled to nothing in others. Even through the water, the blood-rust hue of its tegument was disgusting, and the sickly sweet smell of decomposing flesh made me gag.

Its huge, blobby head swung relentlessly from side to side in parody of a hunting dog. I knew with a deep certainty that I didn't wish to ever be its prey. A bulbous, blood-shot eye peered down at us through the crystal clear water, and for one nanosecond, locked gazes with me. My skin shuddered, threatening to peel itself away from my core. To the depth of my being I felt unclean.

Then it moved on. For long after the *thing*, whatever it was, had gone from sight, we three remained frozen in place.

Eventually I had to ask, "What *was* that?"

Wynter shuddered. Keeva sidled close to her, wrapping around her legs and Wynter splayed her fingers in the cat's deep fur. They both looked uneasy.

"I won't name it, no," she said. "That would be unwise. If you want a label, call it a hellhound. If it'd been hunting us, we'd be dead by now. But it wasn't, so don't worry. Feck!" She shivered again. "I think it's time we went home."

"But what about the summoning?"

"Oh, that's simple now you've had a go. If the druid does it again, get yourself here as fast as you can. I can't tell you exactly what you'll see; it's different for everyone. For me, it's a cone of concentric blue ripples. You'll be at the centre, being drawn towards the point. Assuming you see something like that, make a bubble around yourself big enough so you get stuck, or imagine something like a giant eraser and rub it out of existence. You'll come up with your own idea when you see it. Use your imagination and remember when you're here, you can make things appear or disappear at will."

"I can?" I was sceptical that it could be that simple.

"Well, yes. Mostly. Of course, if he realises what you've done he might be able to counter it, and then it's down to who's the stronger and quicker thinker."

"How do I get here, without Keeva?"

"Keeva says you have your own familiar. A mink?"

I shook my head. "He's Liam's, not mine."

Wynter smiled. "I think you might find otherwise. Try giving him a chance."

My little spy. I'd have to think about that. But for now, I filed the information away in my mind, hoping against hope that I would never need to use it.

Returning involved picturing the empty husk I'd left in Wynter's caravan and mentally pouring myself back into it. This was, of course, the Cassie shell. I wondered if it was because Cassie was still in existence back here, albeit in husk form, that my Morven persona had appeared in the otherworld.

Worryingly, I now had more questions than before. Wynter had no explanation as to why I even *had* a shell, so although I'd had instruction in how to avoid being summoned again, I left her caravan even more disturbed than when I'd arrived.

Recalling the hellhound didn't help, either. It had noticed me, no question about it. That it had allowed me to know this meant I would be seeing it again. I had no idea how I knew this, but I did. And it was not a meeting I contemplated with relish.

As I drove, I picked viciously at an annoying loose thread on my cuff. Between worrying at my sleeve I channel hopped, trying to find something interesting on the radio to distract me. Then I checked my phone for messages. Nothing.

I'd cleared my day's work, but it was still early. Back before I'd lived as a human I wouldn't have cared. I'd have slipped into a nice little stream somewhere and floated a month or two away. A hollow feeling inside forced me to contemplate the likelihood that I would never be able to settle back into my old life.

I needed to *do* something.

I stopped the car, picked up my phone and called Gloria. I barely waited for her to answer.

"Where are you?"

"Watching Liam's workshop," she answered, not sounding at all surprised to hear me. "Do you want to join me?"

"Yes," I said. This whole situation was driving me crazy. I needed it finished yesterday.

Gloria gave me directions. The workshop wasn't far from the site of Liam's mobile home, but instead of being back up into the hills, it sat right down on the edge of Loch Ness. I joined Gloria where she sat in the heather overlooking the anonymous building from a safe distance. Small clouds scudded over the sun, breaking the light into brief flashes of brightness. At least it wasn't going to rain anytime soon.

"He's in there?"

Gloria favoured me with a sideways look. "You think I'd be sitting here if he wasn't?"

"Fair point," I conceded. Why did I *still* come out with such inane comments when I was around Gloria? Even knowing that she'd been going steady with Alastair for the past couple hundred years, I wasn't ready to acknowledge that what I yearned for was doomed not to happen.

Never mind the potential for blowing up Scotland.

"Do you know what he's up to?

At least that sounded a *bit* more intelligent. Gloria shook her head and her cornrows bounced across her smooth, bare shoulders. She was dressed rather inappropriately for the time of year, in a skinny vest top and shorts, but it wasn't as if she was going to feel the cold. All that naked flesh made me gulp.

Of their own volition, my eyes followed the smooth curves of her calves and on, up her toned thighs to where the arc of her buttocks vanished beneath denim. I tugged at the zip neck of my fleece.

"I don't give a shit what he's doing," said Gloria. "I want to kill him."

Direct. And worrying. For a nasty moment I thought she was going to march down the hillside and confront Liam right away.

"Not long now," I soothed, wondering how the hell I was going to prevent this whole situation from spiralling out of control. I wanted it over, yes, but I didn't want anyone to die and I *still* didn't know where Euan had gone; he might even be down there with Liam. The magician had the right ideas but the wrong way of going about things. Could I talk him out of his plans? Get him to give up his hold on Euan and leave?

Or should I try talking Gloria around?

By the fierce glint in her eyes, I might as well have been attempting to hold back a wildfire with a hosepipe.

"I've had enough of this!"

Gloria surged to her feet.

"Wait! Please! Gloria, you can't do this!"

I was upright, standing below her on the hill, hands held out as if I could physically stop her.

<*Fool*>

"Get out of my way, Cassie. How's he going to escape if I set fire to that building? He can go straight to hell!"

I backed down the hill, panic rising, staying barely in front of her. "He'll have magical wards, like before. Don't *do* this, Gloria! All that planning and you're going to throw it away? You'll get caught again; do you want that?"

Her face closed down to a mask of fury. Reminding her that Liam had caught her before had been stupid. She was a salamander, after all—flame up first and think later. It tended to get them what they wanted.

This once, though, I didn't think it would.

Gloria feinted left, then right. I flowed from side to side, always staying between her and the unsuspecting mortal in his workshop below. Any moment now, Gloria would take to the skies and I would never catch her. I had to create a distraction, get her to stop and think.

I bent, reaching for a lump of rock to throw, just as she lunged that way. She managed to stop, teetering mere inches from my outstretched arm. Our faces were so close I could smell her furnace breath. Alarm shone in both our eyes; mutual acknowledgement of our recklessness.

For a fraction of a second the world paused, caught in one of those freeze-frame moments from whence fate might tip one way or the other, with very differing outcomes.

The bushes behind Gloria parted and a lone red deer hurtled towards us. The hind twisted, trying to alter her trajectory, but her momentum was too great.

"*No!*" We screamed in unison as she slammed into Gloria's shoulder.

Time seemed to decelerate as the deer galloped on, and I
watched Gloria fall towards me in slow-motion. I retracted my arm
as fast as I could.

Not fast enough.

The shock when we collided was like nothing I'd ever imagined.
But it *wasn't* catastrophic.

We tumbled down the hill together in a ball of flailing arms and
legs, so stunned that we simply allowed gravity to take us. When we
fetched up at the bottom of the hill a few hundred metres from
Liam's workshop, we sat motionless, staring at each other.

"What?"

"How?"

I shook my head, wondering why it didn't fly off, or explode or
something. We shouldn't still *be* here.

Nor should Scotland.

"That," said Gloria, "should not have happened.

Understatement of the century. Or millennium.

I could *touch* Gloria. *Why* could I touch her?

Could I touch her again?

Without standing up, I shuffled backward away from her.

"You don't say." Shock made me sarcastic. "I don't think we
want to risk trying it again. Perhaps it's something to do with
Liam's spells."

Gloria's head swung back and forth, searching for the magician's
illusive magic. As if it could be seen.

Despite my suggestion, I couldn't smell any magic, but another
idea was germinating in my mind. One that I couldn't explain, but
the possibilities it opened up were staggering.

"Let's get out of here," I whispered. Last thing we needed was for
Liam to come out and find us neatly packaged together ready for
him to gather in.

It seemed our little escapade had knocked Gloria's previous
intentions clean out of her head.

"Okay," she agreed, and we scrambled back up the hill, keeping a safer buffer distance between us than we'd done of late. We kept on going past our point of collision, past where we'd sat and all the way back to the lay-by where our cars were parked. The empty road stretched out of sight in either direction. Our only witnesses were a pair of black grouse, and they were too interested in eating to be bothered by us.

"I think I know what happened," I said.

Gloria stared at me as if I was insane. Come to think of it, I probably was. Crazy idea.

If only I was right.

"I *think* I've ingested something magical, and it's formed a barrier around me."

Now I thought about it, I felt like I was wrapped in clingfilm. Not quite suffocating, but definitely encased. Perhaps that's what it was—magical clingfilm.

"Don't ask me what, I've no idea, but Wynter saw it last night, and this morning she took me on a trip to the otherworld. And that shouldn't be possible either."

Gloria eyes widened. Like any salamander, she had a need to be in control. That she was totally out of her depth here had her rattled.

"What? What do you think you've ingested? How can you *possibly* have gone to the otherworld? Elementals can't!" She was starting to look wild, and the smell of scorched earth wafted into my nostrils, heating me up. Muscles all over my body tautened. A sense of urgency filled me to bursting.

Then I did something I would never have contemplated doing with any other salamander.

But Gloria wasn't any salamander; she was the salamander of my dreams.

I held out a hand. "Touch me."

She recoiled.

Now she worried about safety?

"Are you insane?"

"Possibly," I agreed. "But it's you who's making me crazy."

Oh, dear gods! Even *I* cringed at that.

Gloria's expression changed then. Slowly, but it changed. Her face softened, and her eyes glinted. Her shoulders lifted in a minute shrug, fatalism written plain across her features.

"So," she said quietly, drawing out the single syllable into something that wrapped itself around us, cocooning us away from the real world.

I gulped. My nipples tightened until they were painful. As Gloria's fingers reached towards mine, I had that experience that I've read about so many times—countless eons of life flashed through my mind in a bright stream of memories.

Was this it? Were we about to complete Liam's theory, but without his safeguards?

I had a sudden, terrifying moment of guilt. This was not only *our* lives at stake if I was wrong. Even after the bizarre event on the hill, we might still be risking a whole country's future.

But I wanted her *so* much. I *needed* to know.

Gloria's fingertips touched mine. The same incredible shock—pain, ecstasy, and numbness all rolled into one—spilled over us. I could see it reflected in Gloria's eyes. And the intense desire it engendered.

"We can touch," she whispered, awed.

"We can," I confirmed. "We can."

She looked at me. I looked at her.

"This might not last..."

Gloria drew a body-shuddering breath. "Then let's not waste it."

Goose bumps rose all over me. "Not here," I said, glancing towards Liam's unseen workshop. My voice had deepened by a couple of octaves.

"Get in," Gloria ordered, almost wresting her car door off its hinges. For once, I didn't argue.

22. HEAT

The trip back into Inverness felt interminable. I fidgeted incessantly in my seat. I had no idea how long this magical state was going to last. And besides, my desire was crashing over me in unstoppable waves. I didn't know how long I *could* wait. I needed to be in Gloria's arms, skin against skin, exploring, teasing, loving.

The house she drove to was old, in a road of large granite buildings with gothic towers and crenellated rooflines, the gravel drive immaculate between close clipped lawns dotted with rhododendron bushes. Gloria stamped on the brake pedal and we skidded to a stop. Stone chips clattered in a spray against the steps that led up to the impressive portico entrance.

"This way," she instructed, hurrying along the side of the steps to the head of a narrow downward stairwell. Wisps of smoke trailed behind her and heat haze blurred my vision.

"Careful, love," I cautioned. "I don't know how much heat this shell can handle."

"Well, let's find out." She sounded as impatient as me.

A single bulb lit the dim passageway. Was this Gloria's house? If so, why were we going to the basement?

She pushed open a door at the end of the corridor and flicked on the light.

Oh no, not Gloria's house. Unless she rented out the cellar.

It was decked out like a porno studio, sans cameras. A huge mattress sprawled across the floor, dressed with black satin sheets. At one end of the room stood an old-fashioned set of stocks, and manacles hung from the wall. Piles of soft rope coiled in one corner, and a couple of riding crops leaned against the wall behind. There was also a washstand with a pristine white ceramic bowl, the shelf above stacked with neatly rolled bandages.

Nice.

I've tried some kinky stuff in my time, but this wasn't quite how I'd pictured my perfect consummation with Gloria.

In the far end of the room rested the owner of this cosy little boudoir. His black lacquer coffin lay on a large wooden bench, lid firmly shut.

Watching me take in my surroundings, Gloria smiled, flashing her teeth almost as if she, too, was a vampire.

"Don't mind Alastair. He won't be up for hours yet."

Not wanting to sound ingenuous, I fell back on flippancy.

"I'm sure it wouldn't be the first threesome you've have had down here, but where's your imagination?" I waved a hand vaguely towards the SM equipment. "Most of this stuff is pretty standard."

"*Ooh*, you surprise me again, sprite! Your sort is usually *so* straight laced." She pointed out a cupboard I hadn't noticed before, hidden behind the stocks. "We keep the special stuff in there. Want to see?"

This was not going how I'd planned. I shook my head and used the best excuse I had.

"Let's not waste time. We have no idea how long this thing is going to last. We might miss our chance altogether."

Gloria sighed, her smoky breath scorching my cheek.

"I suppose you're right," she agreed. "Pity, though. There are a few things we could have tried out that are impractical with a human. But hey, let's improvise."

She pointed towards the inviting spread of deep foam on the floor.

"Are you wearing real clothes?"

I nodded, mute. My legs started to tremble.

"Okay, strip!"

I almost lost cohesion, threatening to dissolve into a warm puddle. I like a strong woman. I ripped off my clothes to the soundtrack of tearing threads.

"Now, kneel."

Kneeling was not an option. I slithered onto one buttock, my feet tucked beneath me.

"Just stay there," Gloria hissed. I heard her move away and rummage in the cupboard. My pseudo heart beat rapidly against my ribs. A delicious shiver slid through me.

Gloria's footsteps returned, bare feet padding on the laminate floor. I started to turn, but one sharp word froze me in place.

"Stay!"

What was I, a bitch? I opened my mouth to protest but fell silent as soft black cloth whispered over my eyes and the lights went out. Well, not quite. I could just make out movement as Gloria passed in front of me again.

"But I want to *see*!" I protested.

"Perhaps I'll allow it," she teased. "Then again, perhaps not."

"But—"

Gloria tutted loudly. "You're not going to be wet about this now, are you?"

Wet.

Me?

For some reason this struck me as hilarious and I burst into giggles.

Something pressed against my shoulder, pushing me down to the mattress. I let myself fall back, still giggling. Whatever was touching me, it was soft and fluffy and I rubbed myself against it eagerly.

"Naughty," Gloria admonished. "Lie back and lie still."

I obeyed, yielding to taut anticipation. All around us loomed a profound absence of sound. Not even breathing. I imagined Alastair, lying in his coffin, viewing the proceedings via some weird, voyeuristic vampire sense. Something deep inside me clenched and a tiny gasp escaped my lips, booming into the silence.

I sucked in a breath and tasted sparks. The silence stretched.

Ghost sensations twitched randomly across my skin. When would Gloria touch me? Where? A moan of frustration rose in my throat and suddenly the soft and fluffy *something* pressed against my face, stopping my nose and mouth.

Despite my lack of need for oxygen, panic shot through me.

Before I could react, it moved, trailing down my throat, between my breasts and on down over my bare stomach. Feathers. Or fur. I wasn't certain which, but I didn't care as it tickled along my waist, back up my rib cage and then circled each breast in turn, brushing my areola. My whole body twitched, begging Gloria to get on and touch those places I yearned to be touched, but she kept on stroking. Down the outside of one leg; back up the inside. Across my ribs, my forehead, my shoulder.

I squirmed with increasing agitation. My fingers clutched at the sheets, rucking up handfuls of fabric.

A dark shape blotted out the little light that filtered through the blindfold, and I inhaled fire. Gloria's mouth closed over mine. Our tongues connected and we both jerked. For a frightening moment I thought she would back off. My hands whipped up, fingers tangling in her cornrows as I pulled her tighter to me. If the magic failed now, we would go out in a true blaze of glory. I wasn't about to miss this for anything.

Gloria's lips were scalding against mine. She tasted my mouth hungrily. Transferring one hand to her waist, I dragged her down onto me. The heat of her body was intense, burning like a reactor on the verge of meltdown. Without this amazing magical hide, I would have vaporised.

In a brief moment of coherent thought, I wondered about Gloria's human lovers. She must be supremely vigilant in her passion or she'd incinerate them, like she had her first, all those centuries ago. It was as well vampires healed fast; I'd bet Alastair had been singed a few times. But when could Gloria truly let go her passion?

My hand slid down her back to cup one rounded buttock and she groaned into my mouth. I wanted to see her, but when I moved to slip off the blindfold she slapped my hand away. My lips opened to protest, but a gasp erupted instead as her tongue seared a line of fire down my throat, all thought driven out as her teeth nipped my neck, my shoulder, my breast. That sliver of flame traced a burning pathway down my bare flesh, licked at my inner thigh and then, ah goddess! It slid inside me. A scream tore from my throat as we united in a way that was beyond even my dreams. Ecstasy swept through my body on the leading edge of a wave of wildfire.

My back arched, fingers clawing at the cool sheets. Hips lifted, twisted and jerked, but Gloria mouth stayed locked onto me, tongue driving further inside me than physically possible. For a human.

Why had I never done this before? Another sprite or even a sylph might have obliged. Would it have been the same?

The answer came in another surge of fire. No, nothing would ever match this, because it should never, ever have happened.

And we might be running out of time.

Ripping off the blindfold, I flinched in the blaze of light. I was being fucked by a flame; an intense, blazing miniature inferno.

Did I care? Not one bit.

I plunged my hands into the firestorm. Gloria's smooth brown body re-formed slowly, reluctantly. Her eyes flicked up at me even as her tongue licked up that most sensitive nub of flesh between my legs, and orgasm burst through me. Pulses of sensation swamped my mind, smothering coherent thought. I was on fire; I *was* fire.

My Gloria was truly glorious.

After an indeterminate time, I came back to my senses. Gloria lay alongside me, watching. She licked her lips. "That was novel," she said.

I was speechless for a time, my whole body vibrating.

But where fire burns hot and swift, water flows relentlessly. As the pulses of ecstasy swept through me at diminishing tempo, my mind began to function again. There might still be time.

Swinging upright, I straddled Gloria.

"My turn."

Gloria stretched luxuriously across the black sheets. Her divine body glowed—literally—with the aftermath of our love-making. The smell of charred fabric rose from the sheets beneath her, but the dark colour hid the scorch marks.

"Well that was fun," she said.

Fun.

Not the response I'd been hoping for. I replayed the last couple of hours. For me, exhilarating, exquisite or downright awesome would have covered it.

But *fun*?

My self-esteem plummeted. Was I that inept? None of my previous lovers had complained. In fact, I had distinct recollections of gushing complements. Surely they could not all have lied?

Perhaps salamanders did things differently.

I dragged my gaze away from the flowing curves of Gloria's magnificent nude body long enough to glance at the paraphernalia stashed at the other end of the room. Despite the thrilling pleasure *my* body remembered, it appeared I couldn't give Gloria what she desired. That stuff wasn't me.

I drew my knees up to my chest and hugged them, burying my face into my arms. Where had I gone wrong? I'd tried everything I could to make her love me, yet still it hadn't worked. It wasn't fair! I loved her so much, but my true love had never stood any more chance than a raindrop in a firestorm. Bitter disappointment stabbed me in the gut. I'd been deluding myself, trying to read into the small looks, the moments of interest, something that was never there.

Gloria didn't want *me*, she just wanted an experience.

I had no idea how this whole situation had been possible, but I knew deep down that we should never have taken advantage of it. How irresponsible we were! This spell, whatever it was, might have vanished at any moment, resulting in exactly the kind of explosion Liam was trying to engender.

Fools. Selfish fools. I had to get out of there.

Reaching behind me, I grabbed my clothes and pulled my t-shirt over my head.

"Going already?"

"Somebody should check on Liam," I said, muffling my wavering voice with my sweater. I was *not* going to cry in front of Gloria.

I would be strong; I would get through this.

My traitor hand reached out to touch her one more time, and her skin felt soft and feverish beneath my palm. Almost choking, I added, "Besides, we shouldn't push our luck; this bubble might burst at any moment."

"I suppose you're right," she said, stretching again, cat-like across the silken sheets. My throat slammed shut. "Although we could take a gamble,' she continued, staring at the innocent-looking cupboard. "I have a few ideas I'd like to try out."

That was all this was to her. A game. Not trusting myself to say anything further, I shook my head and finished dressing.

"Want a lift back to your car?" she offered into my silence.

"I'll take a cab," I said without looking round. I *couldn't* look round or I would tear my clothes off again and fall back into her arms. Resolutely, I trudged to the door and pulled it open. As soon as it had shut behind me, the bare passageway beyond echoed to the sound of my running feet, and I burst out at the top of the stairwell as if I had a vampire on my heels. I didn't stop running until I was three streets away and totally lost.

I stopped and leaned against a high brick wall. With my back to the cold stones I slithered to the ground, crumpling into a limp heap.

For the second time in as few days I started sobbing.

Why? Why was this happening to me? What had I ever done to deserve such heartbreak? At that moment I regretted ever trying to live as a human; it was too hard for a simple sprite. If I'd just withdrawn far enough into the mountains I could have avoided their dams and filtration systems, their sewage farms and domestic supplies.

I made a decision. Gloria could deal with Liam however she chose. I would go back to the house, free Minkie and close everything down. Then I would walk out of there, get as far away from human civilization as possible, and slip back into my natural element. I could feel a welcoming torpor washing over my limbs already.

As I fumbled in my pocket for my mobile phone, intending to call for a taxi, it rang.

I squinted through tears at the screen. Alison's name glowed there.

"Yes?" I answered in surprise. I hadn't expected to hear from Alison ever again. Not after our last parting.

"Um, Cassie?"

"Yes." Who else would she be expecting? Then my numb brain caught the quaver in her voice and I knew something was very wrong.

"What? What's happened?"

"I'm sorry to call you. I didn't know what else to do."

"It's okay. Tell me."

"It's Dawn. She's missing!"

"What do you mean, missing?"

"She was supposed to meet me at Tiso's for lunch, but she never showed."

Dawn had missed her lunch appointment. And I should care? I had more important things to attend to, like vanishing from civilisation.

"Maybe she got held up," I suggested, going into autopilot friend-support mode. Meanwhile, I'd dragged myself upright and proceeded to walk along the street looking for a road sign so I'd know where to get the taxi sent.

"But she'd have called," Alison protested.

"She could be out of signal. You know how it is in the Highlands, there's plenty of places you can't get a signal."

"Not between Drumnadrochit and Inverness."

"Well perhaps she went somewhere else first!" I was getting a bit peeved; why was Alison so upset about something that must have a simple explanation?

"No, she didn't, she was coming straight here from home, and Gordon says she left on time. There haven't been any accidents—I've checked with the police—so she's just *vanished!*"

That gave me pause. Where might Dawn have gone, driving along the side of Loch Ness, a road with no side turnings?

Not my problem, I decided, locating a street name at last. I wanted to call a taxi, and I needed Alison off the phone to do that.

"I'm sure she'll turn up. Unless she's been eaten by Nessie."

"Cassie!" Alison sounded shocked. "It's not funny. Saffron's already got the police looking, and Gordon's doing something arcane to try to locate her."

"Oh. Sorry. I thought she was just a bit late."

"Do you really think I would have called if she'd just been running late?" Alison sounded scathing, and I didn't much care for being on the receiving end. It wasn't as if *I'd* called *her*.

"Well I'm sorry, I can't help you."

"I shouldn't have called. Bye."

And the phone went dead. Although that was what I wanted at that moment, it left me feeling rather uneasy. When had I become so selfish?

But there was nothing I could do, lost somewhere in the Inverness back streets, so I went ahead and ordered the taxi. It didn't take long to arrive, and I didn't bother to watch the route as we drove through the city. It wasn't as if I was ever going back to that house.

Sunlight flickered through the swags of steel support cables as we crossed the Kessock Bridge, and my mind flashed in synch, flitting from one concern to the next. What did I need to do at the house? Where was Dawn? Or Euan? *How* had I been able to touch Gloria?

Gloria. Oh gods, I loved her.

I started weeping again, silently brushing tears from my cheeks. If this was what humans went through every time they thought they'd found love, why did they do it? I was more than ready to give it up.

But what could have happened to Dawn? Poor Alison had sounded distraught, and I could imagine what Gordon and Saffron were going through.

I shook my head. Sparkly tears flew against the cab window and streaked downward into oblivion, foreshadowing what I intended to do. Curiosity is a sprite trait, but guilt? Guilt is all human and I was having no more to do with it.

The back of my sleeve dried my cheeks quite effectively and I smiled as I paid the cabby. I was sad about Euan, but humanity and I were done. Decision made.

Entering the pump room, I set about shutting down the big house. None of the pumps were active at the time, but I wanted to be thorough. All the switches were off, and I pulled the mains lever which came over with a very final *snap*. The water supply stopcock was also located in the pump room, and after some struggling I wrestled it shut. After one last, long look around, I breathed in the familiar smell of grease mixed with the sharp tang of metal, then resolutely turned my back and left. For years now this room, of all the rooms in my big house, had supplied me with the comforts and necessities my faux-human life could not. And so, I would forsake that life and return to my natural state. No more worries, no more heartache.

And no more love, squeaked a tiny, traitor sliver of my mind.

"Enough!" I commanded, and scrunched across the gravel to the steading. I wanted no one to have cause to come looking for me, and I had a plan. I composed emails and texts, sending them to all my clients, and to the gym. I had to go away unexpectedly. Family business. Not sure when I would return.

There. Now no one would report me missing.

Not like Dawn.

"Stop it!" I snapped aloud. Guilt was a thing of the past. Like friends.

I grovelled under the sink to locate the steading's stopcock. My hair trailed through mouse droppings and the distinctive musty odour of rodent assailed my nostrils. Apparently a mink was not as much of a deterrent as a cat. Oh well, not my problem anymore.

That was starting to be a mantra for me, and it perched uneasily on my shoulders. I shrugged, trying to dislodge it. What next? Ah yes, the refrigerator.

The fridge yielded a mouldy lettuce and a couple of limp carrots left over from feeding the rabbits. Those went in the bin.

Note to self: remember to empty the bin.

Aside from that, all that remained was a couple of frozen packets of tripe intended for Minkie. Well, even if I was going to set him loose, I might as well feed him first. The plastic bowl for defrosting was in the sink, and I turned on the tap to rinse it. No water, of course. I wasn't going to rummage in the mouse droppings again, so I used the expedient solution of allowing my hand to liquefy. The sensation of scrubbing the bowl was interesting, but then so is stubbing your toe.

The microwave hummed to itself and I wondered where Minkie was. It was unlike him not to arrive the instant the meaty waft of tripe escaped the kitchen.

Even when the timer *pinged* and I took out the steaming bowl, he failed to put in an appearance. Puzzled now, I went looking for him, tripe bowl in hand. Knowing that his favourite haunt was the laundry pile, I headed for the utility. Sure enough, there he was, sitting on the counter.

"Not hungry?" I enquired. He gazed intently back.

"Fine!" I slapped the bowl onto the worktop beside him. "Help yourself. It's the last easy meal you're going to get."

That seemed to get through. He backed away from me, sidling towards the bowl. My heart sank; I'd never meant to frighten him.

"I'm sorry. I'm not in the mood for games. What's that you were guarding?"

For guarding he had been. Sitting on a clear plastic sachet. One of my skin cell packets.

Memory flickered. Was this what humans called déjà vu? Hadn't we had played this scene before?

Precisely this scene. Two days ago.

I picked up the empty packet and stared at it. My mouth dropped open as everything fell into place. Minkie trashing the utility room, sitting on that one very particular packet to hide it from my tidying until it was the only one left. The one I would use to replenish my low DNA as I'd already tossed the rest into a box.

I would never have used that particular packet if I'd indexed them properly. It was my most recent collection, from the towel that Dawn had used after washing my car to remove Liam's spell.

The reason I could enter the otherworld, and why I could touch Gloria without detonating.

True-witch DNA.

23. GUIDE

"*Who are you?*"

I studied Minkie warily. He stared back, whiskers trembling as he sat next to the untouched plate of meat. Perhaps a better question might have been *what* are you? Surely his manipulations were more than a mere animal should be capable of, familiar or no.

I frowned at him, crumpling my face as I pondered the puzzle wrapped in sleek brown fur. His black button eyes locked onto mine and I found myself staring down a dizzying tunnel which grew and expanded, pushing away the light. I slid towards it.

"No!" My squeak of protest was cut short as I was sucked in.

At least this time I knew what was happening. The difference was that Minkie's eyes were black. Keeva's tawny gaze had provided some colour to my passage, whereas now I fell into a black hole. To my relief, the giddiness of last time didn't recur, so perhaps there was something positive to having no visual input. I relaxed and was almost enjoying the ride when my attitude changed, and instead of falling I was careering along a horizontal tunnel without the benefit of headlights.

I was spewed out into the now-familiar amorphous grey landscape of the otherworld. Only it *wasn't* familiar. This time, instead of rocks and mist and stars, I was underground. Grey walls surrounded me and arched above my head. There was no apparent light source, and yet crystals gleamed in the walls and ceiling, glittering in imitation of the stars I'd expected to see. A heavy, loamy smell with salt overtones exuded from walls, floor and ceiling.

As I inspected my surroundings, I reached out a human hand to touch the wall. Glancing down, I found I'd arrived in my Morven Uisce guise. No mega wave form this time. No Minkie either. I'd assumed he would turn up as Keeva had, not long after me, but for now it appeared I was quite alone.

Okay, think. *Why* was I here?

Because I'd looked into Minkie's eyes. I'd done that loads of times without being launched on a trip to the otherworld. But then I hadn't been loaded with true-witch DNA before.

If I was right, and I was ninety nine percent certain that I was, Dawn's true-witch DNA was what formed my magical skin. With this miraculous substance on board I could leave a shell behind as an anchor in the normal world to guide my return, freeing my element to travel to the astral plane. Something that should have been impossible.

Like touching Gloria.

Shaking my head to dislodge an aching memory of smooth brown skin and the evocative aroma of scorched earth, I dug into my recollections of my first trip here. Wynter had said: *'from here you can connect with anywhere in the physical world'*, and, *'I can join with others of my calling, drawn here from the farthest reaches of the globe'*.

At the time it had seemed irrelevant to me. But what if, with Dawn's DNA in my system, I had a connection to the girl that could draw her spirit to this place and allow me to discover what had befallen her?

At the same time I wanted to understand Minkie's intention in all of this. After all, he had deliberately manoeuvred me into consuming that very particular packet of skin cells. Was he was still working for Liam? But that made no sense.

My head began to throb.

Well, nothing was going to get sorted by standing around, dithering. Glancing in each direction along the seemingly endless tunnel, I decided it was time to change my surroundings. I shut my eyes and built up a beautiful thought picture of a fresh mountain stream, sparkling water rushing over rapids that twisted and turned through a deep green, pine-scented, tree strewn glen. Idyllic.

My eyes opened on the same grey tunnel. I must have done something wrong.

I tried again. Same result.

Scanning the irregular and yet featureless walls, I shuddered. I was quite confident this was the otherworld, but this time I didn't seem able to influence it. It had the unnerving air of a prison, or perhaps a rat warren in a petting zoo, and I began to wonder who the keepers might be. I glanced over my shoulder, peering into the gloomy distance. It stretched undisturbed.

"Get a grip!" I said aloud, just to hear a voice. "No point standing here, is there?"

I plumped for one direction and started walking. After a bit I realised that the tunnel was taking a gentle curve to the right. Looking round, I had no idea if I could see back to where I'd arrived. Not that it mattered; there was no exit there.

As I walked, a dark blotch appeared in the centre of the tunnel ahead. I hesitated, and then shrugged. I needed to find *something* soon or I'd go mad. Pretty soon the shape resolved into a large rock with a person sitting on it. All I could make out was the outline of a masculine figure with a mop of thick, wavy brown hair brushing his shoulders.

The man—and I knew I was making an assumption that might prove false, but he *appeared* to be a man—turned his head towards me as I approached.

"What kept you?" he asked, his voice husky as though over-used.

I glanced over my shoulder but no, I was alone. He was talking to me.

"I'm sorry, do I know you?"

For some reason when I tried to focus on his face, my eyes slid away, down to his bare chest. Now *there* was a six-pack any of my clients would pay handsomely to possess. Below that, he appeared to be wearing some sort of skin-tight leggings. Nothing else. His feet were bare.

I tried again to look at his face, but my attempts were deflected in some way I didn't understand. I could study any part of his tightly muscled demi-god physique that I chose, except for his face. I shrugged, accepting for the moment that I was even more naive in the ways of the astral plane than I was back in the ordinary world.

"Would you like me to guide you?" he asked.

"What makes you think I need a guide?" Naive I might be. Stupid, not. Or at least I hoped that was true.

A mild snort of amusement came from the general direction of his face. Not being able to look directly at him was going to get on my nerves.

"Don't you?"

"Not one I didn't ask for, thank you," I said, and resumed my walk along the endless tunnel. As I passed him by, he slipped down off his perch and padded along behind me. I let it go at first, but after a bit it started to creep me out.

"What?" I demanded, spinning round to confront him. "Why are you following me?"

He shrugged. "What makes you think I'm following you?"

"Duh! You're walking right behind me."

"And where else would I walk?" he asked. "Unless you think I should have gone in the opposite direction?"

"That might be a start. Why don't you do that?"

"Do you want me to?"

I thought about it. He hadn't done anything threatening. Yet. Did I need a guide? Maybe.

"No," I said. "I suppose not. Not if you want to tag along."

I couldn't see if he smiled, but his shoulders relaxed. I hadn't noticed the tension in his muscles until then. Suddenly he became a friendlier figure, despite the odd distortion that masked his face.

"Is there somewhere you wish me to guide you?"

I laughed. "What, you're my guide but you don't know where I'm going?"

"Is it a requirement for a guide to also be a mind-reader?"

Touché. I reckoned it was about time I got serious. I had a missing friend to find.

"I'm looking for Dawn. Does that make sense to you?"

"You'd like me to take you to her?"

At about this point, I began to notice that my guide spoke always in questions. Curious. I was also forced to revise my original assumption about his voice, which was becoming softer, more melodious with use. Perhaps it hadn't been rough from overuse, rather from disuse. Which begged the question, how long had he been waiting for me?

"Yes, please," I answered. I'd worry about that little conundrum later.

Guide took the lead now, setting a pace that had me almost jogging to keep up. Damn, but those long legs in their slick leggings were a feast for the eyes.

Rein yourself in there, girl, I self-admonished. How many times of late had I ended up in trouble by letting attraction lead me astray? I wasn't even over Gloria—if I'd *ever* be over Gloria—and here I was, letting myself be distracted by a sexy pair of legs.

"Where are we?" I asked as we walked. "And why can't I change it?"

"Where did you want to be?"

Boy, this question thing was a pain.

"I just want to know why I can't make it change like I did before."

"Did you know that a stronger mind could over-rule yours?"

Uh ha. I'd had a nasty feeling that might be it.

"And whose mind is it making the decisions here?" I asked.

This time he kept silent, and I found that answer enough. This was *his* scenario, and that made *him* the stronger one here. Not a comforting thought. I wished he'd vanish.

"Arghh!"

His inarticulate yell accompanied a prodigious leap that landed him a good five metres further down the tunnel.

"What—"

I threw myself backward, away from the gaping chasm that had opened at my feet. Not until I was certain I wasn't going to slip into it did I look across the stretch of nothingness. My guide stood on the other side, shifting from foot to foot and wringing his hands.

"Why did you do that?" he called back to me.

Astonished, I pointed at myself. "Me? How did *I* do that? I thought yours was the stronger mind here?"

"Did it ever occur to you that what you *think* here might cause some physical manifestation?"

I stared down into the nothingness, then back across to where he stood on the other side. My jaw clenched. Guilty as charged. I'd wished for him to vanish. *Oops!*

"Sorry," I said. "I'll take more care what I think from here on in. Now how do I get across?"

He shrugged and turned away. Not quite the answer I was hoping for. Then I cottoned on. I imagined a solid stone floor where the hole was and, lo, it appeared.

I might not be able to change his overall scenario, but I could affect small details. Now *that* might be useful knowledge.

"What *is* this place?" I asked as I rejoined him.

"Ever heard of a sithen?"

That was *not* what I wanted to hear. A faery mound meant faeries, and the fey don't appreciate strangers in their territory. Then again, as this was my guide's otherworld construct, perhaps it came sans occupants.

"Why a sithen? Are you fey?"

Again, his silence testified for him. So I was being guided by a fey. At this point I gave up trying to figure out what was going on. I wanted to find Dawn and get the hell out of here.

After passing a few dark side turns, the sithen walls grew lighter. Brightness beckoned from up ahead. Thinking that perhaps we were going to exit the claustrophobic mound, I hurried forward only to have my hopes dashed. We were still inside, but the walls had melted into translucency. I blinked; it wasn't quite that simple.

Peering into the faceted walls, I saw landscape within landscape, hundreds of varied vistas refracting through the crystal. Like mirrors within mirrors, layer upon layer of ever diminishing scenes, but each view was different.

Impossible.

Stupid thing to think, considering where we were.

"Won't you take a closer look?" invited my guide.

Puzzled, I stepped closer and something tugged at my core.

"What—?"

"Why don't you follow your instincts?"

His constant questions were getting on my nerves, but this one made sense. The tugging drew me toward a dark patch on the wall. No scenery here, merely darkness. I knew without question that this was where Dawn was being held. My whole being confirmed it.

The crystal was cool to my touch. My palm pressed against it, fingers splayed.

"Shit!"

I jumped back into the centre of the tunnel. A ghostly palm pressed against the wall. *From the other side.*

Size perceptions didn't work in this reality, for the tiny facet of wall was not large enough to accommodate the flattened hand, and yet it did.

"Dawn?" I hurried to replace my hand.

"Cassie? Is that you?"

"Yes, it is. Dawn, where are you?"

"I don't know!" Her voice quavered. "It's dark and I don't know how I got here. Can you find me?"

My throat closed, and I swallowed. "I'm trying my best. So is Gordon. Can you tell me anything that might help?"

"He wants dad to do something. He says he'll let me go if he does, but I'm not sure I believe him. I have to, but I'm scared he might be lying."

"Who is *he*?" I was pretty certain I didn't need to ask, but I did anyway.

"Liam," she snuffled. "It's Liam. I told you he was dangerous."

Dawn's voice faded for a moment, before coming back, coloured with a tinge of suspicion. "Cassie, where are you?"

I glanced round at my guide, at the strange transparent chamber and its myriad panoramas. It was too weird, even for me.

"Don't you worry about that now, just think—is there anything you can tell me about where he's holding you? Can you touch anything, smell anything?"

"I'm tied up and I'm sitting on a mattress on the floor. It's hot and stuffy and there's a funny smell, like from one of those old gas fires, or something like an arc welder in a garage. I tried shouting, but I think the walls are soundproofed; it sort of bounces back at me."

I had a shrewd suspicion I knew where she was. In Liam's workshop, protected by layers of spells that prevented me from getting anywhere near her. Maybe Gordon could break through them. He might even be able to walk in there and back out again; Liam's spells were designed to keep out supernaturals, not humans.

I needed to get to Gordon, fast, before Liam moved her.

"That's great, Dawn. I think I know where you are. I'm going to get your dad."

"No!"

I had started to pull away but froze, startled by the single negative.

"Why not?" I asked.

"Because whatever it is that he wants Dad to do, it's got something to do with you."

Dawn's kidnap suddenly made awful sense. Liam was going to use her to force Gordon into summoning me. How Liam had discovered the druid's ability, I didn't know. What Liam didn't realise was that I had a means of blocking the summoning.

Stalemate.

Except that Dawn's life could be in the balance. Liam might have altruistic motives for his grand plan, but I was convinced that he would be ruthless in his pursuit of it. Whilst I didn't like to think he would hurt Dawn, I wasn't certain enough to take the gamble.

"Don't worry Dawn, I'll be careful. Hang tight and we'll get you out of there."

"Cassie?"

"Yes?"

"Don't take this the wrong way, but you're the last person I would have expected to care. Thank you."

I drew away then, unsure of what to say. Dawn's ghostly pale palm receded into blackness, although I could still feel her presence through the DNA bond we shared. I took a shaky breath.

Despite everything I'd told myself over the last few hours, and all the plans I'd made to wash my hands of the whole human experience I found that, after all, I did still care. No matter what had happened, Dawn was a friend and I wasn't about to turn my back on her. Ultimately Liam was to blame, but the whole mess was because of me, and Gordon and Dawn didn't deserve to suffer as a result.

I had to get back to the real world. Fast.

"I need to go. Do I do the same as last time?"

Guide's shoulders sagged. "Already? Can't you stay a bit longer?"

Suspicion flared, hot streaks running down my back. "Why? Why do you want me to stay?"

Give him some of his own back; answer a question with a question.

"Can't we get to know each other a bit better?"

Frustration hissed through my teeth. "Not now, I don't have time!"

His whole torso slumped, dejection radiating off him. I wondered again how long he had been sitting on that lump of rock, waiting for me. Knowing it was irrational, still I felt guilty.

"Look, I'll come back again, once this mess is straightened out. Okay?"

"You will?"

"As long as I'm able to, yes. I promise. But I have to go now, I'm sorry."

"Are you sure you know how to return here?"

That made me pause. At a guess I'd reckon on repeating the whole falling into Minkie's eyes thing. "Just like this time?" I asked to be sure.

His head bobbed up and down. My stomach roiled queasily as I tried to focus on the distortion that covered his face, and I had to glance away.

"Did you know you can do it remotely too?" he said.

"I can?" I reached out and grabbed his arm, wanting to shake the information out of him. His skin beneath my palm was smooth, like silk, and hot to the touch. This close to him I picked up a faint aroma that I couldn't identify right off; faintly musky, but with sweet overtones. I wanted to get closer, to bury my face against his chest and breathe him in. The urge was almost overpowering, but I suddenly remembered that he was fey, and I drew back, blinking as if waking from a dream.

"How?" I asked, taking a couple of steps backward, away from his seductive pull. He made no move to follow but stayed relaxed, his posture almost jaunty.

"Can you create a mental picture of your familiar's eyes?" he asked.

I nodded.

"Do you think you can expand them, make them big enough to swallow you?"

That simple? That I could do; no problem.

"Thank you, my friend," I said, and I meant it most sincerely. "What's your name?"

He hesitated, and for a moment I thought he was actually going to give me an answer, but no such luck.

"What would you like to call me?"

"Sheesh! I give up. Don't think you're going to keep up this question thing when I come back, or it might be a very short visit," I threatened. "For convenience I'll call you Michael. Is that okay?"

Michael nodded. A non-verbal answer was, at least, better than another question.

"Then that's settled. I have to go now—"

I stopped mid speech. Amongst all the myriad tiny little scenes of life captured within the sithen wall, one figure caught my eye. Why, I had no idea. I didn't know the person cresting the low rise, nor did I recognise the landscape, but I found it impossible to look away and, as I watched, the scene grew in size until it filled a large section of the wall.

Striding through the tussocks, his long sable locks spilled over his shoulders in a shining blue-black cascade that reached to his waist. Where Michael had the build of an athlete, this man was a body builder. And unlike Michael, I could see his face. Perfect proportions, chiselled jaw and deep, deep blue eyes, the sort you could swim in. In his scarlet sleeveless jerkin and leather trousers, he was a breath-taking sight.

I knew I was staring, but when Michael hissed behind me in what sounded like disapproval, my hackles rose. If the fey was not going to let me see his face, he wasn't going to stop me from looking at someone else, and this guy was worth the look. In fact, he was looking at *me*.

A momentary chill crawled up my spine, but turned to rushing heat as the gorgeous stranger winked at me.

"Don't you have somewhere you need to be?"

Annoyed—and guilty—I glanced round at Michael and when I looked back, the vision of masculine beauty was gone, the wall returned to normal proportions. But the stranger didn't need to be there for me to recall every detail of his exquisite face, nor the faint glow of the golden aura that had caressed his skin. I'd seen an angel, of that I was sure.

Had I acquired a guardian angel, along with all the other strange things that were coming my way?

I shrugged. Whatever was going on in this paranormal realm, and regardless of how it impacted my existence, right now I needed to get back to the physical world to rescue Dawn and prevent Liam from getting himself killed. And to see if I could repair any of the mess I'd made of my friendships.

They all deserved better from me.

24. WORKSHOP

Minkie was nowhere to be seen when I dropped back into my body. I guessed he was hiding out in case I wasn't too pleased with him for snagging me like that.

As it was, I didn't have time for remonstrations, and I'd learned so much that in fact I was grateful to the little beast. I dashed back to the kitchen and grabbed my phone. I didn't have a mobile number for Gordon, but I had his land line. I was about to call him when I hesitated, staring at my phone as if it had sprouted antennae.

Saffron had contacted the police. Alison had told me that. Suppose they were listening in? It didn't seem likely they would be taking things seriously so soon, but I could imagine Saffron being pretty demanding. If she'd got them thinking kidnap, any call I made to their house phone could be monitored. I wasn't about to let the local constabulary get caught up in things beyond their abilities. They had enough trouble keeping up with mundane crimes; they didn't need to add paranormal goings on to their workload.

What to do? I could drive out there, tell them in person, but that would take up time I wasn't certain we had. Resolution lodged in my stomach like a lead ball. I was going to have to rescue Dawn myself.

I stuffed my phone in a pocket and hurried outside, dismayed to find how much time had passed. Dark clouds were not the only reason for the gloom that pressed down like a sodden blanket thickening the air; late evening was fast turning into night. I skidded out of my driveway in the sleek little Audi, headlights blazing what I hoped would be sufficient warning for any wildlife out and about to scatter from my path. I tried hard not to think about Alastair waking in his basement. Was Gloria still there? The harder I tried not to think about her, the more images of our twined bodies fuzzed across my vision, blurred by welling tears. I tried to dash them away, tears and visions alike, but they steadfastly refused to be banished.

My fingers tightened on the steering wheel. What would happen if Gloria and Alastair moved against Liam tonight, before I rescued Dawn? They wouldn't be bothered about the life of one mortal, and if she was a distraction for Liam they would use her regardless of consequences.

And I *still* didn't know where Euan was.

My heart pounded against my ribs. What could I do to stop them? They would call me before making a move, wouldn't they? We'd planned this thing together for the three of us, with Wynter's assistance.

Wynter! She'd already demonstrated her empathy for me, and she sure as hell would be concerned for a fellow witch caught up in this mess. If I could get to her first, I could stall things or even use her spells to get in there and back out with Dawn before Liam knew what was going on.

I floored the accelerator. Not sensible on Highland roads, but I had no choice—Dawn's life might depend on it.

The poor Audi jounced and bounced down the rough track to Wynter's caravan, but in vain. The van stood cold and empty. Was she already at the workshop, getting set up to counter Liam's spells? Had Gloria and Alastair decided to go for it without me? My chest ceased to rise and fall. I was suffocating with panic as I drove with reckless abandon along the winding road back to Inverness and through the city centre. Rush hour was in full swing and I hammered the heels of my hands against the steering wheel in frustration until I hit the road that runs down the back of Loch Ness and left the impossible crush behind. I drove as fast as I could through Dores without knocking anyone over, and then floored the accelerator until I reached the lay-by nearest Liam's workshop.

A jolt like an electric shock ripped through me. Four cars sat there, quiet and abandoned. Gloria's, Alastair's and Wynter's ancient Land Rover, plus the Tiguan I'd left there when Gloria and I had—no! I wasn't going to think about that. Gasping like a fish in air I flung myself out of the Audi and across the road. I didn't even bother to try for stealth; I wanted them to hear me coming. This once I didn't care if I alerted Liam, I *had* to stop this!

I crashed through the bushes like a rutting stag but even so, I was too late. I fetched up behind Wynter, and beyond her I saw Alastair with a wisp of flame riding on his shoulder, slipping into the darkened building through a metal door.

"No" I screeched. Wynter's startled face swam past me as I lunged after them, but crashed to a halt against Liam's spell barrier.

"Cassie? What's going on?"

I spun to face her. "That's my line," I spat. "Why didn't you wait for me?"

Ashen-faced, Wynter took a step back. "But...they said you'd backed out, that you didn't want to do this. Alastair *lied* to me?"

"Wake up and smell the shit, woman! He's a *vampire*! Lying is part of his ethos. What? Did you think he wouldn't lie to you because you're a willing snack?"

I knew I was being harsh, but I was shaking with rage. How could they do this?

Dawn! I had to stop them.

"Open it up again." I pointed to the building. "I need to get down there."

Wynter gave a little shake of her head and I noticed then, even under the starlight that was our only illumination, that she was trembling.

"I don't think I can. I've used up all my strength."

"Wynter, please, you must try! There's a young girl down there, a witch like you, and she's going to end up dead if she's still there when they spring this on Liam."

Wynter's hands flew to her face. "No, that's not possible! They assured me no one else would get hurt!"

"And you believed them?"

I was starting to lose it. For all I knew, Liam might have Euan down there as well as Dawn, and if anybody died because of me I didn't think I'd be able to live with myself.

"Come on, Wynter, get a grip and get me in there!"

The witch fell to her knees, and for a horrible moment I thought she was going to blubber, but then I noticed the implements on the ground: a small cauldron, some pouches of who-knew-what. The remains of a fire.

Wynter's hands shook as she tried to re-kindle the fire. For one ironic moment, I wished for Gloria. She'd have lit the charred sticks in an instant.

A tiny puff of smoke wisped upward and Wynter sprinkled dried grass around it, blowing delicately as she coaxed the infant flame. I stopped breathing.

"Find something to burn!" she ordered, and I scanned the hillside, grateful my vision was not as poor as human eyesight in the gloom. I located a cluster of twigs beneath a sheltering gorse bush and scooped them up.

"This do?"

"It'll have to," Wynter said, and now I heard steel in her voice. She sounded well pissed off. Finding out that your lover is using you can have that effect.

She poured a portion of oil into the cauldron and set it on a tripod above the little fire. Then she emptied out the contents of her pouches, muttering as she did so. I didn't listen; I wanted nothing to do with human magic. I stared with laser beam eyes at the invisible spell shield, trying to burn a hole through it. The twined aromas of thyme and lavender swirled around me.

"Cassie, I need your help. Please?"

"What? You know I can't do magic."

She shook her head once. "I know. It's your energy I need. Remember I told you I could use your elemental force to power this spell. Although I'm not sure if I can do it again." She sounded frightened.

"But we're going to try, aren't we?" I found I was nodding my head animatedly up and down, like one of those executive toys some humans find amusing. Wynter's head began to bob in harmony.

"We are, although..."

"What? Wynter, come on! There are lives at stake!"

The witch blinked, her eyes far away for a moment before snapping back into scalpel-sharp focus.

"I have an idea, so I do."

My chest tightened. I wasn't keen to experience another of Wynter's ideas. She must have seen me flinch.

"Don't worry, it'll be easier than last time. I just need you to tap into a ley line. There's one runs the length of Loch Ness. It'll be much easier for me to convert that energy than yours; all you have to do is channel it to me. Yes?"

I wondered why I hadn't thought of it myself. Except that although I knew it was there, I had no idea how to 'tap into' it. If truth be told, I tended to avoid ley lines—their energy frequency put my teeth on edge, like a fingernail down a chalk board.

"I have no idea how to do that," I admitted.

"I'm guessing here," said Wynter, "but based on your ability to travel to the astral, I reckon you should be able to do this."

Suspicion flared. "Why can't you do it?"

She fed a few twigs to the flames before answering.

"Because I can't do it all. I need to speak the words and make the gestures to complete the counter-spell. Can you do that?"

"You know I can't."

"Then this bit is down to you, yes?"

Oh.

"What do I have to do?"

"Reach into the water. You can do that, can't you?"

"I'm a sprite, for gods' sakes!"

She shook her head. "That's not what I meant. Can you do it from here?"

"Oh. Yes, I can. And then?"

"You touch the ley line and you hold my hand. I should be able to draw the energy through you."

Through me. I wasn't convinced I liked the sound of that.

She must have noticed my hesitation.

"It'll be alright, Cassie, so it will. Think of that girl whose life is in danger, okay?"

I didn't much care for having Dawn's predicament thrown back in my face, but Wynter was right. If this enabled the spell, then I'd put up with being used as a power cable.

I grabbed her hand before I could change my mind. Her skin was cold and clammy, and I wondered how exhausted she really was. I hoped I wouldn't be sacrificing one life in an attempt to save another. She squeezed my fingers in encouragement.

I closed my eyes and reached into the dark waters below. My fluid fingers slid into the icy cold, questing for the ribbon of energy that pulsed along the deep, deep crevice at the base of the loch. Once, twice, something brushed against me. Fish? Or something else. I didn't have time to find out.

I felt the warning tingle of the ley line a scant moment before it zapped me. A few years ago, I'd touched an electric fence—this was like that only more so. Pain engulfed my fingers and crept agonizingly up my arm as I clung on with dogged determination. If this was the only way to provide Wynter with the power she needed to complete her spell, I wasn't going to let go. As the power reached my torso I could feel my whole body starting to vibrate. I tried to grit my teeth against the agony threatening to engulf me, but instead a strangled gasp escaped my lips.

I heard Wynter echo my cry. My whole body was rocking now with the violence of the current surging through it, but when I opened my eyes I realised that what had startled the witch wasn't the energy pouring from my hand to hers—it was that I'd lit up like a Christmas tree! For the first and only time in my life, I hoped, my body blazed bright as a beacon, illuminating our surroundings as if Wynter's little bonfire had burst into incandescence.

I prayed to the gods that there was no one around to see this extraordinary spectacle. We were well and truly exposed on the hillside above Liam's workshop. At least at this time of evening, boats on the loch were a rarity.

The pain level increased. My molecules were shaking themselves apart. I believe that if I hadn't been wrapped in the incredible magical skin formed from Dawn's true-witch DNA, I would have disintegrated.

I'd always suspected that avoiding ley lines was a good idea. Now I knew why.

A bright flash burst across my sight and the agony vanished so abruptly that, for an instant, I thought I must have exploded after all.

What would it be like, dying? When you're immortal it's not something you tend to waste time considering. Perhaps this was it: the lack of pain, of light, of any sensory input. Would I simply float around forever in this void, aware but unable to experience anything?

"Cassie? Cassie!"

But surely if I was dead, no one would be shouting at me?

I opened my eyes.

"Goddess be praised!"

Wynter hovered over me like a mother duck. "Feck, I'm sorry, I had no idea it would do that to you."

I groaned and tried to sit up. This was when I discovered I was laying full length on the heather.

"Next time you have an idea, leave me out of it, please?"

Wynter sat down beside me, breathing too hard. The acrid smell of burned herbs clung to her.

"Are you okay?" I asked, sitting up. I put one arm around the woman's thin shoulders. I rather liked the hedge witch and I didn't want her to die. I'd seen it before, a time or two. Witches who'd over-reached themselves. Of course, these days one expected them to be in better health, more robust. Pity a vampire-junkie didn't come into that category.

"I'll be fine," she said, waving her hands towards the dark looming bulk of the workshop. "Get in there while you can, okay?"

"It's down?"

"Yes, it's down, but I'm not sure for how long; it was no more than a minute or two last time, so go!"

I staggered to unsteady feet and stumbled forward. I held my breath as I passed the place where the barrier had been. Nothing happened. I glanced back at the crumpled form of the witch, sitting beside the smouldering remains of her fire. A sudden thought shot ice through my veins and I turned.

"How do we get back out?"

She made shooing motions. "It's a one way spell, you won't have any problem crossing it this way. Go. Save your friend."

Light flashed between us, like static. The barrier was back in place. Too late to back out now.

"Go!"

"I'm going!" I took one last look back at Wynter. "You sure you're alright?"

"I'll be fine, so I will."

I wasn't sure I believed her, but I had Dawn to think about, so I left her there, sitting on the hillside, and pushed my way through the undergrowth to the door I'd seen Gloria and Alastair use. I tugged the handle and the door swung open. If it had been locked earlier, it wasn't now. I slipped inside.

Liam's workshop was a converted agricultural building the size of a small warehouse. I could make out Gloria's and Alastair's voices, but not their words; the acoustics were dreadful.

Tiny pinpricks of colour gleamed from various places on the walls, reds and greens with the occasional blue. Electrical tell-tales, like those back in the old hydro station where this whole nightmare had begun. A shudder rippled across my shoulders.

Light blazed and I flinched, momentarily sure that Liam was responsible.

James Bond material I'm not.

"Cassie! You decided to join the party after all!"

Gloria's voice rang across the open floor space. She and Alastair stood by the far wall. Between us lay a giant replica of Liam's containment apparatus. Huge black cables in concentric rings snaked across the concrete floor, cradling a simple chalk-drawn circle in their centre. Even as I watched, Gloria touched one of the cables and it burst into flames.

"What are you doing?" I cried, my voice rising with incipient hysteria.

"What does it look like?"

"But—"

"No!" Fury crackled in that one word. Gloria wasn't going to listen to reason. She wasn't going to listen to *anything*. She'd gone into full fiery salamander fury and nothing I said now was going to stop her.

She pointed a finger at me. "You had your chance to find another way, and you didn't. We're going to do this *my* way now."

Gloria pointed a finger at a squat black box connecting two cables. Fire streaked from her hand like napalm from a flame thrower. The box exploded.

I needed to find Dawn. She had to be in one of the partitioned rooms I could see at the other end of the building. Attempting not to draw Gloria's attention, I started edging that way.

"Going somewhere?"

A shrill squeak escaped me as I jumped back. Alastair blocked my path.

"Alastair, there's a girl back there, an innocent human. Let me get her out of here."

Whoosh! Gouts of flame shot roof-ward as two more of the connecting boxes exploded.

"Sorry Cassie, I don't believe you. You've tried any number of times now to delay or derail what should be a simple matter of terminating an irritating problem."

He sounded anything but sorry. I didn't bother wasting words because at the basest level, he was right. That didn't negate the fact that I was telling the truth about Dawn. It just wasn't important to him. I tried to brush past him, but he moved with me.

"Sprite, you're not going anywhere."

More flames burst into vivid red life as Gloria continued her wrecking spree. I considered dropping cohesion to get around the vampire but paused, confused now as well as worried. What did Gloria hope to achieve? Wrecking Liam's equipment last time hadn't stopped him. The plan, according to Gloria, was to kill the magician. Setting fire to his workshop wasn't going to accomplish that.

"Why, Alastair? What good will this do?" I waved a hand towards Gloria's handiwork. It was starting to become uncomfortably hot in the close confines of the workshop, and the smell of burning rubber was clogging up my throat.

"Nothing," he said. "But Gloria needs to vent, and she seems to find this satisfying."

Not for much longer, if I had my way. I knew I was going to piss off the salamander, but I was too aware of Dawn's fragile mortality. I let go some molecular bonds, and spread myself a little, reaching for the water sources within the building. One corner of my mouth twitched up as I found a well that piped water to a sprinkler system. Gloria, or maybe Alastair, had disabled the sensor, but as far as I could tell the system was still fully functional. I didn't want to hurt Gloria, but I did want to put out the fires she'd set.

Overtones of the hydro station again.

"What are you up to?" asked Alastair suspiciously. I glanced at myself. A certain degree of translucency had given me away.

"Gloria!" Alastair's shout rang out above the snap, crackle and pop of the flames. "She's up to something!"

'She' most certainly was. As soon as Gloria moved towards us, I loosed the sprinklers. A fine mist filled the air, forcing her to duck beneath a gantry. Sheltered by the wooden slats that floored the overhead walkway, she glared at me. "Are you insane?"

Alastair loomed over me but the threat was empty; he knew he had no way to harm me.

"So do I have your attention now?" I asked, feeling pretty smug with my solution.

Gloria groaned. "Don't tell me. You want to *talk* to him. I suppose it might work. I'm sure you could get a serial killer to confess if it meant getting away from your endless nagging."

Humiliation washed through me. Not only did Gloria not want me, but she thought I was some sort of joke. Acrid bile rose to my mouth.

"Well at least I wouldn't kill one without giving him a chance to change his ways!" I threw back at her. "It's as well your kind are so rare. I doubt the human race would have survived if you'd been common!"

"And you care about them so much you've never killed one?"

I opened my mouth, and shut it again. My teeth collided with a guilty *snick*.

"Thought so," said Gloria. "Miss High-and-Mighty sprite-with-a-conscience."

Stalemate. And this bitching wasn't getting us anywhere. I still had no idea how we were going to resolve the Liam situation, but right now I was more concerned with rescuing Dawn and getting her out of here.

"Turn this damned sprinkler off!" demanded Alastair. He was still beside me, trying to be intimidating.

"I can't," I said flatly. "I can draw the water into the system and get it running, but once the pump's taken over, there's no way I can stop it."

Not strictly true, I could have stopped the water flow at source and left the pump to burn itself out, but having so recently put out one fire I had no intention of starting another. I surveyed the now soggy workshop where just the odd wisp of damp smoke recalled the recent conflagration.

"What *were* you trying to do, anyway?" I asked Gloria. "I can't see Liam throwing himself into the flames in an attempt to rescue his work. He'll write it off and start somewhere fresh. Again."

Gloria smirked, which looked quite silly on the face of someone cowering beneath a flimsy bit of shelter. I ached inside to see my beloved lose her dignity so. But then I thought about how she regarded me, and I clenched my jaw until my teeth hurt. The ache turned to ice.

"It's not about *this*," Gloria answered. "This was a bit of fun. I want him off balance when he gets here. Distracted."

I groaned. Gloria had always struck me as typical of her type—hot tempered, quick to make decisions and damn the consequences. It had never occurred to me that she might also be dim.

"Don't you think this might serve to *warn* him? Didn't it occur to you how strong the smell of burning rubber is, and how far it carries?"

Gloria pouted. "Of course it did. What do you think I am, stupid? How's he to know it's not an electrical fault? I expect him to go for the mains cut off before he does anything else. That's outside, in case you hadn't noticed. I plan on getting him out there, when he reaches for the switch."

Oh. Quite neat as plans go, but I still didn't think Liam would fall for it. Not when he knew there was a salamander around.

"Perhaps if you'd told me what you were planning, we wouldn't be in this mess," I couldn't resist pointing out.

"We can still make this work," said Gloria. "But I need to get outside. Are you sure you can't turn the sprinklers off."

Well I *could*. But I didn't trust Gloria. I wanted Dawn out of here before I considered anything else.

"What's the matter?" I said. "You won't melt in a bit of drizzle."

"Of course I won't, but it's bloody uncomfortable. Now can you, or can you not turn it off?"

"I don't think so," I hedged. "I'll see if I can come up with a way, but first there's something I have to do. Liam's got a human girl captive back there somewhere." I waved a hand towards the far end of the building where I could see at least three doors leading into partitioned spaces. Dawn had to be there somewhere. "I need to get her out of here."

"Whatever," Gloria conceded, giving in far too easily for my liking. I narrowed my eyes until I was peering at her from slits, but she was giving nothing away. She settled a little under her shelter, making a show of getting comfortable for the wait.

Dubious, but determined to find Dawn before the fragile status quo failed, I pushed past the now passive vampire, and headed towards the nearest door. I scanned it as I approached. There was a simple keyhole beneath the handle, and even if it was locked I doubted it would take much strength to break it open. I grasped the handle and pushed.

It wasn't locked. The door swung open onto a dark space. I ran my hand along the wall inside and located a light switch. A single fluorescent tube buzzed into life, and I found myself in a storeroom stacked with boxes at the back, and shelves nearer the door laden with electronic bits and bobs. A cursory glance confirmed that this was not Dawn's prison. I backed out and shut the door.

As I moved to the next one, I glanced over my shoulder at the space beneath the gantry. Empty. I should have known.

A quick scan located Gloria and Alastair threading their way towards the door we'd all entered by. Gloria must have decided to endure the discomfort of getting wet. Steam sizzled where the fine mist touched her bare skin, but she was in no danger.

She reached for the door handle and my heart stopped. Whether it was a sudden burst of intuition, or that I was starting to see patterns in Liam's behaviour, I don't know.

What I did know was that they weren't going to get out that way.

The world around me slowed. My human body's senses abruptly gained sharp-edged clarity. I could see more, hear more, smell more.

I just couldn't do a damned thing *about* it.

My scream of, "No!" came a fraction of a millisecond too late. As Gloria touched the door handle, Liam's trap sprang.

My eyes were dazzled by power flaring in a dome around Gloria and Alastair. The *crack* of displaced air assaulted my ears in tandem with Liam's signature fruity smell filling my nostrils.

Why, oh *why* hadn't it occurred to me sooner? Of course Liam would have a second line of defence. Of course he would want to capture trespassers *inside* his workshop where they would be contained, away from chance prying eyes.

Why were we so *stupid*? Always one step behind him.

Gloria's wail of disbelief echoed around the walls. She struck the dome mindlessly with her fist, snatching it back amidst a shower of sparks. Energy rippled the air and the only upside for Gloria was that she was no longer getting wet.

I quelled the urge to run to her. I was too familiar now with Liam's magical constructs, and knew there would be nothing I could do. This called for someone with powers of the same kind as the magician. This called for a witch.

I spun round and went back to my search for Dawn. For once, we had a witch to hand, and much though I didn't want Dawn to come onto Gloria's and Alastair's radar, I couldn't see any way to prevent it now. And I sure as hell wasn't going to leave Gloria trapped. No matter what she thought of me, I still ached with love.

Misguided love, hopeless love, but love nonetheless.

I flung open the middle door, revealing a carbon copy of the first.

One left. This had to be where Dawn was held. I tried the handle. Locked.

Even more certain now that the young true-witch was lying trussed up on a mattress on the floor behind this door, I yelled, "Don't worry Dawn! I'll have you out any second."

I tried ramming the door with my shoulder. I've seen it done many times on all those TV cop shows. They always make it look easy, and perhaps it is if you have the weight of a large man behind you. But it wasn't going to work for me.

Next, I tried the high kick, equally well demonstrated on the small screen. The door warped a bit, but after three attempts I abandoned that technique too.

I had one left. I hunted the nearest workbench and located the perfect implement: a large wrench. The first blow sent a massive shock up my arm, and I thanked the powers that I wasn't made of flesh and blood in truth. A dozen more belters and the handle started to disintegrate. Two more and it clattered to the concrete floor. I shoved the door in triumph, elated when it swung open.

The room was dark inside, as it had been when I'd talked with Dawn in that strange encounter within the faery sithen on the astral plane. I fumbled for the light switch, and found instead a pull cord dangling against my questing fingers. Grasping the cord, I yanked. Light flooded the room.

I stood in stunned silence.

This was no prison, but an office, with banks of computer screens and electronic gadgetry.

No sign of Dawn.

25. DECISIONS

Heat suffused my body, followed by shivering chills. Air rushed in and out of my lungs, the rapid gasps of a drowning woman.

Why had I assumed Dawn was imprisoned here? My eyes hunted every corner of the office long after my mind accepted that I'd made a monstrous mistake.

I was responsible for Gloria and Alastair getting trapped for no good reason.

Now hang on a minute, remonstrated a tiny voice of reason within my head. *They did a pretty good job of it all by themselves.*

Well, and so they had. That didn't make me feel any less guilty. Perhaps if I hadn't pushed them by turning on the sprinklers they might not have been caught out. Maybe.

Whatever. It was down to me as the only one of us still at large to find a way to free them. My mind turned.

Wynter! Surely the witch could find a way, even if it meant me having to plug myself back into that awful ley line.

Before I could talk myself out of it, I set about finding a way out of the workshop that wouldn't end up with me trapped as well. At the back of one of the store rooms I found a toilet. Perfect.

Well, hardly perfect, but it would do.

"I'm going for help," I yelled. All the answer I got was a curt nod from Gloria. She and Alastair were more interested in peering up at the roof. I frowned. What could be so important up there? It wasn't as if the spell field would stop where it met the corrugated plastic.

Oh gods! Corrugated *plastic*. Not tin, asbestos, or anything solid. Plastic. *See-through* plastic to allow daylight in.

And Alastair was directly beneath it, with nothing to shelter him from direct sunlight when morning arrived. Certain death for a vampire.

I plunged headfirst down the toilet.

This was starting to become something of a habit—escape by effluent. I'm sure there should be some sort of toilet humour involved, but it escaped me at the time.

I skidded round the u-bends and down the pipe into the septic tank. The inspection lid proved to be screwed down tight. Not a huge surprise as the installation appeared quite recent, but frustrating as that would have been my fastest exit. I swam across to the outlet and percolated as fast as I could, which was not by any means as fast as I'd have liked, up through the gravel layers until I oozed out into fresh air. My body coalesced on ground bathed in creamy moonlight. I glanced up. How much time had passed? I couldn't be sure, but the moon was certainly on her downward slide.

Orienting myself, I charged up the hill to where I'd left Wynter.

The hedge witch was gone. No sign she'd even been there. Nary a charred twig or a hint of incense in the air. She'd covered her tracks so completely I'd have defied even Liam to find where she'd worked her spells.

Sweat trickled down my spine. I glanced up at the moon again. I had to do *something*.

All I could think of was finding Wynter. I sprinted up the remainder of the hill and flung myself into the Tiguan. The Audi might have been the faster car, but it wasn't designed to handle the rough track down to Wynter's caravan, and I was relieved to be back in the 4 x 4. The engine roared to life and I careered once more along the dark, narrow Highland roads out to Cannich and beyond.

In the end all my haste was for nothing. Wynter was gone. Moved on. The site where the old showman's caravan had stood was pristinely empty, nothing to show she'd ever been there at all. I sat and stared at the blank spot illuminated by my headlights and it stared vacantly back at me.

How could she do this?

I wanted to curse the witch for abandoning us when she was the only one with the skills to save Alastair. But I didn't. I couldn't. I wished her well. I hoped that wherever she ended up she'd find peace, away from vampires and their corrosive passion.

Instead, I cursed myself. I should have seen it coming—the look she'd given me back there on the hillside, when I told her she'd been lied to. Rammed it down her throat was more like it. I had been far from delicate in my delivery of what was an earth-shattering truth for poor Wynter.

I hadn't known her well, but it seemed to me that she was too trusting for her own good. I hoped she was strong enough to bounce back from this.

But the fact remained, I was witch-less. Is that even a word? Probably not, but it summed up my predicament.

Who else did I know in the witchy business? Gordon and Dawn. Liam was going after Gordon, so that counted the druid out. Which left Dawn.

I *had* to find her.

Groundhog Day came to mind.

Where was my guardian angel when I needed him? I recalled his heavenly face—and body—and how he'd winked at me from the crystal wall of the sithen. But what good was he, when I didn't know how to call him? I needed to go back there to find either him or Dawn; I had no other leads.

I peered upward. Was the sky starting to lighten? When I switched off the car engine and lights, darkness cascaded over me like a tidal wave. I welcomed it. Every moment longer that it stayed dark was a moment more in which I might yet save the day. Or the night, even. Alastair might be a vampire, and he might also be my darling Gloria's preferred lover, but nobody deserved to face the ghastly death that would come to him if I failed.

I scratched an itchy patch of skin on my wrist.

Since when did my body suffer from any form of irritation? I stared down at my unseen hand where it lay cradled in my lap and shuddered. This had to be the first sign that my borrowed witch DNA was starting to degrade. It *had* to be. I could think of no other reason for my body to exhibit such unnecessary symptoms.

I felt like a scene from Star Trek: *'Shields at eighty percent, Cap'n, and falling. I dinna know how much longer we can hold on!'*

If this was ever going to happen, it was going to have to happen right now. There were no guidelines to tell me how long my magical skin might protect me once it started failing, and the gods alone knew what would happen if it packed up completely while I was out of my body.

Closing my eyes I did as I'd been instructed, focussing hard on my mental image of Minkie, of his beady dark eyes in particular. In my mind, he lay snuggled in his favourite spot on top of the dirty laundry. His eyes opened.

This time, I rocketed down the dark slide of his gaze. My breath was snatched away, my vision plunged into a blackness so intense it sparkled. Vertigo gripped me, and I lost all sense of up or down. When greyness appeared around my edges I had an inspired—I hoped—thought and drummed up a clear memory of that strange chamber deep within the sithen, where the crystal walls showed every manner of scene from the outside world.

"Ouch!" I protested, as I landed hard on unyielding rock. A smile of somewhat grim satisfaction twisted my lips. At least I'd arrived in the right place.

All around me the walls shimmered with tiny moving scenes like you see in a TV salesroom, but magnified thousands of times and every scene different.

"So you managed it okay?"

Michael's feet appeared in front of me. Looking up at him, I sighed. Divine body, shame about the fuzzy patch where his face should be.

And we were obviously still playing the silly only-speaking-in-questions thing. Fine. I had other things to worry about right now and, during my dizzying passage into this weird world, I'd had a new idea I urgently needed to explore.

"Indeed," I answered tartly, picking myself up off the ground. "And I need your help."

"What is it you would like of me?" asked the infuriating fey.

"I need to get to where Dawn is. Can I go there from here?"

It hadn't occurred to me to ask last time. Everything about the astral plane was new to me, and I had no idea what was possible and what wasn't. With only the guidance of he-who-speaks-in-questions the onus was on me to invent the rules, or at least to query what might be possible. I wished I had a bigger imagination.

Michael appeared to be struggling for words. Did he not want to answer this question, or was he struggling to find a phrasing that didn't break his rules?

"Where did you leave your physical shell?" he asked after a long pause.

"In the forest," I said, for want of a better answer. I had no idea what Michael knew of my world.

"Is that anywhere near where your friend is?"

My temper snapped. "How do I know? That's why I'm here! Some guide you are; you're no help at all."

I knew I was being petulant, but lives were at stake. Not the best word to use with a vampire involved, but I was beyond quibbling semantics and I needed answers, not more questions.

Michael's shoulders slumped, and remorse filled me. I had no idea what was behind his peculiar method of communication; maybe he found it equally as frustrating.

He tried again. "Did you know that your body will remain where it is until you return to it?"

I hadn't, but that answered my question. No way to physically get to Dawn via the astral.

"Sorry, I know you're trying to help," I said. "I just don't know how I'm going to find her in time."

"Why don't you talk to her again?"

That sounded suspiciously like a suggestion, and if that broke Michael's rules, well I wasn't going to correct him. It was about the one option I had left.

I opened myself to the tugging sensation that would draw me to Dawn. It was there still but I was alarmed to notice how much weaker it had become. I didn't waste time speculating about what this might mean, but allowed it to lead me to the dark crystal facet.

"Dawn, are you there?" I placed my palm to the cool wall.

"Cassie?" Dawn's wraithlike palm met mine. This time I was expecting it.

"Have you found out where I am yet? I don't think I can take this much longer." Her voice trembled through tears I couldn't see.

"I'm getting closer," I said truthfully; at least I knew where she *wasn't* being held. "But I need a few more details."

"What else can I tell you? It's still dark and nothing's changed."

"Let's try a recap. Perhaps we missed something."

"Okay," she said, sounding dubious. I daresay in her situation I would have felt the same.

"You said you're sitting on a mattress. Have you been able to move around at all?"

"A bit, but wherever this is, it's not much bigger than the bed. Oh, yes, it's not a mattress, it's a bed. It's not very high off the floor, and it's all boxed in underneath. There's a narrow space down one side of it and then a wall. I tried kicking, but it's lined with something soft so there's no sound."

"Good, Dawn, that's good. Keep going."

"You know that smell I told you about? Well I've noticed another one too, sort of like strawberries."

No surprises there.

"Anything else?"

"Well, yes," she added, but sounded unsure. "This is going to sound kinda weird, but this place *moves*."

My senses sharpened. "Moves how?"

"Well, it rocks from side to side, a bit like a boat but without the up and down you get on water."

Then I knew.

Not a boat—a *caravan*!

Why had it not occurred to me before? It was the most obvious place. She was in Liam's mobile home up on the muir, protected by all those layers of spells that prevented us from getting anywhere near. Even mounted on concrete blocks as it was, it would rock when he moved around inside it, and the wind would affect it too.

And, of course, it was somewhere I couldn't go. Tears of anger and despair started trickling down my cheeks.

"Cassie? Are you still there?"

"Yes. Yes, I am, and I know where you are."

"That's great!"

The joy in Dawn's voice cut me like paper; sharp and bloody.

"So come and get me!"

If only it were that simple. "Dawn, I'm going to go away for a bit. I have to find Gordon."

"Can't you come yourself? Oh. Of course you can't. Liam's still after you isn't he? But if I'm the bait he's probably watching

Gordon too."

"I know it's a risk, but I can't see any other way. Liam's magic stops me from getting to you."

"Oh. Well then, you'd better find my dad as quick as you can and hope Liam hasn't got to him already."

"I'm on it," I said, backing away from the wall. The spot where Dawn's palm still rested shrank back to blend in with all the other tiny cells, like reflections in an insect's faceted eyes.

"It'll take too long!" I wailed into the void. I halfway expected a comment, or at least a question from Michael, but when I looked up he was further along the chamber, attention riveted to another crystal scene. His shoulder muscles were rigid, fists alternately clawing and closing.

"What—?" The single word erupted from my throat. In the three steps it took me to reach Michael's side he'd swung around and grabbed for me, trying to block my view with his body.

"Let me *go*!" I protested, squirming; and then froze as I caught sight of what had fascinated him.

Two people lay together on a concrete floor, one on top of the other. At first look you might have thought they were making out, but then a sudden flare of brightness touched the figure on the bottom and flame blossomed. The oddly-shaped one on top patted frantically at the blaze until she had it extinguished, and then spread herself out again, trying to cover the body beneath her.

Gloria and Alastair.

I was too late. Night had passed.

Out there in the real world, the new day must be cloudy. Sunlight appeared in no more than brief flashes, but I could see that Gloria's strategy was never going to work. Even stretching her shape to its limits, she simply wasn't big enough to cover every part of Alastair, and whatever clothes she'd appeared to be wearing weren't detachable.

Even as I watched, a shaft of intense light pinned them like the beam of a searchlight and fire blazed from three exposed areas of the vampire—shoulder, thigh and foot. Again Gloria beat out the flames and expanded herself ready for the next onslaught.

I rubbed clammy hands against my thighs. My throat was so dry my breath rasped in and out. I wanted to run, to do *something*, but there was nothing I could do other than watch.

"Wouldn't you like to leave now?" Michael suggested gently. I shook my head. I'd caused this or, at the very least, contributed to it. I was not going to walk away now.

My hand, seemingly of its own volition, lifted and stretched out to touch the rough glass texture of the wall. Sound flowed through my touch; Alastair, accepting the inevitable.

"Gloria, love, enough. It's over."

"No!" she shrieked, a banshee wail of utter denial. "I won't let it be!"

"Arghhh!"

Another eruption of flames interrupted their argument. This time the sun blazed down for longer, until after an eternity a blessed cloud slid above them and allowed Gloria to extinguish the many patches of charring skin on the vampire.

Of all the days for the Highlands to have fine weather, why today?

Alastair took advantage of the shade to move, reaching up to grip Gloria's arms. "Gloria, listen to me. This is *not* working! Sooner or later there won't be time enough to put out the fires. Look at the sky: it's clearing."

As if to back up Alastair's prediction, the sky cleared and they were plunged back into bright sunlight. Both of Alastair's hands where they gripped Gloria's arms burst into flames, as did both feet and lower legs.

Coward that I am, I let my hand drop at this point; I couldn't bear to hear his screams. When eventually the sun vanished again, I dared to raise a trembling arm and touch the wall once more.

"Can't you see? I've had enough! Let me go, please?"

Gloria's head wagged back and forth.

"No, I can't. I won't! I'm not done with you yet."

Sounding incredibly reasonable, which I was pretty certain I would not have achieved if our roles had been reversed, Alastair put his burned hands with their blistered flesh on either side of her face and held her still before saying: "This isn't about you. For once in your immortal life think of someone else. I always expected to be around for longer than this, but if this is it, so be it; I'm ready. All you have to do is let me go."

"No!" wailed Gloria, but I knew she'd given in. I hadn't been entirely certain that she *was* capable of considering anyone other than herself, but perhaps in her own way she did love the vampire enough to let his suffering end.

Alastair glanced uneasily upward. From my view I couldn't see the sky, but I'd bet there was a large patch of heavenly blue up there, creeping inexorably closer.

"Yes," he said, steel threading the word.

Gloria's shoulders sagged. Her head dropped forward and I had to strain to hear her words.

"I'll miss you."

"And I, you, my love. Please, make it quick."

She bent to kiss him and as her lips touched his, an inferno blazed up to fill the spell bubble. Alastair vanished, consumed by the raging conflagration. My knees gave way, and I crashed boneless to the rock floor. Fire raged within the tiny crystal facet, showing no sign of abating. A salamander giving vent to her fury.

Warm arms cradled me from behind, and I leaned back into Michael's embrace. I turned my face and cried against his warm, smooth skin. He stroked my hair and I buried my face deeper, letting the sobs come. My mind relentlessly replayed Alastair's cruel death.

Whilst you could argue that a vampire is already dead, that's not the case; they simply have a different type of life. Like Gloria. Like me.

My chest felt constricted, and pain throbbed behind my eyes. I shook my head, trying to dislodge the ache but it only hurt worse. I snuffled, and then my skin flushed; I was leaving disgusting bodily fluids all down Michael's bare chest. I was mortified. Exuding fluid of any description is plain wrong for a sprite. My whole existence was tilting, teetering on the edge of an abyss. Impossible things were happening to me, and to those around me, however hard I tried not to let them.

I wished I'd taken the coward's way out, done what I'd planned and ditched the entire living as a human thing, then none of this would have happened.

Oh yes it would, my nasty little rational inner voice pointed out. *You just wouldn't have been aware of it.* I mentally stuck my tongue out at it. If I decided to wallow in guilt, that was my choice.

I swallowed, the pain in my raw throat rivalling the one behind my eyes. Being human sucked! If I hadn't still needed to rescue Dawn I'd have given up on it right away. But I had to rescue Dawn so I could free Gloria and besides, there was no way I was going to leave Dawn at the mercy of the crazy magician.

Why was life so complicated?

"Feeling better?" Michael asked. Why I might have been feeling any better so soon puzzled me for an instant until I noticed that I'd stopped crying. Not that the lack of leaking fluid meant I *felt* any better about what had happened. Perhaps the fey didn't understand the depth of human emotions. Damn, *I* didn't understand them, but maybe I was closer to it than he would ever be. Unwilling for the moment to risk answering, I wiped his bare chest with my sleeve (at least when I'd formed my astral body I'd dressed it) and then snuggled closer against him. It was about this time I noticed how well we fit together.

That was also the moment when the first sharp *tug* snagged me. I was being summoned.

26. ANGEL

I gasped. The suddenness of it caught me totally unprepared. As ever, Liam was one step ahead of me.

The tug came again, as if someone had taken hold of the silver cord that bound my essence to my shell and was giving it tiny experimental jerks. Like a fish caught on the end of the line, and Gordon the angler was getting set to reel me in, ready for Liam's net.

A ghostly blue circle formed beside me. As I watched, other circles appeared within the first, concentrically smaller and smaller as they led away from where I sat. Where they intersected the crystal walls and rock floor the now familiar solid boundaries of the sithen chamber ceased to exist, the summoning funnel over-riding even the powerful fey magic. My stomach clenched and I bit back a cry—the circles framed a threatening black vortex.

A firmer tug rocked me where I reclined within the protective circle of Michael's arms. He hugged me closer as if he could prevent me from being dragged from his clutches.

"Do you know how to block this?" he asked urgently, gripping me even tighter as the next jerk almost ripped me away.

The summons began to arrive in increasingly insistent pulses. As if I needed any more sensory input, the blue ringed funnel pulsated sickeningly, the wide end nearest me questing around like a living thing seeking a victim. I tried to remember Wynter's instructions. Why is it that as soon as one is put under pressure, the first thing to vanish is memory? A frightening blank occupied the space where I'd stored that conversation. Something about a beach ball? A giant ball? Balls! What the hell was I supposed to do with them?

Michael and I both grunted as an even stronger wrench tried to pull me towards the open maw of the hideous funnel.

"Can you think of something to block it with?" asked Michael, sounding desperate. At any other time I'd have been thrilled to have him hold me this tight, but my astral body was starting to fracture, to come apart at the seams. Bits of me began to escape his embrace.

Suddenly I remembered. Create a giant ball and stuff it in the top of the funnel. So simple, if I could do it!

The next heave tore me almost in two, bisected by the defensive clutch of my fey friend. I wasn't sure at what point Michael had become either friend or protector, but somewhere along the line both appeared to have happened, and I wasn't sorry. What I was sorry for was that it appeared he was going to fail—this was *his* world to manipulate, not mine.

"*Do something!*" I screeched at him as the biggest blue ring brushed my arm. The whole limb tingled before going dead, an unresponsive lump of pseudo flesh. Latching on like a limpet, the leading edge of the funnel started to crawl up my useless appendage, and I stared helplessly into the abyss.

"Do you remember the hole in the ground?"

What? Why would I—

Yes! Rusty gears crunched in my almost paralysed mind, and the lesson of the hole in the ground surged back even as my shoulder ceased to exist, gobbled up by the voracious funnel. This might be Michael's world, but I could still influence details.

A mental image of my first encounter with Michael flashed into bright relief; he'd been sitting on top of a lump of rock like a pixie on a toadstool.

Numbness spread to the left side of my torso and I resisted looking down; I had no wish to see myself being swallowed alive. I reached out with my thoughts and pictured that boulder stuffed into the top of the funnel, sealing its end.

Sensation flooded me, hot and throbbing. Pins and needles prickled my arm. I gasped, unsure whether this was a good thing or not, but when I looked my mouth stretched into a tight grin. My body was whole again, and that big old chunk of rock was well and truly wedged into the orifice that had tried to devour me.

I fell back limply, enjoying the sensation of warm skin against my back and strong arms encircling me. I felt, even if ever so briefly, safe. Michael rested his chin on the crown of my head and I wondered about him again. Who was he, and why was he here?

Regretting it yet knowing I must, I squared my shoulders and sat up, pulling away from the comforting circle of his arms. I had created a breathing space, nothing more. Gloria and Dawn were still captives and, despite my interference, Gordon's summoning spell persisted. When Liam realised I was able to resist it, I dreaded to think what his next action might be. I had to do *something*.

But what?

Behind me, Michael rose to his feet and walked towards the crystal wall, skirting the aimless weaving of the blocked summoning funnel. I followed his example, cringing away when the tube tracked my movement. It couldn't suck me in, but it sure as hell knew I was there.

Beyond its reach, a glittering patch of wall caught my attention. I forced myself to look.

Gloria still roiled in fiery elemental glory around the confines of her prison. At a safe distance, Liam stood watching Gordon. The druid sat cross legged on the workshop floor before a makeshift altar, his eyes closed in a meditative trance. Sweat stood out on his brow and upper lip. *He* knew something was awry with his spell; it should not have been possible for me to resist him for this long.

Nausea turned my stomach. I was desperate to resolve the stalemate, but the only way I could see to do that was to give in and put myself right back into Liam's hands. Back to square one.

Or was it?

"Can I speak to Gordon without Liam hearing?"

"Have you thought of bringing the druid here?" said Michael in what was clearly a suggestion. His head turned so that his fuzzy almost-face glanced over his shoulder, and it occurred to me that perhaps he was operating under his own set of restrictions that were nothing to do with me. His whole body was tense, as if expecting trouble. When nothing immediate happened, he relaxed a little but reached up to rub his neck muscles, kneading the tops of his shoulders. A tiny portion of my mind wondered what could exert such control over a fey, but I had enough problems of my own without worrying about anyone else.

I considered his suggestion. How to bring Gordon here. I was still so new to this astral manipulation, I was making it up as I went along.

Okay, right. Just do it.

I studied the little scene before me. Like every time I'd peered into one of the tiny facets, this one had grown until it filled a considerable chunk of the wall. I had the feeling that if I were to touch the wall as I had when speaking to Dawn, my voice would be heard throughout the workshop. So what would happen if I strategically touched just Gordon? It was worth a try.

Edging past Liam's figure, I placed myself right in front of Gordon. I reached out gingerly, touching a fingertip to the druid's shoulder. My finger sank into the once-hard crystal of the wall, as though it had turned to jelly. My hand passed through the wall and slid inside the druid's body. I shuddered. It felt like reaching inside a rotting corpse.

A startled look came over Gordon's face, and I glanced anxiously at Liam to see if he'd noticed. Thank the gods, he was watching

Gloria. I closed my ethereal fingers around Gordon's essence and tugged, much as he had done to me earlier. My lips stretched into a brief vindictive grin; now he knew what it was like to be on the receiving end of a summons.

Gordon's astral body popped into being in front of me, and I let my fleeting self-indulgence pass. We had more important things to address. To my surprise, the druid's spirit version was very similar to his real world image. A tad younger perhaps, but the long grey hair and patrician features were much the same. I guessed he was comfortable with his own body, and for some reason that made him seem all the more trustworthy.

"What's going on?" he asked, gazing around in bewilderment. He sounded shaken. Not surprising, when he had thought he was in control.

"We don't have much time," I said. "Liam might realise you're not in your body if we take too long, so listen. He's got Dawn trussed up in his mobile home, down a sidetrack off the Foyers road. There's a sign to an artist's steading; take the next track beyond that. He's left a few magical surprises, so be wary, but they shouldn't be anything you can't deal with."

Gordon's gaze slid over Michael where the fey stood silent behind me, past me in my Morven Uisce guise and locked onto his thwarted funnel. Realisation hit home.

"*Cassie?*"

His eyes swivelled back to me, radiating shock.

I grinned, feeling curiously abashed. "Yeah, it's me."

"But—"

"I know, I know. It shouldn't be possible. Tell me about it! But listen, you have to get back and rescue Dawn. I don't trust Liam."

Gordon's eyes narrowed. "Nor I. But since when did you care what happened to my daughter?"

I was offended, although I understood his question—elementals are not known for their loyalty. "I consider her my friend," I said somewhat stiffly. "And I won't see her hurt on my account."

Gordon's face softened, eyes brimming with unshed tears. "I know your kind, sprite, and I would not have credited you with such altruism." He shuffled his feet and glanced down. "I apologise for not reading you better."

"Yeah, well. You're not the first. But you have to go. Get out of here before Liam realises, and go get Dawn."

Gordon shook his head. "He won't let me go that easily."

So it had come to this after all. I swallowed hard and my guts turned to jelly, but I made my choice.

"He will, if I obey your summons," I said. Michael stiffened beside me, and Gordon stared at me like I'd sprouted a second head. Or two, or three.

"You'd do that, for us? But what does he want with you? That's a salamander he's got caged up in there! He can't be planning to put the two of you together. Can he?"

I shrugged. It would be better if Gordon didn't know Liam's intentions. He might decide to gamble with Dawn's safety for the continued survival of Scotland. For my own sanity, I had to believe that Liam's containment spells along with his electronic wizardry would be successful in confining the inevitable explosion.

Gordon lived up to my expectations, damn the man.

"No, I won't allow this," he said. As if he had any say in it. "I'll find a way to convince him he's being reckless."

"Good luck with that," I said sourly. "You think I haven't tried? He's got this obsession and nothing is going to divert him. You have to get Dawn away. At least if he doesn't have a hold over you, then he can't force you to do anything else. Now get out of here."

I don't like being rude, but this wasn't an argument I was going to prolong. Catching Gordon by surprise, I shoved him hard, pushing him back against the wall through which his spirit had passed. With a startled expression and a mouth open in protest, he fell back through the wall and into his body, which jerked upright as if an electric current has passed through him. Thank the gods Liam wasn't watching.

"Surely you don't mean to go through with this?" asked Michael.

I shrugged. "What else can I do? Gordon's right; Liam will never let him go if I don't put in an appearance."

I was trying to be brave. I knew I was doing the right thing, at least for Gordon and Dawn. For Gloria and me? I wasn't so sure about that, but what choice did I have? My jelly-like innards were doing a good impression of a hula dancer on speed, and my lungs were pumping air in and out fast enough to run a marathon at thought of putting myself back inside that spell bubble, but I wasn't about to let Michael know. We might survive this; it wasn't a given that we'd both die in a blaze of glory.

Just very likely.

"And if there was another way?"

The deep, rich voice came from right behind me.

"Fuck!" I leapt clean off the ground and did a one-eighty in mid-air. The sight that greeted my sore eyes was so beautiful, I almost forgot for a moment that I was about to die.

My guardian angel stood before me in all his radiant beauty.

Up close, he looked every bit as ravishing as he had when he'd winked at me from the tiny pastoral vista, first time I'd seen the crystal wall. If anything, his hair was even glossier, that darkest black that is so black it has a blue hue. His features were strong and even, airbrushed to perfection. Today he wore a black leather jerkin and trousers laced at the sides, showcasing his fully muscled body. He exuded a slightly odd smell, sweet and yet a touch sickly; perhaps too saccharine for my taste.

A polite smile graced his heavenly features as he awaited my answer. Behind me I could hear Michael hissing like an angry cat. Jealousy or dislike? Or both?

Trying to be nonchalant, I raised my eyebrows. "And you are...?"

The divine being bent into a sweeping bow, disarming me even further.

"How rude of me," he observed, and my body vibrated to the resonance of his bass voice. "Allow me to introduce myself. My name is Rafe. And you are Cassie, this I know."

Michael's spluttering reached a new intensity. I looked around at him in concern; it sounded like he was choking. With the fuzziness over his features I couldn't make out quite what was going on, but the hand waving gestures did nothing to suggest distress, merely that he wanted me to come away from Rafe.

Well. And why should I when the stunning creature was offering me an alternative to falling on my sword? I turned back to Rafe.

"Pleased to meet you, I'm sure. So you have a suggestion for me?"

"Indeed," he said with a dazzling smile. "I have watched your predicament and feel that as I have something that may help you, I should offer it."

My skin crawled. The thought of some angelic being watching my every move made me very uncomfortable. There were certain things in my life I'd have liked to remain private, but apparently that choice was not my own. Did I want to accept help from something so omniscient?

Hell, yes! If it was going to stop me from getting killed, I wanted it. I liked being immortal. I wasn't going to give it up if there was an alternative.

An alternative that didn't involve anyone else getting hurt.

"What's the catch?"

I'm not totally naive.

Rafe smiled again, and my legs turned as jelly-ish as my insides. Boy, he was so *hot*! In fact, now I thought about it, he had something of that scorched earth smell about him that reminded me of Gloria. I inhaled like a naughty youth sniffing glue.

"No catch, although you will owe me a favour."

"A favour?" That didn't sound so bad, but I'd have liked something a bit more defined.

He shrugged. "Yes, I might ask you to change a watercourse one day. Something like that."

I glanced uneasily back at Michael. His head was wagging back and forth at high speed, but no words were issuing from that blank space where his face should be. I clenched my jaw. If he wasn't even going to say anything, then I'd make up my own mind.

"Deal," I said, and stuck out a hand. Rafe clasped my fingers in his huge fist and I winced, expecting him to crush them. But his touch was delicate, so sensitive for one so powerful, and my heart flip-flopped inside my chest. He truly must be the guardian angel I'd taken him for.

"Okay, so what have I signed up to?"

His brilliant blue eyes flashed, and his full lips curved into a wicked smile. I took an involuntary step back as a seed of doubt germinated.

Had I done the right thing?

"To save your friends you must still obey the summoning—"

My heart sank. This didn't sound like a solution.

"—but I will give you something to take with you: a spell of your own so that you may defeat this magician."

My heart did a back flip. "What do you mean, a spell? A spell to do what? You've got the wrong sprite. I can't *do* spells."

"All you must do is to activate this one. It will take care of itself."

Sounded promising. "What does it do?"

"You must place it on the outside of the spell sphere as you travel through its surface. Once there, you will be able to activate it from inside with a single word—a word I will teach you."

Better and better. But I still had reservations. "That sounds great, but what will it actually *do*?"

"It will collapse the sphere."

Music to my ears. "How long will it last?" I asked, considering possible ramifications. Liam was more than just a one-spell magician.

Rafe spread his big hands wide. "It has no longevity. Once the spell is negated, it is up to you to escape before he can construct another."

So a slim chance, but better than we'd had scant moments earlier. Long term, I still couldn't see a solution to the Liam issue, but at least we might all live to fight another day. If I could use this spell. And if we could escape all the other traps our sneaky opponent had secreted about his workshop. That was a lot of 'ifs', but a slim chance was better than none at all.

"I'll manage. How do I carry this spell?"

"In the palm of your hand. Give me a moment and I will construct it."

He flashed a look towards Michael which I could not interpret. The fey backed away, shoulders and head slumped. A tendril of unease burrowed through me, but I rapidly forgot it as Rafe began his spell crafting.

Unlike human witches or wizards, my angelic benefactor needed no props beyond the astral substance. His hands grasped and kneaded, twisting in unnatural ways, or what would have been unnatural if we'd been in the material world. This was, however, the astral plane and the rules were different, as I was constantly reminded.

A darkly glittering *something* began to take form between Rafe's fingers. Fine hairs all along the back of my neck stood up, and my stomach roiled queasily. I averted my eyes.

Rafe bent forward to breathe life into his creation. Twisted syllables slithered down his tongue, curling and writhing from his mouth to pollute the air around the *something*, as oil pollutes water. My feeling of unease heightened, clutching at my heart with icy tentacles.

And then the *thing* vanished. *Poof!* Like it had never been.

I wasn't sure whether to be relieved or disappointed. My self-appointed saviour—and I was starting to have a few doubts about him after seeing the *thing* he'd tried to create—had failed.

Or had he?

Rafe bestowed a beatific smile upon me. "It is ready."

"I'm sorry?"

He held out an empty hand towards me. I couldn't help it; I flinched back. I'd always avoided getting involved with any of the powers, and I had an awful feeling I should have continued to do so. Rafe's exquisite face radiated sorrow at my action, and heat rose to my cheeks.

"Sorry," I said again, wishing away the wretched flush from my face. "I don't understand."

Rafe smiled once more, and I relaxed inside. Everything would be alright now, said my conscious mind, although I could still hear a dissenting niggle of doubt somewhere deep inside.

"The spell is here," he said, again proffering his hand. "It is simply not visible."

Duh! Of course it would be invisible. What use would a visible spell be, if I was going to sneak it past Liam? Hesitantly I extended my hand.

I shuddered when it touched me; I couldn't help it. Maggots crawled across my palm, burrowing into my flesh, and I had a sudden violent urge to vomit. I wanted to drop the unseen thing, stomp on it and then run screaming down the tunnel behind me. Of course none of that was going to happen; I would take it with me and do as instructed, and then I might not die. I hoped.

At the second attempt, my voice croaked back into existence.

"So what's the word I have to remember?"

"Salamander," he said.

I blinked. "Really? That's it?"

Rafe grinned, but with a knowing edge that heightened my unease.

"I thought you'd like it."

Well. It was certainly a word I wasn't going to forget. And under the circumstances it was one I'd be able to slip into conversation without alerting Liam.

So, now all I had to do was unblock Gordon's summoning funnel and jump right on in there. Lovely. I *so* didn't want to do it, and yet there was too much riding on this for me not to. Gloria, Dawn and Gordon were depending on me, whether they knew it or not. I squared my shoulders. Time to get this over with.

"Are you sure you want to do this?" I glanced around to the source of my thought's echo. Michael.

I shrugged. "I'm sure I don't, but I'm going to anyway."

I turned to thank Rafe. The chamber was empty. Ah well, he'd done what he came to do, so I guessed he was free to move on. Probably had other damsels in distress to rescue.

I wondered how many of them owed him a favour, and how many of those favours he collected. I stared at my apparently empty hand and shuddered; the invisible spell still clung there, writhing obscenely against my palm.

No time to worry about that now. I glanced at the crystal facet showing Liam's workshop. Gloria had smouldered down to a sullen glow at the back of the bubble as far away from Liam as she could get. Gordon was still in his meditation pose, but Liam was becoming impatient, pacing the perimeter of the containment field.

It was time to go.

Clearing the block of stone from the mouth of the funnel was as simple as *thinking* it back to its original setting. I was finally getting the hang of how things worked in the otherworld. Pity I'd been so slow; I doubted I'd ever return.

Facing that possibility, I turned to Michael one last time even as the newly opened maw of the summoning funnel quested around, sniffing me out like a sightless predator. I shuddered.

"I may not be back," I said, finding my voice catching inexplicably. "Thank you for everything, and I'm sorry if I disappointed you in the end."

Michael struggled for words and finally abandoned his questions-only policy. "You are your own person," he said. "Never be sorry for that. I hope it works out for you. Come back if you can." He shrugged. "I might still be here."

"I will," I promised, even as my body began to liquefy and vanish into the ghastly orifice. I had no time to consider Michael's cryptic final comment, but in my last glimpse of him he was looking over his shoulder with one arm raised as if to ward off a blow. I belatedly wondered if the question thing might have been a geas I'd caused him to break.

One more thing to feel guilty about.

Powerless to stop the process now, I was siphoned down the dark throat between the pulsating blue rings, my incorporeal form vibrating in time with the throbbing beat. Confused images rushed past me in a cinematic montage, too fast to identify.

When my essence left the astral plane and re-entered the corporeal world, my true-witch DNA 'skin' joined me. It was drawn by Gordon's summoning, just as my whole being had been drawn to the coven's altar back at Plodda Falls.

Feeling like a comfortable old t-shirt, it enveloped me in a Cassie-shaped body suit, but I was instantly aware of patches that were thin to the point of transparency. It appeared I had left the astral plane not a moment too soon. The amazing shell that had enabled this whole crazy sequence of events was on its last gasp.

I shuddered. Had it disintegrated before I'd left the astral, my anchor to the human plane would have vanished. What then? Eternity in the otherworld? Intriguing though the visit had been, the prospect of being stuck there did not appeal.

Then I was being dragged through the workshop wall like a ghost in a cartoon towards where the funnel pierced the spell bubble above Gordon's head.

So, to work. Place Rafe's spell as per instructions on the outside of the bubble. I would be glad to be rid of the nauseating thing.

I stuck my hand out. It bounced off the funnel wall.

Shit! Now what?

I tried again. The end of my journey was racing towards me; I had one chance to get this done. I extended my arm more slowly, forcing myself to ignore the panicky voice inside my head screaming at me to go faster. My fingertips touched the gel-like inner layer of the funnel, pushing into it but not passing through. My throat constricted. Suppose I couldn't do this—what then?

I pushed harder, *thinking* my nails into sharper points, willing them to cut through the summoning fabric.

One nail popped through, followed abruptly by the others. Searing pain shot up my arm.

I screamed. Or at least I tried to. I don't think the sound travelled beyond the funnel. Staring in open-mouthed shock at my fingers where they projected into the outside world, I could see them lit up like miniature comets, burning up as they re-entered the atmosphere.

Spell! My nagging inner voice screamed for attention. *Get that spell in position or die.* Survival mode rode roughshod over my shock and hurt. Almost in slow motion I could see the bubble's boundary looming closer. One chance. One chance only. I forced more of my hand outside the funnel.

I whimpered as agony engulfed my whole arm, but forced yet more of me through the tear I had created, the urge to survive blotting out coherent thought. The remainder of my body still inside the funnel thrashed desperately, fighting the inexorable tide that was dragging me to my doom. My arm became a thing of white hot pain, my mind a battlefield between the urges to pull it back inside, and to keep pushing it further out.

The repellent *thing* crawled across my palm, laying a trail of acid in my flesh. I spread my hand wide when all I wanted to do was curl it into a fist around the agony and weep over the misshapen lump of flesh. My body was on the rack, stretched beyond its capacity to remain intact, my arm ripping excruciatingly away from my shoulder.

I thought I felt my palm slap against the outside of the bubble as I fell through the tiny aperture where the funnel terminated, but in my haze of anguish I couldn't be certain. My mind went from tortured soul to gibbering wreck to blank nothing and then I was falling, tumbling through the hot air trapped inside the bubble.

27. DESPRITE MEASURES

I slammed into the floor so hard, I lay stunned for a long moment.

Had I done it? Was the spell in place? I had no way of knowing for sure; I guessed I would find out when I tried to activate it.

Not reassuring.

Gingerly, I sat up and inspected myself. To my surprise every bit of me was still intact. I'd half expected to find at least my right hand, and maybe the whole arm, missing. I shook it to make sure it was still firmly attached. Pain lanced upward from the caustic burns the spell had laid into my flesh when it crawled across my hand. Bile rose in my throat; I was *so* glad to be rid of the thing, even if it had left lasting damage.

I spread my fingers and inspected the livid weals striping my palm. I'd never had any injury that couldn't be repaired by the simple expediency of dissolving my body and reforming, but this felt different, as if the spell had marked me with an indelible red stain. A tremor ran through me. Stomach-churning pain still jangled along my nerves, and I had to swallow hard a couple of times before it began to recede.

Drawing my knees beneath me, I staggered upright onto shaking legs and rubbed at several itchy patches of skin. Dawn's DNA was degrading a whole heap faster than the regular human variety. I didn't know if this was the nature of witchy DNA, or because I'd used—and probably abused—its borrowed powers. Ordinarily I'd have had several days warning, but at this rate it would all be gone within hours, and my ability to hold corporeal form with it. Under normal circumstances, I'd never let it get this far, but today was hardly normal.

I glanced toward Gloria where she sat slumped on the floor as far away from me as possible, sullenly smouldering. My gut knotted and I looked away. I couldn't bear to think of what she'd gone through, knowing that I was at least in part responsible. All things considered, I was pretty certain that she wasn't going to be open to any suggestions coming from me. I could only hope that when it came to it, she would have escape as a higher priority than revenge.

Raised voices drew my attention: Gordon yelling at Liam. So, this time no sound muffling spell. Good, that would make it easier to follow events beyond the bubble.

To my alarm, Gordon appeared about to strike Liam. I tensed, willing Gordon to stay calm. Powerful druid he might be, but Liam's dark magic and youth combined to make him a lethal adversary.

"You made a promise," Gordon snarled. "You said you'd tell me where to find Dawn if I summoned the sprite."

"And I will," said Liam. "But not quite yet. Your daughter is my insurance policy against your interference. Go home. I'll be in touch."

I feared Gordon was going to explode. He struggled visibly to contain his obvious desire to throttle Liam, but after a few painful moments his shoulders slumped in defeat and he turned to leave. With his back to Liam he cast one last glance my way. And winked.

What an actor. He should be Oscar nominated.

I drew a deep breath in relief. Dawn and Gordon would be safe now, and Liam none the wiser that the druid already knew where to find his daughter. I watched the door close behind Gordon and smiled. Now it was just the three of us, ending as it had begun. But this time I had an ace up my sleeve.

I hoped.

I watched in silence as Liam methodically checked the positioning of the thick cables surrounding us. Perhaps he really could produce clean energy by sacrificing just two lives. That would be a triumph over the millions lost to accidents in power production—miners, oil riggers, nuclear plant workers and the like. Were Gloria and I being selfish, wanting to perpetuate our immortality? I couldn't agree with Liam's methods—he'd shown a truly callous side, kidnapping Dawn like that—but I approved of his goals.

Finished with his inspection, Liam turned his attention to us.

"So Cassie, here we are again," he said. "I trust this time you'll be more cooperative? After all, you know you'll be helping to save the planet. That's important to you, isn't it? Besides, you've nothing left to keep living for—you don't have a friend left to your name now, do you? And only yourself to blame."

Not *quite* true. I disagreed, but held my tongue. I was sure that if I investigated I'd find him behind much of my recent woe. The smell of his magic had been all over Euan, and whilst I daresay I'd bollixed my relationship with Alison all on my own, I suspected Liam's culpability in the deaths of Morag's beloved chickens and the resulting animosity of my neighbour.

When I failed to react, Liam shrugged and walked away, secure enough to turn his back on us. Overconfidence can be fatal, I've noticed, and Liam's swagger told it all.

Twisting round, I inhaled heat. Gloria stood behind me, way too close for comfort. The air around her shimmered in waves. Bits of my body began to vibrate, and patches of my DNA wrapping flaked off, exposing my native form to Gloria's dangerous energies. Trying not to appear panicked, I edged away with my back to the bubble's boundary.

"You killed him," Gloria accused, advancing on me again. I backed off, holding my hands up in front of me.

"I'm so, so sorry about Alastair," I said, and I meant it. "But you both knew the risks when you came in here."

"We wouldn't have been in this position if you hadn't pulled that stupid stunt with the sprinklers. And then you fucked off and left us!"

Smoke seeped from Gloria's form as she started to lose definition, and the temperature inside the bubble skyrocketed.

No! I was *not* about to let it end like this. I yielded before her advance. "You don't want to do this. Would Alastair have wanted you to end yourself like this? If you do, Liam will have won. It's *him* you want to kill, not me!"

Gloria paused, and the flickering light blurring her extremities faded. This wasn't how I wanted things to play out, but if I could get her fixated on something other than murdering me, we'd have our chance at escape. Then I'd have to find a way to prevent her from killing Liam, at least until I knew Euan was safe.

"We're all set!"

We both turned toward Liam's excited voice, but he was speaking into his mobile phone, not to us.

Gloria hissed, and I sidled a bit further away while she was distracted. Not that there was anywhere to go inside the damned bubble, but it made me feel better.

"No, I don't foresee any problems this time," Liam assured his listener. "Have you got the press releases ready? My contacts in Greenpeace are all lined up to make a big splash—guerrilla marketing, they call it." He laughed; a mocking edge to the sound made my skin crawl. "Yes, and I spoke to William and Catherine about it at the last summit; they were very interested. Have you got the patent sorted?"

Paperwork, paperwork; bane of my working life. Apparently Liam's too. I wondered who he was talking to.

"No," he snapped, and chopped the air with a stiffened hand. "That wasn't the deal. Fifty, fifty. No more, no less."

"The price of our lives," grated Gloria from beside my shoulder. I jumped away from her once more. My chest tightened. Heat raced from my feet to my head and it had nothing to do with Gloria's proximity. Was Liam talking *money*?

His next sentence confirmed my worst nightmare.

"This is supposed to set me up for life!" His hand sliced the air again. "You might have paid for the equipment, but you sure as hell wouldn't know where to even *start* without me! If you think for one minute—"

The heat that had suffused my body a moment before turned to ice. My hands flew to my throat. My legs shook, and I groped dizzily for non-existent support. At the same time, I found I was seeing the world with more clarity than I had in months.

Liam wasn't motivated by altruism, but by *money*.

The proverbial scales fell from my eyes and a tingling sensation prickled me all over. Had Liam's magic been influencing me all along, or had I really been that naive? I shook my head in horror, knowing that the answer fell somewhere between the two.

And my misreading of the situation, for whatever reason, had resulted in Alastair's death.

My throat closed. I turned to Gloria.

"If you'd just *listened*!" she spat.

I glanced down; I couldn't meet her eyes. The tiny ridges in the concrete beneath my feet demanded intense scrutiny.

Liam's next words completed my humiliation.

"Containment failure? Relax. It'll be years, and by then we'll be rich and living on the other side of the world. Just avoid the coastal regions."

If I could have been any more stunned and horrified, I would have been. As it was, my mind refused to assimilate it, as if this hideous thing was happening to someone else and I was no more than a spectator watching from the side lines.

Liam's experiment was going to fail. Not now, not in any immediate future. But at some time, the spell and the technology he'd combined to buffer the world from the immense energies he planned to release would fail. He knew it. His partner knew it. Yet still they were going ahead, and at some point the world would pay for their greed. Cataclysmic events would be unleashed. A humongous explosion which would probably destroy Scotland, with subsequent earthquakes and tsunamis across the world. The sheer scale of the devastation was unthinkable.

And they were quibbling about *money*!

Liam had to be stopped. If we simply escaped, he would either capture us again or find some other unsuspecting elementals. Even if, gods forbid, it cost Euan's life, this cause would be worthy of that sacrifice in his eyes; I knew him well enough to be certain of that.

This had to end here. Now.

I rubbed at an itchy patch on my neck and skin cells peeled away. We were running out of time, fast.

A final plan formed inside my head. My mind shied away from the probable outcome. If I thought about it, I'd never be able to carry it through. Rationally, I knew what had to be done. Emotionally? That was a whole different kettle of fish. Whatever had happened between us, I would always love Gloria. I knew now that nothing would ever come of my love for her but heartache, but that changed zilch. I couldn't bear to think of harming her in any way, and yet I already had, and now I was going to ask her to risk everything. My whole being, mind and body, felt numb.

Probably for the best.

Images of my beloved Highlands flowed past me, of mountains and lochs, rivers and heather, deer and salmon and red kites on the wing. I could only hope they would all still be here when this was over.

"I have a way out of here," I told Gloria quietly. Liam was still chatting on his phone.

"*Now* you have a way out?"

"I'm sorry it's too late for Alastair but I have it now, so the question is how much do you want revenge? I'm willing, if you are?"

Gloria's eyes blazed. Her glorious full lips stretched into a vicious grin and my resolve wobbled. Could I ask my love to do this? There were no assurances. Moments from now we might both cease to exist.

I gathered the sole hope we had—the tattered scraps of my true-witch DNA. I shrank myself down to as small a size as I could, and covered every scrap of me with what remained. All bar the last millimetre of one set of fingers.

Those fingertips felt very exposed.

"Here we go!" Liam sang out in triumph. I guessed he'd got his way, although I thought he was a fool to trust the mystery person on the other end of the line.

Yeah. Takes one to know one.

He reached for the switch to turn on his electromagnetic thingummybob wotsit field.

"You stupid SALAMANDER!" I yelled at the top of my voice. Gloria and Liam both froze in shock, and in that static moment a tiny change in air pressure lifted the hairs on the back of my neck. The spell had worked.

"Time," was all I said. Gloria nodded once and extended her hand towards me.

Too late, Liam realised that his bubble had popped.

His wide eyes caught and held mine. "What are you doing?" he shrieked.

I couldn't help myself. My mouth curved into a nasty, spriteful little smile.

"Saving the planet," I said, as the DNA-naked tips of my fingers reached for Gloria.

As we touched, I had a brief glimpse of Liam's ashen face, hands raised to ward off the inevitable.

How do you describe the indescribable? I have no words to convey the sensation of being at the heart of a miniature sun. Those I can use are pale in comparison to the reality, but they are all I have.

Fire washed through me. Exquisite. Excruciating. Even as it blossomed inside me, I quenched it. For a microsecond that tiny portion of my essence not protected by true-witch DNA mingled with Gloria. Water and fire, existing together as they were never meant to do. It was simultaneous orgasm and death. In our purest elemental forms we joined, and in that tiny corner of a tiny country on a tiny speck of a world, the very fabric of the universe warped for a bare instant before reacting to the outrage.

My whole being existed in torment; pain beyond account. And yet as Nature reasserted herself and we were torn apart, the pain intensified and I clung to it, for in that one perfect moment Gloria had been mine. As the world faded into oblivion I wept for my lost love and prayed that whatever happened to me, she might survive.

Blackness.

Timeless.

Drifting.

Waking.

To my utter astonishment and woe, I found that I lived. To face continued life with no more than a fading memory of that instant of union seemed cruel and unnecessary. If I'd known how, I would have slipped quietly back into the dark and never woken again. But I had no knowledge of how to achieve such an end—the very thing I'd feared the magician's experiment might accomplish, but which had been thwarted by a few microscopic strands of Dawn's DNA.

Liam was gone. Obliterated along with his workshop and around a twenty metre radius of vaporised rock, leaving nothing but an immense crater. A clean, quick death. Kinder than he'd planned for us.

Gloria, too, was gone. Not in any permanent fashion, but I doubted I would see her again. It was for the best, I told myself as I trudged away from the scene of devastation. Somewhere inside me burned a tiny speck of flame. Imaginary or real, it made no odds; I knew with a dire certainty that I could never bear to be close to her again for fear of re-kindling an impossible dream.

Sirens wailed in the distance, and their melancholy song fitted my mood perfectly. I stepped into the cold and welcoming water of Loch Ness and dissolved.

Epilogue

The new crater beside Loch Ness has caused a huge tourist boom. Ever a popular destination for monster-hunters, the Highlands now have visitors of a new ilk: conspiracy theorists. Rumours range from UFO landings to nuclear testing gone wrong. Thankfully, nothing comes anywhere near the truth.

The police suspect Liam of eco-terrorism. What they imagine he planned to do with a bomb powerful enough to blow a sizeable hole in solid granite, I can't quite fathom. But hey, it's another piece in the puzzle for the conspiracy-lovers, and any tourism is good for the economy.

Still feeling raw inside and out, I have decided to wait a while before rejoining the human race. There's no hurry; I implied an open-ended leave of absence from work, so no one will be concerned when I fail to re-appear. I've yet to decide if I will ever face the world as Cassiopeia Lake again.

I have, however, discounted my original intention of abandoning humanity altogether. The world is ever-encroaching on the wild spaces, and at some future point the human race and I will cross paths again. It is inevitable, so delay seems rather pointless.

Besides, as Gloria noted on more than one occasion, I'm not a typical elemental; I actually enjoy company.

In the interim I have plenty to think about. As I trace my fingers along the deep gouges crossing my palm, I find myself brooding. Was Rafe really the angel I took him for? Surely a being so pure of spirit could not have fashioned a thing as vile as that spell. I wait nervously for his summons to repay my debt.

And Michael. Michael counselled me not to listen to Rafe, but I ignored him. My last memory of the fey cowering before something only he could see plays over and over inside my head. Was I responsible for another death? Or is Michael still there, perhaps trapped on the astral plane as I'd feared I might be. I made a lot of assumptions about Michael without solid basis, and now I might never discover the truth.

At least for now the world is safe. No one will ever have any idea how close we all came to global disaster, and probably just as well. Sadly the world's energy crisis hasn't been solved, but from a personal standpoint I'm hoping Liam's experiment will never occur to anyone else. The remaining loose end preys on my mind—Liam's partner, the mystery person on the other end of that telephone call. I'm not sure how, but I intend to find the asshole who thinks it's acceptable to condemn millions of people for the sake of profit. And when I do—

Let's not go there. Not yet.

In the meantime I've cracked, at least in part, the issue of releasing Minkie from his unsatisfactory living arrangements. Allowing myself a small measure of melancholy pleasure, I watch as he runs joyously up and down the banks of my underground stream, popping in and out of the water and chittering his excitement.

Small mesh wire now seals each end of the stream where it enters and exits beneath the house, allowing the fresh mountain water to flow unimpeded but keeping Minkie contained. Of course it also blocks the access for any fish; they must now keep to the open water where the main course flows past the building. This requires me to continue providing mink food on a daily basis as I still haven't figured out how to let the fish in, but not the mink out.

I recline half-submerged in the shallows and Minkie curls contented in my lap.

At least I can make *someone* happy.

I've always treasured my privacy and now I have it in abundance. With my ultimate, devastating solution the quiet, private life I craved is mine once more, but at what cost?

Euan is gone. I'm assuming he still lives, though I have no proof.

I've taken to haunting his favourite feeding grounds, those sea lochs where briny water mingles with fresh, and fish is plentiful. As yet there is no sign of the selkie. My feelings verge on mourning; I have no idea what's become of him and I miss him terribly. Now Liam's magical influence is gone I want to explain, to explore any possibility of a second chance. But unless Euan re-appears, the ache lodged beneath my heart will continue to deepen day by the day.

Alastair is dead and my friends are all keeping me at a wary distance. A couple of awkward phone conversations give me hope that those friendships are not broken beyond repair, but it will take time to rebuild any level of trust. Dawn and Gordon are making overtures, and their gratitude is smoothing the way, but it'll be slower going with Alison.

I hurt my best friend more than I could have imagined, concealing the truth from her as I did. In recent days I've drifted up to her croft, hanging invisible in the air, watching as she struggles with daily life. Her cats, Jemima and Horatio, watch me back, with eyes that see what humans' do not. Simon continues to plague her, and I'm not there to support her. She turns to Dawn on occasion, but their friendship is still too new and I believe she misses me as much as I miss her.

Soon, I hope we will be reconciled. Until then, my heart breaks for us both.

And eventually, as ever, my thoughts turn to my glorious Gloria. I wonder what she's doing and who she's seeing now, but whilst I ache to see her again, I hope I never will.

Fire burns swift and bright, but in the end it burns itself out. Water endures. And that is what I will do.

Endure.

NOTE FROM THE AUTHOR

Thank you so much for spending your time reading my words. If you liked what you read, would you please leave a short review on Amazon?

Just a few lines would be great!

Reviews are not only the highest compliment you can pay to an author, they also help other readers discover and make more informed choices about purchasing books in a crowded space. Thank you!

If you'd like to find out more about my other novels, find me at my:

Blog: www.deborahjayauthor.com

Facebook: www.facebook.com/deborahjay

Twitter: www.twitter.com/DeborahJay2

If you'd like to be notified when my next novel is released, please contact me via my blog and I will add you to my mailing list.

Also by Deborah Jay

Epic Fantasy

THE PRINCE'S MAN

Award winning novel, THE PRINCE'S MAN, has been described as 'James Bond meets Lord of the Rings' - a sweeping tale of spies and deadly politics, inter-species mistrust and magic phobia, with an underlying thread of romance.

Rustam Chalice, hedonist, dance tutor and spy, loves his life, never better than when he's bedding a gorgeous woman.

So when the kingdom he serves is threatened from within, he leaps into action. Only trouble is, the spy master, Prince Hal, teams him up with an untouchable aristocratic assassin who despises him.

And to make matters worse, she's the most beautiful woman in the Five Kingdoms.

Plunged into a desperate journey over the mountains, the mismatched pair struggle to survive deadly wildlife, the machinations of a spiteful god - and each other.

They must also keep alive a sickly elf they need as a political pawn. But when the elf reveals that Rustam has magic of his own, he is forced to question his identity, his sanity and worst, his loyalty to his prince.

For in Tyr-en, all magic users are put to death.

About the Author

Deborah Jay writes fast paced action adventures featuring quirky characters and mulit-layered plots - just what she likes to read.

Living mostly on the UK south coast, she has already invested in her ultimate retirement plan - a farmhouse in the majestic mystery-filled Scottish Highlands where she retreats to write when she can find the time.

Her taste for the good things in life is kept in check by the expense of keeping too many dressage horses and her complete inability to cook.

She also has non-fiction titles published under her professional name of Debby Lush.

Find more at her website: deborahjayauthor.com

34442861R10185

Printed in Great Britain
by Amazon